I0649902

Penumbra

A Journal of Weird Fiction and Criticism

No. 5 ☾ 2024

Edited by S. T. Joshi

"You will drift into a penumbra."
—W. B. Yeats

Hippocampus Press

New York

Published by Hippocampus Press
P.O. Box 641
New York, NY 10156
www.hippocampuspress.com

Cover art by George Cotronis.
Cover design by Daniel V. Sauer, dansauerdesign.com.
Hippocampus Press logo designed by Anastasia Damianakos.

PENUMBRA is published once a year, in Summer. Articles and letters should be sent to the editor, S. T. Joshi, ℅ Hippocampus Press. Literary rights for articles will reside with PENUMBRA for one year after publication, whereupon they will revert to their respective authors.

ISBN 978-1-61498-459-7 (paperback)
ISBN 978-1-61498-460-3 (ebook)

Contents

Fiction

Nonfiction

Classic Reprints

Poetry

Notes on Contributors

Folktales and Myth in Joel Lane's
Where Furnaces Burn

James Goho

Et nos servasti . . . sanguine fuso[1]

Joel Lane (1963–2013) was a modern master of noir, weird fiction. During his life Lane published two mainstream novels, many short stories and poems, and several collections of stories and poems, along with discerning nonfiction and editorial works. Some of his books went out of print, but Lane appears to be receiving renewed interest in the United Kingdom. In November 2023, Influx Press (a publisher in London) and Voce Books (a bookstore in Birmingham) hosted a day-long celebration of the life and legacy of Lane entitled "The Witnesses Are Here," which featured talks, panels, readings, screenings, and more. On the following evening, attendees explored the streets and canals of the Digbeth area of central Birmingham, which the event brochure claimed may yet be troubled by Lane and his many characters.[2] Moreover, in 2022 and 2023 Influx Press reprinted several of Lane's books with new introductions, including *From Blue to Black*, *The Blue Mask*, *The Witnesses Are Gone*, and *Where Furnaces Burn*, the last of which was originally published in 2012 and

---

1. "You saved us . . . by shedding blood," translated by Burkert (*HN* 22). This is a debated reading of an inscription found in the Mithraeum of Santa Prisca, Rome first reported by M. J. Vermaseren and C. C. van Essen in 1965 as *"Et nos servasti eternali sanguine fuso"* (217). Silvio Panciera argued that their reading was uncertain because only *sanguine fuso* was clearly visible on the wall. Mary Beard, John North, and Simon Price also contest aspects of the transcription in their *Religions of Rome* (2.318–19).
2. As this essay demonstrates, Lane's *Where Furnaces Burn* traverses many areas of Birmingham.

won the World Fantasy Award for Best Collection in 2013.[3]

Joel Lane lived in Birmingham for much of his life. That city and its environs appear as dark settings in much of his fiction, where it seems a vast, neo-Gothic, violent labyrinth. He epitomized this in *Where Furnaces Burn,* which I will focus on in this essay because it exemplifies, in my view, the essence of Lane's literature of the noir city. The book is a compilation of short stories that trace the narrator's progress from constable to detective sergeant in Birmingham. But it is also a novel. In this essay I argue that the detective is a flawed, tragic hero who endures many ordeals in his quest to solve the problem of violence in the city. Many of the stories (chapters) tell of the hero's experiences in the modern maze-like city through story patterns found in traditional narratives. Some of the folktale patterns that Lane's chapters renew include the girl's tragedy, the transformation tale, the magical flight, the combat tale, and the disenchantment tale. His folktales lead to a myth in the last chapter of the book. In the hyper-intense, nearly hallucinatory "Facing the Wall" (2004), Lane rewrote the myth of the Minotaur of Knossos for modern times. He did so because it is only through myth, understood as *mûthos,* that one can truly tell the story of the modern violent city. In that final chapter the unnamed detective, seemingly possessed by the trauma experienced by the victims of violence, confronts the monstrous at the center of the labyrinthine city. Within an overall heroic quest narrative arc and punctuated by folklore ordeals, *Where Furnaces Burn* culminates in a mythic sacrifice that recapitulates an ancient ritual in the modern city that is dramatized as an actual and supernormal labyrinth.

In *This Spectacular Darkness* (2016), Lane argued that "supernatural horror has its roots in folklore" (1). The genre arises from the oral heritage of storytelling about death, fears, and marvels that people have told for ages. In "What Is Folklore?" (1965), Alan Dundes defined "folklore" as a widely inclusive term that includes folktales, legends, rituals, folk art, folk poetry, superstitions, and other forms

---

3. Influx Press also plans to reissue Lane's *The Lost District* and *The Terrible Changes* in 2024.

of folk expression (3). Folk narratives helped people cope in a dangerous world. In general, such tales are often terrifying, violent, and redolent with strong emotions, but also beautiful and sometimes redemptive. According to G. S. Kirk, folktales often involve ingenuity in escaping danger and illustrate wish-fulfillment (*Myth* 38). He also found that characters in folktales often have generic names or are unnamed (*Myth* 39), as is the detective in Lane's book. In *The Morphology of the Folktale* (1929), Vladimir Propp classified the units of plot actions in quest folk narratives into thirty-one functions. The quest is the major narrative arc in Lane's novel. In *The Meaning of Folklore* (1995), Dundes defined these functions as "motifemes" (96–97). A folktale is a fixed sequence of motifemes. All thirty-one motifemes are not found in every tale, but each traditional tale will exhibit a specific pattern of motifemes. Such patterns as the combat tale, the magical flight, and the girl's tragedy exhibit such a motifeme sequence, according to Walter Burkert in his *Structure and History in Greek Mythology and Ritual* (1979). In his six-volume *Motif-Index of Folk-Literature* (1955–58), Stith Thompson classified folktales into thousands of motifs, demonstrating the endurance, scope, and gravity of such tales.[4] Folktales continue to persist in the modern city, and present-day authors use folklore techniques creatively to explore current human conditions.

In the first story (or chapter) of *Where Furnaces Burn,* "My Stone Desire" (2007), the detective says he joined the police force because he needed "to understand" (*WFB* 3). That is why he chronicles his harrowing police work. The novel starts with his early police training and traces his crime investigations through twenty-four years in urban environs where violence is endemic and usually focused on marginalized populations who suffered from economic and social deprivations.[5] The chapters reveal the violence experienced by the detective

---

4. In *The Folktale* (1977), Thompson defined a motif as "the smallest element in a tale having a power to persist in tradition" (15).
5. In *Unutterable Horror*, S. T. Joshi points out that Lane's tales are an especially effective commentary on economic and social inequities (718).

as a child. His police work resurfaces his traumas and causes more as he internalizes the violence of the city. The detective finds no explanations or answers in the city of desolation, where children seem to have been sacrificed to a shadowy god. In "Beth's Law" (2009), the detective aches to know the god to whom Elizabeth Kindling was sacrificed. The story is a modern version of the folktale pattern of the girl's tragedy where a child is taken from her home, abused, and sometimes rescued, which does occur in "Beth's Law." "The Hostess" (2010) is another girl's tragedy story or an exile, return, and revenge story. In this chapter the detective supernaturally liberates Theresa O'Kane from her recurring return to the scene of her misery, murder, and killings. She fades away into peaceful shadows. Lane wrote these tales in a gritty realism haunted by melancholy and fury.

"My Stone Desire" sets the stage for the detective's quest through the city of violence. At first the detective investigates missing persons, who are never found. This chapter illustrates the violence, poignancy, and bleakness of his police work; yet it also reveals an occasional transcendent experience. The detective shares liaisons with Kath under a low railway bridge of dark stone. It seems a space of sanctuary and hope where couples eerily escape the ravages of the deadly city. Formed of tightly packed, embracing naked humans, it is the bridge of sorrows, where missing persons go to die in each other's arms. It is a startling image of despair and love.

Early in the chapter the detective recounts a dream. Dreams are a common narrative technique in folktales. Lane used dreams to reveal aspects of the detective's character and experiences. The detective traverses the dream waste ground to a wall where something waits on the other side. That other side is the unknown, where there is "the lack of answers" he so urgently wants to hear (*WFB* 6). Dreams appear in other stories. For example, in "Dreams of Children" (2012), he dreams of being cut with tiny knives when he was a kid, which alludes to the abuse he suffered when he was young. In "Morning's Echo" (2010), the detective's dreams pinpoint the location of the body parts of the dismembered Denny, which expresses the detective's delusion of putting himself back together and shows Lane externalizing an internal experience of a character.

Dreams are part of the folkloric and mythic logic underlying the novel. In "My Stone Desire," the detective's dream depicts a hidden space in a waste ground. Waste grounds abound in the book. They recall the ancient motif of the wasteland, a magically blighted land that occurs in Celtic and other lore. In the Irish "The Adventure of Art Son of Conn,"[6] Conn's land suffers an enchantment that leaves it barren with "neither corn nor milk" (155). In the third branch of the *Mabinogion,* Manawydan, Pryderi, Rhiannon, and Cigfa find themselves in an abandoned Dyfed where they see "nothing, no animal, no smoke, no fire, no man, no dwelling" (86). It is a country mysteriously emptied. In Lane's novel, waste grounds represent the desolation and despair of people struggling to survive in current economic and social conditions. Such waste lands also depict the ruin of nature.

Lane reshaped traditional folktale patterns to help us experience the nature of the modern, noir city in *Where Furnaces Burn.* It is folklore of loss, dread, and wonder shared around a heap of burning rubbish on a spoil-ground or under a crumbling viaduct. Folktales are alive today because of their primal energy. Lane channeled that energy to illuminate dark and dangerous things at the core of modern urban human conditions. The reprisal of folklore is not trivial because it dramatizes such conditions, as Dundes argued in "What Is Folklore?" He maintained that folklore is an artistic process that helped people make sense of the world and that it continues to be meaningful today. At its end, "My Stone Desire" becomes a transformation tale embodied in the anguished image of lovers converting into the structure of a decaying stone railway bridge. Lane's folktale tells of a wonderful metamorphism driven by desolation. The detective takes Kath to the bridge, but they resist the desire for oblivion in each other's stone arms. It is the first ordeal for the detective.

Another trial occurs in "Blue Smoke" (2012). The story tells of

---

6. *Eachtra Airt meic Cuind* in Irish.

people released from the agony of the city but sentenced to circle endlessly the urban waste grounds in a phantom train. It is a procession of the dead tale. The story is set in 1989, when drunks and the homeless stop showing up in hospitals, at the Salvation Army, or being found on the streets of Digbeth. Digbeth is a "lifeless place" of derelict factories, empty canals, abandoned railways, and mounds of wrecked cars (*WFB* 27). Early in his career, the detective has already worked on cases of inconceivable violence. He drinks to dull the horror of the city. There are two challenges for the detective in this urban folktale. One is his growing alcoholism; a second is to avoid becoming part of that procession of the dead.

The detective and a fellow officer, Terry, discover the reason for the disappearances through a drinking binge. On a cold, snowy night, they stumble through the Digbeth district. In their intoxicated state they respond to the call of a troupe of monks to follow. These monks represent folktale villains who aim to deceive the hero on his quest, which is Propp's function VI. The detective and his friend merge with a crowd of people led by those villains disguised as monks into a bizarre church. The detective longs for a drink and deliverance and rises to approach the church's altar. But Terry drags him out of that mysterious church into the freezing night. The detective suffers frostbite but survives his ordeal. Later, when sober, he sees a phantom train packed with people, bottles in their hands, traveling on a derelict railway to nowhere—a convoy of the dead. The detective avoids that fate because of the intercession of a helper (Terry), who appears in many, but not all, folktales to assist a hero at a critical time, according to Propp (82–83).

There are no helpers in "A Cup of Blood" (2004), which reads like a modern Grail legend. The chapter connects the detective's investigation of a priceless cup reportedly stolen from the house of a disreputable dealer to the origins of the Grail legend. The story takes place in West Bromwich[7] early in the detective's career. Of course,

---

7. West Bromwich is a town about 7 miles northwest of Birmingham in a region known as the Black County because it was a center of early Indus-

there are crimes and murders in the chapter; that is what happens in the nightmare city. But under an abandoned viaduct flanked by derelict factories, unusual travelers reveal a mysterious cup. When filled with water, the cup shines blood-red and heals a man. These mysterious travelers seem like modern Grail bearers. One suspects the cup chose them. When dropped and broken, the cup makes itself whole.

Is it the Grail? Characters yearn for that cup to reveal its meaning or to reveal its value. The cup bears the weight of healing and of magic that is lost. It may be the Nant Eos, the Welsh healing cup, which Arthur Machen in *The Secret of the Sangraal* (1994) suggested is a part of the Celtic origin of the Grail Legend. Robert Sherman Loomis also argued for the non-Christian origin of the Grail. He found it in Irish folktales, as did John Carey, who argues that the core of the Grail narratives arises from Irish folklore of a mystic vessel. He suggests that this folklore was probably first written in the lost *Cín Dromma Snechtai*, which is thought to have been compiled in the 8th century C.E. Carey postulates that early Irish scholars took these written collections to Wales in the early ninth century. And Jeffrey Gantz argues that the "style of *The Mabinogion* resembles that of the Irish sagas in style" (24).

The cup lost for centuries reappears in Lane's story—a cup symbolizing many things. The bowls and cauldrons in the *Mabinogion* suggest rebirth, fertility, and regeneration. Lane's unusual travelers include "a couple and a baby," suggesting this group comes from an enchanted, generative past (*WFB* 50). The travelers move on without the cup. Perhaps they slipped across the canal into that otherworld of lore, as waterways often act as a liminal space between the ordinary and the fantastic. The story implies that within the waste grounds of the modern city marginalized people may find ways to protect themselves against the terrors of the modern city. And the cup symbolizes an unseen power of old animism, intimating that secrets of the land may persist in ruins, hinting that the power of heal-

---

trial Revolution activity. Due to its coal deposits, many coke and brickworks were established, leading to soot shrouding the county.

ing and rebirth may yet be found. It is a mysterious power that is ages old. Lane wrote a marvelous urban folktale that suggests the miraculous persists in the crime-ridden and violent city. This story of a wondrous cup shows the lasting power of folklore. But Lane's chapter also expresses great sorrow and loss. The cup is lost again. The magic is gone. The detective goes for a pint, and we return to an appalling reality.

"Winter Journey" (2008) is Lane's "urban myth" about a savage boy stalking Fox Hollies, which is an area of Birmingham on the edge of the Acocks Green district in the southeast of the city (*WFB* 159). Lane's modern wild hunt tale features a supernatural fox, which often appears in folk narratives. Hans-Jörg Uther traces European fox narrative tales back to antiquity. Such tales also appear across the world, and many feature clever foxes. But foxes also have other characteristics, for example, perfidy, woe, wariness, and heroism. The fox in "Winter Journey" is a complex and shape-shifting figure. Fox Hollies features a sculpture of an "oddly pagan fox" (*WFB* 159). And a homeless boy, Mark, appears feral, like a fox, because he stalks people and sometimes bites them. His sexual liaison with Irena seems to have caused his strange wasting disease, which spread the violence she experienced to him like an infection. The fox also represents the anguish of Irena, who had fled through Europe only to become sex-trafficked and brutalized in the UK.

In this modern wild hunt tale, the detective is the hunter, his ghostly company includes Mark and Irena, and the prey is the fox, or perhaps the real prey is violence itself. As the detective chases the fox, it sheds parts of itself as if fragmenting from its, Mark's, and Irena's agony. Irena's suffering metastasizes throughout the tale. For example, Mark is gnawed to death from the inside, a gruesome image of the effects of violent trauma. Mark leaves a message from Irena, which expresses her agony in a desperate scrawl ending with a plea: "always cold always hungry help me please" (*WFB* 165). This paragraph powerfully expresses the suffering of female refugees in a violent world.

In the *Mabinogion* an animal hunt is usually connected with an uncanny encounter or a way to reach the otherworld, which is Thompson's Motif F159.1. That is what the detective experiences. The hunt ends when the fox disappears into the black water of a canal or passes into the otherworld. The detective does not follow.

Similarly, the detective survives a test on a rancid stairway in "Point of Departure" (2012). Located in the center of Birmingham, the public stairway consists of three flights of stairs with convex mirrors for visibility. These malevolent mirrors present a mode of supernatural surveillance that causes, captures, and conducts violence. The stairway appears to be an ordinary urban space, but it is haunted by people's fears and dreams. This sense of the unusual or the perilous seems to adhere to certain harmed or sacred places. During his late teens the detective would race up the stairs to catch a train back to Wolverhampton.[8] Once he fell. He remembers being attacked by a dog. But he could be wrong because he had no scars. Ghosts leave no fingerprints.

The action starts with the detective investigating the unusual death of a woman on the stairs. More attacks are reported. But the attacks seem more like dreams or hallucinations than reality. One victim claimed a pack of dogs teemed down the stairs and attacked him. But the recently installed CCTVs showed the victim but no dogs. Walking the concrete stairway alone in a snowstorm, the detective senses the mirrors remembering him or his memories and dreams. Or are they collective nightmares of despair and death? From the top landing, a torrent swoops down—people with bony wings rush past and fly away through the snow into the dark sky, escaping the city. This is a wish-fulfillment tale of flight from the despair of the city. They soar down the gray stairway past the detective and lift away into the forgiving dark sky. It is the realm of a timeless, brutal, magical escape on a stairway of dreams and terror. Lane's modern magical flight tale depicts the lost and the damaged escaping from

---

8. Wolverhampton is a metropolitan borough twelve miles northwest of Birmingham.

the dangers of the city into a dark sky, blossoming with snowflakes.

Lane's noir novel shapes a folklore of contemporary society by charting the detective's quest to find answers to the spread of violence in the modern city. Another urban folktale, "The Receivers" (2002), links political corruption with monstrosity. A corrupt councilor had died from blood poisoning, but his body disappeared from the Solihull Hospital.[9] Here Lane crafts a disenchantment story where the detective removes a curse from a place or a people by destroying the source. Lane's chapter recalls Stith Thompson's D763 motif: disenchantment by destroying an enchanter. In this case, the detective kills an enchanter who is already dead.

After the disappearance of the body, the police at the Acocks Green station becomes overwhelmed by an epidemic of thefts, arson, fights, and random attacks on the populace. Pandemonium reigns in this violent city. The detective patrols the allotments in Tyseley,[10] where he lived as a child. It is the return of the hero to his home, but not to bring knowledge. He returns to re-experience the anguish of his youth in a waste ground surrounded by derelict railway shacks, a rusting railway line, and heaps of rusting cars. His memories actualize in distorted forms of pale, needy children, who appear thin and illusive as paper or ash in the falling dark. The detective stumbles away past three brick garages. Later he returns because, in his youth, there were only two garages. One of the garages reeks as if it were the center of the disease of crime. In the underground chambers of that garage the detective overcomes his fear of the dead and ends the enchantment. It is the hero's descent into the underworld, which is a common stage in the classic hero's journey. It is stage VIII in Jan de Vries's outline of the hero pattern. Digging down through moldering piles of trash and cash, the detective uncovers the rotting bones of that dead politician, who appears to be a

---

9. Solihull Hospital is part of the Birmingham hospital system and is located in Solihull, about 9 miles from Birmingham city center.
10. Tyseley is an area in the south of Birmingham, near the district of Acocks Green.

dead god still "feeding on money" (*WFB* 181). It is a disturbing image of corruption persisting beyond death. The detective crushes the bones and removes the curse. The descent into the underworld is a supreme test of the hero because it is a confrontation with one's deepest fears. But this chapter is a prelude to the final ordeal of the detective against the source of violence.

That shadowy figure appears throughout Lane's book. In an early chapter, "Even the Pawn" (2012), the detective investigates the murder in Yardley[11] of the sex-trafficked Tania, who had died in a trash bin after being beaten and sexually abused. One of the suspects is the mysterious Derek, who frequented the massage parlor where Tania worked. But Derek had an alibi that checked out. Months later the detective follows up with Derek. Or did Derek set a trap for the detective? A villain uses trickery and disguises to deceive and harm the hero. Late at night in the Ackers[12] on a patch of waste ground, where the detective seems to have been lured, Derek awaits. He touches the detective's face. By doing this, Derek transfers Tania's agony to the detective. This action is Propp's function XVII, where the hero is branded. Lane expresses this in a fragmented paragraph that screams the terror and pain that Tania experienced. Her dying trauma possesses the detective. This experience intensifies the detective's quest for the thing at the center of violence.

That mysterious villain also appears in a later chapter, "The Victim Card" (2004). This villain may be Dael, Derek, or Dean, or each of them, or none of them. In this tale the villain takes on different forms to confuse the detective. Is that villain a victim of a crime? Did he stage his death? Or did he force the suicide of another man to mystify the detective? But the detective is not deceived; he knows the source of violence is "still there in the shadow" (*WFB* 157). That dark presence draws others into his maze, where they will become his victims. The detective swears that when the evil presence finds him, he will kill it.

---

11. Yardley is an area in east Birmingham.
12. Ackers is southeast of Birmingham City Center.

The detective enters that dark maze in "Facing the Wall." This chapter, or mythic tale, takes readers into the void. Erich Kahler thought a myth "bears with it a kind of awesome breath from regions unreachable" (42). Lane's myth tells of those regions. In *This Spectacular Darkness* Lane argued that although the roots of weird literature could be found in folklore, its current expression arose from the "pressures of modernity," which required a new kind of imagination that could generate "new myths" about the realities of the human condition (2). In "Facing the Wall," Lane imagined a modern myth based on ancient precedent. He focused on the modern, urban environment beset by fear, violence, and monstrosity. Before he left the police force in "Facing the Wall," the detective had been investigating a set of murders with a similar M.O., which suggested one murderer. All the victims were male, and each had been stabbed in the back. The bodies were found in abandoned industrial buildings, and the dead men had a small tattoo of a bull's head on their backs. The police investigation called the unknown serial killer a "real monster," who seemed to be linked to an underground organization christened the "Maze" (*WFB* 212). During his time on the force, the detective had scrupulously searched the maze-like "back-streets of Digbeth and Hockley"[13] for clues or leads about the ritualistic crimes but had found only more confusion (*WFB* 213). These mazes suggest a deep existential fear of imprisonment in the modern city. A labyrinth signifies enclosure, terror, panic, and annihilation. There is no escape. In Lane's novel, city inhabitants seem trapped in labyrinths that end with an encounter with the monstrous. The detective accepts this tragic fate.

It is 2003, at the beginning of the Iraq War, when the detective leaves the police force. The violent city has scarred him. Alone, he faces his final ordeal. He embarks on a journey through the maze-like underworld of the city to make himself visible as a potential victim. In a labyrinth of factories the hero lets the monster find him in

---

13. Hockley is a central district in Birmingham, approximately one mile northwest of the city center.

a rubbish-heaped office in a jail-like building. It is the house of death, as the mythic labyrinth, designed and built by the mythic Daedalus, was a house of death for Athenian boys and girls, and finally for the Minotaur. The ex-detective kills the modern Minotaur with a knife, leaving the human body. This chapter ends the ex-detective's quest. It may be viewed as a folktale or traditional tale as a form of the combat tale. In the chapter, the ex-detective is the heroic champion who faces an imposing and dangerous antagonist. In Lane's story, as Burkert showed, the hero uses "cleverness against brute force" to attain triumph (*SHGM* 33).

But the final chapter is more than a folktale. "Myth" comes from the Greek word *mûthos*, which originally meant "utterance" or what one says. In *Myth*, Kirk traced how it came to mean what one says in the form of a tale. *Mûthoi* are stories but special kinds of stories. Kirk argued that there is no definitive definition of a myth, or, as he put it, "no Platonic form of myth" (7). Yet myths vary from folktales. Lane's tale contains the key elements of myth identified by Karen Armstrong. It is rooted in death. The slayings in the chapter read like rituals or sacrifices, which are also common in myth. It is about the unknown and confronting one's fear. Moreover, myths have a meaningful underlying purpose. As Burkert argued, myths are unique types of traditional tales that tell "something important, serious, even sacred" about a society (*SHGM* 4). Erich Kahler insisted that "myth deals with the fundamentals of our life" and does not explain anything (42). Myths are stories that point out *something of collective importance*" in a society and reflect the "general problems of human society" from which they originate (*SHGM* 23). Lane's modern myth is set in Birmingham, which symbolizes the modern gothicized city of violence.

Lane's myth features a bull image. Bulls frequently occur in mythology and legend. Aurochs appear among the cave paintings at Lascaux. Kirk attested in *The Nature of Greek Myths* (1974) that "[b]ulls were important creatures in Bronze Age Crete" (158). Burkert showed that three-horned bulls appear in Celtic votive practices (*SHGM* 86). In Celtic lore, according to Nora Chadwick, *Tarvos Trigaranus* was a bull god revered as a symbol of fertility and ferocity (145–46). Lane's myth also reminds me of elements of the ancient Mithras cult.[14] The Roman Mithras cult was open only to men, as verified by Chalupa (93), Valerie M. Warrior (91), and Mary Beard et al. (298). Accordingly, Lane's modern Minotaur kills only men. Akin to all the ancient mystery religions, the Mithras mysteries are obscure. But the Mithraea are more allusive than other mysteries, according to Warrior, and to Burkert in his *Ancient Mystery Cults* (1987). Jaś Elsner finds nearly no texts survive about Mithraism (207). But a key icon found in "dozens of Mithraic temples from Syria to Britain" depicts Mithras killing a bull, usually in the innermost of a building (Elsner 206), similar to where the ex-detective kills the modern Minotaur. And "Mithras' weapon in bull-killing is a knife," akin to what the ex-detective used against the modern monster in Lane's book (Beck 288). In ancient times, the sacrifice of a bull was a sacred act atoned for by caring for the remains of the animal sacrificed. A bull's skull would be preserved and honored (Burkert, *HN* 6). Recently the discovery of a sacrificial bull's head in a Minoan cemetery dated to 1850 B.C.E., reported on by Stephanie Makri, confirms this practice. Similarly, the ex-detective keeps the bull's head of the modern Minotaur.

The former detective's actions seem like a ritual, or perhaps more accurately, a re-creation of an ancient ritual. As with many rituals, his act "dramatizes the existing social order" (*HN* 25), that is, it enacts the current rule of violence in contemporary cities. Yet there is more to Lane's story. It is narrative weird fiction constructed from ancient myth melded with ritual performance to illuminate a critical current human condition. In "Facing the Wall," Lane used mythic language to message the danger of, yet also the potential for resistance in, the violent city. He wrote a modern myth remaking the

---

14. See Franz Cumont's original work, first published in 1903, along with revisions and updates on the Mithras Cult by Roger Beck, Per Beskow, Aleš Chalupa, Manfred Clauss, and others.

tale of the Minotaur because only a mythic, monstrous thing can explain the horror of the city of ruins, waste grounds, and unending violence. Lane created a myth for our time—that is to say, a narrative that speaks to something of collective importance, something serious. What is more important or serious in our time than endless violence and endless war?

Burkert warned that institutionalized violence is the essence of all forms of authority (*HN* 1). Confirming this, Hannah Arendt argued that the most egregious violence comes from those in positions of power, from the state or police. She suggested those oppressed or those ill-ruled by power act violently "without counting the consequences" when justice is needed to be enacted (4). This violence arises from rage, but it is not irrational. It is natural and could be the only possible action. But Arendt hesitated. She went on to write that violence changes the world, but "the most probable change is to a more violent world" (80).

"Facing the Wall" revitalizes the meaning of myth from the past, or from our collective memory, into modern times as an antidote to the disease of violence and the feeling of helplessness in the modern noir city. The ex-detective sees something more violent as a way to overcome the violence of the city, symbolized in the form of a mythic urban monster. In the final chapter, the ex-detective accepts violence as a legitimate form of struggle. He is now outside the police system but within the overall societal system, which, in a sense, has compelled him to use violence to express his trapped rage. His violent act, rooted in anger and despair, is an act of resistance; perhaps it is his only way to act. Lane captured the dilemma of violent resistance in a violent world while exposing the seductive, gruesome pathology of institutionalized violence.

The final chapter gives no final answer. Kirk showed that many myths leave problems unanswered (*Myth* 269). There are loose ends and unsolved crimes in Lane's novel, which reveals the modern noir city as a labyrinth imprisoning us in recurring cycles of violence where there is no escape and no wonder or beauty. The noir city walls us in a maze of dread. It takes a grave act, mythic in structure, to shatter those walls.

Where Furnaces Burn is Lane's great work on the nature of violence, told in part through patterns of folktales and myth. Lane had a keen sense of social and economic injustice in modern society. He also responded to the underlying strangeness and foreboding of the world found everywhere. Out of the modern jaws of violence, Lane fashioned a novel revealing not only desolation but also moments of wonder and heroism by creatively deploying traditional narrative patterns and ancient myth through a noir lens to transport readers from the real world of violence into a supernormal world. Through the book's dark power, I feel Lane tells us there is something perilous at stake in our time. Lane's myth relates a modern, labyrinthine journey out of a prison of violence and nihilism. We are meant to experience this myth, like an old myth, as an exemplar of heroic action in dangerous times. A phrase in Lane's poem "Andromeda" from *Trouble in the Heartland* (2004) reads: "Without the stories, this city is / a prison" (59). When we think of *mûthos* as storytelling, as a means of reshaping our understanding of our world, as a way of encountering the void, as a way of living through the long, dangerous urban nights, as a way out of the labyrinth of violence, as the old myths helped the ancients, then we can understand Lane's heroic achievement in *Where Furnaces Burn*.

Works Cited

"The Adventures of Art Son of Conn, and the Courtship of Delbchaem." Tr. and ed. Richard Irvine Best. *Ériu* 3 (1907): 149–73.

Arendt, Hannah. *On Violence*. Orlando, FL: Harcourt, 1970.

Armstrong, Karen. *A Short History of Myth*. Toronto: Alfred A. Knopf, 2005.

Beard, Mary; North, John; and Price, Simon. *Religions of Rome*. Cambridge: Cambridge University Press, 1998. 2 vols.

Beck, Roger. "History into Fiction: The Metamorphoses of the Mithras Myths." *Ancient Narrative* 1 (2001–02): 283–300.

Beskow, Per. "The Portorium and the Mysteries of Mithras." *Journal of Mithraic Studies* 3 (1980): 1–18.

Burkert, Walter. *Structure and History in Greek Mythology and Ritual.* Berkeley: University of California Press, 1979. [Abbreviated in the text as *SHGM.*]

———. *Homo Necans: The Anthropology of Ancient Greek Sacrificial Ritual and Myth.* Tr. Peter Bing. Berkeley: University of California Press, 1983. [Abbreviated in the text as *HN.*]

———. *Ancient Mystery Cults.* Cambridge, MA: Harvard University Press, 1987.

Carey, John. *Ireland and the Grail.* Aberystwyth, Wales: Celtic Publications, 2007.

Chadwick Nora. *The Celts.* London: Folio Society, 2001.

Chalupa, Aleš. "The Origins of the Roman Cult of Mithras in the Light of New Evidence and Interpretations: The Current State of Affairs." *Religio* 24, No.1 (2016): 65–96.

Clauss, Manfred. *The Roman Cult of Mithras: The God and His Mysteries.* Tr. Richard Gordon. Edinburgh: Edinburgh University Press, 2000.

Cumont, Franz. *The Mysteries of Mithra.* 1903. Tr. Thomas J. McCormick. New York: Dover, 1956.

de Vries, Jan. *Heroic Song and Heroic Legend.* Tr. D. J. Timmer. London: Oxford University Press, 1963.

Dundes, Alan. *The Meaning of Folklore: The Analytical Essays of Alan Dundes.* Ed. Simon J. Bonner. Logan: Utah State University Press, 2007.

———. "What Is Folklore?" In Alan Dundes, ed. *The Study of Folklore.* Englewood Cliffs, NJ: Prentice-Hall, 1965. 1–4.

Elsner, Jaś. *Imperial Rome and Christian Triumph.* Oxford: Oxford University Press, 1998.

Ganz, Jeffrey. "Introduction." In *The Mabinogion.* Tr. Jeffrey Ganz. London: Penguin, 1976. 9–34.

Joshi, S. T. *Unutterable Horror: A History of Supernatural Fiction*. 2012. New York: Hippocampus Press, 2014. 2 vols.

Kahler, Erich. *Out of the Labyrinth*. New York: George Braziller, 1967.

Kirk, G. S. *Myth: Its Meaning and Function in Ancient and Other Cultures*. Berkeley: University of California Press, 1970. [Abbreviated in the text as *Myth*.]

————. *The Nature of Greek Myths*. 1974. New York: Barnes & Noble, 2009.

Lane, Joel. *Trouble in the Heartland*. Todmorden, UK: Arc Publications, 2004.

————. *Where Furnaces Burn*. Hornsea, UK: Drugstore Indian Press, 2014. [Abbreviated in the text as *WFB*.]

————. *This Spectacular Darkness*. Ed. Mark Valentine and John Howard. Leyburn, UK: Tartarus Press, 2016.

Loomis, Roger Sherman. *The Grail: From Celtic Myth to Christian Symbol*. London: Constable, 1992.

The Mabinogion. Tr. Jeffrey Ganz. London: Penguin, 1976.

Machen, Arthur. *The Secret of the Sangraal*. Leyburn, UK: Tartarus Press, 1994.

Makri, Stephanie. "Sacrificial Minoan Bull's Head Unearthed on Crete." *Greek Reporter* 31 (October 2022) <greekreporter.com/2022/10/31/minoan-sacrificial-bull-head-unearthed-crete/> [Accessed 1 November 2022.]

Panciera, Silvio. "Il materiale epigrafico dallo scavo del mitreo di S. Stefano Rotondo (con un addendum sul verso terminante . . . *sanguine fuso*." In Ugo Bianchi, ed. *Mysteria Mithrae*. Leiden: E. J. Brill, 1979. 85–125.

Propp, Vladimir, *The Morphology of the Folktale*. 1929. Ed. Louis A. Wagner. Tr. Laurence Scott. Austin: University of Texas Press, 1968.

*Thompson, Stith. *Motif-Index of Folk-Literature*. Rev. ed. Bloomington: Indiana University Press, 1955–58. 6 vols. <ia800408.us.

archive.org/30/items/Thompson2016MotifIndex/Thompson_2016 _Motif-Index.pdf> [Accessed 15 September 2022.]

———. *The Folktale*. Berkeley: University of California Press, 1977.

Uther, Hans-Jörg. "The Fox in World Literature: Reflections on a 'Fictional Animal.'" *Asian Folklore Studies* 65 (2006): 133–60.

Vermaseren, M. J., and C. C. van Essen. *The Excavations in the Mithraeum of the Church of Santa Prisca on the Aventine*. Leiden: E. J. Brill, 1965.

Warrior, Valerie M. *Roman Religion*. Cambridge: Cambridge University Press, 2006.

Black Shells

Katherine Kerestman

Black shells. They were all over the place. In fact, she could hardly avoid stepping on them, crunching them into sharp shards under the soles of her hiking boots. She had never heard of black shells. Clams, she supposed. Oysters? It was all so new to her. It was all so unbelievably wild, she thought as she photographed the beach.

Lost in wonder, Margot almost stepped on a stingray. The sea creature was a soft shade of pink, damp-looking (like a rain slicker), kite-shaped, and it had a kite-like tail. She photographed it, too, thinking of the travel magazines to which she would send her photo-essay. As she walked the deserted beach, she encountered four, five, *six* stingrays and countless black shells. By this time the red-orange sun had liquefied into the horizon and the full moon, which had succeeded it in the firmament, was illuminating the beach the whitish color of a fresh corpse. Margot spied a slow-crawling hermit crab who was intent upon returning to the deep.

She had been walking since morning, exploring the grass-spotted dunes of the coastal island, the only person, apparently, who was enjoying the nature preserve the entire day. Margot had never been to the Outer Banks before, the archipelago of isles positioned between the North Carolina mainland and the raging waters of the Graveyard of the Atlantic and infamous for its thousands of shipwrecks and subsequent pirate tourism trade; and, when she made plans to visit her brother, she decided to combine her vacation with a journalistic project. The diminutive island she was reconnoitering was a dedicated nature preserve and (notwithstanding the fact that, in days gone by, it had been a notorious pirate lair) uninhabited by humans. Few people ever ventured on the lonely island except birdwatchers and the occasional environmentalist. Margot had not seen a living creature all day, except for the black ducks flying in V-formation and blue-headed kestrels who squawked shrilly as they flew back and forth in the winds—which were mounting—and occasional gusts, which were forcing tall, dolloped creamy clouds to skid crazily across the bright blue sky, covering it more and more with white cloudstuff.

Her view of the lone road on the island and the ferry dock was impeded by a minor mountain range consisting of a row of twenty-foot-high sand dunes. Margot sucked in a deep breath, expanding her lungs and relaxing her entire body as she did so, and then she adjusted her backpack and headed inland toward the dunes with a huge grin on her face. The ferry would not be back until noon on the morrow, and Margot would be camping overnight on the island. She checked her phone to learn the time, but found that there was no internet service and that the communication device she was carrying was good for no more than a paperweight. Well, she could tell the time by the sun, easy enough to know when it was noon so that she could be back at the landing, where her brother the fisherman was going to pick her up in his skiff. Aided by the ghastly evanescence of a great full moon, she planted a three-foot stake into the sand (she had a bundle of them on her back) to mark her path back to the landing, before she entered the woods.

As she lifted her foot from the deep, sucking sand, which greedily swallowed her every step, she raised her eyes to look up at the treeline of the forest, and she found the green of it overwhelming. The green was lush, sensuous, erotic, even in the pallor of moonlight, and she thought that color should not be so opulent that it becomes indecent. The flora on the ground and in the leafy canopy was heavy with dew, and the undergrowth caressed her ankles and calves as she penetrated the fringe of the wood. Not only the hue of the forest, but the perfume, too, she found heady, a fragrance like a drug. She fancied she was becoming intoxicated. *Had she had too much sun on the boat ride to the island and on the beach?*

Succulent leaves stirred. *A breeze.* Margot remembered: the forecast had denied any possibility of rain, and without internet she could not check the current prognostication. But she knew that conditions often changed quickly in the Atlantic. Margot parted large fronds with her hands as she ventured further into the interior. Low tree branches scratched red marks on her face and a party of kestrels shrieked in the canopy—hawks, she recalled, members of the hawk family, predators. Squirrels crisscrossed her track in the uncleared brush, in a prodigious hurry to accomplish some dire purpose known only to themselves, and from the gloom several pairs of eyes gleamed at her. Slight, muted beams from the dark-blemished full moon pierced the cover of interwoven branches, illuminating a narrow footbridge. Realizing she had come upon a swamp, Margot reapplied her insect repellant, for the mosquitoes were zeroing in on her.

Sand became sticky mud and adhered to her shoes as if trying to take back what rightfully belonged to it, and the leaves in the high treetops made a rustling sound, as of an hundred accordion-folded fans being fluttered simultaneously by a congregation of overwarm ladies rocking in wicker chairs on a wrap-around porch on a sultry day; the sound made Margot understand that a storm was approaching. Doffing her backpack, she unzipped a compartment to extract her flashlight, which she used to locate the stakes she had planted, having decided upon a retreat. She would try to locate her rendezvous point, if she could, before the rain came.

By gray slivers of full moonlight she saw the branches waving over her head and the saplings bending to touch their roots as if they were performing calisthenics. The rustling fans became a *slap, slap, slap* on the forest floor, although Margot, insulated from the winds by the trees, felt little of the wind.

She hoped to find some sturdier kind of shelter than the folded-up tent she had in her backpack, for, according to the clamor generated by the trees, the onrushing gale was giving no signs of abating. *Perhaps fallen logs strategically piled to protect her from flying debris might serve her purpose. Was it possible there might be a cave on the is-*

land? As Margot backtracked toward the beach, she was dismayed that she could not find her stakes. The strong wind was creating havoc now, causing the bushes to lean left, then right, and the low-slung branches to slap her chest and shoulders—and black clouds were hoarding the moon and its beams, so that she was forced to grope her way nearly blind and cold out of the wood.

Cold: the wind had turned cold for August, and even through the dense tree canopy Margot began to suffer the pinpricks of raindrops on her bare arms. *Drat,* she thought, *everything was beautiful up till now—my camera! Oh, yes it's secured watertight in my backpack, it's okay—I ought to get a good price, maybe a journalism prize even (at the least, prestige) for my piece on this trip: lone woman backpacker hiker camping in wilderness during gale. I can't find my stakes in the dark! I can see my face on the cover of* Time! *I need to find shelter but also want to find the ferry dock first so they can find me tomorrow and I'm not on the other side of the island when they come.*

A frontal assault by a deluge of ocean surfing in on a gust of wind forced her back two or three steps when she first emerged from the trees and stepped onto a waterlogged dune; the wind would have knocked her over had not the wet sand swallowed her feet and held her fast so that she merely bent at the knees in the gusts. Unredeemed blackness was what she saw now, and she felt a twinge not unlike panic—but then a formation of black clouds rolled past the moon's face, allowing one or two fugitive beams to escape. A little illumination helping to steady her nerves, Margot pulled out her flashlight again to find her stakes.

Holding her head down against the wind, she trudged laboriously, sinking to mid-calf with each step in the heavy, wet dune, and still she failed to sight any of her stakes. Could it be that the sticks had been buried by the wind-whipped sand that had swept through in advance of the pelting rain? What if she could never find the stakes—or the ferry dock? In that case, when morning came she should keep to the shore, so that the boat would see her eventually, not in the trees where they would not find her.

As she slogged through the gale, unsticking her feet from the deep, wet sand into which they sank with each stride, Margot experienced the first stirrings of fear. Bolts of lightning illuminated the furling waves in the ocean, chilling her more than the cold wind and rain. Shivering, her fingers and toes numb, Margot hiked her backpack up on her aching shoulders and forged ahead.

The rain was now beating so hard that Margot felt as if she were trying to push headlong through a brick wall, and so she decided it was time to find a place beneath which she could curl up into a ball and hide herself from the elements. Hugging the landward side of a twenty-foot dune, she foraged for debris from the beach, with which to erect a barricade between herself and the tempest. She dragged a plank through the muddy sand, and then a great branch broken from the trunk of a tree by the fury of the storm, and then some large pieces of plastic from who-knows-what, whatever litter she found on the shore, and piled it against the dune, and then she huddled beneath it all, her back to the dune, and closed her eyes and waited.

And then—she opened her eyes and peered through a chink in the rubble wall. *A light!* Margot tore a hole in her improvised wall and looked again—*a light in the distance!* On the beach! She crawled out of her shelter, adjusted her backpack, and began plodding through the sucking sand toward the light. The rain pricked her flesh, stung her eyes, even when she closed them. But the light drew nearer.

A celestial flash revealed a small shanty on the beach, on an inlet from the coast, a sea shack encircled by a ring of dunes—mountains of sand, two dozen, or three dozen, feet high. Through the sheeting rain Margot saw a light in a window of the ghostly shack. She hurried toward it, thinking that it must be a part of the conservation people's apparatus. Edging into a space between neighboring dunes, she entered the ring of sand and went up to the tiny house. Another flash from the sky showed a bowed, frame structure, a roof punctuated with holes. Still, the light shone from the window.

Margot rapped on the sagging door, knocked again, called hello, is anyone in there? Turned the rusted doorknob, she could feel the rust on her palm, called hello again, pushed the door open, and escaped from the storm into the shanty.

She pushed the door shut, turned to look around the house. The light—*a black taper candle burned down to only an inch!*—someone must be there. Hello, she called again, is anyone home?

She looked around the single room. Adding the candlepower of the flashlight to that of the candle, Margot peered into the corners. Built-in shelves covered three of the four walls, all made of time-darkened, hand-hewn planks. Two items filled the shelves: books and seashells. All the shells, of incongruent shapes and size, great conch shells mixed with those of oysters, clams, and mollusks, were black in color. The books were all old, their bindings ripped and stained by damp and time. The only other furnishings were the plain table on which the candle was placed and a straight-backed wooden chair. Margo dropped into the chair and looked at the storm through the window: it was increasing in fury.

Oh, great, I've got myself stuck in a hurricane, she thought. *This little shack can't keep me safe in a hurricane, but at least I'm dry for the moment.*

She laid her head on her hands, sobbing her fear and frustration until she exhausted her store of tears; and then she rose and wiped her face on her wet sleeve. With the aid of her flashlight she perused the titles of the damp, old books. *Tales of Death on the Seven Seas. A Cursed Mariner's Adventures in Olden Times. Dangerous Creatures of the Deep. Poseidon and Other Water Deities. Pirates and Piracy in the New World from the Renaissance through the Eighteenth Century. Sailors' Songs. Poems of the Seashore. Beachcombing Guide for the Beginner. Bird-Watching for the Hobbyist.*

Margot moved to another wall. The books on these shelves were bound in antiquarian, tooled leather, their bindings wrought with curious designs in tarnished brass. She could not decipher the strange figures on the bindings—an Eastern language, she wondered, or an ancient one—written in a script she did not recognize.

She pulled one from the shelf. Its cover was frayed and its pages curled. Carefully she opened it to the first page. Inscrutable characters covered the friable paper. Margot strove to recognize a single symbol, but she could not. She turned the pages and found illustrations—giant octopi crushing ships in their tentacles, an oyster swallowing a man, mermaids feasting on human eyeballs. She threw the book to the floor. This was not the time to enjoy nonsense like this!

She shone her beam on another book, one with a faded red cover embellished with eroding gold writing of a sort she could not characterize. She removed the volume from the shelf. Its cover was decorated with golden swirls, concentric rings that curled into one another, like a wire coil or a seashell. Turning the mildewed sheets, she discovered more inscrutable glyphs; there were many illustrations, too, drawings of shell-clad ocean creatures—crabs, lobsters, shrimps, and others she did not recognize. All the crustaceans were colored black and drawn upon white backgrounds.

The walls shuddered in the wind. A breeze extinguished the candle, now burned two-thirds of the way down. Margo could hear the shingles fleeing from the roof as she watched the water pouring in through the two holes in it. *It must be nearly morning,* she thought with some relief. *I've made it this far, I'll wait out the storm and my brother will come for me. He may have to search, but he'll contact the authorities and they'll get me out of here in one piece.*

The floor began to rumble as the shanty vibrated crazily, throwing Margot to the floor.

She heard singing . . . melodic intonations . . . she could not make out the words . . . *they had come already! I'll be rescued!*

"I'm here!" she cried. She threw open the door: "I'm here! Help me!"

The singing continued. The song was plainly audible, even over the ululations of the winds. She shined her flashlight through the open door, and the water streamed in torrents down her face and body.

Margot had to hold onto the door frame to avoid being knocked off her feet, for the house was swaying and rolling as the earth shuddered. The song on the wind continued undeterred.

A flash of lightning disclosed a mountain coming over a sand dune—a mountain coming toward the house! Margot stared: lightning flashes came in quick succession now. Thunder booms followed by flashes. More thunder heralding more flashes. Nature's fireworks. In the strobe-light Margot thought she saw a black crab of gargantuan proportions scaling the dune and coming toward the house.

Get hold of yourself, Margot. You're losing it, she chided herself.

As the mountain drew nearer, Margot trained the beam of her flashlight upon it. Four hairy red legs were crawling over the largest dune, a pair of eyes close behind, and more legs—a crab beyond all imaginable proportions. She tried to run back into the shanty, but the black crab picked her up in its pincer and raised her to its eyes, inspecting her, most likely to determine whether she were good to eat.

Margot struggled to extract herself from the monstrous claw—beat upon it with he hands, kicked her legs, screamed at the horrible eyes.

Yet she nearly forgot her own predicament for a second or two—because from her new height she could see a gigantic reptile emerging from the ocean, dragging its long, scaled body from the churning waters with its webbed feet. It opened its elongated, razor-toothed jaws—and the song grew louder, louder than the storm, more pronounced than the thunder and the surf. A phantasmagoric serenade as of sirens calling to night-things. The reptile's tail curved and then thumped the beach, shaking the shanty and levelling two dunes.

Margot began screaming a high-pitched, never-ending scream.

"Margot! Margot! Are you okay? Say something, Margot!" Paul was shaking her as he choked out the words.

Margot opened one eye with difficulty, and her brother began to come into focus.

"I'm—" she fell back, unable to speak any more.

"It's okay, it'll be all right," he repeated as the Coast Guard rescuers bound her to the gurney and carried her to the ambulance boat. One rescuer was holding an IV bag high over his head and watching the drops enter the tubing.

Margot looked around. The sky was a brilliant blue, the sand white-gold heaped up into dunes and dotted with clusters of sea grass. Black ducks glided overhead. There was no sign of the shanty.

"The hurricane—" she faltered.

"There was no hurricane, Margot. The weather's been beautiful all week," Paul answered. "Just relax, honey, you've had too much sun. You're dehydrated. What's that you're clutching so tightly in your hand?"

Margot looked at her clenched fist, raised her hand to her brother. Gently, Paul pried her fingers loose, removed a torn sheet of paper.

"What's this, Margot? A page from a book?"

He unfolded the crumpled paper. It was a woodcut drawing of a nameless and loathsome black crustacean.

Autumn

Anna Taborska

The old man loved the trees that separated his house from the rest of the street. They grew densely, providing him with the solitude he craved, and spoke to him through the sighing of their branches and the rustling of their leaves. The only problem was that one of them had fallen in last week's storm and needed to be replaced.

A sudden gust of wind stirred the russet and crimson leaves, sending them swirling and crackling along the damp pavement. Bill pulled his coat tightly around him and hurried on into the mist. He had to be nearing the place by now: the houses were thinning out and the paving stones were becoming erratic, as though civilization were petering out all around him. And sure enough, the road turned into a dirt track and the suburban landscape gave way to what seemed like a wilderness of mud, grass, and trees, the wilting leaves still clinging to the branches for dear life, but some already beginning to drop like tears of blood.

The man on the phone had said that his house was the last one on the street, past all the other houses and through a small wood. But Bill hadn't counted on the sharp chill in the air and the mist that pooled among the trees that now crowded around him, confounding his sense of direction. He paused for a moment to get his bearings, and the wind that had followed him down the street gathered in strength, rustling the dry leaves and rattling the branches in a way that made him shiver. Perhaps this had not been such a good idea after all. Bill needed a car badly, and the price the man was offering on the Ford was exceptionally good, but the walk to the man's house was making Bill feel increasingly nervous.

As Bill ascertained which way he was meant to go, he imagined he saw movement out of the corner of his eye. He spun round, but it was only a tree—its boughs swaying in the wind. Bill moved off, but not before he saw something move to his left. He looked over his shoulder, but saw only leaves and the branches of trees, obscured by the grayish-white mist.

Bill hurried on, but soon found himself slowed by the protruding limbs of the trees all around him. They seemed to be pressing in on him, and he had to be careful not to sustain a nasty scratch on his face or have an eye poked out. He hadn't noticed when the trees had become so dense, and figured that he must have strayed off the path in the mist. He looked around, trying to spot the dirt track he'd come in on, but all he could see were the dark-barked trees with their blood-colored leaves, which rustled at him in a manner that somehow seemed hostile. Bill chastised himself silently for such a ridiculous notion and decided to press on, but almost impaled himself on a branch as he did so. A partially formed thought flashed in his mind: surely trees didn't grow so close together; surely they had to have some space between them, not to block out each other's light and steal each other's nutrients from the ground. He took a step back and hit his head hard on a low bough. Everything went black for a moment, as Bill reeled from the blow to the back of his head.

A few seconds later Bill regained consciousness as a heavy weight pushed against his chest. Something rough was scratching his face, and there was a loud crackling in his ears. Bill opened his mouth to scream, but the trees between which he was wedged forced all the breath from his lungs. Then his body convulsed as twigs and branches, suckers and bark grew all around and into and through him, rooting him to the ground on which he stood. His skin hardened and cracked; his arms twisted and burst out in a thousand gnarled shoots. And as Bill's face froze and hardened and dissolved beneath a coarse wooden crust, he finally released his last scream: it was the rustle of russet and crimson leaves over the spot where he vanished from sight.

The old man came out into the yard and listened to the wind whispering in the trees. He stroked the roof of his battered old Ford and smiled.

Come Figures, Shadows, and Reflections: The Timeless Appeal of Rod Serling's *The Twilight Zone*

Jason V Brock

Rodman Edward Serling (25 December 1924–28 June 1975) of Syracuse, New York (his family moved to Binghamton, New York, when he was a child), had been a reader of various pulp magazines and anthologies dating all the way back to his service in World War II, and possibly even earlier. His time in service had been difficult and traumatic; he was stationed in the Pacific Theater during the war, where he was wounded in combat (he served from 1943 to 1945, earning a Purple Heart and a Bronze Star). The whole experience left him with deep psychological scars, as it did for many who served. Although a reader, he had never really been a serious writer prior to his military involvement, aside from editing the Binghamton Central High School newspaper. After the war, he seemed to take comfort in the process of creating stories, perhaps as a way to grapple with his personal demons, and writing became a way of relating not only with the world, but also to himself, almost rising to a compulsion at times.

Upon his return to civilian life, Serling in 1948 married a young woman named Carol Kramer, whom he met at Antioch College while attending on the G.I. Bill. They would ultimately have two children, daughters Jodi and Anne. In 1949, Serling won a writing contest for his radio script "To Live a Dream," and the couple visited New York City as a result; future *Twilight Zone* scribe Earl Hamner, Jr. (later the creator/writer of *The Waltons* [1972–81]) was also there, having placed in the contest as well. In 1950, Serling earned his B.A. in Literature from Antioch.

After graduating college, Serling began working a staff position at a radio station in Ohio, WLW, which had not only recently been vacated by his friendly rival Hamner, but had also been key in the career of one of their mutual early influences, the radio giant Norman Corwin ("On a Note of Triumph" [1945]), another lyrical writer known for his keen insights about the human condition and sharp political commentaries. By 1951, Serling started to write for television in addition to radio, leaving once more for New York City to become a full-time writer for the new medium in 1952. His big break would arrive in 1955 with his seventy-second produced script: "Patterns," aired on the *Kraft Television Theatre*. The production was an immediate, resounding success and catapulted Serling into the stratosphere of public consciousness. It would go on to win the 8th Annual Primetime Emmy Awards (1956) for Best Original Teleplay Writing (the first of six in his career). As a result, offers poured in, and the Serlings relocated to California. This triumph would be followed in short order by several other milestones in TV writing.

Thus, by 1958 Rod Serling was a major force in television, having accumulated three Primetime Emmys ("Patterns" was followed by "Requiem for a Heavyweight" [1956] and "The Comedian" [1958]), as well as a Peabody Award ("Requiem for a Heavyweight") for his outstanding efforts; by this time, he was rightfully lauded as one of the most significant, original writers of serious televised drama. Highly regarded by the networks, critics, and the general public alike, Serling's name was already a fixed star in the constellation of teleplaywrights of the Golden Age of TV, right alongside other such vital creators as Paddy Chayefsky ("Marty" [1953]), Reginald Rose ("Twelve Angry Men" [1954]), Gore Vidal (*Myra Breckinridge* [1970]), and Horton Foote (*The Trip to Bountiful* [1985]).

Unbeknownst to the viewing public, however, Serling had already been long frustrated by the tightening grip of sponsors (corporate interests that financially underwrote the shows being produced). He was eager to get away from the ridiculous demands that were increasingly expected of his scripts, demonstrated by this quote from a 1959 interview with journalist Mike Wallace:

Somebody asked me the other day if this means that I'm going to be a meek conformist, and my answer is no, I'm just acting the role of a tired non-conformist, and I don't want to fight anymore. I don't want to have to battle sponsors and agencies. I don't want to have to push for something that I want and have to settle for second best. I don't want to have to compromise all the time, which in essence is what the television writer does if he wants to put on controversial themes.

Undeterred, and despite his reservations, Serling pitched his idea for a show rooted in science fiction, fantasy, and horror traditions, but he was met with skepticism by broadcast executives. His thought process, based on interviews during this time, was that if he wrote what he wanted but used the filter of fantastical genres as a frame-of-remove to address his thematic interests, he would be able to skirt the censors (sponsors) while keeping his personal integrity intact:

> **WALLACE:** Well, you're not going to be able to cop a plea or chop an axe because you're going to be obviously working so hard on *The Twilight Zone* that, in essence, for the time being and for the foreseeable future, you've given up on writing anything important for television, right?
>
> **SERLING:** Yeah. Well, again, this is a semantic thing ... "important for television." I don't know. If by important you mean I'm not going to try to delve into current social problems dramatically, you're quite right, I'm not.

Protestations aside, Serling crafted a teleplay, "The Time Element" (1958), which, while thoughtful and well realized, was a departure from—although soon to be a signature of—his previous trajectory as a dynamic and important writer for the burgeoning small screen medium. It was a bold move, especially at the time—arguably during the height of his career—and given his position in the firmament of TV writers during this period. After being shelved for a time, it was eventually produced in late 1958 for *The Westinghouse Desilu Playhouse*, an anthology series from Lucille Ball and Desi

Arnaz. As a result of critical acclaim and enthusiastic public support for the episode, Serling was finally given the green light to undertake his own weekly anthology show, *The Twilight Zone,* in 1959.

The Twilight Zone (1959–64), notwithstanding Serling's cachet, was by no means guaranteed to be a success, though the signposts ahead were pointing in the right direction.

Context, since nothing happens in a vacuum, and *dramatis personae:* By the 1950s, in addition to declining print sales from pulps and digests (e.g., *Weird Tales, Black Mask, Gamma*), upcoming slicks such as *Man's Adventure* and *For Men Only* (soon superseded in popularity by lifestyle magazines—*Playboy* [1953f.] and its imitators, notably including *Rogue* [1956–65]), as well as sundry paperback originals (mostly novels and anthologies) featuring classic and neophyte authors alike (to include the phenomenal Ray Bradbury [*The Martian Chronicles* [1950], from Doubleday]) were available during this era at newsstands. Not to be outdone, lurid comic books such as *Tales from the Crypt, The Vault of Horror,* and *Weird Science-Fantasy* from EC Comics publisher William M. Gaines (1944–56) were very popular and widely copied (though soon to be troubled, thanks to later debunked claims of contributing to juvenile delinquency in psychiatrist Dr. Fredric Wertham's notorious *Seduction of the Innocent* [1954], which powered the eventual primacy of superhero offerings once horror titles were essentially banned). EC also worked with Bradbury and rendered several of his short stories into the comic book medium.

In the meantime, other media continued (or revisited) this genre-related trend. Of course, there had been numerous efforts in mass media prior to this post–World War II resurgence in more esoteric popular fare—which owed much of its 1950s rise to the then-novel concept of the "teenage consumer" and car culture—in radio, film, and television, capitalizing on renewed enthusiasm for all things fantasy, horror, and science fiction in the escapist-oriented wake of the war and the atomic bomb. Some offerings were inevitably more successful than others.

Precursors to Serling's vision included both long-running and short-lived attempts in all media, with broadcast radio boasting several notable shows in the pre-TV, post–World War I/1918 Flu Pandemic period—galvanized in part by the sensational Mercury Theatre production on Halloween 1938 of Orson Welles's adaptation of H. G. Wells's novel *The War of the Worlds* (1898), which stunned a traumatized nation—such as *The Witch's Tale* (1931–38; the first horror-oriented offering on air nationally), *The Hermit's Cave* (1937–44; an early influence on later *Zone* alumnus Charles Beaumont), *Lights Out* (airing 1934–47; later taken over by Arch Oboler and brought briefly to television), *Inner Sanctum* (1941–52), and several others. In this light, even more mainstream forays into the fantastic—such as Frank Capra's immortal *It's a Wonderful Life* (1946), itself a reimagining of Charles Dickens's holiday ghost classic *A Christmas Carol* (1843)—could be seen as artistic predecessors to Serling's creation.

The 1950s also initiated what is now understood as the "Monster Kid" craze, fueled by the reissue in theaters of now iconic (and heavily imitated) Universal Studios monster movies from the 1930s and '40s, featuring pictures adapted from well-known literary sources—including Bram Stoker, Mary Shelley, and Edgar Allan Poe—as well as Hollywood originals: *Dracula* (1931), *Frankenstein* (1931), *Murders in the Rue Morgue* (1932), *The Mummy* (1932), *The Invisible Man* (1933), *The Black Cat* (1934), *The Wolf Man* (1941), and many others.

During this time, upstarts such as American International Pictures (AIP) jumped into the fray. From 1955 until finally closing down in 1980 after a name change to Filmways, Inc., it was during its tenure as an independent studio that AIP would turn out many genre features, in the process driving the careers of numerous important figures, including prolific and influential filmmaker Roger Corman (*The Intruder* [1962], adapted by Charles Beaumont from his 1959 novel), producer Alex Gordon, and later writers who would eventually be key to *The Twilight Zone*'s success (as well as Corman's

"Poe Cycle" [1960–64] of film adaptations): Richard Matheson (*The Shrinking Man* [1956]), Charles Beaumont (*The Hunger and Other Stories* [1958]), and *Playboy* editor/writer Ray Russell (*Sardonicus and Other Stories* [1961]); the former two were also recommended by later *Zone* contributor and Serling favorite Ray Bradbury. (As an aside, Corman's fine adaptation of *The Intruder* would also include a solid performance from Beaumont, in addition to cameos from his writer friends William F. Nolan, George Clayton Johnson, Frank M. Robinson, and OCee Ritch.)

Timely treatments of the unthinkable also prevailed in the guise of intergalactic "alien" invaders, paranoid social interactions, and identity-stealing lifeforms (*The Day the Earth Stood Still* [1951], *Invasion of the Body Snatchers* [1956], and others), in addition to the body horror levels of nuclear unease on display in Japanese *kaiju* films, including the watershed 1954 classic *Godzilla*. Hammer Film Productions Ltd.—pivoting to monster horror in the 1950s (*The Quatermass Xperiment* [1955], based on the original 1953 BBC serial by Nigel Kneale)—would carry the village torch for a bit, though by the end of the 1960s audiences were again ready for change. *Rosemary's Baby* (1968) would reset the scene with another, less secular repackaging of what scared people, leading to *The Exorcist* (1973) and its legions of imitators before morphing audience fears further with new subgenres of fright, including everything from eco-horror, disaster films, and Slasher movies, to—even later—opening the Void to Lovecraftian cosmic horror.

All this activity would feed a building frenzy for the strange, horrific, and tawdry in all phases of teen life, leading to the magazine debut of *Famous Monsters of Filmland* (1958–83; original run) from publisher James Warren, edited by science fiction pioneer (and Bradbury friend) Forrest J Ackerman, who also acted as literary agent to many writers in the science fiction and horror fields at this time. As the decades wore on, top-notch creators such as Georges Franju (*Eyes without a Face* [1960]), Michael Powell (*Peeping Tom* [1960]), Bradbury, and Ackerman soulmate Ray Harryhausen (*Jason and the Argonauts* [1963]), and Alfred Hitchcock (*Psycho* [1960]; adapted from the famous 1959 novel by the prolific and formative writer Robert Bloch, which was itself loosely based on the crimes of killer Ed Gein) began to remake the genre into different shapes and shades of monster. The configurations were less menacing simply due to physical deformity (and/or revulsion tied to the uncanny or supernatural), and instead harkened back to exotic legends from other cultures, or the twisted psyches of "human fiends" from earlier movies, such as German Expressionistic masterpieces *Der Golem* (1920), *The Cabinet of Dr. Caligari* (1920), and Fritz Lang's classic modernist takes such as *Metropolis* (1927) or the chilling *M* (1931). These older efforts, particularly, appeared to resonate within the mental/emotional space increasingly swarmed by creeping modern-ist/postmodernist real-world concerns, social upheavals, and terrors. Later on, as technology progressed, many of these same trends and apprehensions would inspire Serling and his confederates in a bur-geoning, volatile mediascape. Like Sputnik 1 in 1957, entertainment and technology were fast approaching cultural escape velocity.

In another nod to the preoccupations of the era, on TV—sandwiched between the ubiquitous Westerns on offer—the fare was becoming more wide-ranging and spooky as well, reaching for adults in addition to kids. Shows included mysteries, crime, and re-lated programming along with ghastly and futuristic treatments, these latter two gradually reflecting Atomic Age contemplations, post-Rosenberg paranoia, and Red Scare McCarthyist/Hollywood Ten anxieties, which were all touched upon in series such as *Tales of Tomorrow* (1951–53), *Alfred Hitchcock Presents* (1955–65), *One Step Beyond* (1959–61), Roald Dahl's *Way Out* (1961), *Thriller* (1960–62) with Boris Karloff, and more. Things would even veer into the bizarre and camp with comedic takes on the strange in the guise of such macabre programming as *The Addams Family* (1964–66) and *The Munsters* (1964–66).

As much of this was happening, in 1957, a 52-set package of pre-1948 Universal Horror films were made available for TV syndication by Screen Gems, part of Columbia Pictures. It would be known as *Shock Theater* and sold as *Shock!*. Beginning on local TV stations and spreading coast-to-coast, the (mostly) weekend offerings developed into miniature events as horror hosts such as Vampira and Zacherley presented classic horror flicks to horrified small screen audiences along with scary music, visuals, and chutzpah.

Meanwhile, novelty songs such as "The Purple People Eater" (1958) and "Monster Mash" (1962) wafted from car radios everywhere in their freakish lope to the top of the charts, as other horror tie-ins replicated like some bioluminescent graveyard fungus. In 1961, Aurora model kits released "Frankenstein's Monster" to avid aficionados and collectors as monstrous Halloween costumes for children proliferated faster than ghosts from a major disaster; at the same time, high-quality rubber masks from places like Don Post chilled devotees to the bone. It was quite a time for neophyte Monster Kids, as store shelves sagged under the increasing weight of proliferating "Creature Feature"–oriented product, from posters, makeup manuals, and clothing to trading cards, clubs, novelizations, and so on. In the modern era, even theme parks would be in on the creepy action.

This intoxicating background set the stage for *The Twilight Zone,* and Monster Kids everywhere—including future cultural titans such as directors Steven Spielberg, John Landis, Joe Dante, George A. Romero, John Carpenter, David Cronenberg, as well as writers Stephen King, Greg Bear, Dan O'Bannon, and others—were soon to be whisked into a fifth dimension from whence they would never truly return.

Once the show, remarkably with no recurring characters aside from Serling as host/narrator, was approved to go into production by the network due to acclaim from "The Time Element," Serling got to work in earnest. The name of the pilot episode for the new speculative series *The Twilight Zone*—Serling's "Where Is Everybody?"—seemed to be both a cry into the depths of some existential chasm as well as a veiled challenge to naysayers. Debuting in October 1959, the show was slow to attract viewers at first, so the episode title also served one other function at its launch—irony.

The close of the 1950s, as noted, was the apparent end of one version of America and the dawn of another. Even as World War II and its attendant horrors retreated—including the Holocaust as well as the twin artificial suns of Hiroshima and Nagasaki—there was an unfocused, protean angst about what was looming on the hazy, distant horizon, politically, culturally, socially. The postwar era was a period of rapid expansion and disorienting change unlike others before it, and the maturation of its modernist shockwaves rippled across the spirit of the age like an atomic blast; cultural and societal touchstones would be redefined in multiple realms by the kaleidoscopic repercussions to follow.

For example, just in U.S. domestic politics there was the civil rights movement, the induction in 1959 of Alaska and Hawaii as states, a creeping escalation of the cold war with the USSR, interventionist wars in both Korea and Vietnam, and Castro's successful revolution in Cuba among them.

In other areas, humanity was shaken by the gamut of nascent American art movements such as Abstract Expressionism (perhaps owing a debt to Francis Bacon and a few others)—represented on one side by Jackson Pollock's "Action Painting" and on the other by the subliminal Color Fields of Mark Rothko—and Pop Art (lead by notable tastemakers such as Andy Warhol and Jasper Johns). Meanwhile, in the domains of science and medicine, even as the chilling specter of nuclear war spread like some dark cloud from the ashes of the old order, several advances were made, including Watson and Crick's discovery of the double-helix structure of DNA, the creation of an effective polio vaccine led by Dr. Jonas Salk, the unsettling launch of Sputnik 1 by the Soviet Union (which would kick off the space race), the development of the transistor, the founding of NASA, the advent of the contraceptive pill ("The Pill"), and the beginning of passenger airplane service. (Much of this would become fodder for the outstanding modern TV show *Mad Men*

[2007–15], part of the so-called "Second" Golden Age of TV.)

In the world of literature and entertainment, there was the previously stated rise and fall of EC comics, *Playboy* magazine's arrival, and an upsurge in youth and car culture, while, simultaneously in popular music, there was the birth of rock-'n'-roll, an explosion of jazz, and a revival of the older idiom of folk. Novels were events that informed personal and social discourse in ways not equaled since, and the bestseller lists were populated by authors as diverse and influential as J. D. Salinger (*The Catcher in the Rye* [1951]), Ernest Hemingway (*The Old Man and the Sea* [1952]), Ralph Ellison (*Invisible Man* [1952]), Ray Bradbury (*Fahrenheit 451* [1953]), and Vladimir Nabokov (*Lolita* [1955]). Writers such as James Baldwin (*Notes of a Native Son* [1955]) and Mary McCarthy (*The Group* [1963]) were also popular, while the Beat Generation, among them Allen Ginsberg (*Howl and Other Poems* [1956]), Jack Kerouac (*On the Road* [1957]), and William S. Burroughs (*Naked Lunch* [1959]) pushed literary culture ahead as they reflected on the gods and monsters of the human condition.

In film during this time there were several key figures—directors Alfred Hitchcock, Federico Fellini, Ingmar Bergman, Akira Kurosawa, and Lina Wertmüller among them—who would reform the cinematic experience. Along the way, many low-budget science fiction movies (again, like *Godzilla* and the various offerings from Ray Harryhausen), Italian Spaghetti Westerns (e.g., director Sergio Leone's output), and the French New Wave (e.g., filmmakers Jean-Luc Godard, Éric Rohmer, François Truffaut, et al.) impacted audiences with blasts of energy and creativity that were both shocking and exciting. As cited, television was also in the midst of its Golden Age, exemplified in part by such writers as Rose, Chayefsky, and, of course, Rod Serling.

Despite all this largely positive forward momentum, and though the 1960s would commence with a fragile hope—personified by the ascension of youthful Massachusetts senator John F. Kennedy to the presidency in 1960—much of this expectant confidence would soon give way to political strife and turbulence, including the Bay of Pigs debacle in 1961, the Cuban Missile Crisis (precipitated by shoe-banging USSR leader Nikita Khrushchev, which climaxed in October 1962), and finally the tragic assassination of JFK on 22 November 1963; under the new presidency of Lyndon Johnson, Vietnam would intensify.

Before this sudden shift, however, Serling would introduce something new to television screens—though it would obviously have echoes of previous efforts in differing media—that would continue the overall social trend of general optimism (albeit tinged with wistfulness and unease), and combine it with a curious reflective progress characterized by a fear of machines and an embrace of the supernatural. The result would be a worthy vehicle to extend the immense potential and artistry of television's First Golden Age.

In *The Twilight Zone,* Serling's aforementioned frustrations with television's corporate interference would be tackled obliquely; the outcome would usher in a whole new way of considering the world and human experience in the media across its 156 remarkable episodes (a staggering 92, many of them classics, would eventually be written or adapted by Serling as part of his commitment to CBS to get the series on the air, among them "The Midnight Sun" [1961]). Equal parts surrealist delusion, critique of humanity's hubris, social autopsy, and technological warning bell, the series was a thematic and dramatic departure for audiences and creator alike, detonating perfectly into the already explosive intellectual psychosphere and resulting in an uncanny, satisfying *gestalt.*

The energetic creative engine of *The Twilight Zone* was comprised primarily of Serling and his core writers working in concert with many talented producers, actors, directors, and composers. The atomic structure of this arrangement would come to revolve around the charismatic and driven Charles Beaumont (the most prolific contributor to the show after Serling, with 22 episodes to his credit, such as the unforgettable "The Howling Man" [1960]; some of them would be ghostwritten due to his tragic final illness). Other writers would muster around Beaumont, who was himself not only employed by Serling but previously mentored by Bradbury.

This congregation of writers, much like the Beats, the Lovecraft Circle, and the Lost Generation before them, were an exclusive yet welcoming pack of determined young men (mostly). Known collectively to themselves as "The Group" after McCarthy's famous novel (and more formally as "The Southern California School of Writers"), at its nucleus this assemblage of Beaumont's writerly friends included the previously mentioned Richard Matheson (16 shows for the series, including "Nick of Time" [1960], showcasing a pre–*Star Trek* William Shatner, who also starred in Corman's *The Intruder*), John Tomerlin (writer of "Number 12 Looks Just Like You" [1964], based on a Beaumont story), and George Clayton Johnson (story for four adaptations, scripter of four others, including the poignant "Nothing in the Dark" [1962]).

Other key players included William F. Nolan (*Logan's Run* [1967; with Johnson]), who along with Matheson would later be critical to the output of genre director/producer Dan Curtis (creator of *Dark Shadows* [1966–71]), and who co-authored an unproduced fantasy *Zone* episode with Johnson ("Dreamflight"); novelist Jerry Sohl (whose three episodes, such as the creepy "Living Doll" [1963], were ghostwritten and uncredited to him in order to assist the terminally ill Beaumont); the writer/editor Charles E. Fritch (*Negative of a Nude* [1959]); Chad Oliver (*The Winds of Time* [1957]); Mari Wolf (*Mari Wolf Resurrected* [2011]), the only female who was not married to a member of The Group; Kris Neville (*Bettyann* [1970]), and others.

Several established creators also crossed orbits with The Group, both privately and professionally, including not only Bradbury (who provided one episode for Serling's venture with "I Sing the Body Electric" [1962]), Bloch, and Russell, but also Ian Fleming (creator of James Bond), *Rogue* editor Frank M. Robinson (*The Power* [1956]), early Serling friend Earl Hamner, Jr. (writer of eight *Zone* episodes of his own, including "The Bewitchin' Pool" [1964], the final show aired of the original series), and Harlan Ellison (*Dangerous Visions* [1967]; also an editor for *Rogue* under Robinson), as well as filmmakers Corman, Otto Preminger (*Anatomy of a Murder* [1959]), and George Pal (*7 Faces of Dr. Lao* [1967], scripted by Beaumont and the legendary, uncredited, Ben Hecht).

Overall, the collective impact of these youthful innovators on popular culture—especially considered through such a narrow aperture of time—is difficult to overstate; in fact, it transcends the present.

With respect to their influences, all were impressed to some degree by timeless writers of the past, such as L. Frank Baum, John Collier, Franz Kafka, Edgar Allan Poe, and H. P. Lovecraft, but also by contemporary mainstream novelists and playwrights, as well as more directly by Bradbury (many became his close friends) and newer fantasists. In addition, they shared a strong desire to address social issues of the day, and infused it into the subtext of their multifarious output. In addition, their avid consumption of pop culture—from auto racing, science fiction, and hobby rocket launches to jazz, comics, and movies—also factored into the ways they expressed themselves. At the end of the day, given the delirious speed of societal progress and technology, as well as the complexity of a darkening geopolitical landscape under the cold war, there was probably no community of artists anywhere better suited to tackle the myriad issues facing the modern social order as it evolved. Spearheaded by the caduceus of Bradbury and Serling (though their working and personal relationship would eventually cool), The Group would join them in crafting a generally hopeful, although wary, outlook with respect to the cynical approaching oblivion that seemed to shift in the shadowed fringes of an increasingly bewildered populace, awash in postwar anomie and disillusionment, especially following the Kennedy assassination.

In this way, *The Twilight Zone* would define a gold standard in the horror and science fiction fields while widening them further through generous sprinklings of the "Dark Fantastique," modernist literary concision, novel psychological approaches, and a final "touch of strange" by way of magical realism. A broad swath of topics and themes—ranging from the breakdown of society and human interactions to the delicate balance of human reliance on the more destructive aspects of technology and science to the mysteries of the supernatural brought tantalizingly into focus through sharp writing and provocative stances—would fearlessly explore both the cryptic, everchanging human interior and the rugged frontiers of tangible reality. No ideas were explicitly off limits, though care was made to treat thornier subject matter so as to be palatable to most audiences (and to keep these areas opaque from undue sponsor influence, always an issue). To this end, in addition to the fine original works from the regular *Zone* contributors, Serling and his production team also recruited from a wide selection of classic and newer authors, including excellent adaptations of contemporary genre writers such as Jerome Bixby (the Serling-adapted "It's a Good Life" [1961]), Damon Knight (Serling's treatment of "To Serve Man" [1962]), Ambrose Bierce (the 1963 Academy Award-winning *Zone*-acquired French short film adaptation of "An Occurrence at Owl Creek Bridge" [aired on the series in 1964]), and others.

Along the way, there were many products and tie-ins to the series, including original albums (such as Marty Manning and his Orchestra's *The Twilight Zone: A Sound Adventure In Space* [1961]), books collecting stories adapted by Serling from scripts in the series (*Stories from the Twilight Zone* [1960], *More Stories from the Twilight Zone* [1961], and *New Stories from the Twilight Zone* [1962] among them), *Twilight Zone* comic books (1962–82 and other iterations later), and even a board game from Ideal in 1964. By 1963, another short-lived entry into Serling's space would launch with the arrival on TV of *The Outer Limits* (1963–65), produced initially by *Psycho* screenwriter Joseph Stefano, who also wrote for the show.

Despite these entries into the popular consciousness; despite the quality of the writing and production values; despite the warm critical receptiveness; and despite multiple industry accolades (the series would garner two Primetime Emmys [1960 and 1961] against four nominations, as well as a 1963 Golden Globe for Serling as producer), *The Twilight Zone* always struggled to entice a wide viewership. Every year since its debut there were scraps with executives over renewal of the show, and the struggle was finally lost over low ratings in 1964. In the end, Serling would breathe a sigh of relief, freer now to pursue other opportunities after a protracted term in the creative trenches.

The final impact of *The Twilight Zone* would not be fully understood for a while. In the end, it is obvious that the show was more than the sum of its parts; today it is seen as one of the greatest shows in history. Its creators, especially Serling and his stable of writers, are revered as masters of the craft of television and literature, and they are together regarded as perhaps the most influential collective of creatives in any medium. On the whole, the series was wildly successful artistically, and its legacy (including revivals) stands as an unshakable testament to its staying power, influence, and prestige. Of course, there were a few episodes that missed the mark or were too "on the nose," but this is to be expected over the course of a collaborative effort that went on as long as *The Twilight Zone*. It remains as a bold testimony to the powers of invention, implementation, talent, and fearlessness; no other TV presentation really comes close, and it has inspired not only casual viewers but creatives alike in the years since to consider the unexplored idea, to reflect, to have greater empathy, to view events not with a distorted mirror of presentist narcissism, but through the long lens of historical perspective. This kind of insightful perception can only be found in truly astonishing works of art; the result is that the show embodies a timelessness and beauty of execution that is generally reserved only for the greatest artists and creators in all human history, irrespective of tradition, culture, era, medium, or time. The final analysis reveals Serling's creation to be not only a triumph, but noble as well.

The Group, in the post-*Zone* aftermath, began to capitalize on their unrelated prospects, having diversified deeply into various areas of print (e.g., stories and articles in *Playboy, Rogue,* original anthologies, collections, novels, and so on), film (with Corman, Pal, et al.), and television. Indeed, if *The Twilight Zone* represented a sort of creative "marriage" which kept The Group employed and busy, they were not above the occasional "affair" with other series, such as *Alfred Hitchcock Presents, Thriller, Route 66* (1960–64), and several more. As a consequence, they began both individually and collectively to influence pop culture, and they would continue as a loose consortium for a time (including a short-lived venture called "The Green Hand"). Their final dissolution would result from the untimely death of Beaumont due to a degenerative neurological condition (probably Frontotemporal Dementia [FTD]) at age thirty-eight in 1967; after this event, there was no longer a strong enough force to bind them together. In the aftershock of their grief, they would fly apart to engage in their singular destinies.

Their impacts individually, as a result, would continue in very concrete ways.

Though *The Twilight* Zone was ending, 1964 saw other cultural shifts in the media come to the fore. In the immediate wake of The Beatles' early 1964 appearances on *The Ed Sullivan Show*, American tastes by the mid-'60s were moving away from the more rigid social norms of the initial postwar phase. So long Rat Pack, Doo-Wop, and Elvis; hello Hippies, Flower Power, and Rock bands.

As the seasons turned, Serling stayed as in demand as ever, combining his writing duties with teaching, appearances on TV, and lecturing. He wrote the holiday-themed TV movie *A Carol for Another Christmas* (1964) based on the Dickens classic, as well as the screenplay for a political thriller, *Seven Days in May* (1964), created and wrote for a short-lived, poorly received Western (*The Loner* [1965–66]), and later another TV thriller entitled *The Doomsday Flight* (1966) which he came to regret after people began to call in terroristic threats triggered by the show. (Interestingly, Serling's older brother Robert J. Serling, an aviation expert and writer, served as technical adviser to the movie.)

In the meantime, the other *Zone* writers were also keeping busy.

In addition to magazine appearances, books, periodic film work, and some episodic TV credits, the social climate—heating up in conjunction with the escalating stakes in post-Kennedy Vietnam—was making a big impression on The Group and their output. The youth movement had transformed, and the Hippie countercultural era was rapidly taking to the streets and dividing universities with new energy and purpose. Parents and their children saw an increasingly wide rift open between them sociopolitically, and everything from music to art to TV and movies began to reflect these cultural changes.

In the latter half of this tumultuous period, TV shows began to harness this unrest with the spikier youth-oriented elements quickly becoming the new normal; as post–World War II ideals eroded under withering political protests and dissent amidst an uptick in global activism and broader social unrest, people were openly questioning realities (e.g., for the poor, for women, for minorities) they had previously ignored. In this new age, everything was suspect; older people were seen as likely "enemies" and the U.S. government was increasingly viewed as complicit in undermining human enterprise and potential as the decade wore on.

One of the most interesting developments in television during this time was a renewed curiosity in the ways entertainment could address these issues. In the late-1960s, right alongside TV programming such as the previously noted horror movie reruns and campy monster fare such as *The Munsters* and *The Addams Family*, new socially reflective shows such as *The Monkees* (1966–68) and *Rowan & Martin's Laugh-In* (1968–73) gained status; though Westerns were still quite popular, the entry of a modestly budgeted new series set in space called *Star Trek* (1966–69) would not only capture imaginations (switching the "frontier" from the West to the stars), but also serve to represent a sort of post-Group reunion vehicle.

Several familiar names from *The Twilight Zone* would have bylines on *Star Trek*. Though Serling himself was not involved in the series, creator/writer Gene Roddenberry and his cohorts, showrunner/writer Gene L. Coon ("The Devil in the Dark" [1967]) and story editor/writer D. C. Fontana ("Journey to Babel" [1967]), obvious-ly valued similar themes and appreciated strong writing. Since The Group was still communally active to some degree (though Beau-mont would never write for the show due to his condition; he died in 1967, a year after the debut of *Star Trek*), the other members were still seeking work where they could find it, with an obvious prefer-ence for science fiction, horror, and fantasy.

Strangely, much like *The Twilight Zone*, *Star Trek* struggled to find an audience even though it was well written, entertaining, and progressive. Looking back, it seems absurd that people were so reti-cent to embrace these iconic shows—now considered major intellec-tual properties with enormous fanbases—but it is a fact nonetheless. At present, *Star Trek* has become an institution, much like *The Twi-light Zone*, and it is hard to fathom the realms of current speculative television or literature outside of their twin cultural influences. The shows' production staff, writers, and actors, against all odds, wound up creating something, once again, greater than the sums of their parts. Not an easy feat, even now.

Not to be outshone, Serling was once more feverishly at work on several projects, including films; a few of them had an astonishing cultural influence in the near-term. In the first instance, he flexed his pro-social ideals and insights in ways that short-form TV (and its sponsors) would not have been able to permit at the time. To that end, he poured his incredible talent and drive into adapting a French novel: *La planète des singes* (1963) by Pierre Boulle—into a screenplay (with noted screenwriter Michael Wilson); in the process he managed to imbue a gritty realism to the fantastic story while in-fusing it with masterfully misdirected social critique. The result—*Planet of the Apes* (1968)—was to spawn a pop cultural phenomenon and inspire a whole franchise that is still relevant today. *Apes*, as not-ed, would be a watershed in several ways, though one unanticipated, and sadly noteworthy, aspect of its history (especially given some of its subtext) was its debut on 3 April 1968—*one day* before the heart-breaking assassination of American civil rights leader Dr. Martin

Luther King, Jr. As this tragedy unfolded, only a few short months later the United States reeled again from the senseless murder of Democratic presidential candidate Robert F. Kennedy on 6 June 1968. Their premature deaths would complete a terrible quadfecta that included the death of Kennedy's brother, President John F. Kennedy, only five short years previously and had continued with the shooting of Malcolm X in 1965.

As the year dragged on, the 1968 Democratic National Convention in Chicago devolved into an authoritarian nightmare as police attacked conventioneers and war protestors live on TV. Later, Monster Kid George A. Romero would unleash his haunting vision, *Night of the Living Dead* (1968), in an apparent bid to reflect the growing discontent of the times; his film even included the awful killing of a black protagonist at its climax, although the picture had been completed well before King's murder. In fact, he was shuttling the film around to find distributors when he heard of King's death on the car radio.

By all appearances, the 1967 Summer of Love vibes, perhaps best symbolized by The Beatles' *Sgt. Pepper's Lonely Hearts Club Band,* was dying; in late 1969 it would be finished, finally killed during the disastrous Altamont Speedway Free Festival in California, presided over by The Rolling Stones, with "security" provided by the Hell's Angels. With the murder of black festival-goer Meredith Hunter, captured in the documentary *Gimme Shelter* (1970), the entire horror show was an effective rebuke to the idealistic 1960s ethos of "Peace and Love" displayed a mere few months prior at the Woodstock Music and Art Fair in rural New York.

Alas, the '60s were dead.

As the '70s took form—shambling into view during a uniquely grim and opaque period—the spirit of the age appeared intent on shrugging off the afterglow of the naïve optimism of the hippie/peacenik aesthetic. As the Baby Boomers aged into adulthood, such blind hopefulness appeared more and more at odds with the looming social and material entropy of progressively complicated global *realpolitik* considerations; the modern and postmodern world was increasingly understood to be unpredictable, paranoid, dangerous—a bleak contrast to the way the decade of the 1960s had begun. After all the hope and excitement on offer in the post–World War II era, the changes blowing through the mediascape and geopolitically would forever burst the cheerful bubble of U.S. superpower hegemony on display in the wake of conquering the twin threats of Nazi and Imperial Japanese ultranationalism, the "defeat" of the Soviet Union in the Space Race, and the rise of personal fortunes after the war. Dragging on the collective (un)consciousness were not only an escalating Vietnam War, but also growing awareness of financial disparities between minority groups and whites in the aftermath of desegregation and the dissolution of Jim Crow, as well as the specter of rising international tensions over resources such as oil, food, and water, in addition to blowback from the American public with regard to U.S. intervention in foreign geopolitics and the ever-smoldering embers of the Cold War.

Although his main vehicle for examining these various social ills was now long gone, Serling was not oblivious to the churn and change of the world around him. Ever observant, ever political, he would have been acutely aware of such gathering storms moving in off the metaphorical horizon. With all this going on, the general pace of life began an acceleration trend that has only increased in speed and profusion in the decades following, and this would afford him one more major foray into their analysis via broadcast television (now available in higher sonic fidelity and glorious color); this consumer-driven technological period was a precursor of the digital revolution soon to manifest in the Information Age. The end product of this new vehicle for Serling would present (perhaps as a reflection of his mood) in a more pointedly Gothic and chilling exhibition—leaning decidedly into personal horror, shock, and psychological examination, and away from cautionary tales of modern technological achievement or the unmasking of squishy moral dilemmas: *Rod Ser-*

ling's Night Gallery (8 November 1969 [pilot]; 16 December 1970–
27 May 1973 [series]).

As all this coalesced, Serling himself couldn't have written a
more bracing coda to end one era and begin another—but he was
about to try, nonetheless.

Return of the Revenant

Carl E. Reed

In the briny deep moves a withered beast
     of rictus'd grin & skeletal claw,
stumbling forward in the Stygian dark
     in defiance of natural law.

One hundred years to the day he drowned
     Oliver Grenville makes the coast;
off Old Head of Kinsdale, Ireland:
     revenant escorted by fishy host.

Boom-crash of the waves: spumed muted thunder
     on that stretch of desolate beach;
the cry of the gulls harsh, piercing shrieks—
     a derelict corpse has returned to teach.

This modern world of idiot idols
     passing fads & fatuous manias
thrusts tragedy down the memory hole—
     Remember the Lusitania!

The Misting at Emerald Oaks

Joshua Green

Finn remembered a time when Ingrid brought him to the graveyard.

He thought of one particular summer day when the oaks were in bloom. They looked like crooked hands with bent fingers. But the green was beautiful, and Ingrid usually loved the way the light peeked between the leaves, occasionally hitting their faces as they played and danced.

But it was Ingrid's final summer. A Saturday, which meant they had a few hours of free time before Ingrid's next Session.

They stopped upon a small, unmarked grave. There were many like it. The graveyard was bigger than the town they lived in.

"This is where she is buried," Finn said. "This is where Baby is buried."

"Your sister?" Ingrid asked. "I didn't know they buried her."

Finn nodded. "Mom's labor was hard, but she gave birth to a healthy girl. Ms. Johnson had her doubts, though. She said something was wrong."

"She always thinks something is wrong."

"I know. And my mom didn't believe her. But she didn't say anything, either. I never saw her so happy in my life."

"What happened? You never told me."

"I went to check on her one day. Mom was growing her arm back, but had mustered some strength. Enough to go to Baby's room and back. But when I walked to the crib, she wasn't breathing. Nothing happened. It was like she just stopped living."

They stared down below in silence, the warm wind blowing through their clothes.

"I'm sorry," Ingrid finally said. "I've never had a sibling, Finn. I can't imagine having one and then not."

"Have they told you where you're going yet?" Finn asked, trying to change the subject. He wiped a tear from his eyes. "How long do you think

they'll wait to tell you?" They left the grave and moved to the great oak farther out in the forest clearing.

"I've asked my parents, but they won't say," Ingrid said, fixing her brown hair into a bun. "They said they don't even know. Apparently Mother Superior keeps things like that from everyone else."

"You mean Ms. Johnson?" Finn asked. "She's going to kill you if you're late. We should really go back."

Ingrid continued fixing her hair, ignoring Finn's plea. "You know her as Ms. Johnson. And you'll know her as that until the summer you leave. The upper age Sessions are different."

"Different?"

"They're more serious. She demands respect. Says that our bodies are ready for what's to come. That we need to be prepared." Ingrid paused, then gave a smirk. "But you know what?"

"What?"

"I'm not going back."

The words hit Finn like a brick wall. "Not going back? To class? You have to."

"No, Finn. To Emerald Oaks. I'm leaving. Right now."

Finn didn't respond. How could he? No one ever left. Not without graduating. "You can't leave," he said after a moment. "You never told me. We still had weeks to see each other. You never . . . you can't." Finn paused, trying to find the words to say. "Your parents. Ms. Johnson. They'd never allow it. It's against the rules."

Ingrid laughed, but there were tears in her eyes. Finn could see the pain she carried, the way she wanted to tell him but couldn't. "I'm sorry, Finn. I should have told you. But I couldn't. It's not that I don't trust you—"

"—but it's that you don't trust me," Finn said.

At that, Ingrid embraced him. Her body was warm as she held him tightly under the great oak. Stone graves leaned carelessly all around them. "Never," Ingrid said. "Truthfully, I didn't know how to tell you. There's something about this place, Finn. Something isn't right. And it's weird thinking it's not right because we grew up here. Finny, I overheard *some things. After Sessions one day. Last year. I never told you because I didn't know what to make of it. But I went to Mother Su—Ms. Johnson's office to ask her for something. I must have been pretty quiet, because to this day I don't think she ever heard me. But I heard her.*

"Finn," she continued, pushing him back so that their eyes met. "She's old."

"I know," Finn said with a smirk. "She hobbles quite a bit. And she's going to get older if you don't go back."

"No. It's not a joke, Finn . . . I mean she's really old. Not like our parents. She was in the office with someone. Another adult. But I overheard her say that they needed more children this year."

"I don't get it," Finn said. "Are you talking about the Misting Season? When the adults all leave for the graveyard party?"

"I don't think it's a party."

The sound of a bell screamed through the trees, startling Finn. He looked away from Ingrid and through the oak branches. When he turned, she was crying.

"I'm going to miss you, Finny. But I need you to promise me something." She darted her eyes toward the town, as if she knew they were coming.

"What's that?" Finn asked. Tears were beginning to well again in his eyes, too.

"I'm going to leave. But I'm going to come back. Finn, I want you to take care of yourself. I want you to be safe. I'm going to leave and see where all the other kids go—where they live after Emerald Oaks. If I can't find them, I'm going to come back and get you. I don't know where we'd go, but it wouldn't be safe here at Emerald Oaks. Not if they're lying." She hugged him one last time before detaching and turning away. After taking a few steps, she turned around one last time and said, "Be curious, Finn. I know you're confused. But try and finally see things for yourself. Ask your parents questions. Careful ones. But listen to how they dodge them."

And with that, she turned away.

It was the last time he saw her.

Finn followed the forest path with an earnestness he'd never experienced before. Towering oaks with twisted branches blocked the light of the falling sun, but failed to prevent the autumn breeze from stealing away his breath. He used to walk this path with his best friend Ingrid, but she had moved away just over a year ago. He thought about her often, the way they grew up together as neighbors. He smiled thinking about how they used to prank Ingrid's parents during the Misting Season. One time they sprayed the garden hose at Mr. Benson's headless body as it lay outside, watched as it twitched and flung around, as the blood seeped out from his body and onto the grass. They would laugh, hear his dying voice from the forest edge as his head cursed well into the rising night.

"Finnegan! Finnegan Wilson!" he heard from behind. Finn turned and looked back down the path, his mother racing toward him. He kicked the dying leaves in frustration. A few floated and landed on the decaying limbs that had been placed last week. He eyed a pile of maggots feeding upon a festering hand. He wasn't supposed to be walking toward the graveyard. Children weren't allowed to see what lay down this path during autumn. Most children didn't wander here anyway. The smell was awful, the flies a terrible nuisance.

"Finn!" she said once more when she was close. "What are you doing? I've been looking all over."

He inhaled her breath. "I'm just going for a walk," he said, pointing down the road. "My Session work is done. It's a nice day."

"It's cold," said his mother. She reached out and grabbed his arm. "You shouldn't be out right now. You'll get sick."

Finn planted his foot and jerked his arm away. "Mom," he said, "I'm fine. What could happen to me? I'm just walking. I just wanted to see Baby. I miss her. And there's no one else around. Are you worried about seeing other people not from Emerald Oaks?"

"Of course not," she said, eyeing the forest path ahead. She had wide eyes, though Finn couldn't tell if it were fear of this place or pure annoyance. "That would never happen."

"Then what?"

Finn's mother faltered for a moment, trying to figure what to say. Her gaze fell back onto his. "You will listen to me, Finnegan. We will not argue about this."

Finn opened his mouth to speak, but no words came out. *Disobedience is sickness,* he thought. He took a deep breath and sank his shoulders in defeat. "Yes, Mother," he said.

At those words his mother pulled a knife from her pocket. With one quick movement she sliced off her little finger and let it fall to the ground. She squeezed the new wound, let the blood pour out in front of her. In front of Finn. After dipping a finger from her other hand where her pinky once was, she wiped a bit of blood on Finn's forehead and smiled.

She smiled the way every loving mother at Emerald Oaks does at her child.

They walked back together, her good hand gripping his. Finn stole a glance behind him and he swore he could see the Mist as it fell deep within the forest.

It was Misting Season after all.

That night Finn lay in his bed sleepless. His father, Kenneth, had reprimanded him at dinner, told him that there was always a price to pay for disobedience. And Finn agreed. He had been foolish to wander toward the graveyard this time of year. He knew that his insubordination had led to his mother having to sacrifice a bit of herself to the Mists. It had always been this way. Adults kept the town safe by offering a part of themselves, indemnification for the sins of all, and especially the sins of disobedient children.

But everything seemed to grow back in Emerald Oaks.

Everything.

Finn reached into the nightstand and pulled out a letter Ingrid had given him a month before she left, before she made the insane decision to leave Emerald Oaks without finishing her time at Ms. Johnson's Sessions. Ingrid Benson was someone he loved. She was one year older than him, and far more beautiful than any of the other girls he knew. And yet, they had just remained friends. Best friends. He was glad for her, and was happy that he got to spend the time he did with her before she moved away.

I will miss you, Finnegan, the letter read. *My parents say that I'm to move away soon. I'm nervous . . . but I promise I won't go too far, okay? I've been thinking about where everyone goes when they graduate Ms. Johnson's classes. It has to be close, right? Ugh, I hate how secretive my parents are over it! It seems so ridiculous. But then again, they're secretive about a lot of things . . . just try asking your parents if they can die. Ask them about death and what really kills a person. I bet they won't answer!*

But maybe wait until the pain of losing Baby passes. Maybe it's not a good time for you to ask such things.

Well, at least I won't have to be here during another Misting Season. I hate the way the Mists wander around the edge of the forest. I hate the way they seem to stare at the town. I swear I can see their mouths open. Sometimes I feel like they're screaming.

Before you leave, you should figure out what that really is, okay? Then when we find each other you can spill everything.

Finn dropped the letter on his lap, tears in his eyes. It was signed *Ingrid Benson,* as if he would forget her last name. He missed her so much.

Finn raised his head and peered through the tiny slit in his window. The other houses were shuttered as well, as if a great storm were about to pass by. He swore he could see curious eyes, much like his own, peeking through the other windows. The other children didn't talk much about the Mists between Sessions. But they had to be at least curious, right?

What if he just took a peek at the edge of the forest? Just to see why the Mists were settling near the graveyard. Why they didn't come any closer than the edge of town. Ingrid deserved to know. Didn't she?

Escaping his thoughts, Finn got out of bed. He wore pajama pants and a white cotton shirt. He slid his slippers out from underneath and put them on quickly and quietly, being sure to peer through the tiny vent in his window once more. Was anyone watching? Was anyone out? He moved to the door and opened it slowly, the creak of the hinges straining like the sound of a dying shrew.

It was the only door in the house that squeaked.

The hallway lights were off. The house was completely dark. But there were a few places down over the balcony that were lit with moonlight.

He moved from his room to the staircase, trying to find all the spots in the wood that didn't creak. His father's snores echoed all throughout the house, which was more than fine to Finn. His steps felt less intrusive.

The front door was at the bottom of the stairs and the door was locked. Finn furled his brow and paused with his hand outstretched. He'd never gone outside at night before. Why would he? He unlocked the door, the deadbolt slamming against the latch. Then he opened it and stepped outside.

Cool air invaded his lungs. Moonlit fog had settled upon the forest far in front of him, and he couldn't help but shiver at the thought that he was being watched. Houses were lined on either side, and while most of the windows were closed and shuttered, he couldn't help but think that everyone was staring at him through the slits, wondering what it was he was going to do next. And if Finn were honest, he didn't quite know what he wanted to do. The night seemed unkind, the fog a heavy burden upon this sleeping town, a burden on his mind. He was being disobedient. What would this cost his parents if he were caught? What kind of horror would he have to live with?

Finn crouched down, as if to make himself smaller on the sidewalk. He swore he could see something with form walking along the forest edge, the very path he had taken earlier in the day. He strained his eyes in the moonlight, squinting them to try and see what he was missing. Something was raising what looked to be a hand, though it was too far away to truly see. There were others like it, others that passed by and stopped to raise their hands. Others that—

"Finn."

Finnegan turned, his father towering above him like the great oaks that littered the forest. He looked unnatural in the night, under the light of the moon.

"Dad, I'm—"

"Do not speak," he said quietly, his voice barely a whisper. He waved his hand, beckoning for Finn to follow, which he did without hesitation.

Later that night, which was now almost early morning, Finn lay in his bed with his father standing by the door.

"I'm sorry," Finn said.

"You should be."

Finn could hear his mother groaning in the other room. His father had told him that she was in a great deal of pain. Slicing off a finger had been easy work. Growing one back, however, was an incredibly agonizing thing to experience.

"I'm sorry," Finn said again, sitting on his bed. "I just don't get it. I just want to see the Mists like the adults do. Why can't I see like you?"

"Because," his father said, "children are untrustworthy. It has been hundreds of years of life for us. Hundreds of uninterrupted years. There are rules, ways of doing things that ensure my survival."

"Couldn't you just build a fence?"

For the first time tonight his father smiled. "A fence would just provoke you kids to climb it."

"True, but—"

"It's time for bed."

Finn's father stood without tucking him in. He held his hands behind his back, his posture looking more strained than relaxed. "Goodnight, Finnegan. Get some sleep. Sessions are tomorrow."

And with that, his father retreated to his bedroom, toward the soft whimpering of his wounded mother.

The next day was like any other. Finn awoke to the rising sun and had breakfast with Mother and Father. Her pinky finger was easily noticeable, slightly shorter than it probably should be and with no grown nail. She walked back and forth between the kitchen and table with warm buttermilk biscuits, fixing Finn and his father their favorite omelettes.

They were happy. Far happier than they should be.

"Must I go to the Sessions today?"

Finn's mother gave a scowl but otherwise maintained an upbeat spirit. His father said nothing. He ate with one hand, his other somewhere hidden on his lap. "Finnegan," his mother said, "what has gotten into you the past couple days?"

"I just miss Ingrid," he said.

"She was a very disobedient child, Finn," his mother said. "I knew I should have never let you two continue playing together. Is that all this is?"

"Well," Finn said, "no, it's just that . . . I don't know, she snuck away. I don't know if I ever told you that. She never finished her Sessions. She said that she was going to come back for me. Come back to see me."

His parents passed a glance toward each other. His father gave a nod, and his mother sighed.

"Finn," she said. "Ingrid is dead."

The words hit Finn square in the chest. His mind wandered aimlessly searching to make sense of such a lie. "I saw her leave, Mom," Finn said. "She isn't dead. She left!"

"No," Finn's mother said. "She came back. Maybe she came back to get you as she said she would. But she was caught with a rather large knife at Ms. Johnson's house, trying to sneak through her bedroom window at night. Now why would that be, Finnegan? Do you think she wanted to talk to your teacher?"

"I——"

"No, Finn. I can tell you she wasn't. She was going to murder her. Is this who you are trying to become like? Are these the kinds of children you enjoy spending time around? Do you understand what we've been through, Finn?" She paused, her voice rising in contempt. "Do you understand what we've given up to live? We already had Baby. Must you go so soon?"

"Nora!" his father said. He looked at her gravely, as if she had said far too much. "That's enough."

Finn had already been crying for some moments. "I—I don't understand. How did she die?"

Finn looked at his father. He couldn't read his face. Was it one of sympathy or one of warning?

Finally he looked back at Finn and said, "She is dead, son. Isn't that enough? The details aren't important. What's important is that you don't end up like her. For our sake as well." Then he forced a smile and said, "Besides, I need my head today. I have a lot to do."

"Can't I just stay home one day?" Finn said through muffled cries.

"Of course not," his mother said. "You have to go to the Sessions. Plus, you could use the lessons. What is it that Ms. Johnson has you say in the morning?"

Finn composed himself, or at least made an attempt. "We learn to obey, obey to live, and live to serve the ones that gave us life."

"One more time," his father said, fork scraping across the almost empty plate.

Finn straightened up a bit in his chair, knowing his father wouldn't relent without him saying it properly. "We learn to obey, obey to live, and live to serve the ones that gave us life."

"Good," his father said. "Nora, would you walk him today? I need to rest a bit longer."

"Certainly, dear," she said, moving to grab their coats.

Stepping outside, Finn was met with a brilliant blue. The sun was poking over the tops of the trees far in front of him, and the once-shuttered windows all around were now open, ready to let in the new morning light. They walked side by side in silence, and Finn noticed—not for the first time, actually—that no one walked alone. Every child had an adult with them, and all the adults looked quite normal. Small, even. But then Finn made another observation, one that he had never made before.

"Mother?"

"Yes?" she said, not looking down. They rounded the sidewalk toward the small building used for the Sessions.

"Why is it that Baby didn't come back?"

His mother kept her gaze straight ahead.

"I don't understand the question, Finn."

"I'm just thinking," Finn said, trying to work it out in his mind. "Everything seems to grow back here. Everything. You give parts of yourself to the Mists to keep us safe. But everything you give grows back. Is it possible that Baby could come back? If I died, could I come back? Could Ingrid come back?" He looked up and studied his mother's face. He couldn't quite make out the issue in his head. Baby was the only death he'd ever witnessed, and it was strangely occurring to him that there was a lot he was confused about.

Finn looked up again, and this time he swore he could see real anger in his mother's eyes. "That's enough questions for today, Finn. It's time for your Sessions."

And with that she stopped. The doors were open wide in front of him. The stained glass windows above poured colored light onto the concrete below. In the past he always enjoyed looking at the glass, playing in the purpled light that covered the green grass. He loved the way the children in the picture danced away from the fog, painted in such a way as to seem so far off yet like some lingering, awful danger. He used to love the way the parents looked to be laughing and clapping as they circled the children. And yet, the more he stared at it today, the more it felt wrong. The once-happy expressions of the glass children now looked sad, even horrified. And the more he looked, the more he could see the strain on their faces, their wide-eyed look of primal fear. And the parents . . . their faces were something different now entirely. Twisted and contorted and aged beyond all belief, their teeth were sharp and bared as if hungry. The older children looked to be running away toward the forest, running far far away. He tilted his head in wonder, as if the glass were changing before the sun, as if—

"Finnegan!"

Finn looked down. Ms. Johnson was smiling and waving for him to come inside. "Are you just going to stand there?" she asked.

Finn turned. His mother was nowhere to be found. Then he looked up once more at the glass.

The children were smiling.

At recess, a boy named Erik walked up to Finn with a half-deflated basketball.

"Wanna play?" Erik asked.

"I'm good," Finn said. He eyed Ms. Johnson. Erik was a few years younger than Finn, but he talked extremely well for his age.

"I heard about last night. My parents said that you snuck out. That you were a very disobedient child."

"Yeah?" Finn said. He looked at Erik with dead eyes.

"Yeah," Erik said. Then he got closer and said, "But I have a se-cret. And I'll tell you if you promise not to get mad."

"Mad?" Finn said. He was curious now. He eyed Erik with in-terest.

"I—I saw through my window and told on you. My parents called yours. I tell on all the kids. You're not the only one that sneaks out sometimes."

"Why are you telling me this, Erik?"

Erik shrugged. "I was told to. My mom said it would make you stop. Sometimes when I tell on kids they disappear. Like Ingrid. I told——"

"Ingrid?" Finn said, his face quickly changing. "What did you say? What did you see? When did this happen?" He took a step for-ward, looming above the poor boy.

"I—I don't know. It was last year. I saw her walking around down the street. Near where you and I live. But she didn't look like she was going anywhere. It looked like she was coming back."

"Erik," Finn said, trying not to scream, "tell me what you saw. Was she holding a knife? Was she going toward Ms. Johnson's house? Did someone take her?"

"What? No. A knife? Why would she have a knife? I don't know who took her. And why do you care? She was being disobedient. The parents took her, the way they take everyone when they get bigger. And they come back with blood. But there's just so much, I don't know if it's theirs or not. They took her away to the forest, toward the graveyard, I think. It was winter, so the Mists had just gone away. I guess that means it was safe."

Before he could respond, Finn found himself on top of Erik, pummeling his face into the concrete below. A slew of punches broke the boy's nose, but it wasn't enough. Finn couldn't stop. He wouldn't stop. He was crying, hardly able to think as Erik's head bounced off the cement over and over and over again, his head bleeding all over Finn's hands.

Finn didn't notice the children gathering around. Things like this never happened. Not in Emerald Oaks. A moment later Ms. Johnson was between them, screaming at Finnegan to stop whatever madness had overtaken him.

When he stood up, Finn was a bloody mess and his hair was disheveled. He looked at the work he'd done. Erik's newly disfigured face was one of frozen terror, and the boy was breathing in gurgled sobs while his eyes searched for some coherent shape somewhere beyond the pooling blood. Shame and guilt poured into Finn. He had nearly killed a small boy. And over what?

"Over what?" he said to himself, weeping into his hands. Erik was only a few years younger than him. He did what he was told, just like everyone else. He didn't mean any malice. He couldn't have. Ingrid was dead, and it was Erik's fault. But what did Erik know of what happened to children at the hands of adults? If Finn wasn't sure, how could Erik be?

Once, a few years back during the Misting Season, his mother had said that children had no business with ghosts.

And yet, it seemed as though the adults didn't really care if they became one.

Later that night Finn lay in bed thinking of the day as the moon rose above the town like a great spotlight. Through the slit in his window he could barely see the forest edge. But the Mists were thick tonight.

Erik would survive Finn's assault—at least, that's what his parents had said. Ms. Johnson had set quickly to work fixing him. The rest of the Sessions that day had been canceled.

After classes, Finn had told his headless mother that he was sick and had apologized to her for hurting Erik and for wandering off the other day. Finn's father was holding her severed head, hands dripping with her blood. He was on his way to the forest to place her there for the night. She responded by saying, "Disobedience is sickness." A few days ago Finn would have never questioned it. But at that moment he couldn't help but think that his mind was being twisted like a wet rag.

He had walked right up the stairs after their conversation, shoes jacket and all, with his head hanging low.

No one bothered him for the rest of the night.

But of course he had lied. He wasn't sick. And he wasn't sure at all anymore if disobedience made one feel ill at all. He stood now with his shoes and jacket on, his eyes looking through the tiny window slit in his room. His heart fluttered in his chest as he heard the wailing of his mother far away.

Moving to the end of his room, Finn put his ear to the door. He heard his father snoring, occasionally moaning from the pain of his growing hand. He didn't think he would wake. And if he did, Finn decided he would run. He would run straight into the forest, into the Mists. Into Ingrid's arms, wherever she was.

Moving downstairs and out the door, he left the house and began to walk the street listlessly under the moonlight. It wasn't that he didn't feel anything, or that he wasn't nervous . . . but that he felt numb as the Mists swirled in the distance. It were as if they were goading him to apathy, yet somehow convincing him to take step after step toward the forest.

Finn stole a look behind him, half expecting to see his headless mother or an angry father. But the door to his house remained shut, the window to his room shuttered like the others all around him. *Why do I feel this way?* he asked himself. *Why don't I care?*

Finn stopped exactly where he was. There were figures in the forest again, foggy forms of light that seemed to wander that very path he had been on days ago. One of them stopped and seemed to look his direction.

I heard that they come back.

Erik had said this on the playground before Finn beat him.

Finn took another step but stopped once more when he saw that there were more, that each one took turns stopping and looking upon the town. He couldn't see their faces, but they were children. Every single one of them. Their posture was one of great sadness, as if their expressions had been replaced by pure feeling. Within moments Finn started to cry, the apathy he felt melting into a heavy depression he'd never felt in his life.

He stayed this way for minutes and hours, his face one of intense weeping as these Mists took turns looking upon him and the town. He would have stayed this way until morning had it not been for one particular form. It passed like all the others, slowly and almost passionless. But Finn thought he recognized it. Not the face, but whoever or whatever made this formed mist the way it was.

"Ingrid?" he said. Then, he started to walk again. And before he knew it he was running wildly down the street, staring at the one he *knew* was Ingrid. Behind her, mists and ghostly figures continued on behind her, stopping periodically to stare as if looking for a friend, teacher, or parent.

Someone who truly loved them.

When he arrived Finn hardly noticed the gore in front of him: the fingers, hands, his mother's putrid head as it screamed for him to stop, as it screamed that his blood would be next. He couldn't bear to look at the limbs that bordered the path, the violence of adults. He was too busy looking at the figure in front of him, a faceless thing made of mist and fog that held something so remarkable and precious.

It was Baby.

Everything grew back.

Everything.

"Ingrid?" Finn said, trying to catch his breath. Tears still fell upon his face. "Ingrid, is that you?"

Nothing moved but the line of wisps behind her. But then it reached out to touch him, the formless thing drawing enough mist unto itself to lift what seemed to be an arm.

"Ingrid!" Finn said. "It is you. It—"

But then it stopped, unable to cross the freshly cut limbs beneath them.

"Finnegan! Finnegan Wilson!"

Finn turned and saw father running down the street, a terrible tower in the night. His teeth glistened under the moonlight, sharp and awful.

His decrepit mother was in tow a few yards behind.

When he turned back toward Ingrid, he said, "I don't know what to do. They did something to you, didn't they? Your parents. My parents. They found you. They just get rid of us, don't they? They just dispose of us before winter. When we're big enough to drink. When we're too old to love. That's all this is, isn't it."

The form remained without expression, hand still raised upon whatever barrier existed between them. But Finn could feel her pain, the suffering she endured and the suffering she still felt. Even though she had no body left, he could feel her pain.

Did she want him to come with her? To join her in the graveyard for whatever happened during the Misting Season?

Finn raised a hesitant hand. He would go with her. He loved Ingrid, had loved the friendship they shared for as long as they had known each other. He missed his sister greatly, and he knew she deserved someone who really loved her.

But was it enough to abandon the town while the other children suffered?

He reached out through the barrier to touch Ingrid, and to his surprise he felt her hand. It was familiar to him. But she didn't pull. He looked at her curiously as he heard his parents' footsteps from behind.

But then he looked down and saw the limbs and gore, the work of adults to keep the ghosts at bay.

"No," he said to Ingrid, and to Baby as well. "You're coming back. You're all coming back."

Then he pulled with all his might.

Monsters, Mazes, and Edward Lucas White

Lee Weinstein

"The Snout," a horror story by Baltimore author Edward Lucas White (1866–1934), is based on one of his bizarre nightmares and is one of his more effective, although lesser-known, tales. He wrote it after experiencing a vivid nightmare in February 1909 (Wetzel 69), although, like several of his horror stories, it remained unpublished until 1927.

The Maze (1945) is a weird novella or short novel by Swiss author Maurice Sandoz (1892–1958). Sandoz had a Ph.D. in chemistry but also pursued a career in writing, and wrote two collections of macabre short stories as well as the play *Spring-Heeled Jack*. While little-known today, *The Maze* (as well as several of his other books) was illustrated by Salvador Dali and was filmed, with the same title, by John Cameron Menzies in 1953.[15] It resembles White's story in plot, structure, and atmosphere, although it is unlikely that Sandoz knew of White's horror fiction. The inspiration for it, as well as the inspiration for *Spring-Heeled Jack*,[16] came from the realm of urban legend.

Both "The Snout" and *The Maze* involve wealthy and powerful families; remote, isolated estates; and quasi-human monsters.

White, the author of a small body of notable weird fiction, deserves to be better known today than he is. H. P. Lovecraft said of him that he "imparts a very peculiar quality to his tales—an oblique sort of glamour which has its own kind of convincingness" (72). Or, as S. T. Joshi says of White's stories, "their most salient feature is perhaps the sheer bizarrerie of their weird manifestations" (43). In

---

15. *The Maze* was filmed in 3-D by John Cameron Menzies for Allied Artists. Starring Richard Carlson, Veronica Hurst, and Katherine Emery.
16. *Spring-Heeled Jack* (1927) was filmed in Britain as *The Curse of the Wraydons* (1946).

his own day, primarily in the 1920s and 1930s, he was well regarded as a historical novelist, specializing in classical antiquity,[17] but it is his tales of supernatural horror that have survived the test of time, especially those included in his collection *Lukundoo and other Stories* (1927). He transcribed most of his weird fiction from his vivid and weird nightmares. "Lukundoo," a horror story involving African witchcraft, is probably his best-known, or at least the most frequently reprinted. "The House of the Nightmare," possibly his nearest tale to a traditional ghost story, is a close second. "Amina," about an encounter with a female ghoul in Persia, and "Song of the Sirens," about a deaf sailor's encounter with the titular sirens of Greek myth, have also been occasionally anthologized.

"The Snout," while equally bizarre, is not as well known. The main setting of this novelette is an isolated walled estate somewhere in North America. It is occupied by Hengist Eversleigh, the mysterious master of the estate and heir to a great fortune.

The body of the story is narrated by the unnamed accomplice of a thief named Thwaite, who has reconnoitered the grounds inside the estate walls on several occasions and has determined that there is a fortune in gold and diamonds somewhere within. Thwaite relates to his accomplices that Eversleigh resided at the estate with his father until his father's death. He has never been outside the walls, nor has he been seen by anyone except his small retinue of servants, who have all been sworn to secrecy.

He describes the estate as "an infinity of structures . . . with pinnacles and roofs . . . [a] complication of buildings that make up the castle or mansion-house or whatever" (White, *Lukundoo* 103). He explains that Eversleigh is sent large monthly payments in gold from his wealthy siblings in other parts of the country and that there is very little in the way of security. There are no watchmen's cottages, no regular patrols, no alarm wires or traps, and no dogs. He recruits

---

17. The relevant novels are *The Unwilling Vestal* (1918), *Andivius Hedulio* (1921), and *Helen* (1926). He also wrote a historical monograph, *Why Rome Fell* (1927).

the narrator and a third man, named Rivven, in his scheme to burglarize the estate.

There is a growing sense of something seriously amiss as Thwaite relates various clues he has overheard in the conversations of the servants. As Joshi puts it, "White's leisurely narration is designed to build up an insidious atmosphere of horror by the slow accretion of bizarre details" (44). He relates to his cohorts that Eversleigh can't abide the presence of women and that married servants are obliged to live in a separate walled-off area within the enormous grounds. Eversleigh also can't tolerate the presence of dogs or even cats. However, Thwaite says he heard one servant tell another of a chauffeur-driven limousine with a pet monkey as the only occupant.

The thieves scale the walls, and the ominous atmosphere continues to build as they explore the grounds. They enter a building and search the labyrinthine interior with its numerous rooms and galleries. They find a wine cellar filled with small-sized wine bottles, "splits," labeled with the device of an angel tethered to an alligator and the motto "Let not your baser nature bring you down / Utter no whimper, not one sigh or moan / Hopeless of respite / Live out your life unflinching and alone" (126).

They find rooms with child-sized furniture and galleries full of paintings of animal-headed people, signed by the owner. While the human figures mostly have various types of animal heads, many of the paintings also feature a larger-than-life figure, all with the same head: "long-jawed, like a hound's; the triangular shape of the whole head; the close-set, small, beady, terribly knowing eyes; the brilliant patches of color on either side of the muzzle" (124).

The escapade (and White's nightmare) ends as they open a final door and are viciously attacked by Hengist Eversleigh himself, who is revealed to be a dwarf with the body of a man and the doglike head of a mandrill. He attacks Rivven, ripping out his throat, and a panicked Thwaite beats the monster to death.

* * *

The Maze similarly involves a large isolated estate with a dark secret in the form of a monster. In this case it is Craven Castle, a remote Scottish castle belonging to the McTeam family.

Edith Murray, a McTeam relative, narrates the story to the author, just as the unnamed third thief in "The Snout" narrates the story, presumably to White. Gerald McTeam, the next baronet in line and newly engaged, is summoned to the castle on the death of his uncle, the baronet. But instead of returning home as he had promised, he suddenly breaks off his engagement to the young woman and remains uncommunicative in the castle. Edith, who is also a friend of the jilted fiancée, goes to the castle to investigate and finds a preoccupied Gerald looking prematurely aged and behaving in an uncharacteristically nervous fashion.

There is again a growing sense of things seriously amiss as she observes a number of odd clues that, as in "The Snout," only come together at the end of the story. There is a rule against young women staying in the castle overnight. The baronetcy always passes from uncle to nephew because the baronets are not permitted to marry. She relates that the guests are locked in their rooms at night, she hears footsteps accompanied by strange thudding sounds at night in the hallways outside the bedrooms, and on two occasions hears something inhuman, once in the hallway and once in the titular hedge maze behind the castle. "It was a voice. And yet it wasn't a voice. That's what frightened me" (67). From a window she glimpses a large, dark, but indistinguishable shape in a horse-drawn carriage. There is a mysterious book Gerald has, which is later revealed to be a treatise on teratology.

In both stories the secret uncovered at the end is a semi-human monster. In *The Maze,* the unseen true patriarch ruling the castle, Sir Roger Philip McTeam, is revealed to be, literally, a human-sized toad "with human intelligence and the heart of a man" (106). Hengist Eversleigh is also quite intelligent, being described as fearful "for his awful wisdom . . . He's that wise, no man is more so" (110). In both stories the monster dies at the end; but in this case it is from natural causes after 175 years.

There is no explanation given for the monster that is Hengist Eversleigh, but in *The Maze* the monstrous Sir Roger is explained as a case of arrested development. According to a discarded biological theory, a developing fetus passes through earlier stages corresponding to the adult forms of more primitive species, i.e., a fish stage, an amphibian stage, a reptile stage, and so forth. A human fetus does briefly have, at a certain time, gills. Sir Roger's pre-natal development had stopped at the amphibian stage.

Some of the parallels between the stories, such as the fact that both are set in a frame story as they are told to the respective authors, are doubtless coincidental. But the deep-seated similarities of large isolated estates concealing an intelligent, partially human monster within are undeniable and suggest a common source for both stories.

The Maze was evidently based on the Scottish legend of the monster of Glamis Castle. There are numerous stories and legends attached to the Scottish castle, the childhood home of Elizabeth II, which is owned by the Bowes-Lyon family and dates back at least to the fifteenth century. In fact, the novel is essentially a thinly fictionalized version of the legend. George T. Wetzel notes that "the whole plot, atmosphere and local[e] of *The Maze* was in truth based upon the legends of Glamis Castle near the Scottish border" ("Glamis Castle" 43). He further elaborates that in both there is a forbidden section of the castle, a walled-up window to a secret room, and unusual sounds heard at night by guests (43–44). A member of Lord Glamis's family committed suicide after his fiancée broke their engagement. In *The Maze*, it is the protagonist who breaks the engagement. In both the "secret soul-burdening legacy" is handed down to succeeding generations.

While there is no maze behind the castle, and many of the legends are typical ghost stories,[18] this one, which tells of a monstrous

---

18. Legends such as the ghost of the "Grey Lady" who had been burned for attempted murder of the king in 1537 and the ghost of an unknown woman without a tongue. Another legend tells of the Earl of Beardie who played cards on the Sabbath and lost his soul to the Devil.

ancestor kept hidden in a secret room, is the inspiration for *The Maze* and probably "The Snout" as well. It tells of a seriously malformed heir to the title, the Earl of Strathmore. Contemporary records show that Thomas Lyon-Bowes, the first-born of the 11th Earl, Thomas Bowes-Lyon and his wife Charlotte Bowes-Lyon, was born on 21 October 1821 and died shortly after birth on the same day. But it was rumored that he actually survived and was kept hidden away in a secret room through many generations of heirs. As he grew older, he was taken for walks along the battlements of the castle at night even as Sir Roger of the novel was taken for exercise at night in the titular hedge maze. As each succeeding presumptive heir to the title of earl reached the age of twenty-one, he was shown the secret: the true holder of the title, as happened to the fictional Gerald McTeam. According to various versions of the story, Thomas, the monster, lived until 1905, 1921, or even, in some versions, 1941. In some nineteenth-century accounts he was described as a human toad (Dash).

There is an oft-repeated tale that a group of guests in the castle wanted to find the secret room and hung towels out of all the windows. One version says this happened in 1850, when the 12th Earl's wife asked her guests to aid her in a hunt while her husband was away. One window, viewed from outside, had no towel, but there was no visible entrance to the room on the inside.

Another story dating to about 1865 tells of a workman on the estate who went through a door into an unfamiliar corridor and saw something he shouldn't have. He anxiously reported what happened to the estate's factor. He was given a large sum of money and requested to leave the country and relocate to Australia.

A more recent source is *The Queen Mother's Family Story* (1967) by author and journalist James Wentworth Day. In interviews with family members he was given this description of the monster: "His chest an enormous barrel, hairy as a doormat, his head ran straight into his shoulders and his arms and legs were toylike" (122).

While White's immediate inspiration for "The Snout" was a nightmare, his nightmares, in turn, were often inspired or colored by his reading material. White, who was well versed in Greek mythology, noted that the nightmare that resulted in "Song of the Sirens" was modified from its mythological background. He said, "it was the more marvelous since there is nothing, either in literature or art, suggesting anything which I beheld in that vision of the two living shapes" (*Song* v–vi).

Of his story "The Flambeau Bracket" White said in a letter: "There is no doubt that 'The Cask of Amontillado' forms the background of the very vivid dream on which [it] is founded," referring to the carnival setting (*Sesta* 264). Both are also tales of revenge, but the actual plots are quite different.[19] While his story "Lukundoo" was also literally transcribed from a nightmare, he said he would not have dreamed it if he hadn't read H. G. Wells's short story "Pollock and the Porroh Man" beforehand (*Lukundoo* 327). Both include an African setting, witchcraft, disembodied heads, and concerns of distinguishing reality from hallucinations, but the plots are quite different. In the Wells story, the man responsible for the murder of a witch doctor is pursued by a possibly hallucinatory skull, while in White's the cursed man is plagued with tiny heads emerging from his body.

In a similar way, the nightmare he transcribed as "The Snout" may have been influenced by the Glamis Mystery, if he had known of it.

It is likely that White, although in America, did know of it.

From perhaps the 1840s until 1905, the Earl's ancestral seat at Glamis Castle, in the Scottish lowlands, was home to a "mystery of mysteries . . . and the talk of Europe" (Dash). References to the story of the secret room, the hidden monster, and the secret passed down from generation to generation repeatedly appeared in the British journal *Notes & Queries,* going back as early as 1884 in a thread on the topic of "The Glamis Mystery." This journal had a running subtitle, "A medium of inter-communication for Literary Men, the General Public, etc.," and in some ways was the equivalent of a modern-day online newsgroup. Correspondents, often anony-

---

19. White became obsessed with Poe's fiction early on but later destroyed all his Poe-influenced stories, with the exception of "The Flambeau Bracket."

mous, communicated with one another on various topics. A communication published in 1885, in response to a previous posting, summed up the legend quite nicely. The correspondent (M. Gilchrist) wrote that the monster was a human being, "above the waist formed as a frog, below as a man. He was kept in a concealed chamber in the house and his existence was only known to the reigning earl, the factor, the family lawyer, and the next heir on his attaining majority" (35).

In 1908, a letter, in response to a previous posting about the "Glamis Mystery," was published less than six months before the year White had the nightmare resulting in "The Snout." It said:

> The mystery was told to the present writer some 60 years ago, when he was a boy, and it made a great impression on him. The story was, and is, that in the Castle of Glamis is a secret chamber. In this chamber is confined a monster, who is the rightful heir to the title and property, but who is so unpresentable that it is necessary to keep him out of sight and out of possession. (241)

White was an academic who had been teaching at the Boys Latin School, a private college preparatory school in Baltimore, since about 1900 and had researched and wrote historical novels set in ancient Greece and ancient Rome. He may well have been familiar with this journal.

References to the "Glamis mystery" also appeared in American newspapers around the country at the time White was writing his short stories, many around 1904 and 1905. The *New York Sun* printed an article in early 1904 headlined, "Mystery of Glamis Castle. Secret of Hidden Room Never Disclosed," followed by the subheadings: "Curious Country Folks Have Decided that a Semi-Human Monster Is Confined There. Death of Lord Strathmere Revives Interest in Strange Legend" (7).

Closer to Baltimore, the *Washington Times* ran an article on the subject under the headline "Does Glamis Harbor a Monster?" (13 March 1904). Again, in the fall of 1905 the same paper ran the article "Strathmore Heir Has Mystery Revealed to Him upon Coming of Age and Returns Livid" (15 October 1905). This was followed on the second page with the headline "Glamis Mystery Again the Subject of Club Talk." Similar articles probably appeared in the Baltimore papers at that time. Evidently, talk of the Glamis mystery and its horrible secret was in the air, possibly into early 1909.

Notably, White knew the editor of the *Baltimore News* and, beginning in May 1908, wrote a column about foreign affairs for it (Wetzel 125). Perhaps a search through the microfilms of his columns would reveal that one of those foreign affairs involved the Mystery of Glamis Castle.

Works Cited

Dash, Mike. "The Monster of Glamis," *Smithsonian* (10 February 2012). www.smithsonianmag.com/history/the-monster-of-glamis-92015626/ accessed 10 March 2024.

Day, James Wentworth. *The Queen Mother's Family Story.* London: Robert Hale, 1967.

[Gilchrist, M.] "The Glamis Mystery." *Notes and Queries* (10 January 1885): 35.

Joshi, S. T. "Edward Lucas White: Dream and Reality." In Joshi's *The Evolution of the Weird Tale.* New York: Hippocampus Press, 2004. 39–45.

Lovecraft, H. P. *The Annotated Supernatural Horror in Literature.* Ed. S. T. Joshi. New York: Hippocampus Press, 2nd ed. 2012.

[Outis.] "The Glamis Mystery." *Notes and Queries* (26 September 1908): 241.

Sandoz, Maurice. *The Maze.* New York: Doubleday, 1945.

[Unsigned.] "Does Glamis Harbor a Monster?" *Washington Times* (13 March 1904): Colored Section.

[Unsigned.] "Mystery of Glamis Castle. Secret of Hidden Room Never Disclosed." *New York Sun* (21 February 1905): 7.

[Unsigned.] "Strathmore Heir Has Mystery Revealed to Him upon Coming of Age and Returns Livid." *Washington Times* (15 October 1905): 2.

Wetzel, George T. "Edward Lucas White: Notes for a Biography." *Fantasy Commentator* 5, No. 1 (Winter 1983): 67–70, 74 (Part IV); 5, No. 2 (Winter 1984): 124–27 (Part V).

———. "Glamis Castle and Sandoz' *The Maze.*" *Nyctalops* No. 14 (March 1978): 43–44.

White, Edward Lucas. *Lukundoo and other Stories.* New York: Doran, 1927.

———. *Sesta and Other Strange Stories.* Ed. Lee Weinstein. Seattle: Midnight House, 2001.

———. *The Song of the Sirens and Other Stories.* New York: Dutton, 1919.

Wind Tarot

Ann K. Schwader

Last divination dealt from skyclad trees
before the snow, they drift unnoticed down
in pavement spreads. These strange arcana, brown
beyond their days, or set alight to freeze
in darkness are not ours. Some elder hand
inscribed each symbol twisted through their veins
invisible until November rains
revealing mystery. To understand
costs more, perhaps, than sanity. Mere sight
suffices only as a warning: turn
away before the next leaf drops reversed
into its pattern. Shattering what light
still clings somehow to branches, meaning burns
along naive synapses like a curse.

The Enmity of Xubalba and Zardaak

Wade German

In the ninth chronicle of Gulnooz, that ancient historian collects many strange tales concerning the wizards whose unbridled sorceries resulted in the epochal Witch Wars that nearly extinguished their entire age; but one of the strangest and most curiously morbid of those tales relates the long-lasting antagonism between the warlocks known as Zardaak the Red and Xubalba the Green.

Amongst members of the many witch-cults and other magical societies of that era, Zardaak and Xubalba were legendary not only for their profound enmity, but also for their respective catalogues of enormous and sundry evils. No one claimed to know the origin of that reciprocal animosity; but theories were abundant, and some speculated that the two warlocks had initially met at some unknown cross purposes in the astral worlds, somewhere upon the occulted highways of interdimensional travelers. Whatever the reason for the mutual hatred, their sorcerous clashes were well known and earned them deep respect from their peers in wizardry.

In astral form the two sorcerers took on aspects of phantasmal titans or demigods as they stalked each other across the immeasurable voids and stellar gulfs. It was said that during their fierce magical exchanges they hurled planets like cannonballs at each other, and fashioned the cores of dead or decaying suns into inconceivably powerful munitions to detonate on their cosmic battlefields; they were also known to gather and condense the gaseous contents of nebulae and ignite them for similar terrible purposes. Entire constellations were said to have been rigged into pit traps or snares against the other's star-treading steps; and as they battled, the dark substance of space itself warped around their colossal forms as they pursued each other across the horizons of incredibly vast black wells, which were believed in theory to swallow all matter into irretrievable and infinite oblivions. Entire planetary systems—yea, entire galaxies—all populated with the teeming souls of innumerable alien life forms, were annihilated in the mad quests of Xubalba and Zardaak to destroy each other.

But these prolonged psychic exertions had their deleterious effects, and the aftermaths of conflict required both wizards to retreat and recuperate their depleted magical energies. And so they would retire to their respective demesnes, at opposite ends of the same continent in our mundane reality, and there renew or reformulate tactics and strategies for their next potentially fatal encounter.

It was said that by all outward appearances the two wizards formed a remarkable study in contrasts, far removed from the demigod-like avatars they projected in astral aspect.

Xubalba was an obese, green-tinged sybarite. Rich beyond calculation for all the magic he conjured for his clientele, he lived in a mansion near Pfsosz, the most ancient city on the western edge of the continent, where he often wallowed in drug dens and attended orgies of incubi and succubi at the city's famously luxurious bordellos. He was forever clouded in purple tobacco smoke and partook in huge quantities of exotic liquors and other intoxicants, including fungoid hallucinogens. His skin had turned a vibrant green due to a peculiar side-effect caused by the combined abuse of these substances, which, aside from the inducement and prolonging of carnal pleasures, also afforded him access to other planes and dimensions, from which he could summon spirits of the otherworld for strange counsel or even command.

Zardaak's was a hermetic existence, lived alone in the extreme austerity of a desert anchorite. His entire body, which he kept shaved from head to foot, was covered in red-inked hieroglyphs and runes that were the eldritch charms and prayers of an all but defunct sect of demon worshippers. His home was at the site of an ancient, abandoned temple in a remote region of the East. He was gaunt, but not only for a regime of self-imposed subsistence: he also partook in weird, self-distilled elixirs and imbibed tremendous quantities of stimulants—especially the narcotic petals of the illicit *sotula* poppy, which he chewed perpetually and stained his teeth a lacquer-bright crimson, so that when he smiled he appeared to have been drinking blood like a cannibal at some fireless feast. This potent drug helped him to sustain deep meditative stupors, wherein he conversed with ultramundane entities and chthonic spirits that harnessed outré supernatural forces and dark subterranean currents. These meditations had many times taken him to the threshold of madness, and perhaps even beyond it.

The mutual disrespect between Xubalba and Zardaak carried on for centuries. Then one day, in a truly inspired moment, it occurred to Zardaak that he could traverse the continent and assassinate his adversary in person. Thunderstruck by the practical utility of this epiphany, he broke down and wept, and praised all the darkest gods of his pantheon for gifting him the evil inspiration.

And so he quickly gathered the few gems and coins that amounted to his entire worldly wealth, buckled on an old scimitar that he used for chopping fruit and vegetables, and, galvanized by a sense of adventure he had not known since youth, was by the next day searching out supplies in the reeking bazaars of Izupzaal, the town nearest his habitation. When all necessities had been gathered, he then visited the stables where there were many beasts and purchased a *vamgorvipant,* a flying steed that somewhat resembled an albino pterodactyl. Soon his avian creature was harnessed and Zardaak himself was saddled. Both were eager for flight as they lifted into the air upon a transcontinental voyage.

Zardaak was excited, not only by the prospect of bathing in his archenemy's blood, but also by the exhilarating panoramic vistas of variable terrain that were swiftly passing beneath him. But the journey was fraught with perils. When flying over the southern jungles, there were missile-throwing lizard-people to avoid; and more than once evasions had to be made to escape a species of nearly invisible aerial parasite that fed upon other airborne creatures. And when camping for the night, there were concerns over roving mutant hordes that dwelt in the desert spaces and wastelands, as well as nomadic raiders of the steppes, and the monster-haunted hills, forests, and mountains. But despite these threats, Zardaak found the very novelty of his transit quite pleasurable. As evening came down, he relished the stars and the moons in their various phases and thrilled at the spectral beauty of green and violet auroras that flowed eerily in the welkin, a phenomenon wholly unobservable in his own land.

Eventually Zardaak saw the turrets, steeples, and towers of Pfsosz rising through mist in the twilit distance. Having nearly reached the terminus of his voyage, he noted with some jubilation that the stars had formed auspicious alignments as he approached Xubalba's castle of indolence on the sea, the location of which was no secret.

He landed his *vamgorvipant* on a grassy knoll behind the beetling sea cliffs so as not to herald his arrival inadvertently. Securing his steed, he stealthily approached the house of his enemy.

The mansion, which squatted on a sea-sprayed cliffside, was a vast pile of black, purple, and red obsidian stone, which to Zardaak's mind bore all the appearance of a dead god's mausoleum and stood as testimony to Xubalba's funebriously decadent tastes.

Conducting a covert reconnaissance of the grounds, Zardaak's sorcery-enhanced perception detected a host of roving phantoms around the walls of the place, which Xubalba had obviously summoned from the beyond for a sentinel purpose. Zardaak easily dispersed these otherworldly sentries with a spell of banishment. Then he searched around the now unguarded lower floor and found his point of ingress at an unlocked window.

Skulking through darkness inside the manse, he was quick to scoff at the opulence of the place. All the chairs and couches were sumptuous and gaudy; and hideous statues, paintings, and other objets d'art decorated the tables and walls of the shadowy interior. The entire place was pervaded by a cloying odour of incense, and an annoying amount of dust had settled over everything, much to Zardaak's distaste. Then, at the bottom of a wide spiral staircase, Zardaak heard the soft strains of a stringed instrument playing a weird but pleasantly soporific melody; beneath this he also heard faint murmurs of jovial voices. He stalked up the stairway, following the music and voices, which were now discernible as the sounds of male mirth and feminine merriment. On the upper landing there were several chambers, but only one of which emitted a soft, tremulous glow of candlelight. He peered in from around the corner. This room was strewn with carpets and plush floor pillows; and here Zardaak again heard a woman's laughter, which was followed by a deep-throated chuckle. Much to his amusement, Zardaak fully expected to surprise his old foe in the midst of lovemaking.

Still keeping to the shadows, he entered the chamber, where he now espied a sitar-like instrument leaning against a pillar, its strings being plucked as if by invisible fingers; and Zardaak had no doubt that Xubalba had here conjured the ghost of some former musician to provide the queer musical ambiance. But the playing went on unperturbed by Zardaak's presence as he crept across the deep-pile carpets and approached the two figures who were intimately entangled amongst the pillows.

Zardaak silently caught his breath as he spied his intended victim, whose head was buried between a naked woman's breasts, but was otherwise completely wrapped in the coiled embrace of the woman's black and yellow-mottled serpent tail. Zardaak was not at all surprised to learn his ancient enemy Xubalba would choose to couple with a lamia; but as he pondered over the perversion, his presence had caused a slight shift in the air, and the plumes of incense that rose from a burning brazier now wavered and wafted in the draft.

The lamia noticed this change immediately and turned to face the intruder in the shadows, which also alerted Xubalba; both now had seen him. In an instant of reversed glamour, the lamia's beautiful face metamorphosed into its true demoniacal visage, and she hissed at Zardaak through her fangs. Xubalba, too, howled in surprise, but also in recognition of his old adversary, even though it was the first time they had ever met on the material plane.

The lamia, who Zardaak inferred was a spellbound creature for all the talismanic enslavement sigils tattooed upon her sleek back, rapidly uncoiled from the corpulent warlock, and like a bolt of lightning escaped through a portal hole in the wall, which Zardaak assumed led to a lair in some sub-level of the house. Xubalba, now left sprawling naked and defenseless amid the cushions, tried to back away from his assailant as Zardaak leapt at him and completely severed his head with a single swipe of his scimitar.

Xubalba's head flew from his blubbery neck in a gushing fountain of pink blood, then bounced with a grisly splash on the floor and rolled away across the carpets. But to Zardaak's dismay and horror, the still rolling head was rapidly sprouting a pair of bat-like wings from its ears and was already flopping about on the floor like some hideously awkward fledgling; then, with newfound agility, it flapped its leathery appendages and lifted off the floor in flight.

Zardaak gave chase, swiping his sword wildly at it, but the thing was flying evasively and erratically about the chamber and out of his reach. Zardaak stumbled and fell, knocking over statues and smashing his shins on low-lying tables as he gave desperate pursuit, as all the while the otherworldly sitar music continued in an incongruous accompaniment to this grotesquely comical pantomime. The chase now sped from the chamber onto the staircase, where Xubalba's high-flying head hurled grievous insults at his foe while circling above him, then flew outside through an otherwise inaccessible transom.

Unable to give further chase, Zardaak stood a while in bafflement. But he quickly decided to set about destroying Xubalba's body, so as to lessen the possibility of its ever being magically rejoined with its head. He began the macabre task forthwith; but this, too, proved a considerable challenge. For as he approached the corpulent green corpse, the thing began to grope and kick at him with a blind fury, apparently aware of its impending fate. Zardaak's initial attempts to sever the limbs from the torso were clumsy and futile; but after some further floundering, he succeeded in the vivisection of his old adversary's quivering cadaver. Even after complete dismemberment, the separated parts exhibited a terrible animation for some time, until the twitching and shuddering altogether suddenly ceased. The red wizard sighed with relief and wiped the sweat from his brow and pink blood from his hands as he stood over the motionless remains. All that was now left to do was to destroy them.

And this he set about doing quite gleefully by forming an impromptu pyre, which was quickly assembled from the many wooden artifacts and other flammable furnishings in the chamber. When sufficient fuel had been heaped together, he heaved the flabby pieces of the green wizard's corpse upon the pile, then tossed several burning candles upon the lot to set it all ablaze.

Zardaak watched as the flames slowly engulfed the gory assemblage, then shrieked and giggled with a hitherto unknown joy as he hopped and skipped down the staircase toward the ornately carved front door of the mansion, which, much to his consternation, he found to be locked. He fumbled with the lock ineffectually before thinking to mutter a simple cantrip of opening; but this also had no effect. The matter was of some pressing concern to Zardaak, as the crackling blaze continued to spread above and behind him; and as ceiling timbers began crashing down the spiral staircase from the floor above, he knew his arson had already become an unquenchable inferno that would soon claim the entire house.

And then he heard a weird rustling and scratching noise from above him. Searching out its source, he looked up to see Xubalba's disembodied head as it bobbed and hovered at the high window above the front door, its eyes reflecting the leaping flames like those of an exuberant pyromaniac, its terrible face bearing an insane and retributive smile.

And the hovering head of Xubalba continued to smile a smile that, if he could wish it from a genie, would go on smiling and laughing forever. For, while Zardaak had been occupied with the horrible disposal of his enemy's corpse, the winged head of Xubalba had secured a large feather between its teeth; and using his own jugular blood for ink, had been flying with great haste outside and around the blazing mansion to paint crude but efficacious warding sigils upon all the exits, be they door or window, thus sealing them shut with binding magics.

Zardaak screamed, shook his fists, and spat invectives at his floating opponent, for he understood his terrible predicament. But this did not stop him from running madly through the burning mansion to seek out every possible site of egress, which all refused him.

As the inexorable flames licked at the walls around him, and realizing his doomed plight while at the same time unable to fathom it fully, Zardaak was completely beside himself with spite and outrage, and uttered a shrill, ear-splitting litany of the evilest imprecations imaginable against his hovering, maniacally grinning nemesis, who was more than happy to observe the destruction of his own residence if it housed the heart of his hate.

It is not known if any of Zardaak's curses reached their intended recipient to cause any effect. What is known is that when the vast conflagration was exhausted of its fuel, and only a few feeble flames guttered in finality amid the smoking ruins of Xubalba the Green's mansion, all that remained of Zardaak the Red was a blackened cinder of kindling.

Robert Nelson, Charles D. Hornig, and the *Fantasy Fan:* A Motley of Young Talents

Marcos Legaria

> The first II stanzas of verse, from Duane W. Rimel's "Dreams of Yith" are little verbal jewels that are worthy of praise and admiration. And I prefer to think of Clark Ashton Smith's "The Epiphany of Death" (Dedicated to H. P. Lovecraft) as something that is truly deathless, immortal. If you have planned to use this in the Aug. Our Readers Say of *TFF* please do not do so. Please do not print this. No one seems to care for my comments or writings in *TFF* anyway. Please do not print what I said. If you print it, I shall not continue to read *TFF*.[1]
>
> I dwelt in Shadow's lonely home
> And thought that all the light was there.
> But now I know how wrong the tome
> I had so needlessly to bear.
> —Robert Nelson, "I Dwelt in Shadow's Lonely Home"

At the start of the summer in 1933, a circular appeared among the science fiction community announcing the forthcoming appearance of a magazine called the *Fantasy Fan* (September 1933–February 1935). Intriguingly, the publication was instigated by Charles D. Hornig (1916–1999), at the age of seventeen from Elizabeth, New Jersey, and typeset and printed by Conrad Ruppert. Upon its debut, Hornig's *Fantasy Fan* made such a huge splash that publisher Hugo Gernsback hired Hornig on the spot to edit the science fiction magazine *Wonder Stories*. This precocious editor's tastes soon proved eclectic, as he accepted fantasy and weird fiction from such authors as

---

1. Robert Nelson, postcard to Charles D. Hornig [postmarked 1 August 1934]; ms., Forrest J Ackerman Papers, Syracuse University (hereafter SU).

H. P. Lovecraft, Clark Ashton Smith, and a neophyte poet hailing from St. Charles, Illinois, named Robert Nelson (1912–1935).

Aside from stories, the *Fantasy Fan* soon welcomed an interesting variety of articles, news, poems, and miscellany. Hornig's greatest feat was the serialization of the revised version of Lovecraft's "Supernatural Horror in Literature" (October 1933–February 1935). One of the first features Hornig created was a column designated "The Boiling Point" (September 1933–February 1934), itself a controversial forum whereby Forrest J Ackerman initiated "A Quarrel with Clark Ashton Smith." Ackerman, a science fiction fan already with some notoriety, was upset when *Wonder Stories* ran Smith's Martian macabre story "The Dweller in Martian Depths," a tale he vehemently stressed was better suited to *Weird Tales* magazine. Ackerman's rant began as such in its premier issue:

> It seems to me that *Wonder Stories* is going far afield when it takes such a horror story as Mr. Smith's "Dweller in Martian Depths" and, because it is laid on the Red Planet, prints it in a magazine of scientific fiction. Frankly, I could not find one redeeming feature about the story. Of course, everything doesn't have to have a moral. The thrilling scientifilm, "King Kong," for instance, has no moral to it—except, perhaps, to be careful of Fay Wray, if you are a great prehistoric ape—but it has a point, at least: to interest. And "Dweller in Martian Depths" didn't interest me. I don't know, maybe it did others. But it disappointed me very greatly to find it in a stf publication. In *Weird Tales*, all right. I don't like that type of story, I wouldn't read it there. I fail to find anything worth-while in an endless procession of ethereal lines, phantastic visions, ultra-mundane life, exotic paradises, airy vegetation, whispering flutes, ghastly plants, and dirge-like horrors. May the ink dry up in the pen from which they flow! Or, at least, Mr. Smith, direct those tales elsewhere—NOT to a stf publication, because I do like your science fiction like "Master of the Asteroid" and "Flight into Super Time." But "stuff" like "The Light From Beyond" . . .

Staunch supporters of Smith's, such as Lovecraft, defended him and "The Dweller in Martian Depths." Sloppy editorial tampering was to blame, so the deficiencies in the story were not Smith's fault. In addition to Lovecraft, Smith's main advocate during this wrangle was Robert Nelson, who defended Smith and "The Dweller in Martian Depths" in the November 1933 issue:

> The Ackerman–Smith controversy assumes all the aspects of a mad comedy. To assail and reprehend the writings of Clark Ashton Smith is as preposterous and futile as a dwarf transporting a huge mountain peak upon the tip of his tiny finger. Either Forrest J. Ackerman is daft for an imbecile or a notoriety-seeking clown and knave. Clark Ashton Smith stands alone in the realm of present-day weird and fantastic literature, and, therefore, above all his contemporaries. He is still King: and has yet to be dethroned.

Again, Nelson defended Smith against Ackerman in the February 1934 issue:

> When you shout, pertaining to Smith stories, "May the ink dry up in the pen from which they flow!" you affect the refined and sensitive minds of the admirers of beautiful things, and cause them to exclaim, "Here, indeed, is one who endeavors to do something in words as terrible as in actuality: cleave the head of a genius in twain!" Hence our fitting denunciation of you, Mr. Ackerman, for attempting to backbite one of the greatest writers America has ever produced.

Nelson then sent Hornig a personal letter on 21 April 1934 from his address at 1030 Elm Street:

> My Dear Mr. Hornig:
> I hope you did not misinterpret my last personal card. When I said, "You show very good logic: one should *never* make promises!" I was serious, of course, and meant no "slam" or sarcasm to you. The unnecessary adding of the exclamation mark would have been the misleading factor. You, of course, made no promise *when* you

would print my dialog.[2] You only said "probably in the so-and-so issue." All of which shows good logic on your part. One should *never* make promises. (Don't tear up this letter, yet Charles! There's more to come!) [. . .] Five years ago; when I was much younger and more foolish than I am now, I loaned $100 to a best friend (he was supposed to be a friend) and he promised to pay it back. Needless to say, he still owes me $100. Moral: *never* make promises![3]

This friendship of Nelson's wouldn't be the last he would lose among family members and friends in the last year of his short and troubled life. The unpaid loan to Nelson was money from a recently matured insurance policy he had just collected on. For all Nelson's sarcasm, he held his correspondence with Hornig in high esteem when he said: "Seriously, I want to thank you again for the addresses you gave me. And thanks a lot for publishing some of my letters in *TFF*. [. . .] You *do* understand life, Charles."[4]

Good news arrived for Nelson to share in time with Hornig in his characteristic sarcastic manner:

> You may or may not be interested but my first published poem, "Sable Revery,"[5] will appear in a forthcoming issue of *Weird Tales*. I sent the poem to Clark Ashton Smith[6] for criticism and he thought it "quite remarkable and something outstanding in substance and inspiration." And to him I owe much in aiding me in bringing the poem to its final perfection and acceptance. The acceptance, besides Smith's letter of praise to Farnsworth Wright, also necessitated me to make four trips in person to the *W.T.* office, in the matter of fixing lines, etc. besides also my first introduction to Wright.[7]

---

2. "The Weird Tale (A Dialogue)," *Fantasy Fan* 1, No. 9 (May 1934): 141.
3. Nelson, letter to Hornig (21 April 1934); ms., SU.
4. Ibid.
5. "Sable Revery," *Weird Tales* 24, No. 3 (September 1934): 351.
6. For more on Nelson's turbulent working relationship with Clark Ashton Smith, and to a lesser extent editor Farnsworth Wright of *Weird Tales*, see my three-part series "Clark Ashton Smith and Robert Nelson: Master and Apprentice."
7. Nelson, letter to Hornig (21 April 1934); ms., SU.

A little over two weeks later, on 9 May 1934, Hornig received a poem and a short story from Nelson for his inspection:

> Thanks a lot for praising my poem[8] and "The Last Feast."[9] You may be very interested to know that the latter was never submitted to Farnsworth Wright with the view of publication in *Weird Tales*. It was written especially for *The Fantasy Fan;* and you are the only person beside myself who has ever read it. However, the weird and poetical part, uttered by Exphele, is substance taken from an original poem of my own, entitled "Under the Tomb," which I sent to Clark Ashton Smith for criticism. Smith said of it, "you seem to have had a vision of a strange realm of hidden horror beyond death but have not succeeded in embodying it. (I think I have embodied it, but in a different way of course, in "The Last Feast.") I believe you can do far more with the theme if you will let your imagination play over it awhile before attempting the revision of the poem. (Aw, the hell with it, Smith.) The best lines at present are the last two of the third stanza." ("A moon of steel drips blood upon a sky Darkened by what mad phantoms prophesy.") This poem on the whole, I really did not care for myself, and decided not to submit to *W.T.* But I thought I could use it to good advantage in some other way: hence "The Last Feast."[10]

Nelson was pleased with Hornig for his kind comments regarding the "The Last Feast," and that it was "better than half the stuff you've read in *Weird Tales*."[11]

Less than a month after, Hornig sent Nelson extra copies of the May 1934 issue of the *Fantasy Fan,* containing Nelson's sketch "The Weird Tale (A Dialogue)." Nelson thanked Hornig for the issues and was happy that the printed version looked fine with no typographical errors, but the only exception was the excusable (A Dialogue). Nelson further wrote: "But it all looks great, and if it 'goes over' in the same manner with the weird fans, (which I don't suppose it will) then

---

8. An early version of the poem "Under the Tomb."
9. The story "The Last Feast" is nonextant.
10. Nelson, letter to Hornig (9 May 1934); ms., SU.
11. Ibid.

perhaps my efforts will not have been entirely in vain. (This last is an old phrase, Charles, but it's all I can think of at the moment.)"[12]

"The Weird Tale" by Nelson ran as follows:

Gerald: So you say that science fiction has fallen into decay?

Sidney: Precisely. By its own outlandishness and inflated ridiculousness it has been reduced to the tedium and monotony of everyday life.

Gerald: Oh, but you make me laugh, Sidney! What of weird fiction? How can any one endure these everlastingly infernal vampire stories with their boorish waving of crosses to defy and fight off the vampire! I dare say that if I should fling a putrid tomato at one of the accursed things it would run helter-skelter!

Sidney: It is very true. Vampire stories are a bit worn, and deserve to have gone out of existence long ago. But it is the weird tale, Gerald, the sort of tale as produced by Lovecraft and Smith, that truly makes weird literature, something far more noble and beautiful than most modern fiction, with its silly tea-lady romances, modern love, and high society twaddle.

For an illustration of weird fiction, Gerald, let us take Clark Ashton Smith's most superb tale, "The Double Shadow." Here we have one of the most beautiful weird tales in the English language. When we read it we experience the sensation of a sweeping and stirring symphony. We read of Pharpetron, "the last and most forward pupil of the wise Avyctes," and how he and his master live in the marble house above the "loud, ever-ravening sea." We see the wind-swept sea, the white towers, the eerie demonisms and necromancies, the Double Shadow. It creates for us a life which we would wish to live, and fills us with a sense of eternal, majestic beauty of which we have been ignorant. All of this is so beautifully weird. Is not this more appealing than science fiction?

Gerald: Of course it all depends upon the individual. But I suppose the weird and macabre is more appealing, and rightfully, perhaps, it is. But you mentioned and inferred that the weird tale, as executed by Lovecraft and Smith, is the most worthwhile of the whole. Personally, I like Robert E. Howard the best of them all.

Sidney: My dear boy, all three are great writers. We know that,

---

12. Nelson, letter to Hornig (19 May 1934); ms., SU.

but it cannot be denied that Smith is a truer artist, and that makes him the greatest. Oh, Gerald, if more people could only appreciate and understand the significance of the weird tale! And if scribes could only emulate Smith or Lovecraft or Howard! If they would only strive for originality and beauty! But no! We poor and insignificant readers of the weird tale must continue to be plagued with time-worn vampires, witches, rituals, and other weird senilities!

Gerald: Well, why don't you try to write a weird tale, Sidney? You seem to know all its merits and demerits.

Sidney: Well, because I—er—well, I just haven't the time.

This sketch is a perfect exposition of Nelson's belief of what a true weird tale should be, and of those writers he highly regarded.

A couple of months in, the *Fantasy Fan* was already having trouble securing submissions. Finances kept Nelson from securing a year's worth subscription, otherwise he would have been glad to "swell the *TFF* treasury."[13] If this wasn't enough, Nelson wanted his short story "The Last Feast" returned to him. At the end of May, Nelson convinced Hornig:

> I am enclosing a self-addressed and stamped envelope, for you to return my manuscript, "The Last Feast." I have never submitted it to Wright. And I have been thinking (ever since I received your letter praising it) whether I should not have sent it to Wright in the first place. I do things, perhaps, in too hasty a manner; and you might even think me a bit daft or something. If Wright will not take it then I'll send it back to you. I hope this won't create any hard feelings. I have a short weird piece[14] in mind, that I hope to write shortly for *TFF*, in case Wright takes "The Last Feast."[15]

Things were looking up: "Below the Phosphor"—one of Nelson's earliest composed poems, written in 1928 and containing traces of the style and content of Edgar Allan Poe—appeared in the June 1934 issue of the *Fantasy Fan*:

---

13. Ibid.
14. Nelson is referring to his upcoming sketch the "Trilogy of Death."
15. Nelson, letter to Hornig (28 May 1934); ms., SU.

The swaying corpse upon the wall
Grows rotten with the waning;
And crawling shadows of the night
Lie on the body like a pall

Dead spirits dance upon the slope;
Blatant are bat-things overhead;
But now the revenants have fled,
The glad fantasias grope.

Only the ghouls are gently stirred
By tainted gusts lost from the gale;
And in the faun-infested vale
Wild screeches of a fiend are heard.

Impending o'er the noisome spawn,
In glaucous haze the Phosphor steals—
Thence to Azrael's eyes reveals
The wrestling wraiths on death's dark lawn—

Fast scaling up the ebon sky
To cull and slay the gnawing blight,
All cool of the corpse's mute delight,
Or if the baneful fiends should die.

If Nelson had some more matters of interest to get off his chest
and mind, he'd soon unload them as he warned Hornig: "I am sure
looking forward to you coming to Chicago. I'm marking off the days
on my calendar, and it won't be long![16]

The meeting in Chicago between Nelson and Hornig occurred
on 24 June 1934, a Wednesday. Nelson wrote to Clark Ashton
Smith of the meeting on 6 July 1934:

> Meeting Hornig was quite interesting. [. . .] Hornig and I were
> standing side by side on the steps leading to the Art Institute, on
> Michigan Boulevard [. . .]
> There really is no use in going into further detail about our
> meeting. We sat on a park bench, viewing the Outer Drive and

16. Nelson, letter to Hornig (28 May 1934); ms., SU.

Lake Michigan. We [. . .] talked on science-fiction. And I listened. I endeavored to start on another subject [. . .] Hornig posed for 23 or older, but is really younger. But he will not confess his exact age. I imagine him to be about 21 or 22.[17]

Later, in the evening, we went to a theatre. On the whole, I found Hornig a really interesting fellow [. . .] But I don't believe I made a very good impression on Hornig. Not that I care, but perhaps it only goes to prove once more than I never, or rather, very seldom I appeal to either man or woman, more especially to woman.[18]

After Nelson deprecatingly put himself down, he wrote Smith a little more about his interaction with Hornig a week later: "Regarding Hornig again: he really is a fine young fellow, and is worthy of all the success that he has thus far achieved. [. . .] He lives in Elizabeth, New Jersey, only a comparatively short distance from New York City."[19]

Worries plagued Nelson two months after the publication of his sketch "The Weird Tale (A Dialogue)." A letter of explanation was quickly printed in the July 1934 "Our Readers Say" section: "Some will perhaps wonder what I precisely meant, in my dialogue in the May issue, when my character, Sidney, exclaimed, 'And if scribes could only emulate Smith or Lovecraft or Howard!' I meant, of course, that writers should strive to these three in *greatness*—but a greatness of a different sort. For there can only be *one* Clark Ashton Smith, *one* H. P. Lovecraft, *one* Robert E. Howard. But the aspiring writer can always form himself on a good model; and in time, he will find his *own* individuality."

If Nelson was closely guarded about his correspondence, he was no less so with his writings as he recommended Hornig to do with his latest poem: "Change slightly the title of my poem 'The Unremembered Realm' to 'Fragment: The Unremembered Realm.' And the very last three lines could be separated perhaps from the preced-

17. Nelson wasn't even close, as Hornig just turned 18 the previous month, on 25 May 1934.
18. Nelson, letter to Smith (6 July 1934); ms., John Hay Library, Brown University (hereafter abbreviated JHL).
19. Nelson, letter to Smith (14 July 1934); ms., JHL.

ing five of the original second and last stanza when printed, for they are of iambic hexameter, while the others are of troches and iambic hexameters, septameter, and octameter."[20]

"The Unremembered Realm" soon appeared in print, sans the three lines and keeping its original title. The poem appeared as follows:

> Nameless: that unremembered realm of the temporal universe
> Which the sundry gods have slighted to complete:
> These azure ice-peaks thrive and wane in wild exult,
> And shift their freezing heights in tremulous tumult;
> The wan ice-forms are vanished creatures lost in time.
>
> Nameless: that unremembered realm of the temporal universe
> Which the sundry gods have slighted to complete:
> There the youthful moon is like a fount of living flame;
> The eldern sun moves in a clique of pallid dying mist;
> Dark birds flow endlessly to turn the dawn to amethyst;
> When moon and sun and birds are gone the dead make fires
> In reeking, foul-swept skies above the great ice-spires,
> And view the cold-fraught land with last and mad proclaim.

Although Nelson didn't consider "The Unremembered Realm" to be one of his best poetic efforts,[21] the poem does resonate with the horrors that would come upon the universe at the end of time. Remarkably, the three excised lines Nelson didn't utilize for the poem would later make its way into another poem, of which more later.

On 1 September, Nelson congratulated Hornig on the excellent August issue of the *Fantasy Fan*. The only item Nelson wanted to see more of was more the "Dreams of Yith" poems by Duane W. Rimel.

By the autumn of 1934, Nelson had been toying with various writings. The first would be devoted to a sketch he called the "Trilogy of Death." After working on a premature version of this sketch,

---

20. Nelson, postcard to Hornig [postmarked 12 August 1934]; ms., SU.
21. Ibid.

Nelson lamented to Hornig about the revisions for this second version: "I'm sorry about my changes. I am training myself as much as possible to govern and control my emotions and sharpen my discriminating faculties. I am returning 'Trilogy of Death' once again, revised in the latter part. It is really written in all seriousness."[22]

At the same time, Nelson would also appear in the *Fantasy Fan* with his series "Lost Excerpts," as he told Hornig: "Also, I am submitting III., IV., and V. of 'Lost Excerpts.' Please do not change anything in the 'Lost Excerpts' series without letting me know."[23] The first two "Lost Excerpts" episodes were personally handed over by Nelson to Hornig when the two young men visited each other in Chicago several months before in the summer. These comprised the episodes "In Living Darkness" and "The Feast of the Centaurs."

The origins of the "Lost Excerpts" can be traced in a letter Nelson wrote to Clark Ashton Smith earlier in the year, on 3 April 1934:

> Recently I completed a group of six short works in prose. My aim has been to make them of "fine and practical writing." But I don't suppose I have succeeded. I have had a vague idea to have them privately printed, if ever possible. They are not short stories, in the sense that each one adheres to any certain architectural norm. And they are not weird, although one or two tend to be fantastic. The present titles are *Painting in Love*, *The Man in the Street*, *The Ray of Happiness*, *The Pure Honeymoon*, *Woman of Gold*, and *Revelation*.[24]

Nelson would keep these sketches on the fantastic-weird side, with a change to the titles for their later appearances in print. The first of the "Lost Excerpts" to appear was published in the November 1934 issue and entitled "In Living Darkness":

---

22. Nelson, letter to Hornig (15 October 1934); ms., SU.
23. Ibid.
24. Nelson, letter to Smith (3 April 1934); ms., JHL.

In dreams agone I walked aimlessly and long in far and distant realms.

I have seen wretched and depressed women feed with their milk the famished spirits that swelter and moulder amid the rank noisomeness of charnel hells. By blue and rotting trees I have seen colossal and cankered white worms fawning to their young and devouring themselves.

I have seen evil and demented dwarfs fling flaring torches into the faces of maids who were playing sad violins and dying with nameless sins and melody. And I have stood on red rocks overlooking a black and ever-surging sea where in dread things stabbed and slew and shrieked in exaltation to the molten dripping skies.

Considering the daring concepts already apparent in this premier episode, Hornig was willing to take a chance for their inclusion in the *Fantasy Fan*.

Then the news hit Nelson that the magazine was hanging by a thread. Nelson was bothered to hear from Hornig that he received only twenty-three inquiries from readers about the *Fantasy Fan* through an advertisement in *Weird Tales*.

One matter remained certain. Nelson was adamant on copyrighting his "Lost Excerpts," as he had revealed to Clark Ashton Smith all the way back in April. He also brought this up with Hornig on 17 October: "I have been thinking whether or not I should have the first seven of the 'Lost Excerpts' series copyrighted by myself. What do you think? You already have the first five. And I have two more ready."[25] Hornig suggested that perhaps a deluxe volume of "Lost Excerpts" would be better, but Nelson didn't think this was a good idea:

> At the present time I can't afford to have any deluxe volumes made. And I am wondering if Ruppert would undertake to print just two copies of the first seven of "Lost Excerpts" in *TFF* format-size. But perhaps he is already occupied with enough work. I was wondering if he would undertake to print the seven "Lost Ex-

---

25. Nelson, letter to Hornig (17 October 1934); ms., SU.

cerpts in just two copies on the cheapest paper possible—and what his charge would be. Naturally, and inevitably, they will appear in *TFF*, as I originally planned, but I should like to have them copyrighted.

Let me know what you think of this proposition.[26]

Hornig replied to Nelson, but the feeling one gets is that it wasn't practical at the time. Unforeseen events would soon take a turn for the worse. By 23 October, Nelson wrote Hornig: "Thanks for your advice regarding the copyrighting of 'Lost Excerpts.'"[27] So far, with the first two "Lost Excerpts" published and episodes III–V waiting in the wings, Nelson had two further episodes ready: "I am enclosing two more 'Lost Excerpts'—VI, and VII. This is all in the series I shall submit to now: I won't be sending you any more material until I see the reaction from the fans to 'Lost Excerpts.'"[28]

Positive feedback for Nelson's writings among readers of the *Fantasy Fan* wasn't his only concern, but he was now worried that some may have misperceived his sexual preferences from his writings, as he wrote Hornig: "Do you think of my writings a bit effeminate, Charles? Some of my few friends, whom I am fast losing, are accusing me of being a pansy, because they think I look and act like one."[29]

By his next letter, Nelson was slightly in better spirits, thanking Hornig for his interesting letter and his nice compliments regarding "Lost Excerpts." Aside from his own writings, Nelson shared some of his outside interests on 29 October: "I very seldom go to a movie—if I do it is one in which stars John Barrymore[30] or Fredric March[31] or Norma Shearer."[32]

---

26. Ibid.
27. Nelson, letter to Hornig (23 October 1934); ms., SU.
28. Ibid.
29. Ibid.
30. John Barrymore (1882–1942), American actor well received in such pictures as *Dr. Jekyll and Mr. Hyde* (1920), *Sherlock Holmes* (1922), and *The Sea Beast* (1926).
31. Fredric March (1897–1975), Academy Award–winning actor for his role in *Dr. Jekyll and Mr. Hyde* (1931).

His interest in the female sex was practically nil:

> I do not associate with any girls whatsoever at the present time, chiefly because of lack of finances. Even so, I have seen only a few girls who would be really worth loving. And even the few I have loved, all have been deceiving in one way or another, or else they did not care for me because I was too serious. The girls who *have* "fallen" for me I never cared for myself. And the ones whom I have "fallen" for either tricked me in one way or another, or cared little for me because I was too serious, saying so to my face. So now I associate with no girl whatsoever. In fact, I associate hardly with anyone. And I don't believe, Charles, I could really say that I have even *one* friend! This may sound a bit unusual, but it's the truth.[33]

Another outside interest Nelson shared with Hornig but had no luck with was vacationing: "Travelling is wonderful, if you can afford it. And when I do travel I enjoy it immensely of course."[34] Up till then, Nelson had made short trips into Chicago, meeting Farnsworth Wright at the *Weird Tales* office, and of course Hornig the previous summer; the latter would soon make trips to visit H. P. Lovecraft in Providence, R.I., C. L. Moore in Indianapolis, and other writers who contributed to the *Fantasy Fan*. Nelson himself would soon move to Chicago for a short time.

For some time, illness plagued Nelson by the form of tuberculosis: Lovecraft mentioned to correspondents that Nelson constantly imbibed milk. When it came to drinking, Nelson verified the following to Hornig: "I don't care for coffee, thank you! Milk and beer and wine for me. Milk always for breakfast and lunch. Beer always for dinner. And wine occasionally in midnight drafts."[35]

Friction between Nelson and his parents came to a head, forcing him to move alone to Chicago. Nelson had also started to feel sui-

---

32. Norma Shearer (1902–1983), Canadian-American actress known for playing spunky, sexually liberated women in films during the years 1919–42.
33. Nelson, letter to Hornig (29 October 1934); ms., SU.
34. Ibid.
35. Ibid.

cidal, as he explained to Hornig upon his submission of the second version of the sketch "Trilogy of Death" in an undated postcard:

> "Trilogy of Death" revised once again, in the last part. Compare this present version with the one you have, and see which you now have, and see which you think is best. This one I am sending you now better than the other version—it is, of course, the sensations of a suicide while dying.
>
> Don't send me a card or letter commenting on this now. I'll write you a letter very soon telling you why.[36]

Nelson also had this short notation added to his undated postcard to Hornig concerning the latest version of "Trilogy of Death": "If you like this version, then burn the other one."[37] In the meantime, here is the original last paragraph to Nelson's second incarnation of "Trilogy of Death":

> Death is in red ink. . . .
>
> Death is in red ink. "I am surprised how calmly I can do it," scrawled in red ink. "Already begin to feel warming a little . . . get dizzy, and it is only three minutes. Sleep is coming on. My eyes grow heavy. Now my head aches. I begin to ache in the arms . . . heart is pounding. My vision is not much blurred. I have no special pain now. I am trying to keep awake, but won't hold out much longer . . . very pleasant just now . . . mouth seeming to be a bit dry. My throat seems to beat slower . . . would not chance . . . drug heart . . . pretty . . . light when I look around . . . chest and eyes growing heavy . . . heart pounding . . . hear airplanes . . . arms . . . friends . . . about sleepier . . . it is a grand sensation . . ." Death is in red ink . . .[38]

Before getting to Nelson's final version of "Trilogy of Death," a notice of Nelson's address change to Hornig should be mentioned in a postcard written from Chicago and postmarked on 30 November:

---

36. Nelson, undated postcard to Hornig; ms., SU.
37. Ibid.
38. Ms., SU.

Dear Charles:
   You can send the Dec. *TFF*
   To 5245 Magnolia Ave.,
   Chicago, Ill.
     Best Wishes,
     Robert Nelson[39]

The move didn't last long. By 15 December, Nelson wrote to Hornig (as he did to Clark Ashton Smith) of a reconciliation with his parents, prompting him to return to his home in St. Charles. All future issues of the *Fantasy Fan* beginning with the December issue were to be sent to his home. Nelson told Hornig: "I am back at 1030 Elm St., St. Charles, after having been literally begged by my parents to come home. And they now realize and admit that they were not as sympathetic with me as they should have been. [. . .] And so, this recent little comedy has ended. And I have taken a new lease on life."[40]

Sadly, this new lease on life wouldn't last long. Nelson's turbulent view on life can be found in his second "Lost Excerpt" titled "The Feast of the Centaurs," published in the December 1934 issue of the *Fantasy Fan:*

> The enormous chamber was aflare with myriad lamps. There were long tables covered with seemingly endless varieties of meats, wines, cheeses, birds, and other viands and edibles. Drunken centaurs carried other intoxicated creatures across the tables trampling everything that came their way, causing both wrath and mirth to others. Wine was spilled heavily all about; and centaurs fell and grappled with one another on the lubricous earth. Two there were who fought for the possession of a fried grasshopper; and three belabored each other's heads with weighty stools. Some threw great platters of food from the tables and demanded more wine. And the exhalation that arose from the food and creatures became heavier; and the rejoicing and the swearing and debating of tongues increased.

---

39. Nelson, postcard to Hornig [postmarked 30 November 1934]; ms., SU.
40. Nelson, letter to Hornig (15 December 1934); ms., SU.

There were huge mirrors of multiplied convexity in the vast room and these seemed to enhance and sharpen the ebbing and flowing luminosity from the immense wax lights and bright vases. The mirrors caused much confusion among the inebriated and over-gorged creatures, for they crashed and careened with one another against the mirrors and cut themselves, and laughed and cursed at their own grotesque and misshapen likenesses.

"Lost Excerpts" were certainly ahead of their time, and it isn't surprising that readers' responses in the *Fantasy Fan* weren't vocal enough. And yet, Nelson had a third version of the sketch "Trilogy of Death" ready for Hornig: "Am enclosing revised version of 'Trilogy of Death.' This is positively the last time I shall do any revision on 'Trilogy of Death': I think this last one more appealing and better (though not anything extraordinary) than the preceding versions. Let me know what you think of it."[41]

Here follows Nelson's third and final version of "Trilogy of Death" as it appeared in the January 1935 issue:

Death is a wheel . . .
Death is a wheel, grinding, rending, crushing. The little boy skipped gayly to the grocery store for his mother. Crossing the street, he did not see an oncoming truck. It was too late and— Death is a wheel, grinding, rending, crushing. Death is a wheel.
. . .
Death is a dollar bill . . .
Death is a dollar bill. A gust of wind swept a vagrant dollar bill into the gutter. It sped onward through the streets. Onward to a jutting pier. Onward it went. A man espied it. He ran for it. Stumbled. Ran on. He came to the end of the pier. Fell into the water. But he grasped the dollar bill. "I've got it!" he cried. And then he sank beneath the waves. Death is a dollar bill . . .
Death is a dream . . .
Death is a dream. "Death, too, mustd be a dream," said the man in his dream. "Petty hills. Endless. Light all about. Light . . . gladness . . . music . . . voices of women. But my throat. How

---

41. Ibid.

tight. I am choking . . . Breath, breath. My breath. Pretty hills. Endless. My breath. God, my breath. Light . . . breath . . . hills . . . music . . . voices of women. Breath . . ."

Death is a dream . . .

Nelson's third version of "Trilogy of Death" is a marked improvement from its previous incarnations, shying away from the theme of suicide and instead choosing the subtle flame of a candle to appear in the form of death.

Unfortunately, this sketch and the next poem, a "Fragment," would be Nelson's last writings for the *Fantasy Fan* (not including his letters written to the magazine). As previously pointed out, "Fragment" was salvaged from the poem "The Unremembered Realm." Nelson made good use of it by adding one or two additional lines for the January 1935 issue, making this two appearances for Nelson in one issue. "Fragment" reads thus:

With the red bewitchment of the moon canines collect
And feasts and howl o'er carrion and orts and bones
In green and putrid grots that echo shrill sea-moans;
And huge and hoary plantigrades on crags most high,
Hearing the maddened carnal ravings of the hounds,
Huddle together on the topmost frozen mounds
To hurl immense boulders on them until all die.

"Fragment" resumed the subject of horrors that lead the universe toward its imminent demise. On the subject of demise, the *Fantasy Fan* proved too costly to continue as a monthly publication, and its readership remained low. Nelson's other market, *Weird Tales*, would soon reach its end for Nelson, as he jokingly advised Hornig to replace Farnsworth Wright: "My proposition about you becoming editor of *Weird Tales* was half in jest and half in seriousness. But I do say *this* in utmost seriousness: most of us (the seemingly few who are discriminating) are 'fed up,' so to speak with the lax and prejudiced editorial standard of *Weird Tales* and the whole magazine in general, and in all probability we will, sooner or later abandon the reading of the magazine altogether."[41]

On 5 March, Nelson had a new poem for Hornig called "The Dead Poet."[42] He wrote to Hornig: "Enclosed is a brief poem of mine entitled 'The Dead Poet' to be used as 'filler' for *TFF* or your favorite waste receptacle."[43] At this time, Nelson was worried over the delay of the arrival of the February issue. The death of the *Fantasy Fan* was now a reality. Hornig told Nelson that the magazine was no more. Nelson blamed the termination on Farnsworth Wright:

> A thousand apologies for my last letter—after now knowing the final fate of *TFF*.
>
> [. . .] But let me say one thing, Charles, and let me say it out loud: *The Fantasy Fan could have been in existence for a long time to come if it were continually advertised in Weird Tales. But you couldn't do it, Charles! You couldn't do it! Farnsworth Wright wouldn't let you!!!*
>
> Oh, that is what you needed more than anything else. You did a great job, handicapped as you were by lack of advertising. No one could have done a better job than you. And I'll say that out loud to anyone. Farnsworth Wright, if he wanted to, could have permitted things so that you could advertise *TFF* in *WT*. He could have done so, till at least you could have gotten a build-up and a reputation that you *existed*. And his "charitable" mention of *TFF* in the Eyrie columns in the September, '34 issue was misrep-resented—wholly misrepresented! Read it over again, and see if I'm not right.
>
> Oh, it's all very tragic, Charles. It's all very tragic. You did a great job for *TFF* and you're doing great at *Wonder Stories*. Keep it up![44]

Now came Nelson's final demands: "But now I want you to return my manuscripts. I may send them later to *FM*.[45] But I don't know. I feel sad about the whole thing. But now please send back

---

41 Nelson, letter to Hornig (4 February 1935); ms., SU.
42. The poem "The Dead Poet" is nonextant.
43. Nelson, letter to Hornig (5 March 1935); ms., SU.
44. Nelson, letter to Hornig (7 March 1935); ms., SU.
45. *Fantasy Magazine*, edited by Julius Schwartz.

the rest of the unpublished 'Lost Excerpts' and that small poem, 'The Dead Poet.'"[46]

What an unfortunate circumstance. Two of Nelson's "Lost Excerpts" would find print in future issues of Donald Wollheim's magazine, the *Phantagraph*, while three episodes would be lost for good. The poem "The Dead Poet" also suffered a similar fate of oblivion.

Nelson continued to lament the sheer back luck of his writings and continued to criticize Farnsworth Wright:

> Wright has two of my poems on hand for future publication in *WT*,[47] if he will ever print them. He doesn't care for my poetry, and neither do the half-educated, half-illiterate readers of *WT*, who bombard the Eyrie month after month with childish letters and erroneous, incomprehensible criticisms. So I am no longer writing for *WT*—I am definitely through with it. All my work that will appear will be printed and copyrighted by myself or appear in magazines of higher quality, (for I shall not confine myself wholly to weird literature: one's mind is apt to become a bit one-sided by doing so.) I know I never held this latter view a year or so ago. But we live and learn.
>
> And so, goodbye Charles for now. I hope we may be able to see each other again some day. Please send back the remaining unpublished "Lost Excerpts" and poem to me. All best wishes.
>
> And in closing, please know that your job of editing *TFF* has not been done in vain—there are those of us who will remember it to our dying day.[48]

Ironically, for all his attacks on Wright and his publication, Nelson would have one more letter published in *Weird Tales*, in its March issue:

> I was deeply disappointed to see no note of comment whatsoever on H. P. Lovecraft's "The Music of Erich Zann," which appeared in the reprint section for last November. This is one of the finest

---

46. Nelson, letter to Hornig (7 March 1935); ms., SU.
47. "Dream-Stair" (*Weird Tales*, April 1935) and "Under the Tomb" (*Weird Tales*, May 1935).
48. Nelson, letter to Hornig (7 March 1935); ms., SU.

of eery short stories ever written, and is included in at least one of our leading anthologies. Few know and can realize the terror and anguish and sadness and unnamable visions which the powers of music can evoke. All of this is ably suggested in the "The Music of Erich Zann." And rereading this tale, the suggestions grow and mount on one, with the result that the entire aspect becomes something of a very serious nature. "The Dark Eidolon" by Clark Ashton Smith seems to me even to surpass his "The Colossus of Ylourgne"—a magnificent living piece of work.

Two weeks later, Nelson pressed Hornig to return the remaining "Lost Excerpts" immediately. Things became direr a week after this last note, as Nelson wrote an even more urgent and final postcard to Hornig: "No matter of how small worth they may be, I am still waiting for the return of the rest of my unpublished 'Lost Excerpts.' If they are not in my hands within the next 14 days, then, I fear, I shall have to resort to very drastic action."[49] Hornig did eventually send the "Lost Excerpts" and the poem "The Dead Poet" back to Nelson, creating another fractured relationship that ended the correspondence between Nelson and Hornig.

Eventually, in three months' time, Nelson would suffer a nervous breakdown or a suicide attempt, landing him at the Elgin State Hospital early in June 1935. Three weeks later, he died on the eve of his birthday on 22 July 1935. Robert Nelson's mother, Mrs. Elmer Nelson, told Hornig 27 August 1935 of her son's Robert's passing:

> Dear Mr. Hornig:—
> As a friend of my son Robert's I want to write you and inform of his death on July 22nd after but two week's illness. Among his literature and correspondence I find letters and cards from you time to time, and I believe you should know of this fact, as I know he subscribed to the *Fantasy Fan* magazine and had business dealings with you.
> [. . .] We received notice a week after his death that three of his poems were accepted by the Galleon Press on 5th Avenue, New

---

49. Nelson, postcard to Hornig [postmarked 29 March 1935]; ms., SU.

York City and believe he would have eventually made something of his writings had he lived.[50]

Nelson finally did break away from the weird pulp magazine field and had his poems enclosed within hardcover editions. In the meantime, Charles D. Hornig's tenure at *Wonder Stories* ended in its April 1936 issue.

It is apt to memorialize editor Charles D. Hornig for those writers he gave a chance to be included in the pages of the *Fantasy Fan*. As for Robert Nelson, his final poem could be considered something an elegy: it is entitled "The Rememberer," and was published in *American Lyric Poetry—1935*:

> He stood a-top the highest hill and swept
> His gaze across the vales of yesteryear:
> Undimmed by shattered hope and futile fear,
> And cloaked his hands o'er woeful face and wept;
> Illusion reigned upon his bleak threshold
> And made outrage of his impressive strife,
> Rendered the pain and pleasure of his life
> To urgencies that should have been foretold.
> But yet, were he endowed, would he go back
> And tread once more those gloomy, happy hills?
> As with the never-ending surge of seas
> Would he again know all life's chills, its thrills?
> Could he but die and sleep in memories
> And drift forever on that lonesome track!

Works Cited

Legaria, Marcos. "Clark Ashton Smith and Robert Nelson: Master and Apprentice." *Spectral Realms* No. 9 (Summer 2018): 105–13; No. 10 (Winter 2019): 113–22; No. 11 (Summer 2019): 115–26.

Nelson, Robert. "Below the Phosphor." *Fantasy Fan* 1, No. 10 (June 1934): 158.

---

50. Mrs. Elmer Nelson, letter to Hornig (27 August 1935); ms., private collection.

———. "Fragment." *Fantasy Fan* 2, No. 5 (January 1935): 75.

———. "I Dwelt in Shadow's Lonely Home." In Gerta Aison, ed. *Modern American Poetry—1935*. New York: Galleon Press, 1935.

———. Letter. *Fantasy Fan* 1, No. 3 (November 1933): 40. (The Boiling Point)

———. Letter. *Fantasy Fan* 1, No. 6 (February 1934): 81. (The Boiling Point)

———. Letter. *Weird Tales* 25, No. 3 (March 1935): 399.

———. "Lost Excerpts: I. In Living Darkness." *Fantasy Fan* 2, No. 3 (November 1934): 45.

———. "Lost Excerpts: II. The Feast of the Centaurs." *Fantasy Fan* 2, No. 4 (December 1934): 63.

———. "The Rememberer." In Gerta Aison, ed. *American Lyric Poetry—1935*. New York: Galleon Press, 1935.

———. "Trilogy of Death." *Fantasy Fan* 2, No. 5 (January 1935): 78.

———. "The Unremembered Realm." *Fantasy Fan* 1, No. 12 (August 1934): 188.

———. "The Weird Tale (A Dialogue)." *Fantasy Fan* 1, No. 9 (May 1934): 141.

Angels Can Poison the Sacred Wine

Scott J. Couturier

Who shall say if I created the painting or if it created me?

There's little for me to do but fiddle restlessly with my brushes, entertaining such thoughts. Little for me to do but wait until He arrives, to contribute His part. Having made Him you'd think He'd come at my command, but I never give commands, even when not imprisoned. It runs counter to the creative process. The artist should be receptive, a vessel filled to brimful so it may overflow. I am compulsively sensitive to beauty, they tell me in little notes they slip under the door. As such, they won't let me out until I finish painting Him to their satisfaction. That's the catch, and I feel transfixed by it, especially when He's not here to entrance my eye.

Beauty—the eye. Stimulation and response. I try not to focus on the chemicals percolating misery in my brain, instead rendering a potted pansy with wilted flowers. I haven't seen a real flower in years, but memory is its own form of experience. Most things become more poignant in the abstraction of their absence, and everything is absent for me except Him. Have I mentioned Him? Has He come yet? Longing explodes in every nerve as my teeth gnash and eyes roll. A carrion crow preens in the window-slit above, daylight carving a luminous path on the far wall, marked by shadows of bars. It shines on fungus growing in cracks, rusted shackles, smears of blood so old they look black. I close my eyes, moaning as want and need commingle.

I put Him together from pieces they passed to me. A bundle of body parts, needle and thread, a note telling me what to do. At first I was repulsed. I gagged and thrust the severed arms and legs, hands and feet back through the slot, insisting I would never do what they asked. However, after long months of isolation it dawned on me that giving in was the only way to escape my loneliness. I began accepting the limbs, the cast-off bits of organs and viscera, clippings of skin like putty-patches, preserved by some clear solution. I took the coarse twine and began to stitch. With tender care I rendered a creation to defy their grotesque agenda, my magnum opus gaping at his own perfection in the glass where newborn breath also pooled. Perhaps I even enchanted them, because then came the paints and the canvas.

A key turning in a lock. The prisoner's ear is attuned to this sound. It goes round and round inside their head, forever and ever. The *click* meaning freedom, a forbidden world of wonder and pleasure and experience held at bay by grim portals of iron and the grimmer guards who ward them. A machine would envy their diligence. Only one key works here, made of silver; I've seen it glinting in grubby, cloth-clad hands on those rare occasions they open my cell. Usually it's just the meal-and-waste slot, random bangs and knocks, and occasional notes written in hen-scratches I can decipher only due to my artistic inclination.

As for Him—He enters by a different way. They let Him down from above, through the oubliette hatch.

He wears a mask of white cloth, but not so I won't recognize him. I'm as intimate with Him as I once was with my dear mother's womb. I kissed His face when it lay cold and insensate before me, composite of twelve different faces, one for each lamentable month spent on its assembly. But I never complained, especially once they promised to release me after I did a suitable painting of Him. A simulacrum esteemed over the genuine article seems an inversion, but then art is perhaps more valuable than object. I abide by what the scribbled notes instruct, even though they reject effort after effort as imperfect, fresh brushes, paints, and canvas coming to me more often than meals.

I hear the hatch wrench open above me, shrieking of metal accompanied by a rain of rusty flakes. My hands tremble so furiously I upend the paint pots, splays of color running everywhere into the dark. I stain my smock of sackcloth, and the rubbery lump attached at my breast twitches, leech's maw suckling at my supernumerary teat. A necessary alliance for creating Him, alongside electricity from a crude pedal-generator once used for torture: what it is I don't care to know. It feeds for an hour each day, like a sorcerer's familiar, before crawling up to suspend itself in a damp, cobwebbed alcove. I can only think of it as a tool, or at the worst a burdensome accomplice, though my blood gets thinner even as the food runs lean, and I wonder what will happen if I don't soon paint a picture free of "imperfection." All this flashes through my mind as the shriek dies away, rust now pattering gently on my shoulders. I look up as the slimy thing detaches, slithering off in satiation.

He stands like an angel on the very lip of hell, gazing at me with eyes containing utmost love. I start to gibber and hop from foot to foot, a rude little perverted gnome before this display of masculine paragon. Maybe my mouth begins to water, maybe I get hard; after His completion I used His perfect body, though it has but rude soul to animate it, pleasure for Him lying almost wholly in being observed. Baser ardors slaked, brushes and paints appeared. I felt thrilled to create in any medium other than chilly dead flesh.

Unlike the painting, I'm sure I made Him. The painting is an unachieved result, an echo moving forward in time, a reflection of incarnation thus far revealing only the artist's inadequacy. I've tried to capture perfection all my life, but never had a source of inspiration sufficient to spur true greatness. Now, here, in this bleak and foul-smelling pit, I possess stimulus in surfeit. The ideal painting hovers beyond all my efforts, and I pursue it through paths of time and space, this refined offering my purpose, that which creates me and moves me to action. And the promise of freedom on its completion . . . I wonder, does my desire to escape dull my ability to capture Him? Is that part of their agenda? I must merely adore Him the more, then.

Curls of gold, silver, raven black, and auburn frame His masked face. One eye is green, the other chocolate-brown, framed by languid lashes. I know his lips show a pale plum red beneath the mask; this only comes off when I begin painting. All signs of my stitchery have healed, and His body stands hale and naked, muscles subtle under flesh lean and fatless save where flattering, long fingers like those of a musician or prostitute, bulging legs patched with varicolored skin. Between His legs—but no. That must be saved for my brush to convey, though it skitters with giddiness at each attempt. From His shoulders fan a useless set of wings clipped from an albatross, aesthetic in effect (both their majestic span and patent uselessness). Part of His beauty lies in His entrapment; implications of freedom only sweeten slavery's barb. Don't birds in cages always sing the prettiest songs? Even so, somehow perfection confounds my paintings, though it found ready home in Him. *Why* must the inevitable nevertheless elude?

They lower Him down in a bucket once used for carting waste. All the stink of Babylon's excrement couldn't dull my fervor. I call out a greeting, and He raises His chin with proud detachment, a noble light fiery in one eye, sultry in the other. The whole scene would be ludicrous if not for my worship, art's baseline one of absurdity—it's up to the artist to make it otherwise. Demons are preferable to jesters, when the calling is high-minded. Angels can poison the sacred wine with their sensibilities, oh-so-delicate. I impatiently watch the bucket descend, carrying my angel, tainted by dint of His making but impeccable of line and feature, ideal in every observer's sense. As to His own sense—who can say? I never gave Him a tongue.

He alights like an actor on the ultimate stage, stepping from the slop-bucket with a delicacy normally reserved for movements in nature. Willow boughs weaving in the wind, or a palm frond's luxuriant flutter: things I recall from previous lives, here signified by a body of mishmash parts assembled by my own quaking hands. Has any artist been blessed to achieve such vital perfection, save those painters of cathedral frescoes who put God in His Heaven? There is a primacy in His movements as He approaches me, and I huff out a fetid breath, my teeth clogged with the flesh and fur of rats. Sometimes they do feed me, but often they forget, and a man must live, after all.

He looks at me directly now, and I swear I see a little impudent smile twist behind the mask. No doubt they've all had their way with Him, pawing over and defaming my masterpiece with their unclean lust. But here, in this pit, all is wholesome and aesthetically whole. I extend a hand to touch Him, and He suffers me to caress His shoulder, to trail my fingers delicately atop one protuberant nipple.

Then—He pulls away, mounting the dais of raised stone in a corner of my cell. Lowering His mask, he stands exposed, immobile as the clay flesh is fashioned from, eyes upraised as if in supplication, face handsome in the way of a marmoreal monument, body tense with perfectly held torsion. I draw back and pick up my brushes, eager to paint while the rush of inspiration, borne on the horny tide of my blood, animates my imagination. Blues, reds, oranges, and yellows, violet and cerulean, crimson and incarnadine, greens and blacks and earthy browns: somehow I manage to work the whole spectrum into His aura. The painting comes alive under my hands, seeming to stare at me with impatience as I strive to complete it. Or is it completing me? *Am I about to be finished?*

My brushstrokes grow more fevered. He looks at me from the corner of those fairie-eyes, as if sensing something is different. Can He feel perfection at last revealing itself? My hand trembles, and I think of my promised freedom. Will I leave Him here, to be fouled by their gruesome and twisted hungers? What will He do after I leave? Can I take Him with me? Fears mounting, blots of distracting darkness dance at my vision's edge. A rat scuttles over my toes, and I raise my foot and stomp down reflexively, bending to scoop up what would be my evening meal. But if I'm freed—what will I eat? What will I do? Where will I go? I squeeze the dead thing in my hands, and a dribble of blood pours from gagging mouth and bulging eyes. I slather it onto my hands, then look to Him, who watches me in stolid and magisterial silence, though a flush in His one light-skinned cheek betrays disgust at my act. I see that flush—I look to my blood-slicked fingertips. Leaning forward, I daub the painting to mimic His revulsion.

He sees, and His varicolored eyes go wide, filled with a detestation deeper than any love. Turning, He staggers halfway down from the dais, freezing as the silver key turns, the door to my cell thrown wide open. They enter in a rush, bodies cloaked in folds of moldy burlap, eyes like dying coals gleaming out from tattered slits in the cloth. They have seen it—have come to acknowledge my accomplishment. They have come to set me free. It's miracle and tragedy in the same moment, and tears stream down my face, dappling the blood and paint smeared over my hands.

As for Him—they've caught my angel by His albatross wings and hauled Him back to the dais. Comparing my work to what inspired it, they nod and titter to each other in vulgar, slurping voices, as if language itself abhors their enunciation. I've never seen so many in one place: they jostle me, pat me on the shoulder or caress my inner thigh, tongues flickering from holes in the burlap, some gurgling with happiness, others eyeing me ruefully while they finger whips and heated irons, loath at my new-won freedom. With a smile I turn back to see them tearing Him apart limb from limb and organ from organ, a brutish disemboweling by filthy bandaged hands that grope and gouge. The look on His face—while He still has a face—one of them grabs my head and forces me to watch, all while fawning fingers trail over the painting, marring perfection in form and reflection as His guts pile in a mound of stinking coils, wings torn off and held up with mocking flaps, a cacophony of grunting and squealing such as swine would flee.

I scream and start flailing against my captors. It's an act of defiance, my first in years. Emboldened by my own voice, I reach out and snatch at the sack covering one of them, gripping the rough cloth and ripping it aside like a magician unveiling the results of conjuration. What is exposed—no malformed and shambling thing, but a muscular back bent deliberately to give an impression of fee-bleness. A face so beautiful as to defy description, such that almost I think He has come back to life, that it has all been some sick trick and the thing on the dais being butchered is an impostor.

Then, horribly, I see that this man is alike to Him only in the vagaries of perfection. A different nose, and eyes that match, burning a too-light blue. Not quite as tall, but proportioned ideally for his height and build, and between his legs—ah, but beauty takes many shapes. He gnashes his pearly teeth at me, fighting to pull the cloth back over himself, but the illusion is broken. Others turn and cast off their coverings to reveal themselves, male and female and intersexed, all presumably stitched from disparate parts, all of subtle and faultless line, their faces distorted by a feral anger but breathtaking regardless. I fall to my knees as they surround me, the last out-slopping of His guts reaching me like the sound of a receding tide.

"Who are you?" I demand, voice tremulous, breath coming in halting and painful gasps as they set exquisite hands on me, gripping tight enough to bruise. "What are you?" I choke on the words as if a gag were placed in my mouth. Fiendish faces of divine proportion close in around me, grins of immaculate teeth scissoring across my sight line. I feel their collective grip tighten as they answer in one voice:

"We are perfection that could not be imitated."

They haul me from the chamber kicking and crying, away from Him forever. My work is completed: He was not so realized as them, to allow Himself to be replicated. Given no tongue, He couldn't speak—His dumbness marred Him. Hideous voices gabble in my ear, in the most honeyed and dulcet of tones. We weave through a comb of stone passages, innumerable iron doors leading deeper underground to chambers where the same infernal experiment plays out in perpetuity. Dimly I hear the wailing strain of instruments, the cracked and haggard voices of poets raised in recitation. The guards here make no attempt at concealment, standing as though wrought of granite, with an imperious and remote awareness, as one might attribute to natural objects: a mountain's gaze, or the fearsome spirit of a maelstrom at its eye. They have many graceful limbs and sport multiple heads, most more animal than human: chimera colossi of ravishing aspect, phalli and breasts of massive proportion, each hand or claw clutching a platinum cleaver. I spit and struggle as I'm dragged past these sublime scions, stitched from dead tissue by hands maddened to the task. Often the artist fails to capture their magnificence, and the creation joins its jailers, donning ill-fitted gunnycloth rather than risk a second likeness. So my overseers tell me between my cries; I have seen too many of them, hundreds on hundreds. Surely I won't be allowed to survive.

"Survive?" one snorts, as if reading my mind—and who is to say they cannot? "Are you a common man, to fear death rather than calling it friend? Freedom we promised you, freedom you shall have."

There is the truth of it. I laugh and loll my head as they haul me upwards. Someone is carrying Him behind us—His limbs, His organs, even His mocking wings—in an engraved brass bowl, sloshing to the brim with blood. I see His cock drooping over the rim like a limp cocktail shrimp, withered and laced with flaccid veins. He will be reused, I am told: in fact they reassure me numerous times that none of this is going to waste. I have fulfilled my purpose, meaning my parts will go into in the next stitch-up. I should rejoice.

Death comes cool and easy, not like I ever expected it would. A knife of bone is drawn ever-so-graciously across my neck, rill of blood erupting in a pulse before ebbing to dribble down my throat and chest. A wave of heat baptizes my chilling skin as the darkness circles, lit intermittently by smiles of perfect, wicked teeth: if I didn't know better I'd think they planned to eat me. I twitch as they start hacking me up while consciousness lingers. Turning my head, I see my own hand placed reverently in the brass bowl, melding with His remnants. No ghoulish act this, driven by compulsive and degenerate hunger, but a transmutation I can hardly understand, a fate I can't fathom.

Everything goes dark, and with a sigh I close my eyes. When I open them, each peers out from a different patchwork face, viewed in the planes of two breath-fogged mirrors. One is mismatched to His eye of fiery green, His other complementing my own chocolate-brown iris.

Beach Shanty

Katherine Kerestman

The old house on the beach,
Where gales scrape the paint from the wood before it is dried,
Its skeletal boards bleach,
And its warped shingles fling out at the red, roiling tide,

Crouches under two dunes,
Watching the waves thrashing themselves up into typhoons,
Launching wat'ry harpoons,
Growing strong and upsurging with the pull of two moons,

Watches the scaled sea-beast,
The indigo, twenty-legged, seven-headed mer-beast,
Swim from dark realms due East,
Devour schooners and sailors in grisly blood feast,

Spit out their gnawed-on bones,
Swim south, stirring black whirlpools that suck down the freighters.
Dark night echoes their moans,
As carnivorous eels race grotesque alligators.

Darling Daughter

Carla Ward

I stood at the railing of our second-story deck, drinking straight from the bottle of Scotch I'd grabbed on the way out. I couldn't pour it over my eyes to sanitize them, so I settled for steeping my brain in enough alcohol to erase the horrific scene I'd just witnessed.

My husband, Trey, was still inside, dealing with the situation. Waiting for him (and for the booze to kick in), I stared absently at the horizon as the setting sun bled out in murky shades of crimson. Shadows covered our small acreage, and when I glanced over the railing, the walkout patio below looked more like an abyss than the oasis where we usually drank our morning coffee.

I blinked back tears. After what happened tonight, there would be no more quiet mornings together.

Finally the sliding glass door opened and shut behind me. I turned around and found Trey wrapped in the white terrycloth robe I'd given him on our last anniversary. With his bare feet and disheveled brown curls, he looked more handsome than he had a right to after killing our marriage.

"She's gone." He took a hesitant step forward. "Trish, look, I'm not proud of this, but—"

"Is she a student?" I struggled to keep my voice steady. "She can't be more than twenty."

"Twenty-three," he corrected, as if those few years made a difference. "She's an undergrad, graduating this semester."

I shook my head, disgusted. "I never thought you'd be one to rob the cradle." I took another pull of Scotch, wincing as it burned my throat. Ordinarily I watered it down with soda, but after catching Trey in bed with that voluptuous blonde, there hadn't been time to mix a proper drink. "How long have you two . . .?"

"A few weeks."

"Well, I hope she was worth it, because she'll cost you your career. I'm going to tell the dean first thing in the morning."

He held up a hand. "Hold on. I understand this was a shock," he said, in his pretentious professor voice, "but let's be rational."

"I *am* rational!" I didn't worry about my volume. Our home sat in the middle of three acres outside the city limits. The closest neighbor lived half a mile away. "The university has every right to know you're taking advantage of your students. Once I remind the dean of his legal obligations, you'll either be fired or asked to resign."

He pinned me with a solemn gaze. "Have mercy. I'm about to be tenured." A gentle breeze lifted a few ringlets of his dark hair—hair I'd once adored running my fingers through but now was the playground of a younger woman. "Please, just this once, don't think like a lawyer." He moved closer, bringing him within arm's length. Thankfully, he kept his hands to himself. "I never intended to hurt you, and I'm truly sorry you found out this way."

His word choice was right, but his delivery didn't quite ring sincere.

I glowered at him. "Don't bother with fake apologies. Nothing you say will change my mind."

"Of course not. Words are superfluous now." Trey lifted his chin defiantly, and the sorrowful expression he wore was replaced by a placid, unreadable mask. "Actions speak louder, don't you agree?"

Then the unthinkable happened.

He shoved me hard in the chest. My tailbone slammed into the railing's edge, and I flipped over. After falling a full story, I landed head first on the cement patio below with a sickening *crunch* in my neck. Somewhere nearby, the Scotch bottle shattered, and my world faded to black.

When I opened my eyes I expected pain or paralysis or some combination of the two, but for reasons unknown I ended up standing in the grass several yards from the walkout patio, unscathed and unaware of how I'd arrived there.

Stranger still, the backyard looked different from the way it had a moment ago. The sun had disappeared entirely, and the pale twilight had succumbed to utter darkness. I had no trouble seeing, however, because all the exterior lights were on, blazing brightly into the void of night.

Questions flooded my mind. Why wasn't I hurt? How much time had passed? And why had Trey turned on so many lights?

As I struggled for answers, I realized there was something far more distressing to worry about. Looking up at the deck, I mentally measured the trajectory of my fall and determined I should have ended up on the patio directly below.

That's when I noticed the two men in light blue uniforms. They were crouched over something in the area where I should have landed. As I crept closer, a black body bag came into view. The men worked the zipper around it, hefted the figure onto a stretcher, and sidestepped broken glass as they carried it around the side of the house toward the driveway.

Before I could fully process what I'd seen, I heard Trey's voice overhead. I backed up a little so I could see the deck better. Trey strolled up to the railing, now fully dressed in a green cardigan and khaki slacks. A policeman sidled up beside him, and the two of them peered over the side of the deck to study the area below.

I waved to them. "What's going on?"

Trey didn't react to my voice, not even a flinch. He turned to the officer and said, "She was sitting on the railing here, teasing me by pretending to lose her balance. I told her to be careful." He wiped his eyes. "Then she really did lose her balance, and she fell."

"No, I didn't," I said, but Trey and the officer ignored me.

"Had she been drinking?" the officer asked.

My husband nodded. "Unfortunately."

"I didn't fall." I projected my voice this time to ensure I was heard. "Trey pushed me."

The officer didn't acknowledge my accusation. He patted Trey's shoulder, and the two of them walked back inside.

Minutes later, my husband returned to the deck, this time alone. He held a glass of wine and lifted it as if making a toast.

"Here's to you, Trish. Sorry I had to do that, but to be fair, you threatened me. I acted in self-defense."

And that's when it sank in.

I was dead.

After my demise, Trey orchestrated a chintzy funeral. Instead of a satin-lined casket and cemetery burial (the way I would have wanted it), he opted for cremation. The urn he provided the funeral home for my ashes was a plain wooden box from Hobby Lobby that he'd sprayed with shellac, a DIY project that cost him a whole twelve bucks.

The flowers he ordered to decorate the chapel were bouquets of wilted sunflowers. The florist gave Trey a deep discount, since the wedding for which they'd originally been ordered had been canceled.

My husband knew full well I didn't care for sunflowers. In the past I'd mentioned to him they looked pretty growing in ditches out in the country, but to me they were like dandelions, closer to a weed than a flower. He could have used one of my favorite blooms—white roses or orchids or lilies—but instead he went with what would keep the most cash in his wallet.

But I'll give him credit for the performance he put on at the service. He could have handed out playbills as mourners entered the chapel: THE HANDSOME WIDOWER, a one-man show starring Trey Landis as the Bereaved English Professor.

My "grieving" husband made a brief appearance at the luncheon afterward, just long enough to hand my ashes over to my parents, then raced home, changed out of his suit into a T-shirt and cutoff sweatpants, and set to work purging our home of all my belongings.

Within an hour he boxed up my clothes, jewelry, and books. After dropping the boxes off at Goodwill, he returned home and threw away everything that couldn't be donated, including our wedding pictures, my makeup, hair products, dirty clothes, and leftover feminine products.

Then he waged war on my office. Everything related to my current caseload—briefs, notebooks, copies of reports—were neatly boxed up and set aside. He called my employer, the district attorney's office, and offered to drop them off next week. This wasn't out of the goodness of his heart; it was to keep up appearances. The last thing he wanted was a visit from one of my fellow prosecuting attorneys.

After he eradicated all traces of my existence from every surface of our home, he got out his phone and made a call. "I just got back from the funeral," he said, then released a melancholy sigh. "Are you free? I would love some company."

I assumed he was talking to the chippie I'd caught him with last week. It was too bad he taught English, because with his acting skills he could have been a sensational theatre professor.

He listened to her response with a dreamy, contented expression on his face. "Great. See you soon." Then, lowering his voice like a bashful schoolboy, he added, "Oh, and Jess, could you wear that red thong? I'm ashamed to admit this, but I've been fantasizing about you in it all morning."

"All morning?" My shrill words didn't reach him, but I blasted him anyway. "You thought about her in a thong during my funeral?"

I swung my fist at his chiseled jaw, but it was no use. I didn't even stir a breeze.

Over the next few weeks I wandered the halls of our home, observing my husband and the blonde from his American lit class. I learned her name was Jessica Atkinson, and that she loved kittens, Hallmark movies, and shopping for shoes. When she wasn't with Trey she was hitting the books, working hard to maintain her 2.0 grade point average.

At first I couldn't understand why someone as intelligent as my husband would want to be with someone like her, but once I stopped thinking like a woman, I began to see the attraction for Trey. In his eyes Jessica was the perfect package: a great body, an insatiable libido, and too little intellect to challenge his authority.

What wasn't to love?

I told myself this fling wouldn't last, but soon weeks turned into months, and before I knew it the fall semester was over and they were celebrating Christmas together.

The chippie had staying power.

I'll admit, at this point, I was tempted to stop watching my husband's new life and travel toward the white light that appeared in the distance sometimes, beckoning me to step into it, but the idea of letting Trey get away with killing me held me fast to my tentative place on earth.

I wanted revenge.

On New Year's Eve, after a vigorous round of lovemaking, Trey and Jessica sipped champagne in bed.

"I have a belated graduation gift for you." Trey leaned over and pulled a little black velvet box out of the nightstand. "Now that we don't have to sneak around anymore, I'd like to make our relationship more permanent."

Jessica's big doe eyes bulged. "Oh my God, Trey. Is it—"

"Yes, it is." He popped the box open, revealing a platinum band with a monster solitaire diamond. "Will you marry me?"

She squealed and tears rolled down her flushed cheeks. "Of course. Yes. Yes!"

I hovered closer to get a better look at the rock he'd given her. It was three times the size mine had been. My heart clenched with envy.

"You should move in." Trey set their glasses on the nightstand. "Then we can do this all the time."

"Okay."

He pulled her close and kissed her deeply. "You took your pill today, right?"

"Yeah."

"Good." He kissed her again. "The last thing we need is a kid running around here."

She leaned back. "What's wrong with kids? Maybe I wanna have some."

"We can worry about that later." He nibbled her neck. "After I have you all to myself for a couple of years, or ten."

And just like that, she was putty in his hands.

A few days later I was sitting, well, existing, in the backseat of my husband's Volvo as he and Jessica headed across town to their appointment at a quaint bed-and-breakfast, a possible venue for their wedding.

The situation seemed surreal. In the span of only a few months I had been erased. Not a trace of me lingered in our home, nor apparently in my husband's memory. It was as if I'd never been his wife.

"I'm so excited." Jessica reached over the console for Trey's hand. "I can't wait to be Mrs. Trey Landis."

He looked her way, beaming. "Has a nice ring to it."

If I'd had lungs, I would have huffed a disgusted breath. It had taken Trey three years to propose to me, but in just three months he'd decided Jessica, the writer of pithy love notes like *I'll never take you for granite,* was wife material.

Did he want a simpler woman? Someone less complicated than a prosecuting attorney with strong opinions about justice? Or was it a power thing? Trey loved being king of his castle, revered, worshipped, and unchallenged by his subjects. Did I not bow enough when I was still alive?

During the tour of the bed-and-breakfast, Trey yawned several times, glancing repeatedly at his watch. Jessica, on the other hand, stared wide-eyed, nodding with enthusiasm at everything the B-and-B owner showed them about the grounds.

"If the weather doesn't cooperate, we can move the reception in here," the owner explained as she led them into a small reception hall. "But typically, early May is lovely, so I think an outdoor affair is a perfect plan A."

I could tell Trey wasn't into it. Half kidding, I whispered in Jessica's ear, "You'd better ask his opinion about all this, or he'll feel left out."

And do you know what happened? She turned to Trey, batting her gorgeous blue eyes, and murmured, "What do you think, babe? Do you like it?"

His gloomy expression lightened, and he grinned at her. "You know, I think I do."

It wasn't until later, when they returned home, that I started to wonder if Jessica had actually heard me. I decided to try it again, curious to see if what had happened at the B-and-B was a fluke or if she really was susceptible to suggestion.

As Jessica began preparing dinner, in what I used to think of as *my* kitchen, I stayed close to her side. She gathered produce from the fridge to make a salad and put everything on the counter next to a cutting board.

Before she could start chopping lettuce and carrots and cucumbers, Trey joined her at the island, sidling up behind her, and wrapping his arms around her waist. "How about we go work up an appetite first?"

She turned to face him and draped her arms over his shoulders. "Good idea."

They began devouring each other, a sight I was sick of seeing by this point, but then it occurred to me this might be a good time to stage my experiment.

I wasn't sure what directive to use as a test balloon, but I knew it had to be something odd, out of left field, so I would know for certain the idea came from my influence.

"Lick his face. He likes that," I whispered in her ear, fighting the urge to burst out laughing.

And abracadabra—she did it.

Trey pulled away, holding his fiancée at arm's length. "What are you doing?"

She shrugged and giggled. "I don't know. I just had the urge to lick you."

"Lick if you must." He flashed a crooked grin. "But try a different region, maybe a little farther south."

As usual, she obeyed him, so I had to leave the room.

During the next two months I whispered into Jessica's ear, coaching her on ways to please my husband, giving her legitimate suggestions, not just silly ideas for my own amusement. I had come up with a plan, and in order for it to work I needed Trey to be entrenched in a stable, happy relationship.

So I informed Jessica about all the things Trey liked to eat, the things he liked in bed, the way he liked his socks folded, things to say when his ego needed stroking, and ways to include him in the wedding planning. By the time their ceremony rolled around in May, the couple's connection was rock solid.

After they exchanged vows, they honeymooned in Acapulco, eating, drinking, and screwing at regular intervals. I hung out by the beach most of the time, letting them have some fun. Because once the honeymoon was over, *fun* would be in short supply.

When they came home, Jessica fell into a good rhythm with her wifely duties. She made recipes she saw on Food Network and catered to Trey's needs in the bedroom like a pro.

I let them have a month of domestic bliss before I started to interfere. Then, each night while Jessica slept, I whispered instructions in her ear.

"He wants a baby," I told her, "so stop taking the pill."

Each morning, obeying my orders, Jessica would brush her teeth as usual but then skip taking her birth control pill.

A few weeks later she was late.

When Jessica told my husband she thought she might be pregnant, his handsome face creased with worry. "How late are you?"

"Two weeks."

I'll admit it was satisfying to watch my husband squirm as they waited for the results of the home pregnancy test. When that stick showed parallel lines, I thought he was going to faint, but he managed a weak smile and patted his wife on the head like a dog. "I guess we're having a baby," he said.

She was too thick to pick up on his obvious condescension, but she did seem aware that his mood had shifted.

"Don't worry. We can still have sex," she said.

This seemed to revive him from his stupor. "We can? Why didn't you say so?" Then he promptly carried her to bed.

It was irksome to see him rebound so quickly, but I didn't let Trey's temporary victory get me down. I was playing the long game.

After the happy couple fell asleep that night, I entered their bedroom. This time I wouldn't be talking to Jessica. I'd be serving the spirit in her womb with an eviction notice.

Nine months later, Jessica found herself slapped with a huge dose of reality. The pain of childbirth overwhelmed her, and she begged for an epidural the moment she entered the hospital. Twenty-four exhausting hours later, their daughter entered the world.

Shortly after, the doctor handed Trey the baby and stitched up Jessica's episiotomy. When he finished he said, "Remember, no sex for six weeks."

Trey shifted the baby in his arms and sniffled.

"You're so sweet, babe," Jessica said. "I've never seen you cry happy tears before."

"Happy tears . . . sure."

I knew better. He was crying because he wouldn't get any for another month and a half.

The nurse looked down at the little bundle in Trey's arms. "Your daughter has lovely eyes."

"I guess," Trey murmured, failing to notice what should have been blatantly apparent. The little eyes staring back at him were pale green, like sea glass, the exact shade mine had been.

Months rolled into years, and seven years later a lot had changed. Jessica and Trey had new titles—Mom and Dad—though Trey didn't do much to earn his. He left most of the parenting to Jessica, who, surprisingly, proved to be a good mother to me. Of course, she might have treated me differently had she known I had hijacked her pregnancy so I could rejoin the living. But what she didn't know wouldn't hurt her. To her I was just Skylar June, her darling daughter.

The happy couple's unstoppable chemistry also changed, deteriorating over the years since my birth. Jessica's maternal duties cut into the time she could spend with Trey, and his jealousy grew just as steadily as I did. An ego the size of Trey's needed to be nourished regularly, and thanks to me, his was starving.

Now that I was seven, I was old enough to enact the next phase of my plan. My birthday party, held at the house I could now call home again, would serve as the perfect stage for what came next.

While all our friends and relatives were in the backyard playing horseshoes and croquet that March afternoon, Trey and I were in the kitchen. He was fetching another tray of pinwheels to replace the empty one on the buffet table outside.

"Enjoying your party, Skylar?"

"Yes, Daddy."

"I should hope so. I spent a pretty penny on it." He reached into the fridge and pulled out the tray he needed, setting it on the counter.

I tilted my head, feigning innocence. "Can I ask you something?"

"I suppose."

"Why did you kill your first wife?"

His head snapped in my direction, his face chalky white. "What did you say?"

"You heard me," I said. "Why did you kill her?"

He looked around as if worried someone might overhear us. "Is this a joke? Did someone tell you to say that?"

"No, love," I said, using the pet name I'd had for him when we were together. "It's not a joke. It's justice."

He squatted to my level and looked me in the eye. "What do you mean, *justice?*"

"You shouldn't have pushed me off the deck, Trey."

His eyes widened. "Trish?"

"In the flesh." I smiled sweetly. "And I plan to make your life absolutely miserable." Wagging my index finger, I added, "Don't even think about killing me again. Criminals who kill children don't fare well in prison. Just accept your sentence. If you cooperate, I might give you time off for good behavior."

His mouth flapped open and shut a few times, but no words escaped.

"Oh, and just a word of warning," I went on. "You'd probably better drop that little brunette who came over last week while Mommy was at the spa. I might have been watching cartoons, but I know what you did with her in the bedroom." I blew him a kiss, then skipped out the back door, leaving him standing there, speechless.

Outside, Jessica found me and spirited me away to the cake table, saying it was time to sing "Happy Birthday" and open gifts.

I glanced up at the house and saw Trey peering out the little window of the back door, looking as hopeless as an inmate trapped in his cell. Jessica threw him a friendly wave.

He didn't wave back.

She shrugged him off. By now she was used to his moodiness. She fished a lighter out of her pocket to light the candles on my pink unicorn cake. "Is there something special you're going to wish for, sweetheart?" she asked.

"No, Mommy." I hugged her around the waist. "My wish already came true."

A Union in Carcosa

Ngo Binh Anh Khoa

To marry Royalty, is it a dream—
Where one may relish in great wealth and fame
And add a fancy title to one's name—
Or nightmare where things are not what they seem?

My thought was of the former when I found
My foreign lover at the time hailed from
An ancient lineage that had long become
A whispered legend in deep secrets bound.

Then, I was but a humble man with naught
But grand ambitions for a brighter day
When I could leave the mire and live the way
I wished—a freedom for which I'd long sought.

And there it was, just dangling in my grasp,
A tantalizing prize before a man
Imbued with so much yearning that he can
Do anything till it's clutched in his clasp.

And thus, I toiled and fought till at long last,
I won the war and claimed her ardent heart
Once twelve months had elapsed since my rough start.
Worthwhile were all the sacrifices past.

Or so I thought until that fateful day
When she told me to come and meet her Sire.
"And this is it," I thought, "The trial by fire,
The final challenge that obstructs my way."

I bit the bullet, spent all I had left—
Each dime, each crumpled bill, each nickel found—
On some high-fashion clothes, the best around,
And prayed this plan would not leave me bereft.

I was prepared (I thought I was prepared)
For any question and for anything
Her Sire would throw at me. I strived to bring
My prize home—to myself I thus declared.

I packed my bags, all ready for the flight
Until I learned that we'd not go by plane
Or ship or intercontinental train.
She simply took me to her flat at night.

From her bookshelf, she grabbed a flesh-bound tome
On which a yellow sign flashed, bright and weird,
And chanted till the glitched world disappeared
Around me, leaving me estranged from home.

The new realm's sky was in thick darkness drowned,
An inky black that dripped and stained the sea
Where thrashing cloud-waves roared unendingly
And shattered as they grazed the shadowed ground.

Above my head were flickering stars that rose
Beside the circling moons, whose wavering light
Would further make this most phantasmal night
Much more morose with their strange, corpse-pale glows.

The cold air softly hummed an eldritch tune
Composed of woeful sighs of mist-formed ghosts
From aeons past, condemned to haunt these coasts,
Along which their wind-scattered ash was strewn.

So lost was I midst such bewildering sights,
I did not feel my body being dragged away
Toward a ruined castle where I'd stay
For countless dreadful and disquieting nights.

When my blank mind at last dispelled the haze
Brought forth by this unnatural shift in time
And space, I was told that 'twas time to dine
With He who rules this shade-infested place.

"But where or what is this place, actually?"
I asked my lover as we waited for
Her Sire. Her eyes stayed on the massive door,
Whose carving showed a cloaked monstrosity.

"This is my birthplace," reverently she said,
"The timeless city of Carcosa, where
The great Hyades glows, forever fair,
And sings primordial melodies to the dead."

At her reply, much more confused I'd be,
But not another word would leave my lips,
For I was suddenly wrapped in Terror's grip
When that door opened up and silenced me.

A towering figure in a tattered cloak
Emerged from out the writhing shadow and
Approached us. He was large within the grand
Hall, baleful in his yellow garb. He spoke.
His voice was not one voice, but manifold,
A gross amalgamation of harsh cries
And growls and shrieks and murmurs. His cold eyes
Behind the mask gleamed with a might untold.

At once, I felt a pressure push me down.
My body folded as I retched and kneeled
And felt His piercing gaze that cruelly peeled
Me to my rotten core. In fear I drowned.

The chillness of the marble floor would burn my skin,
The dampness of the thickened air would choke
Me to the point that I could barely croak.
My vision, in my terrified state, grew dim.

I hardly noticed when the noises died,
And in the lengthened shadow of this god
With twisting tentacles, grotesque and odd,
Protruding from his robe, I sobbed and cried.

A presence pressed down on me and embraced
My shivering body in a stifling clutch.
The once familiar hold became a touch
Most alien and most toxic that emblazed

My mortal being, but I could do naught
To break free from her suffocating hold.
Between the King in Yellow and her cold
Hands, I was just a fly in their webs caught.

My life and dreams were crushed beneath Their weight,
I am a Royal now in this cursed, gloomy place
Beneath the God-King of this wretched space.
Far worse than death is such a damnable fate.

Eden in Mercia: Recovering Paradise in Bram Stoker's *The Lair of the White Worm*

Geoffrey Reiter

Though long dismissed by interpreters, Bram Stoker's final novel, *The Lair of the White Worm* (1911), is finally receiving the critical attention it deserves. Scholars have primarily focused on Stoker's complex and often troubling interactions with race and gender in the novel. What has received less attention is the way in which *The Lair of the White Worm* interacts with the prevailing scientific notions of Stoker's day (particularly in the field of paleontology) and how he connects them to the novel's explicit religious imagery.

As *The Lair of the White Worm* begins, the young hero Adam Salton, born and raised in Western Australia, moves back to England to claim his inheritance in Mercia, where he meets his last living relative, his great uncle Richard Salton, as well as his uncle's friend, local historian Sir Nathaniel de Salis. Nor is Adam the only one emigrating; the imposing Edgar Caswall, who was born in Italy in exile, also returns to the countryside and an ancestral estate, bringing with him his African servant Oolanga. These new eligible bachelors draw the interest of Mercia's female population, including the mysterious Lady Arabella March, who flirts with Adam but sets her sights on Edgar. Edgar, meanwhile, is interested in the fair Lilla Watford, though not necessarily for pure motives, as he engages in a series of psychic staring matches that appear to drain her strength. Lilla is zealously guarded by her half-Burmese cousin Mimi, who is the subject of Adam's attentions.

As the novel progresses, Edgar Caswall begins to descend into a dangerous madness, continuing his psychic attacks on Lilla, meddling with occult forces, and terrorizing the countryside with a monstrous bird-shaped kite flown from his castle. An even more sinister force, however, is the Lady Arabella, who is in fact not a lady at all but a human form taken by a monstrous ancient reptile of local lore, the White Worm. Edgar Caswall and Lady Arabella facilitate their own demise, however. Caswall is killed when lightning strikes the kite flown from his tower, destroying his entire castle. Meanwhile, the electricity from the lightning strike travels through a wire that the Lady Arabella has stretched from Caswall's residence into her own subterranean lair, igniting a large portion of dynamite that Adam has secretly planted and blowing up the cave and the White Worm with it.

As even such a cursory summary suggests, *The Lair of the White Worm* is a singularly strange novel, prompting Stoker grand-nephew and biographer Daniel Farson to suggest that "It might have been written under the influence of drugs, a 'trip,' along 'the high road of mental disturbance', to use a phrase from the book" (217). While this particular theory has been generally disregarded, most critics have followed Farson's lead in suggesting that its "plot is so bizarre, almost ludicrous, that it is hard to imagine anyone taking it seriously" (218). Indeed, it has become something of a rite of passage for critics to couch all their analyses with assurances that they understand just how badly written *The Lair of the White Worm* is. After an in-depth analysis of the novel, David Glover calls it in passing "without a doubt Stoker's worst book" ("Why" 358). For Phyllis Roth, it is "laughably bad" (84) and "the weakest of all [Stoker's] novel-length fictions, revealing impatience with plotting and characterization, inconsistency in action and tone, and a lack of overall vision or design organizing and unifying the story elements" (80).

Even so, *The Lair of the White Worm* received generally favorable reviews upon its initial publication (Murray 264). And recent criticism has not only brought more attention to the novel but discovered certain unifying factors, so that Roth's charge of "lack of overall vision or design organizing and unifying the story elements" now seems premature. Lisa Hopkins, for example, has suggested that the work's peculiar imagery can be explained in part due to Masonic influences (138–48). Kate Hebblethwaite adds that the surrealist art may have affected Stoker's writing, "emancipating imagination itself from the formal world of logic" (xxx). And more than anything, most critics agree that Stoker's book is intimately tied to his theories regarding race and gender, presenting them in a vivid, hyperbolized manner. Even so, there has been little attention paid thus far to the thematic role of religion in the novel. I believe that understanding the religious underpinnings of *The Lair of the White Worm* is crucial to grasping its treatment of nature. If, as Hebblethwaite notes, there is at times a hallucinogenic quality to *The Lair of the White Worm*, there is also an order to it as well. "Nature," Sir Nathaniel maintains, "is a logician" (250), and it follows the logic of what Stoker refers to in *Dracula* as the "scale of creation" (206).

Stoker's conflation of what might be called geological and biblical time, along with his adoption of a more purposive theory of evolution, are not mere abstract points but have profound implications for the novel. By retaining a textual ambivalence regarding the earth's age, Stoker is able to mingle freely the prehistoric world with imagery from his favorite biblical story, the narrative of Eden. Playing with Tennyson's prehistoric imagery from *In Memoriam* (1850), Stoker posits a natural world that is "red in tooth and claw" (56.15) because it is fallen. This gives hope that "God and Nature" are not "at strife," as Tennyson feared (55.5), but that rather the natural world's brutality stems from the evil caused by the Fall. In the events that ensue in *The Lair of the White Worm*, Stoker goes about creating a second Eden, one that is made pure through the destruction of evil forces and the promise of physical, moral, and spiritual rebirth.

Curiously, *The Lair of the White Worm* never quite tips its hand regarding the age of the earth. Clearly, however, Stoker is still wrestling with all the issues raised by nineteenth-century scientists and intellectuals, even if those issues were more or less settled for many by 1911. This conflict can be seen when Sir Nathaniel first begins to realize Arabella March's true identity. He tells Adam, "We are going back to the origin of superstition—to the age when dragons of the prime tore each other in their slime" (280). This is a clear allusion to Tennyson's *In Memoriam*:[1]

> "So careful of the type?" but no.
>   From scarped cliff and quarried stone
>   She cries, "A thousand types are gone:
> I care for nothing, all shall go.
>
> "Thou makest thine appeal to me:
>   I bring to life, I bring to death:
>   The spirit does but mean the breath:
> I know no more." And he, shall he,
>
> Man, her last work, who seem'd so fair,
>   Such splendid purpose in his eyes,
>   Who roll'd the psalm to wintry skies,
> Who built him fanes of fruitless prayer,
>
> Who trusted God was love indeed
>   And love Creation's final law—
>   Tho' Nature, red in tooth and claw
> With ravine, shriek'd against his creed—
>
> Who loved, who suffer'd countless ills,
>   Who battled for the True, the Just,
>   Be blown about the desert dust,
> Or seal'd within the iron hills?
>
> No more? A monster then, a dream
>   A discord. Dragons of the prime,
>   That tare each other in their slime,
> Were mellow music matched with him.
>
> O life as futile, then, as frail!
>   O for thy voice to soothe and bless!

---

1. I quote Section 56 in its entirety, as it is so significant to Stoker's thought regarding the tensions between the biblical and scientific accounts of creation. He would invoke the same passage to similar effect (*Jewel* 184) in "Powers—Old and New," a controversial chapter in *The Jewel of Seven Stars* that was excised from some editions of the novel.

What hope of answer, or redress?
Behind the veil, behind the veil. (56.1–28)

In making his allusion, then, Stoker was subtly invoking one of the Victorian era's most acclaimed and agonized literary struggles with doubt. Tennyson desperately seeks to reconcile any religious notion that "God was love indeed" with the brutality he sees in "Nature, red in tooth and claw." The dragons represent one manifestation of this Nature, their own claws clearly red from "tar[ing] at each other in their slime." And for Tennyson, there is little doubt that these "dragons" are distinctly prehistoric, extinct and long since fossilized.

Stoker is far vaguer in his approach to time. He frequently conflates seemingly obvious prehistoric references with far more recent periods. In one of his earlier speculations Sir Nathaniel discusses various Anglo-Saxon dragon myths, then adds,

> In both these legends the "worm" was a monster of vast size and power—a veritable dragon or serpent, such as legend attributes to vast fens or quags where there was illimitable room for expansion. A glance at a geological map will show that whatever truth there may have been of the actuality of such monsters in the early geologic periods, at least there was plenty of possibility. In the eastern section of England there were originally vast plains where the natural plentiful supply of water could gather. There the streams were deep and slow, and there were holes of abysmal depth, where any kind and size of antediluvian monster could find a habitat. In places, which now we can see from our windows, were mud-holes a hundred or more feet deep. Who can tell us when the age of the monsters which flourished in the slime came to an end? If such a time there was indeed, its limits could only apply to the vast number of such dangers. (187)

This passage demonstrates well Stoker's habit in the novel of collapsing historic and prehistoric time. Here, as later, he alludes to Tennyson's poem in describing "the monsters which flourished in the slime," which are apparently also the "monsters in the early geologic periods." Yet Sir Nathaniel takes a slightly skeptical approach to the science he is citing, telling Adam, "whatever truth there may have been of the actuality of such monsters in the early geologic periods, at least there was plenty of possibility." The existence of such creatures is of course borne out, but it is never clear what the "early geologic periods" are. The geological references in this passage are bracketed by discussions of legends or recent occurrences of "veritable survivals from earlier ages" (187). The White Worm herself is apparently such a monster, yet she is thousands of years old, not millions, and is in fact connected to biblical history: Sir Nathaniel elsewhere asserts that they should defeat her with modern means, for "there is no use in trying means that were familiar to her at the time of the Flood" (323). In fact, she is specifically linked to Tennyson's poem, even as her age is also specifically delimited, as "a monster *of the early days of the world*—a dragon of the prime—*of vast age running into thousands of years*" (284; my emphasis). If the monster's age "run[s] into thousands of years," and yet the monster is "of the early days of the world," it would seem to follow that the early days of the world occurred thousands of years ago, not millions or billions. Stoker's use of "days" in reference to the early earth may even be a subtle allusion to the six days of creation in Genesis 1.

This is not to say that Stoker was necessarily advancing a young earth chronology. Young earth creationism would not hit its cultural ascendancy for several more years;[2] at this stage, even a strong contingent of American proto-fundamentalists believed in an earth millions or billions of years old. Indeed, three years prior to publishing *The Lair of the White Worm,* in a passage that quotes Tennyson, Stoker had written in *Lady Athlyne* about "the whole world with its million years of slow working" (44). Such ambiguity on his part cannot thus be the result of mere ignorance. With its countless ref-

---

2. Of course, an earth thousands of years old was the default church position in all quarters until the end of the eighteenth century. However, for those believers who did not ignore geology entirely, a variety of interpretations were available, some "young" earth, some "old" earth, and some involving the "gap theory" synthesis of the two.

erences to local Mercian geology and archaeology, *The Lair of the White Worm* ranks with *Dracula* and *The Jewel of Seven Stars* as one of Stoker's most thoroughly researched novels. Indeed, as Carol A. Senf notes, Adam's knowledge of geology is instrumental to the heroes' victory (116). Words such as "dinosaur"[3] and "prehistoric"[4] were in use before Stoker was even born, yet they never almost appear in the work. Rather, his favorite term to describe the White Worm and others of her kind would probably be "antediluvian," which could generally mean "ancient" but literally means "before the Flood"—again, a biblical connotation.

Stoker does use the word "evolution," yet he uses it specifically regarding the White Worm's ability to transform itself into a human being, which Sir Nathaniel calls "the natural process of evolution; not taken from genii and species, but from individual instances" (284). Thus, even this evolution is taking place over thousands, not millions, of years. Moreover, it is non-Darwinian evolution, resembling more an accelerated version of Lamarckian transmutation: "In the beginning, the instincts of animals are confined to alimentation, self-protection, and the multiplication of their species. As time goes on and the needs of life become more complex, power follows the need" (284). For Darwin, evolution occurred through natural selection, a process of random mutation. Stoker's evolution "follows the need"; in other words, species evolve to adapt to their environments, much as in Lamarckian thought. This kind of evolution retains a sense of directedness that is missing from the random mutation in Darwin's theory.

Stoker's conflation of geological and biblical time, along with his adoption of a more purposive theory of evolution, are not mere abstract points but have profound implications for the novel. By re-

---

3. Stoker does refer to a specific genus of dinosaur, *Diplodocus,* as a passing comparison to the White Worm (290).
4. The one use of the word prehistoric again serves to blur temporal distinctions: Richard Salton speaks of Sir Nathaniel as one who "knows all the old legends of the days when prehistoric times were vital" (163), suggesting here too that prehistoric and historic times are not that widely separated.

taining a textual ambivalence regarding the earth's age, Stoker is able to mingle freely the prehistoric world with the biblical imagery of Eden. His use of Lamarckian evolution, even in the case of so malevolent an entity as the White Worm, circumvents the fear, inherent in Darwin, of a hands-off God. If evolution can "follow the need," it could potentially be directed by forces other than just blind chance, whether those forces are evil—as in the case of Arabella March—or good.

There are many sources of evil or fallenness in the novel. The African servant Oolanga, with his ability to "smell death," represents a primitive past in the ethnological terms Stoker often invokes, but also might serve as a reminder that the consequence of Adam and Eve's expulsion in Genesis is death. Edgar Caswall, meanwhile, is often given demonic or devilish descriptions. He is, moreover, associated with predators, especially the hawk, which becomes embodied in the immense hawk-shaped kite he flies over the land. At one point the kite moves from hovering over Diana's Grove—Lady Arabella's home/lair—to the Watford home of Mercy Farm, which he and Arabella will attack in various ways. This would seem to indicate the movement of natural predation from its source with the serpent toward the naturally religious and Edenic environment.

Because Lady Arabella is the obvious literal serpent in the garden. She has a "snake nature" (286). Sir Nathaniel and Adam agree that she is a "survival," an ancient being described in physiological terms, yet one whose long life span has "overlapped the Christian era" (286). She is literally and metaphorically "cold-blooded" and "a monster without heart" (303). As Oolanga notes, her lair—associated with paganism in its formal name of Diana's Grove—is filled with death, new and old. She is, on the one hand, nature "red in tooth and claw" (figuratively speaking, since she may not have claws); but she is also emblematic of the possibility that nature's brutality is an external imposition.

Of course, this serpent is ultimately overwhelmed by the Eden that Stoker establishes for his new generation. And of course, this

Eden has its literal Adam, Adam Salton. Adam may seem a strange choice for Stoker, whose heroes are usually British. But, as Coral Lansbury points out, Victorian writers often held an idealized view of Australia as an Arcadian paradise, a land that invoked an ancient pastoral Golden Age, and "this Arcadian Australia" became "the most favoured interpretation in English literature" (2). Stoker gives indications that Adam is from just such an Arcady, for he wakes early "after the pastoral habit to which he had been bred" (160), and he owned a farm with over one thousand horses. Like the biblical Adam, he is a man who works the field, someone who tames nature. He is also a man of faith who explicitly identifies himself as a Christian (272) and who can assert in final climactic battle, like so many of the heroes in *Dracula*, "We are in the hands of God" (358).

This Adam needs an Eve, and in *The Lair of the White Worm* Mimi Watford is the Eve figure. Like most of Stoker's heroines, Mimi is not purely British, being part Burmese. This gives her a vitality that her more obviously British or Caucasian counterparts— her cousin Lilla or Arabella March—lack. Even more so than her eventual husband Adam, Mimi articulates Stoker's faith perspective. While Adam is most often matched against Lady Arabella, Mimi tends to be put in opposition to Edgar Caswall. In a warning speech to him, she notably articulates the difference between his non-teleological view of nature and her providential approach:

> Oh, I am not afraid of you or your accomplice . . . I am content to stand by every word I have said, every act I have done. Moreover, I believe in God's justice. I fear not the grinding of His mills. If needed, I shall set the wheels in motion myself. But you don't care even for God, or believe in Him. Your god is your great kite, which cows the birds of a whole district. But be sure that His hand, when it rises, always falls at the appointed time. His voice speaks in thunder, and not only for the rich who scorn their poorer neighbours. The voices that call on Him come from the furrow and the workshop, from grinding toil and unrelieved stress and strain. Those voices he always hears, however frail and feeble they may be. His thunder is their echo, His lightning the menace that is borne. Be

careful! I say even as you have spoken. It may be that your name is being called even at this moment at the Great Assize. Repent while there is still time. Happy you if you may be allowed to enter those mighty halls in the company of the pure-souled angel whose voice has only to whisper one word of justice and you thenceforth disappear for ever into everlasting torment. (337)

Edgar's kite, according to Mimi, is his god because he views nature entirely as a series of predator/prey relationships, as symbolized by the hawk-kite. Mimi, on the other hand, interprets natural processes as the moving of God's justice toward an eschatological end. Here and elsewhere she anticipates a final judgment, which is frequently alluded to in the novel. Sir Nathaniel's property is, in fact, known as Doom Tower, "doom" always used in the general sense of judgment, not with intrinsically negative connotations.

Though both Adam and Mimi experience a brief period of doubt, they overcome it to become the new Adam and Eve who restore nature to its prelapsarian condition, in which floral and faunal relationships are rightly and peaceably ordered. A storm arrived, described as the "rolling majesty of heaven's artillery . . . which seemed to shake the whole structure of the world" (360). Lightning destroys Edgar Caswall in his home of Castra Regis, and its collapse in turn sets off explosive set by Adam that violently destroy Lady Arabella, the white worm leading to an eruption of "a mass of blood and slime" (364). When Adam and Sir Nathaniel survey the landscape the next day, they find a "corruption" that "attracted every natural organism that was in itself obnoxious" (368). Elsewhere, though, "All nature was bright and joyous, being in striking contrast to the scenes of wreck and devastation" (366). Adam and Sir Nathaniel turn away from the sight of carnage toward a cliff trop, "where a fresh breeze from the eastern sea was blowing up" (369) before Adam returns again to his wife.

No one doubts that *The Lair of the White Worm* is a bizarre book, and it probably isn't a masterpiece in the same league as *Dracula*. Stoker's research, imagery, and thematic development for the novel, however, are far more complex and coherent than they have been given credit for. His own life cut across the Victorian and Edwardian periods, with their ongoing search to find some resolution between perceived scientific and religious truths. That search seems to have fascinated Stoker endlessly, and from his first book to *The Lair of the White Worm*, his last, he never ceased exploring such themes.

Works Cited

Farson, Daniel. *The Man Who Wrote* Dracula: *A Biography of Bram Stoker*. London: Michael Joseph, 1975.

Glover, David. "'Why White?': On Worms and Skin in Bram Stoker's Later Fiction." *Gothic Studies* 3 (December 2000): 346–60.

Hebblethwaite, Kate. "Introduction" to *Dracula's Guest and Other Weird Stories*. London: Penguin, 2006. xi–xxxix.

Hopkins, Lisa. *Bram Stoker: A Literary Life*. Houndmills, UK: Palgrave Macmillan, 2007.

Lansbury, Coral. *Arcady in Australia: The Evocation of Australia in Nineteenth-Century English Literature*. Carlton: Melbourne University Press, 1970.

Murray, Paul. *From the Shadow of* Dracula: *A Life of Bram Stoker*. London: Pimlico, 2005.

Roth, Phyllis A. *Bram Stoker*. Boston: Twayne, 1982.

Senf, Carol A. *Science and Social Science in Bram Stoker's Fiction*. Westport, CT: Greenwood Press, 2002.

Stoker, Bram. *Dracula*. 1897. Ed. Nina Auerbach and David J. Skal. New York: W. W. Norton, 1997.

———. *The Jewel of Seven Stars*. Ed. Kate Hebblethwaite. London: Penguin, 2008.

———. *Lady Athlyne*. 1908. Chicago: Valancourt, 2007.

———. *The Lair of the White Worm*. In *Dracula's Guest and Other Weird Stories*. Ed. Kate Hebblethwaite. London: Penguin, 2006. 151–369.

Tennyson, Alfred. *In Memoriam*. 1850. Ed. Susan Shatto and Marion Shaw. Oxford: Clarendon Press, 1982.

Cold, Colder thy Kiss

Oliver Smith

As friendly embers faded, to dead cinders, in the grate,
a song shivered, late, beyond leaded panes of diamond glass.
It called me from my familiar bed; on down the darkened stair,
and out. Nightshirt clad, along winding paths, I followed
seeking the singer in the snowy garden's lonely hollows,
its frozen fountains, it's pool of swirling, midnight mist
where a marble angel slept, deep, in winter's frigid grip.

I believed no human throat could form such honeyed song,
so expected that there perched some night-bird; serenading,
a longed-for mate in the lustrous light of the white-skulled moon.
The music's enchantment led, in cold, strange, shivering night,
to where sweet notes thrilled and dreamed and danced in ringing ice,
beyond the rotted flowers, beyond the icicles' glitter,
beyond woods of naked pine; grown broken, bleached and bitter.

The track meandered further; through the fog and winter gloom,
past ragged rocks that mourned like frozen giants in the frost,
to where an ancient, granite mausoleum grimly loomed.
Once padlocked and iron-barred, the massive doors hung askew;
shattered by some awful force, their hinges torn from the wall.
Here, other muse-drawn pilgrims had braved snow and cold and storm
to worship a wakened angel, that stood at the open tomb.

These others came; faint, fogbound shadows, marching, two by two
on crooked legs, to celebrate saturnalia and feast.
Vile beasts which should, long ago, have died, yet were not dead;
but passed beyond their death and to some unhuman form regressed;
with bloody jaws, they gnawed upon the disinterred, and mocking life,

they delighted in worm-skin, grave wax candle, and rattle bones,
and piled high borrowed skulls to construct a monstrous throne.

All in harmony, they howled and before the angel, bowed;
like a frail spirit she danced; beauty in the falling snow
softly on the moonlit field, a song upon her pale lips,
as revenants waltzed between the graves and made their banquet,
upon grey stones. They took my hands in their cold clawed paws
and I joined their wild jigs and danced in the ghoulish ball,
all through the night I danced, until, to me, the angel called.

She plucked me into the air and on feathered-wings we flew
to delight in tooth and claw; quotidian worlds transformed
in the ghostly radiance of long-dead stars that swirled
against the endless, absence of the heaven's deepest void.
I heard such songs as must be sung beside the Lethe
and in her arms, I drank a death so dear and found such release
that ever-more without her, I would never more know peace.

Now, hid in my room, unbearable languor stills my limbs.
Behind the tightly pulled drapes, I abjure the sun's warm light
on summer fields, and love not the garden's bloom, but desire
autumn's dank decay; I am joyful at October's storm.
Raw November frost delights my heart and, in winter's dark,
as my mistress's sweet song rises from the distant tomb,
as falls the snow, with joy, I dance beneath the pale, cold moon.

The Tree-Man

Henry S. Whitehead

[The text of this story is derived from its first publication (*Weird Tales*, February/March 1931), augmented by a partial typescript found among the papers of R. H. Barlow. The typescript was given to Barlow by E. Hoffmann Price. In a letter to Barlow dated 1 March 1933, Price wrote: "I have decided to make you an indefinite loan [. . .] of a piece of manuscript which I believe you will appreciate. ¶ It is a carbon copy of Henry S. Whitehead's THE TREE MAN. This carbon as you will note was corrected by Dr. Whitehead and partly—witness 1st few pages—rewritten in order to cut it down to 7500 words to fit into a collection of weird fiction several of us hope to have published sometime this or the following year. All corrections were made by Dr. Whitehead in person." The anthology Price was assembling never appeared.

This typescript contains numerous passages that Whitehead omitted when preparing the final draft. These passages are enclosed below in brackets. Other, more minor alterations have been made silently.—Ed.]

My first sight of Fabricius, the tree-man, was within a week of my first arrival on the island of Santa Cruz not long after the United States had purchased the Danish West Indies and officially re-named its new colony the Virgin Islands of the United States.

My ship came into Frederiksted harbour on the west coast of the island just at dusk and I saw for the first time a half-moon of white sand beach with the charming little town in its middle. In the midst of the bustle incident to anchoring in the roadstead, there came over the side an upstanding gentleman in a glistening white drill uniform who came up to me, bowed in a manner to commend itself to kings, and said:

"I am honoured to welcome you to Santa Cruz, Mr. Canevin. I am Director Despard of the Police Department. The police boat is at your disposal when you are ready to go ashore. May I see to your luggage?"

This was a welcome indeed. I was nearly knocked off my feet by such an unexpected reception. I thanked Director Despard and before many minutes my trunks were overside, my luggage bestowed in the police boat waiting at the foot of the ladder-gangway, and I was seated beside him in the boat's sternsheets, he holding the tiller-ropes while four coal-black convicts rowed us ashore with lusty pulls at their long sweeps.

Through the lowering dusk as we approached the landing I observed that the wharf was crowded with Black people. Behind these stood half a dozen knots of White people, conversing together. A long row of cars stood against the background of waterfront buildings. I remarked to the Police Director:

"Isn't it unusual for so many persons to be on the docks for the arrival of a vessel, Mr. Director?"

"It is not usual," replied the dignified gentleman beside me. "It is for you, Mr. Canevin."

"For me?" said I. "Extraordinary! What—for me? Certainly,— my dear sir,—certainly not for me. Why,—it's . . ."

Mr. Despard turned about and smiled at me.

"You are Captain McMillin's great-nephew, you know, Mr. Canevin."

So that was it. My great-uncle, one of my Scots kinsfolk, my great-uncle who had died many years before I had seen the light of day, my grandfather's oldest brother, the one who had been in the British Army and later a planter here on Santa Cruz. He had been the very last person I should have thought of, and now—

The police boat landed smartly at the concrete jetty. Mr. Despard and I landed, and in the lowering dusk I could not help noticing the quietly-expressed but very genuine interest of the thousand or more negroes who thronged the wharf as they courteously parted a way for us while we proceeded towards the groups of White people, thronging forward now with an unanimous and unmistakable greeting shining from dozens of kindly faces.

I will pass over the rest of that first evening ashore. At the end of it and all its lavish hospitality I found myself comfortably installed in a small private hotel pending the final preparations to my own hired residence. I found every estate-house on Santa Cruz open to me. Hospitalities were showered upon me to the point of embarrassment, kindnesses galore, considerate and timely bits of information, help of every imaginable kind. I learned in this process much about my late great-uncle, all of which information was new to me, and it was not long after my arrival when it was arranged for me to visit his estate, Great Fountain.

I went with Hans Grumbach, in his Ford car, a bumpy journey of more than three hours up hills and through ravines and along precipitous trails on old roads incredibly roundabout and primitive.

All the way Hans Grumbach talked about this section of the island, now rarely visited. Here, up to ten years before, Grumbach had lived as the last of a long line of estate-managers which the old place had had in residence since the day, in 1879, when my Scottish relatives had sold their Santa Crucian holdings. It was now the property of the largest of the local sugar-growing corporations, known as the Copenhagen Concern. Because of its inaccessibility cultivation on it had finally been abandoned and Hans Grumbach had come to live in Frederiksted, married the daughter of a respectable *creole* family, and settled down to keeping store on one of the town's side streets.

But, it came out, Grumbach had wanted for all those ten years, to go back to the northern hills. This trip to the old place stimulated his loquacity. He sang its praises: the beauty of its configuration, its magnificent views and vistas, the amazing fertility of its soil.

We arrived at last. All about us the vegetation had grown to be ideally tropical, the "tropical" of old-fashioned pictures on calendars! The soil appeared to be rich, blackish "bottom-land."

The old estate was in a sad state of rack and ruin. We walked over a good part of it under the convoy of the courteous Black caretaker, and looked out over its rolling domain from various angles and coigns of vantage. The Negro village was half tumbled-down. The cabins remaining were all out of repair. The characteristic quick tropical inroads upon land "turned out" of active cultivation were everywhere apparent. The ancient Great House was entirely gone. The farm buildings, though built of sound stone and mortar, were terribly dilapidated.

[. . . of it at home but which had disappeared—it was a mere pencil sketch—when I was still a child and never afterwards turned up to my knowledge. Upon the basis of this recollection I constructed a mental picture of my great-uncle as I had heard him described; portly, rotund, yet tall and commanding; presiding over a groaning board in his great dining-room; a mahogany table glisteningly reflecting ancient cut-glass and silverware; his guests about him; and he, if it were a formal occasion, arrayed in his Captain's red uniform coat of the British Army, wherein he had risen to that rank before he sold out his commission to come to Santa Cruz, and which garment he is said to have affected on such occasions.

From my recollection of the sketch I endeavored to explain to Hans Grumbach and the caretaker something of what the Great House had looked like, and in even that scrap of information they seemed almost unduly interested. I was later to learn that my great-uncle, of whom there were many old tales current still, and at least one negro folk-song, had been something of a personage on the island; tales with which I will not delay my story, interesting and amusing as some of them were.

I was, too,] on that visit to Great Fountain [to have] my first experience [with what has come to be known as] the "grape-vine" method of communication among Africans. I had been perhaps four days on the island, and it is reasonably certain that none of these people had ever so much as heard of me before; [certainly none of] these obscure village negroes cut off here in the hills from others the nearest of whom lived miles away. Yet, we had hardly come within a stone's throw of the remains of the village before we were surrounded by the total population, of perhaps twenty adults, and at least as many children of all ages.

As one would expect, these Blacks were of very crude appearance; not only "country negroes" but that in an exaggerated form. Negroes in the West Indies have some tendency to live on the land where they originated, and as it happened most of these negroes had been born up here and several generations of their forebears before them.

We had brought our lunch along, and this Hans Grumbach and I ate sitting in the Ford under the shade of a grove of magnificent old mahogany trees, and afterwards Grumbach took me up along a ravine to see the "fountain" from which the old estate had originally derived its title.

[We walked up a ravine towards it, along a sandy stream-bed which, this being an exceptionally dry season near the end of a three-years' drought, was now a mere trickle.

But I saw something on which Grumbach had descanted as a sure sign of fertility, in the bed and along the sandy banks of the little stream—gold-colored sand, like mica and perhaps iron pyrites, and which Grumbach had called "the golden sand."]

The "fountain" itself was a delicate natural waterfall, streaming thinly over the edge of a high rock[, a source of the one unfailing stream on an otherwise "dry" island since the tropical rain-belt shifted, many years before, south to the latitude of the island of Dominica several hundreds of miles south of Santa Cruz; thus making it entirely dependent upon rain-water and, modernly, the great holding reservoirs which the American Government has provided in the hills.] It was when we were coming back, by a slightly different route, for Grumbach wanted me to take in everything possible, that I saw the tree-man.

He stood, a youngish, coal-black Negro, of about twenty-five years, scantily dressed in a tattered shirt and a sketchy pair of trousers, about ten yards away from the field-path we were following and from which a clear view of a portion of the estate was obtained, and beside him, towering over him, was a magnificent coconut-palm. The Negro stood, motionless. I thought, in fact, that he had gone asleep standing there, both arms clasped about the tree's smooth, elegant trunk, the right side of his face pressed against it.

He was not, however, asleep, because I looked back at him and his eyes,—rather intelligent eyes, they seemed to me,—were wide open, although to my surprise he had not changed his position, nor even the direction of his gaze, to glance at us; and, I was quite sure, he had not been in that village group when we had stood among them, just before our lunch.

Grumbach did not speak to him, as he had done to every other Negro we had seen. Indeed, [catching sight of him as I turned to him for some possible comment,] I observed that his face looked a trifle,—well, apprehensive; and I thought he very slightly quickened his pace. I stepped nearer to him as we walked past the man and the tree, and then I noticed that his lips were moving, and when I came closer I observed that he was muttering to himself. I said, very quietly, almost in his ear:

"What's the matter with that fellow, Grumbach?"

Grumbach glanced at me out of the corner of his eye, and my impression that he was disturbed grew upon me.

"He's listening!" was all that I got out of Grumbach. I supposed, of course, that there was something odd about the fellow; perhaps he was slightly demented and might be an annoyance; and I supposed that Grumbach meant to convey that the young fellow was "listening" for our possible comment upon him and his strange behaviour. Later, after we had said good-bye to the courteous caretaker and he had seen us off down the first hillside road, with its many ruts, I brought up the subject of the young black fellow at the tree.

"You mentioned that he was listening," said I, "so I dropped the matter, but, why does he do that, Grumbach—I mean, why does he stand against the tree in that unusual manner? Why, he didn't even gee his eyes to look at us, and that surprised me. They don't have visitors up here every day, I understand."

"He was listening—*to his tree!*" said Hans Grumbach, as though reluctantly. "*That* was what I meant, Mr. Canevin." And he drew my attention to an extraordinarily picturesque ruined windmill, the kind once used for the grinding of cane in the old days of "muscovado" sugar, which dominated a cone-like hillside off to our left as we bumped over the road.

[Between getting settled in my house, attending to the preliminary work of my mission, and fulfilling the almost numberless social engagements which crowded upon me, I cannot say that I forgot about the tree-man; but, certainly, he and his queer behaviour were anything but prominent in my mind.] It was not until months later, when I had gained the confidence of Hans Grumbach, that that individual gave me any further enlightenment on the subject of the man and his tree.

Then I learned that, along with his nostalgia for the life of an agriculturist,—an incurable matter with some persons I have found—there was mixed in with his feelings about the Great Fountain estate a kind of inconsistent thankfulness that he was no longer stationed there! This inconsistency, this being dragged sentimentally in two opposite directions, rather intrigued me. I saw something of Grumbach and got rather well acquainted with him as the months passed that first year of my residence. Bit by bit, in his reluctant manner of speech, it came out.

To put the whole picture of his mind on this subject together, I got the idea that Grumbach, while always suffering from a faint nostalgia for his deep-country residence and the joys of tilling the soil, felt, somehow, *safe* here in the town. If he chafed, mildly, at the restrictions of town life and his storekeeping, there was yet the certainty that "something"—a vague matter at first, as it came out—was not always hanging over him; something connected with a lingering fear.

The negroes, it appeared—this came to me very gradually, of course—up there at Great Fountain, were not, quite, like the rest of the island's Black population; in the two towns; out on the many sugar-estates; even those residues of village communities which continued to live, in that mild, beneficent climate, on "turned-out" estate land because there was no one sufficiently interested to eject these squatters. No—the Great Fountain village was, somehow, at least in Hans Grumbach's dark hints, different; *sui generis;* a peculiar people [as the biblical phrase runs].

They were, to begin with, almost purely of Dahomeyan stock. These Dahomeyans had drifted "down the islands"[—in the general southerly direction, that is,—] from Hayti, beginning soon after the revolt against France in the early Nineteenth Century[, a fact which was familiar to me even then from my reading]. They were tall, very black, extremely clannish Blacks. And just as the Koromantyn slaves in British Jamaica had brought to the West Indies their Obay-i-, [("obeah")] or herb-magic, so, it seemed, had the Dahomeyans carried with them from Guinea their *vodu,* which properly defined, means the practices accompanying the [vague Guinea] worship of "The Snake."

This worship, grown into a vast localised *cultus* in unfettered Hayti and in the Guiana hinterlands down in South America, is [a vastly intriguing matter,] very imperfectly understood [even to this present day]. But its accompaniments, all the charms, *ouangas,* philtres, potions, talismans, amulets, "doctoring" and whatnot, have spread all through the West India islands, and these are thoroughly established in highly developed and widely variant forms. Hayti is its West Indian home, of course. But down in French Martinique its extent and intensity is a fair rival to the Haytian supremacy. It is rife on Dominica, Guadeloupe, even on British Montserrat. Indeed, [allowing for local variations,] one might name every island from Cuba to Trinidad, and, allowing for the variations, the local preferences, and all such matters, one might say, and truly, that the *vodu,* generically described by the Blacks themselves as "obi," is very thoroughly established.

According to Grumbach, the handful of villagers at Great Fountain was very deeply involved in this sort of thing. Left to themselves as they had been for many years, forming a little, self-sustaining community of nearly pure-blooded Dahomeyans, they had, it seemed, reverted very nearly to their African type; and this, Grumbach alleged, was the fact despite their easy kindliness, their use of "English," and the various other outward appearances which caused them to seem not greatly different from other "country negroes" on this island of Santa Cruz.

[Hans Grumbach did not supply all this information either in one definite account, or, indeed, as fully as I have here summarized the matter. It took months before I got from him, in disjointed fragments mostly, or by means of hints, head-shakings, and almost incidental remarks, any clear-cut idea of what was going on up there in the hills at my great-uncle's ancient domain. Besides, I am supplying, in this brief account of what was toward, subsequent years' results of study and first-hand contact with the subject of the magic of the Caribbean peoples.

On the subject of] Silvio Fabricius[, for that was the tree-man's rather fanciful name—however, my original information was derived directly from Grumbach. He had, you see, known the young negro] since he had been a pick'ny on the estate. He knew, so far as his limited understanding of Black People's Magic extended, all about Silvio. He had been estate-manager at the time the boy had begun his attentions to the great coconut palm. He had heard and seen what he called the "stupidness" which had attended the setting apart of this neophyte. There had been three days—and nights; particularly the nights—when not a single plantation-hand would do a piece of work for any consideration. It was, as Grumbach bitterly remembered it all, "the crop season." His employers, not sensing, businessmen as they were, any underlying reason for no work done when they needed the cane from Great Fountain for their grinding-mill, had been hard on him. They had, in Santa Crucian phraseology, "pressed him" for cane deliveries. And there, in his village, quite utterly ignoring his authority as estate-manager, those Blacks had danced and pounded drums, and burned flares, and weaved back and forth in their interminable ceremonies—"stupidness"—for three strategic days and nights, over something which had Silvio Fabricius, then a rising pick'ny of twelve or thirteen, as its apparent centre and underlying cause. It was no wonder that Hans Grumbach raved and probably swore mightily and threatened the estate-hands.

But [the expression of] his anger and annoyance, the threats and cajolings, the offers of "snaps" of rum, [and bonuses,] and pay for piece-work; all these efforts to get his ripe cane cut and delivered, had come to nothing. The carts stood empty. The mules gravely ate the long guinea-grass. The canetops waved in the soft breath of the North-East Trade Wind, while those three days stretched themselves out to their conclusion.

This conclusion, which was ceremonial, took place in the daytime, about ten o'clock in the morning of the fourth day. After that, which was a very brief and apparently meaningless matter indeed, the hands sheepishly resumed the driving of their mule-carts and the swinging of their canebills, and once more the Fountain cane travelled slowly down the rutted hill road towards the factory below. On that morning, before resuming their work, the whole village had accompanied young Silvio Fabricius in silence as he walked ahead of them up towards the source of the perennial stream, stepped out into the field, and clasped his arms about a young, but tall and promising coconut palm which stood there as though accidentally in solitary towering grandeur. There the villagers had left the little black boy when they turned away and filed slowly and silently back to the village and to their interrupted labor.

And there, beside his tree, Grumbach said, Silvio Fabricius had stood ever since, only occasionally coming in to the village and then at any hour of the day or night, apparently "reporting" something to the oldest inhabitant, a gnarled, ancient grandfather with pure white wool. After such a brief visit Fabricius would at once, and with an unshaken gravity, return to his tree. Food, said Grumbach, was always carried out to him from the village. He toiled not, neither spun! There, day and night, under the blazing sun, through showers and drenching downpours, erect, apparently unsleeping—unless he slept standing up against his tree as Grumbach suspected—stood Silvio Fabricius, and there he had stood, except when he climbed the tree to trim out the "cloth" or chase out a rat intent on nesting up there, or to gather the coconuts, for eleven years.

The coconuts, it seemed, were his perquisite. They were, Grumbach said, absolutely *tabu* to anybody else. It was over the question of some green coconuts from this superior tree that Grumbach himself, with all his authority as estate-manager behind his demand, had come to grips with Silvio Fabricius; or, to be more precise, with the entire estate-village.

I never succeeded in getting this story in detail from Grumbach, who was plainly reluctant to tell it. It reflected, you see, upon him; his authority as estate-manager, his pride, were here heavily involved. But, as I gathered it, his house-man, sent to that particular tree for a basket of green coconuts,—Grumbach was entertaining some friends and wanted the coconut-water and jelly to put in a Danish concoction based on Holland gin,—had returned half an hour late, delivered the coconuts, and, later, it came out that he had gone *down* the hill to a neighboring estate for the nuts. Taken to task for this duplicity, the house-man had balked, "gone stupid" over the affair, and upon the dispute which followed the village itself had joined in. The conclusion, as Grumbach gathered it, to his great mystification, was that the coconut tree "belonged to" young Silvio Fabricius, was *tabu,* and that the village was solid against him on the issue. He, the manager, with control of everything, could not get coconuts from the best tree on the estate! This, attributed to the usual Black "stupidness," had rankled. It also more or less accounted for Grumbach's attitude towards Silvio Fabricius, an attitude which I myself had witnessed. That his "fear" of this young negro went deeper than that, I sensed, however. I was, later, to see that suspicion justified.

For a long time I had no occasion to revisit Great Fountain. But six years later, while in the States during the summer, I made the acquaintance of a man named Carrington who wanted to know "all about the Virgin Islands" with a view to investing some money there in a proposal to grow pineapples on a large scale. I talked with Mr. Carrington at some length, and in the course of our discussions it occurred to me that Great Fountain estate would be virtually ideal for his purpose. Here was a very considerable acreage of rich land: the Copenhagen Company would probably rent it out for a period of ten years for a very reasonable price since it was bringing them in nothing. I spread before Carrington these advantages, and he travelled down on the ship with me that autumn to make an investigation in person.

Carrington, a trained fruit-grower, spent a day with me on the estate, and thereafter with characteristic American energy started in to put his plan into practice. A lease was easily secured [on terms mutually advantageous], the village was repaired and the fallen stone cabins rebuilt, and within a few weeks cultivating machinery of the most modem type began to arrive on the Frederiksted wharf.

After a considerable consultation with Hans Grumbach, to whose lamentations over the restrictions of town-life I had been listening for years, I recommended him to Mr. Carrington as manager of the laborers, and Hans, after going over the matter with his good wife and coming to an amicable understanding, went back to Great Fountain where a manager's house had been thrown up for him on the foundation of one of the ruined buildings. At Carrington's direction, Grumbach set the estate laborers at work on the job of repairing the roads; and, as the village cabins went up, one after another, laborers, enticed by the prospect of good wages, filled them up and ancient Great Fountain became once more a busy scene of industry.

During these preparatory works I spent a good deal of time on the estate because I was naturally interested in Joseph Carrington's venture being a success. I had, indeed, put several thousand dollars into it myself, not solely because it looked like a good investment, but in part for sentimental reasons connected with my great-uncle. [On these occasions,] being by then thoroughly familiar with the odd native speech, I made it a point to visit the village and talk at length with the "people." They were courteous to me, markedly so; deferential would be a better word to describe their attitude. This, of course, was wholly due to the family connection. Only a very few of them, and those the oldest, had any personal recollection of Captain McMillin, but his memory[, aided by the folk-song to which I have alluded,] was decidedly green among them. The old gentleman had been greatly beloved by the negroes of the island.

In the course of my [studies of negro matters, especially African manners and customs, which had included a wide course of reading, for which I wished to master that abstruse subject,] I had run across the peculiar affair of a "tree-man." I understood, therefore, the status of Silvio Fabricius in that queer little Black community; why he had been "devoted" to the tree; what were the underlying reasons for that strange sacrifice.

It was, on the part of that handful of nearly pure-blooded Dahomeyan villagers there at my great-uncle's old place, [an attempt, a recrudescence perhaps,—] a revival[, certainly—,] of a custom probably as old as African civilisation. For—the African *has* a civilisation. He is at a vast disadvantage when among Caucasians, competing, as he necessarily must, with Caucasian "cultures." His native problems are entirely different, utterly diverse, from the white man's. The African's whole history among us Caucasians is a history of more or less successful adaptation. Place an average American businessman in the heart of "uncivilized" Africa, in the Liberian hinterland, for example, and what will he do—how survive? The answer is simple. He will perish miserably, confronted with the black jungle night, the venomous reptilian and insect-life, the attacks of wild beasts, the basic problems of how to feed and warm himself—for even this last is an African problem. [African nights chill to the very bone.] I know. I have been on *safari* in Uganda, in British East Africa, in Somaliland. I speak from experience.

Africans, supposedly static in cultural matters, have solved all these problems. And, very prominent among these, especially as it concerns the agricultural peoples; for there are, perhaps, as many Black nations, kindreds, peoples, tongues, as there are Caucasian; is, of course, the question of weather.

Hence, the "tree-man."

Set apart with ceremonies which were ancient when Hammurabi sat on his throne in Babylon, a young boy is dedicated to a forest tree. Thereafter, he spends his life beside that tree, cares for it, tends it, listens to it; becomes "the-brother-of-the-tree" in time. He is truly "set apart." To the tree he devotes his entire life, dying at last beside it, in its shade. And—this is African "culture" if you will; a culture of which we Caucasians get, perhaps, the faint reactions in the, to us, meaningless jumble of negro superstition which we sense all about us; the "stupidness" of the West Indies; faint, incomprehensible reflections of a system as practical, as dogmatic, as utilitarian, as the now well-nigh universal system of synthetic exercise for the tired businessman which goes by the name of golf!

These negroes at Great Fountain were, primarily, agriculturists. They had the use of the soil bred deeply in their blood and bones. That, indeed, is why the canny French brought their Hispaniola slaves from Dahomey. Left to themselves at the old estate in the north central hills of Santa Cruz the little community rapidly reverted to their African ways. They tilled the soil, sporadically, it is true, yet they tilled it. [Those magnificent tannia plants had been set out. They did not grow merely through the Providence of God.] They needed a weather prognosticator. There are sudden storms in summer throughout the vast sweep of the West India Islands, devastating storms, hurricanes indeed; long, wasting periods of drought. They needed a tree-man up there. They set apart Silvio Fabricius.

That fact made the young fellow what a White man would call "scared." Not for nothing had they danced and performed their "stupid" rites those three long days and nights to the detriment of Hans Grumbach's deliveries. No. Silvio Fabricius, from the moment he had clasped his arms about that growing coconut-palm, was as much a person "set apart," dedicated, as any White man's pundit, priest, or yogi. Hence the various *tabus* which, like the case of the green coconuts, had puzzled Hans Grumbach. He must never take his attention away from the tree. There, beside it, he was consecrated to live and to die. When he departed from his "brother" the tree, it was only for the purpose of reporting something which the tribe should know; something, that is, which his brother the tree had told him! There would be drenching rain the second day following. A plague of small green flies would, the third day later, come to annoy the animals. The banana grove must be propped forthwith. Otherwise, a high wind, two days hence, would nullify all the work of its planting and care.

Such were the messages that Silvio Fabricius, austere, introspective, unnoticing, his mind fully preoccupied with his brotherhood to the tree, brought to his tribe; proceeding, the message delivered, austerely back to his station beside the magnificent palm.

All this, because of my status as the great-nephew of an old Bukra whom he remembered with love and reverence, and because he discovered that I knew about tree-men and many other matters usually sealed books to Bukras, the old fellow who was the village patriarch, who, by right of his seniority, received and passed on from Silvio the messages from Silvio's brother the tree, amply substantiated. There was nothing secretive about him, once he knew my interest in these things. Such procedure as securing the possession of a tree-man for his tribe seemed to the old man entirely reasonable; there was no necessary secret about it, certainly not from sympathetic me, the "yoong marster" of Great Fountain Estate.

And Hans Grumbach, once he had finished with his road-work, not being aware of all this, but sensing something out of the ordinary and hence to be feared about Silvio Fabricius and his palm tree, decided to end the stupidness out there. Grumbach decided to cut down the tree.

If I had had any inkling of this intention I could have saved Grumbach. It would have been a comparatively simple matter for me to have said enough to Carrington to have him forbid it; or, indeed, as a partner in the control of the estate, to forbid it myself. But I knew nothing about it, and have in my statement of his intention to destroy the tree supplied my own conception of his motives.

Grumbach, although virtually Caucasian in appearance, was of mixed blood, and quite without the Caucasian background of superior quality which makes the educated West Indian *mestizo* the splendid citizen he is in so many notable instances. His White ancestry was derived from a grandfather, a Schleswig-Holsteiner, who had been a sergeant of the Danish troops stationed on Santa Cruz and who, after the term of his enlistment had expired, had married into a respectable colored family, and remained on the island. Grumbach was without the Caucasian aristocrat's tolerance for the preoccupations of the Blacks. To him such affairs were "stupidness," merely. Like others of his kind he held the Black people in a kind of contempt; was wholly, I imagine, without sympathy for them, though a worthy fellow enough in his limited way. And, perhaps, he had not enough Negro in him to understand instinctively even so much as what Silvio Fabricius, the tree-man, stood for in his community.

I had, too, you will remember, known something in those six years, of his viewpoints, his reactions to the "stupidness," and, specifically, some knowledge at least of his direct reaction, his pique and resentment, as these arose from his contacts with the tree-man. As I have indicated, the element of fear colored this attitude.

He chose, cannily, one of the periods when Fabricius was away from his tree, reporting to the village. It was early in the afternoon, and Grumbach, having finished his road-work several days before, was directing a group of laborers who were grubbing ancient "bush"—heavy undergrowth, brush, rank weeds, small trees,—from along the winding trail which led from the village to the fountain or waterfall. This was now feeding[, for the drought was no longer plaguing the island,] a tumbling stream which Carrington intended to dam, lower down, for a central reserve reservoir.

The majority, if not all, of these laborers under his eye at the moment were new to the village; members of the increasing group which were coming into the restored stone cabins as fast as these became habitable. They were cutting out the brush with machetes, canebills, and knives; and, for the small trees, a couple of axes were being used from time to time. This work was being done quite near the great tree, and from his position in the roadway overlooking his gang, Grumbach must have seen the tree-man leave his station and start towards the village with one of his "messages."

This opportunity—he had, unquestionably, made up his mind about it all—was too good to be lost. As I learned from the two men whom he detached from his grubbing-gang and took with him, Silvio Fabricius was hardly out of sight over the sweep of the lower portion of the great field near the upper edge of which the coconut-palm towered, when Grumbach called to the two axemen to follow him, and, with a word to the rest of the gang, led the way across the field's edge to the tree.

About this time Carrington and I were returning from one of our inspections of the fountain. We had been up there several times of late, since the scheme for the dam had been working in our minds. We were returning towards the village and the construction work progressing there along that same pathway through the big field from which, years before, I had had my first sight of the tree-man.

As we came in sight of the tree, towards which I invariably looked when I was near it, I saw, of course, that Fabricius was not there. Grumbach and his two laborers stood under it, Grumbach talking to the men. One of them as we approached—we were still perhaps a hundred yards distant—shook his head emphatically. He told me later that Grumbach had led them straight to the tree and commanded them to chop it down[directly, one worker on either side, opposite each other, the axe-strokes to alternate with each other. Detailed instructions such as these are invariably given to such laborers in the West Indies].

Both men had demurred. They were not of the village, it is true, not, certainly, Dahomeyans. But—they had some idea, even after generations away from "Guinea," that here was something strange; something over which the suitable course was to "go stupid." Both men, therefore, "went stupid" forthwith.

Grumbach, as was usual with him, poor fellow, was vastly annoyed by this process. I could hear him barge out at the laborers; see him gesticulate. Then from the nearest, he seized the axe and attacked the tree himself. He struck a savage blow at it, then, gathering himself together, for he was stout like the middle-aged of all his class, and unused to such work, he struck again, somewhat above the place where the first axe-blow had landed on the tree.

"You'd better stop him, Carrington," said I, "and I will explain my reasons to you afterwards."

Carrington cupped his hands and shouted, and both negroes looked towards us. But Grumbach, apparently, had not heard, or, if he had, supposed that the words were directed to somebody other than himself. Thus, everybody within view was occupied, you will note—Carrington looking at Grumbach; the two laborers looking towards us; Grumbach intent upon making an impression on the tough coconut wood. I alone, for some instinctive reason, thought suddenly of Silvio Fabricius, and directed my gaze towards the point, down the long field, over which horizon he would appear when returning.

Perhaps it was the sound of the axe's impact against his brother the tree apprehended by a set of senses for seventeen years attuned to the tree's moods and rustlings, to the "messages" which his brother the tree imparted to him; perhaps some uncanny instinct merely, that arrested him in his course towards the village down there, carrying the current "message" from the tree about to-morrow's weather.

As I looked, Silvio Fabricius, running lightly, erect, came over the distant horizon of the lower field's bosomed slope. He stopped there, a distant figure, but clearly within my view. Without taking my eyes off him I spoke again to Carrington:

"You must stop Grumbach, Carrington—there's more in this than you know. Stop him—at once!"

And, as Carrington shouted a second time, Grumbach raised the axe for the third blow at the tree, the blow which did not land.

As the axe came up, Silvio Fabricius, a distant figure down there, reached for the small sharp canebill which hung beside him from his trouser-belt, a cutting tool with which he smoothed the bark of his brother the tree on occasion, cut out annually the choking mass of "cloth" from its top, removed fading fronds as soon as their decay reached the stage where they were no longer benefiting the tree, cut his coconuts. I could see the hot sunlight flash against the wide blade of the canebill as though it had been a small heliograph-mirror. Fabricius was about a thousand yards away. He raised the canebill in the empty air, and with it made a sudden, cutting, pulling motion downwards; a grave, almost a symbolic movement. Fascinated, I watched him return the canebill to its place, on its hook, fastened to the belt at the left side.

But, abruptly, my attention was distracted to what was going on nearer at hand. Carrington's shout died, half-uttered. Simultaneously I heard the yells of uncontrollable, sudden terror from the two laborers at the tree's foot. My eyes, snatched away from the distant tree-man, turned to Carrington beside me, glimpsing a look of terrified apprehension; then, with the speed of thought, towards the tree where one laborer was in the act of falling face-downward on the ground—I caught the terrified white gleam of his rolled eyes—the other, twisting himself away from the tree towards us, the very personification of crude horror, his hands over his eyes. And my glance was turned just in time to see the great coconut which, detached from its heavy, fibrous cordage up there, sixty feet above the ground, struck Grumbach full and true on the wide pith helmet which he affected, planterwise, against the sun.

He seemed almost to be driven into the ground by the impact. The axe flew off at an angle past the tree.

He never moved. And when, with the help of the two laborers, Carrington and I, having summoned a cart from the nearby road-gang cutting bushes, lifted the body, the head which had been that poor devil Grumbach's, was merely a mass of sodden pulp.

We took the body down the road in the cart, towards his newly erected manager's house. And a few yards along our way Silvio Fabricius passed us, running erectly, his sombre face expressionless, his stride a kind of dignified lope, glancing not to right or left, speeding straight to his brother the tree which had been injured in his absence.

Looking back, where the road took a turn, I saw him, leaning now close beside the tree, his long fingers probing the two gashes which Hans Grumbach, who would never swing another axe, had made there, about two feet above the ground; while aloft the glorious fronds of the massive tree burgeoned like great sails in the afternoon Trade.

Later that afternoon we sent the mortal remains of Hans Grumbach down the long hill road to Frederiksted in a cart, decently disposed, after telephoning his wife's relatives to break the sorrowful news to her. It was Carrington who telephoned, at my suggestion. I told him that they would appreciate it, he being the head of the company. Such *nuances* have their meaning in the West Indies where the finer shades are of an importance. He explained that it was an accident, gave the particulars as he had seen them with his own eyes—Grumbach had been working under a tall coconut-palm and a heavy coconut, falling, had struck him and killed him instantly. It had been a quite merciful death. . . .

The next morning[—we were at that time sleeping at Great Fountain as we oversaw in person the carrying out of the basic works there—] I walked up towards the fountain again, alone, after a sleepless night of cogitation. I walked across the section of field between the newly-grubbed roadside and the great tree. I walked straight up to the tree-man, stood beside him. He paid no attention to me whatever. I spoke to him:

"Fabricius," said I, "it is necessary that I should speak to you."

The tree-man turned his gaze upon me gravely. Seen thus, face to face, he was a remarkably handsome fellow, now about thirty years of age, his features regular, his expression calm, inscrutable; wise with a wisdom certainly not Caucasian, such as to put into my mind the phrase: "not of this world." He bowed, gravely, as though assuring me of his attention.

I said: "I was looking at you yesterday afternoon when you came back to your tree, over the lower end of the field—down there." I indicated where he had stood with a gesture. Again he bowed, without any change of expression.

"I wish to have you know," I continued, "that I understand; that no one else besides me saw you, saw what you did—with the cane-bill, I mean. I wish you to know that what I saw I am keeping to myself. That is all."

Silvio Fabricius the tree-man continued to look into my face, without any visible change whatever in his expression. For the third time he nodded, presumably to indicate that he understood what I had said, but utterly without any emotion whatever. Then, in a deep, resonant voice, he spoke to me, the first and last time I have ever heard him utter a word.

"Yo' loike to know, yoong marster," said he, with an impressive gravity, "me brudda,"—he placed a hand against the tree's smooth trunk—"t'ink hoighly 'bout yo', sar. Ahlso 'bout de enterprise fo' pineopples. Him please, sar, yoong marster; him indicate-me yo' course be serene an' ahlso of a profit." The tree-man bowed again, and without another word or so much as a glance in my direction, detaching his attention from me as deliberately as he had given it when I first spoke to him, he turned towards his brother the tree, laid his face against its bark, and slowly encircled the massive trunk with his two great muscular black arms. . . .

I arrived on the island in the middle of October, 1928, coming down as usual from New York after my summer in the States. Great Fountain had suffered severely in the hurricane of the previous month, and when I arrived there I found Carrington well along with the processes of restoration. Many precautions had been taken beforehand and our property had been damaged because of these much less than the other estates. I had told Carrington, who had a certain respect for my familiarity with "native manners and customs," enough about the tree-man and his functions tribally to cause him to heed the warning, transmitted by the now nearly helpless old patriarch of the village, and brought in by the tree-man four days before the hurricane broke—and two days before the government cable-advice had reached the island.

Silvio Fabricius had stayed beside his tree. On the third day, when it was for the first time possible for the villagers to get as far as the upper end of the great field near the fountain, he had been found, Carrington reported to me, lying in the field, dead, his face composed inscrutably, the great trunk of his brother the tree across his chest which had been crushed by its great weight when it had been uprooted by the wind and fallen.

And until they wore off there had been smears of earth, Carrington said, on the heads and faces of all the original Dahomeyan villagers and upon the heads and faces of several of the newer laborer families as well.

The Ogham Stone

Frank Coffman

In sight of Tara Hill he found the cave,
Long-hidden in the foliage of the Sidhe.
Venturing in, his torch beam caught the stone!
No way to know its age. It eerily gave
Off a faint greenish glow. Expectancy
Grew as he realized that he alone
Could claim discovery of this wondrous prize
Not seen for—who knew how long?—by human eyes.

He quickly scanned the markings lichened o'er.
Clearly in ogham. But an ancient tongue!
Proto–Celtic? No, these words must date before
Even that! To before that tribe was young!
Yet along each stave the marks were well-defined.
Below the lines were shapes . . . strangely designed.

Etched deep into that ancient long-lost rock
Were images that filled him with misgiving.
Along with the thrill of finding it, the shock
Of those shapes that showed no creature living
Nor any long extinct! *What warped soul drew*
Such things? So awful, yet so very real-seeming?
Perhaps the text, once solved would give a clue
About these forms—from Hells of darkest dreaming.

He noted all the ogham signs with care
They must read right to left, he realized.
Well, that's the reverse of normal. But there
Were some uncommon marks that were incised

Along with the letters that were all well-known.
Still, he felt sure that he could solve the stone.

He did not try to sketch the horrid shapes,
But photographed the stone. The shadows thrown
By the flash were . . . odd? Reality escapes
Sometimes when one is in an alien zone.
Just the excitement of the find, he thought.
Yet, those brief, weird shadows seemed to show
Things in that mystic cave that clearly were not
Present as shapes in the red, dim sunset glow!

He hurriedly left the cave before nightfall,
Covering the entrance with the cut and broken brush
He'd cleared away that morning. A strong call
Was beckoning him back to camp. Yet he would not rush
The decipherment of those weird, ancient signs.
The photo first! His mind plagued by those vile designs.

*   *   *

The photo of the stone was well-exposed;
Nine rows of ogham and the shapes below
Stood out against the darkness of the stone.
The things depicted there were all opposed
To any reality a *rational* mind could know.
They showed *beings!* But what abysmal zone
Could hold such things! He cut the print in two—
So only the ogham writings were in view.
The lower half he hastily concealed
Inside the drawer within his writing slope.
To solve this ancient puzzle was his hope,
Find what secrets the ancient marks revealed.
And so, he worked on into that stormy night,
Epigraphy more difficult by lantern light.

The ogham letters themselves were clear enough,
But the language they conveyed was none he'd seen.
Also, the weird glyphs that seemed part of the script
Were alien. Those pictographs made for only rough
Guesses at possible meanings he might glean.
Those eldritch markings were weird oddities to decrypt.
And so, he guessed, *Perhaps from the previous eon?*
Ah yes! A form of Proto-Indo European!

But a most strange dialect of that wide-spread tongue,
This predates that! Humankind was very young
When this strange language was last spoken!
But with that key the secret would be broken.
The linguist knew more labor would reveal
What those who hid the stone wished to conceal.

Yet some of the words were beyond the linguist's ken—
Some words are in no language known to men!
They must be names! He thought. The context made that clear.
But names so strange their mere utterance brought on fear!
Cthulhu, Azathoth, Shub-Niggurath,
Nyarlathotep, Tsathoggua, Yog-Sothoth . . .
The list of vile, malifluous names when on,
Including it seemed these beings and their spawn.

The transcription proved it was an incantation.
To be chanted by nine men circled 'round the stone.
Call them forth! Say their names! Bring them here!
Not merely shadows! Bring their incarnation!
Call them hither from Night's Nether Zone!
Each passage he transcribed increased his fear.

All through next day and night, and next and next
He labored with success upon the text.
A few words here and there—then more came clear.

Then, suddenly, in horror—at last he knew!
But this can't be! he thought. Mind-numbing fear
Grew in him as he realized it was true!
With trembling hand, he drew out the bottom part
Of the photograph that he had hidden away.

Examining it, cold horror clutched his heart.
Those images! The Old Ones on display!
The chant in those weird runes confirmed it all.
They were coming! Some were here! Humankind's fall
Would be summoned by the words upon the stone—
Those beings from the Cosmos' darkest zone.

Those words were not some chant from Druidry
As he had first surmised—no Celtic mystery
Was etched in lines and symbols on that stone.
. . . Just then he knew that he was not alone
In that rude tent. For shadows on its walls
Showed *Them! . . . Their Shapes at least*—though not yet here.
And only a tenuous barrier forestalls
Their coming. But *They* are drawing near!

Merely to translate this vile chant had invoked
A testing of that Veil that keeps them back
Beyond our realm. *Reading it has provoked*
The sending of these shades that substance lack!
He'd read the words of awful summoning
He knew well what performing them would bring.
All through the next day he labored at the cave,
With stones he blocked the entrance with a wall
Of treble thickness, covered over with soil
And brush he'd cut. Some uprooted, replanted gave
A "natural" look. For his hope was to foil
A future finding of the cave and stone within.
By twilight, back at his tent and finished with all

But the final act. He trembled to begin
The terrible but necessary deed.
At least our world will—for a time—be freed
From the summoning of those horrid Things.
With that, he poured the extra kerosene
On every tent wall, the photographs, his translation . . .
Then over himself! The horrible text he'd seen . . .
His memory too would die in the conflagration.
His last act was to swing and smash the lamp,
Immolating himself . . . destroying all that camp!

But fluttering in that blaze's whipped up wind,
A strip of negatives remained intact.
The image of the stone survived! That artifact
We must hope no living soul will ever find.

How to Speak to a Cyber God

Maxwell I. Gold

There weren't instructions for this, for the inevitable cruelties where in the beginning I found myself isolated from reason and smiles; confined to the dank, putrid closets of my brain. That's where *they* found me—the Cyber Gods, fourteen billion years at the edge of the universe, they waited for me, and others like me. There were thousands like us—so desperate to become their flesh-conduits. A cyber-trash-hole on the dirt and sod spinning in the middle of the dark nothingness, we were the mouthpieces for the Infinite and the Demented.

Laughter, it always began with laughter like the whispers and scratches beneath my skill, welling up into some bemoaned song as if I were calling out for the death of the stars themselves. They laughed at me—continuously and for what seemed like forever—without a discerning thought, the Cyber Gods cared not for language. Their treasons against language made me snigger.

Next, came the taste of blood and metal under my lips. They said I didn't need my teeth, tongue, or primitive faculties except the throbbing mass within my brain, a broken consciousness filled with laughter. Bodily pain from the loss of blood and bile quickly numbed with each belly laugh and brain scratch. Words weren't important when communicating with the Cyber Gods, but only the inevitable, the unthinkable which felt as normal as the blood-soaked rain drops pulsing across the remnants of my shattered self. These nightmarish signifiers sung in awful music of what-could-be cackling in pulchritudinous death-songs that littered the world with the laughter of the Cyber Gods. Don't worry, though, they'll be here soon, *you* won't need instructions for anything—ever again.

Threnody for the Witch of Kings Cross

Manuel Pérez-Campos

Panther of silence; god of Night; Lord of the wild inhuman stars:
—Rosaleen Norton, "Black Magic"

Norton was once asked: "What would be the state of the world if evil ruled?"

She replied: "Precisely what it is."
—Marguerite Johnson, "Pan or the Devil?
The Polytheistic Beliefs of Rosaleen Norton"

I. *An Act of Will*

Enswathed in a white funebreal gown of gauze
spun by spiders which have fallen out of parted
lips, she of the pointed ears who has never
been weaned of moonlight has been collecting
strength in a wheelchair from incantation throughout
the painshriek-haunted hospice she is immured in
that once more a favorite of Hecate she may
lurch out skyclad with grey hair dishevelled
and stand wind-numbed in a dry-fountained
courtyard waked by briar and eglantine so
that the ghosts of birds panicking like small
mountain gods because their former mentors,
the hamadryads, keep dissolving into fizzling
particles under siege of black-twirled
flames may quell their thirst at cylix held aloft.

II. Self-Judgment

Extending succour to whoso is fortune-chafed
but invisible, regardless of hideous hazard to herself
is how she has resolved to rebel against the indifference
of so many galaxies and more immediately against
that rambling labyrinth interminable of casements
erratically erected by madmen that is Kings Cross:
O has she not sibilated the rumble of a Luciferian blessing
while rocked forward by imp-possessed besom under
the massive crackle of a dark buffeting to a ram-horned demon
as tall as the stars, an antediluvian annihilator of worlds,
who had been parallelizing her in imploration and who was
already translucent because half ripened into a hollow shell
that wrenched out of it a vision of incipient doom within
which it was able to invent a path and regain—if only
for a glorious moment—the power of being substantial?

III. Augury

Having exo-somatized, she wanders in billowed dalmatica
and watarah blossom in hair an effulgent shoreline
as though its gathering storm's bird bride, in intimate inner
conversation with the holy beings of an inscrutable future
which writhes like a sublime vapour under the bar.
Strangely they murmur until—immobile lest she swoon—
she probes through their vast inhuman minds what to them
is an archaic past, the unprecedented depletion of Pan's kingdom
through whirlwinds spawned by the wizards of that
presumptive age to whom her nocturnal paintings
of transpagan outcry are a thorn: until she groks
that the twentieth century is like a magical ceremony to disjoin
from every living thing those aeons of creative play on which
nature, that dangerous flourisher, is made on: and meanwhile
her hand-mirrour tells her there is no hearth at journey's end.

IV. Dematerialization

Imperceptible in her wheelchair beside a thunderhead-
tremored windowpane, that wide-spanning protean she
of the taloned feet who has already vanished from the aubade
of the cicada and of whom all that shall soon remain
is scattered foam with superfluity inexhaustible
insufflates a spinning carmine mist of serpentine
intrigue which adjures psychopomps out of her spectre-saturated
subconscious and whose loose whisperings beguiles the nuns in
their candle-litten cells into combing further their long-crimped hair:
and meanwhile irremediably absent feral cats
she has cared for and who have been removed without
consent from dayside thought begin to look at her
with alacrity from the ends of continually twisting
corridors and from behind half open doors: yet silent,
and always at a distance which cannot be overcome.

Ave, Nightmare

Carl E. Reed

We fall each night into weirdling sleep
to hallucinate, quite insane;
limbs akimbo 'neath thrashed-out sheets
our worlds-of-wonder brains

"knit up the raveled sleave of care"
by staging surrealist life:
We wander, argue, fight & flee
the unconscious mind midwife

to many a startling, illogical scene
of menace & rising tension.
How call this rest? Such rest, at best:
but panic, rage, frustration!

Worst of all: sad, tawdry tales
quotidian, tepid, banal—
fool-films played to dispiriting ends:
lost lucre, loves, bacchanals.

Bring on the nightmare bold & rare!
Relief from the grind of tedious
problem-solving in mundane dreams—
far better the outré, the hideous!

Forfend, I say! Drear clock-punch dreams
that find us hard at work—at work.
Queue the monsters! Mayhem! Mars!
scares to awaken us with a jerk.

Witch-Hunting Literature 101

Katherine Kerestman

I. A Brief Historical Overview of Western Attitudes toward Witches

From time immemorial there have been wise women and men, people who possess a knack for healing wounds, calming fevers, reducing anxiety. They might know how to make a cow more productive of milk or a parcel of land yield a greater harvest. They might recite prayers or sing softly while massaging oil or unguent into your aching temple. The wise ones live in every corner of the globe, and it is to them that people went for help with their troubles in the days before medicine became a science and a profession. Sometimes, though, people asked the wise ones to aid them in matters of vengeance and evil deeds; when these malevolent efforts were found out, the perpetrators were prosecuted in the arena of secular law, for murder or theft and so forth, but not for the practice of magic.

In the eleventh century, however, when the Catholic Church was vigorously trying to consolidate its temporal and spiritual hegemony over Europe, it kept running into resistance. From the Cathars, who popped up in Southern Europe in the twelfth century, to the pious baptized and catechized simple folk in the villages of England, who continued to seek out the wise ones for help warding off early frost in the fall or drought in the spring, the church kept encountering freethinkers whose unorthodoxy threatened the centralized theocracy it was building. The church labeled divergent views "heresy" and freethinkers as "heretics." And it created the Inquisition to test the orthodoxy of people's faith and to cleanse the church of suspected heretics. Most lapsed Catholics were tried, sentenced, and given penances. More blatant departures from official doctrine resulted in burning at the stake. Canon law divided the legal responsibilities between ecclesiastical and civil courts, and these divisions varied between different countries and over time.

In the thirteenth century, Pope Innocent III crusaded lustily to wrest the Holy Land from the Muslim infidels and to put down the Cathars and other heretics on the home front; furthermore, he declared that all heretical views were a de facto worship of Satan. Pope Innocent VIII was equally zealous in his enforcement of strict orthodoxy—and that is why, in 1484, Inquisitor Heinrich Kramer sought and obtained His Holiness's official sanction for his personal brand of witch-hunting and witch-extermination. Alarmed at the sudden outbreak of witchery in Germany which Kramer had brought to his attention, in the aftermath of the Black Plague, when post-traumatic manifestations such as "mass flagellation and dance mania" (Summers 20) betokened a society run amok, Innocent VIII issued his endorsement of Kramer, which took the form of *Summis desiderentes affectibus*. In *Malleus Maleficarum*, his 1486 pope-approved witch-hunting manual, Kramer expounds his theory of witchcraft and offers guidelines for finding out witches, proving witchcraft in courts of law, and sentencing convicted witches (Jacob Sprenger is listed as Kramer's co-author).

II. Witch Lit

Around 1440, Johannes Gutenberg invented the moveable-type printing press, inaugurating the literary phenomenon of the bestseller featuring horror, sex, and violence. In 1499, for instance, German pamphlets featuring gruesome woodcut pictures of Vlad the Impaler dining in the shadow of his Forest of the Impaled sold as fast as the monks could print them. For those with deeper purses, books such as *Malleus Maleficarum* and Henri Boguet's *Examen of Witches* found eager readers and became the authority and precedent that witch-hunters and tribunals in Europe and colonial America would cite to validate their own work over the next three centuries.

While witch-hunting literature details many of the marvelous things witches can do, flying remains the perennial favorite. In *The*

History of Witchcraft and Demonology, a modern witch-hunting manual published in 1926, Montague Summers (an Anglican cleric and latter-day Catholic, as well as a prolific author of popular books on witchcraft and the occult) asks: if saints and mediums can levitate, why cannot witches? (122–24). That witches generally fly to their blasphemous meetings in the woods is a matter of general agreement among demonologists of every sort, including Summers, Kramer and Sprenger, Boguet, and John Hale. Reverend Hale, in *A Modest Enquiry into the Nature of Witchcraft* (1697), looks back upon the Salem witch trials of 1692, candidly commenting upon the deadly errors committed in Salem's flawed implementation of the witch-hunting protocols; and yet, he maintains that witchcraft still thrives and that witches continue to fly to their meetings on sticks or poles.

Afflicting is another recurrent motif of the witch-hunting manuals: witches harm other people, animals, and the natural environment. Cotton Mather relates the terrible afflictions suffered by numerous witch victims: for example, in his description of the brutalization of the Goodwin family of Boston, he meticulously delineates the evil actions of their washerwoman, who was eventually hanged as a witch:

> The variety of their tortures increased continually; and tho about Nine or Ten at Night they alwaies had a Release from their miseries, and *ate & slept* all night for the most part indifferently well, yet in the *day* time they were handled with so many *sorts* of Ails, that it would require of us almost as much time to *Relate* them all, as it did of them to *Endure* them. Sometimes they would be *Deaf,* sometimes *Dumb,* and sometimes *Blind,* and often, *all this* at once. One while their *Tongues* would be drawn down their Throats; another while they would be pull'd out upon their *Chins,* to a prodigious length. They would have their *Mouths* opened unto such a Wideness, that their *Iaws* went out of joint; and anon they would clap together again with a Force like that of a strong *Spring-Lock.* The same would happen to their *Shoulder-Blades,* and their *Elbows,* and *Hand-wrists,* and several of their joints. They would at

times ly in a benummed condition; and be drawn together as those that are ty'd *Neck* & *Heels;* and presently be *stretched out,* yea, drawn *Backwards*... (Hill 19)

In his *Daemonologie,* King James I/VI tells us that witches "make spirits to follow and trouble persons, or haunt certain houses, and affright oftentimes the inhabitants" (Tyson 130)—and, worse, they raise tempests—"either upon sea or land, though not universally, but in such a particular place and prescribed bounds, as God will permit them so to trouble" (Tyson 130), so that they may commit regicide and topple the Christian Church. Additionally, they sicken livestock and diminish a cow's milk, wither crops, and are generally responsible for every ill occurrence.

It is children who tend to receive the brunt of the witches' penchant for afflicting; for, in addition to "blasphemously offering them to devils" (Kramer and Sprenger 150), witches steal unbaptized children and kill them in order to prevent their entering the kingdom of heaven. Witch midwives "surpass all other witches in their crimes" (Kramer and Sprenger 275), for they have the greatest opportunity for afflicting, and many miscarriages are blamed on the evil meddling of the witch midwives: "For in the diocese of Basel at the town of Dann, a witch who was burned confessed that she had killed more than forty children, by sticking a needle through the crowns of their heads into their brains as they came out of the womb" (Kramer and Sprenger 150).

Montague Summers states that the witches waste no parts of the babes they kill: "Their blood, brains, and bones were used to decoct magic philtres" (160), and one witch made a candle out of an infant's arm and baked the rest of the child in a pie. He states that this practice continues today in Africa and Haiti (163).

Sexual congress and fertility are other especial targets of witchy affliction of their neighbors: "First, when they directly prevent the erection of the member which is accommodated to fructification . . . Secondly, when they prevent the flow of the vital essences to the members in which reside the motive force, closing up the seminal ducts so that it does not reach the seminal vessels or so that it cannot be ejaculated, or is fruitlessly spilled" (Kramer and Sprenger 126). Sometimes they make a man's member disappear entirely.

The witch-hunting manuals wax eloquent not only on the subject of killing children and the prevention of live births, but on witch-sex as well; to wit, Antide Colas of Betoncourt in the district of Baume, in prison on suspicion of witchcraft, was subjected to a body search,

> and it was found when visiting her that she had a hole beneath her navel, quite contrary to nature. This hole was examined on the eleventh of July, 1598, by Master Nicolas Milliere of Regnaucourt, Chirurgeon, who thrust his probe deeply into it in the presence of his servant, and witnesses; and then the witch confessed that her Devil, whom she called Lizabet, had sexual connexion with her through this hole, and her husband through the natural hole. (Boguet 33)

In *An Examen of Witches* (1603), Henri Boguet expounds upon the monstrous births attendant upon such diabolical couplings.

Witch-hunting manuals assert that sex with Satan is one of the lures the Prince of Darkness uses to recruit his followers:

> The Devil uses [women] so because he knows that women love carnal pleasures, and he means to bind them to his allegiance by such agreeable provocations. Moreover, there is nothing which makes a woman more subject and loyal to a man than that he should abuse her body.
>
> And since male witches are addicted no less than female to this pleasure, the Devil also appears as a woman to satisfy them. (Boguet 29)

These relations usually occur during orgies at the Sabbat, in the woods to which they fly on their brooms or sticks. Part of the ceremonies includes the Satanic Kiss, the oscular salutation upon the bum of Old Nick. Montague Summers often refers to the "artificial penis" (98), a utensil required because Satan must service large numbers of his followers. Unfortunately, although Satan tempts his sex partners to join his fold with the promise of carnal pleasure, witches report that they do not find sex with Satan entirely pleasurable. Accused witch Jacquema Paget stated "that she had several times taken in her hand the member of the Demon which lay with her, and that it was cold as ice and a good finger's length, but not so thick as that of a man" (Boguet 31). Other witches complain of discomfort, bodily pain, and cold semen.

Accusations are another feature common to witch-hunting manuals. In the context of the witch trials, accusations are *evidence*. The more people who accuse a suspected witch, or the greater the standing of the accuser, the stronger the evidence provided by accusations. Children frequently accuse their mothers or fathers. People with whom one has previously quarreled may become accusers; also, people who have experienced misfortune and who are looking for somewhere to cast the blame may become accusers. Once accusations are hurled, guilt is assumed, and an accused witch must prove her innocence. Notwithstanding the fact that many fakings have been documented over the centuries—accounts of people who knowingly pretended to have been bewitched, or to have had seizures or other afflictions—still each accusation is given due consideration by the legal and ecclesiastical divisions of society.

In *A Modest Enquiry into the Nature of Witchcraft*, Reverend John Hale tries to make sense of the Salem witch trials, through which tragedy he had just lived. Although Hale has no doubt that witches exist and that they must be found out, he expresses doubts about some of the means and methods used. While an accusation made by an accused person "hath been accounted sufficient proof by Common Law" (85), it is known that some officers promise confessors favors in return for accusation of others, and even that some people falsely accuse others; thus, Hale asserts that accusations made by accused persons ought not to be counted as evidence. Traditionally, the more accusations against a person, the greater the evidence; but, for Hale, it was "the number of persons accused" that tipped him off that they were going too far in Salem (38). In *A Discourse of the*

Damned Art of Witchcraft (1631), William Perkins quotes the Judicious Bernard of Batcomb, who, in his *Guide to Grand-Jury Men* (1627), places, on his list of "shrewd Presumptions of a Witch," accusations made

> by one or more Fellow-Witches, Confessing their own Witchcraft, and bearing Witness against others; if they can make good the Truth of their Witness, and give sufficient proof of it. As, that they have seen them with their Spirits, or, that they have Received Spirits from them; or that they can tell, when they used Witchery-Tricks to Do Harm; or, that they told them what Harm they had done. (Trask 135)[1]

And "The Testimony of the Party bewitched" is proof, too, according to John Gaule, the author of *Select Cases of Conscience* (1646); Gaule is also quoted in the Perkins book (Trask 134).

Accusations, of course, are not the only form of evidence available to witch-hunters. In the case of the Goodwin family of Boston, discussed above, Cotton Mather relates that the magistrates applied several time-honored tests to ascertain the guilt or innocence of the accused. That the laundress was unable to recite the Lord's Prayer was proof of her diabolical nature; and when her home was searched they found poppets therein—and, furthermore, whenever she took the poppets in her hand the children fell into fits. To top it off, Mather states that the laundress had been previously accused, and accusation equals evidence: the laundress in question was the daughter of a woman "whose miserable husband, before he died, had sometimes complained of her, that she was undoubtedly a witch" (Hill 18).

The witch's mark is a principal feature of witch-hunting manuals. According to Summers, "The Devil give them a Mark, which Marks they renew as often as those Persons have any desire to quit him," and the mark is the "most important point in the identifica-

---

1. "On the very first day of the first Salem Village examination, Rev. Parris was presented with a William Perkins volume describing the proper method of detecting witchcraft" (Trask 132).

tion of a witch" (70). Marks do not produce pain; neither do they bleed when pricked with a pin. They may serve as witches' teats, for suckling their familiars who drink their blood. In a protracted exposition of many pages on marks, Summers quotes numerous authorities and provides detailed explanations of the moles, skin tags, warts, and other blemishes and how professional "prickers" (who are paid per witch discovered) locate marks on women's pudenda, inner thighs, necks, and so forth—after the witches are stripped of their clothes, their bodies shaved and offered up to the close scrutiny of inquisitors. Matthew Hopkins, the Witch-Finder General, in *A Discoverie of Witches* (1642), a treatise in which he defends himself from accusations of witch-finder quackery, states that, while some marks may be natural warts, piles, and so forth, trained prickers know the difference between natural and unnatural marks. Hopkins traveled with female assistants, his professional prickers. The Reverend Hale, while advocating a more judicious application of all these time-honored tests, outright rejects the mark as evidence, believing marks to be no more than natural blemishes.

Another recurring element of the handbooks is the water test, and that was one of Hopkins's personal favorites. His method was tying the accused's hands and feet to a chair and then throwing it into a body of water. Floating is a sure sign of witchcraft, for the water rejects witches as they rejected the water of their baptism; drowning proves one's innocence. (Hopkins writes that he never tortured a witch, that the accused all volunteered of their own free will to undergo the water test, and they also went days without sleep of their own accord, the better to practice their black magic.)

Among the recurring motifs in witch-hunting handbooks is witches' inability to pray, considered hard evidence of guilt, as Cotton Mather describes in his story of the Goodwins. The inability to cry provides further confirmation. And then there is the Evil Eye, which casts evil onto the recipient of its gaze, another common proof of sorcery. In chronicling the saga of the Carys of Charlestown, Massachusetts (in which Captain Nathaniel Cary helps his wife Martha escape from the Salem jail after her arrest for witchcraft), in *More Wonders of the Invisible World* (1700), Robert Calef exposes what he considers the kangaroo nature of the judiciary proceedings of Salem. Calef particularly has it in for Cotton Mather, Salem's resident demonologist and the New World's preeminent authority on witch-hunting. Calef reiterates that saying the Lord's Prayer is a test still in use,[2] and he states that, in the court, the prisoners' eyes had to remain always on the judges, lest their gaze fall upon the afflicted girls. (It is true that every time the accused looked at the girls they would resume their writhings and cryings-out.) Spectral (i.e., invisible or visible only to the afflicted girls) evidence is the most salient feature of the American witch trials. The accused would send their spirits to torment the afflicted girls, not only in their bedrooms in the dead of night, but in the courtroom as well. Calef also relates the application of the Touch Test: whenever the accused would touch the convulsing afflicted girls, their afflictions would instantly cease. The gaze and touch tests count as verifiable evidence. He relates how Cary, after his wife's transfer to the Salem jail, follows her to Salem:

> The trial of Salem coming on, I went thither, to see how things were managed; and finding that the spectre evidence was there received, together with idle, if not malicious stories, against people's lives, I did easily perceive which way the rest would go; for the same evidence that served for one would serve for all the rest [i.e. the Afflicted Girls' writhings] . . . if she were carried to Salem to be tried, I feared she would never return. (Hill 70)

Torture was often required to obtain the necessary evidence in witch-hunting, for the Devil gives the power of silence to his witches. Part III of *Malleus Maleficarum* is distinguished by chapter titles

---

2. When the Reverend George Burroughs faced his executioners, he was able to recite the Lord's Prayer, free of errors, but he was hanged anyway, for Cotton Mather, seated on his horse, told the crowd that Burroughs's guilt had been established in court, and that the Devil could lie through him.

that read like this: "Of the method of sentencing prisoners to examination by torture" and "Of the method of proceeding with the torture, and how they are to be tortured; and the provisions against silence on the part of the witch." Torture must not be applied too hastily, nor without preparation, for a prisoner must first be worn down: "Unless God, through a holy angel, compels the devil to withhold his help from the witch, she will be so insensible to the pains of torture that she will sooner be torn limb from limb than confess any of the truth" (Kramer and Sprenger 220). Witches don't really feel pain, unless they are *involuntary* servants of Satan, that is: "And it is such whom the devil deserts without any compulsions by a holy angel; and therefore they readily confess their crimes, whereas others, who have from their hearts bound themselves to the devil, are so protected by his power and preserve a stubborn silence" (Kramer and Sprenger 220–21).

A confession must be obtained one way or the other, for that is the clincher, the conclusive proof which they are after: "Wherefore, that the truth may be known from your own mouth, and that henceforth you may not offend the ears of the Judges, we declare, judge and sentence on this present day and at such an hour, you be placed under the question and torture" (Kramer and Sprenger 221). Just imagine hearing that pronouncement in court!

Since "it is as difficult, or more difficult, to compel a witch to tell the truth as it is to exorcise a person possessed of the devil" (Kramer and Sprenger 221), *Malleus Maleficarum* offers an easy-to-follow guide for torture. First, keep postponing the questioning, so that the accused may rot in jail and think about what is to come. Then, strip the person forthwith and search her clothes (note: in the torture section of *Malleus Maleficarum* the authors switch from the generic "he" to almost exclusively female pronouns) for instruments of witchcraft sewn into the seams. Then,

> The third precaution to be observed . . . is that the hair should be shaved from every part of the body. The reason for this is the same as that for stripping her of her clothes, which we have already

mentioned; for in order to preserve their power of silence they are in the habit of hiding some superstitious object in their clothes or in their hair, or even in the most secret parts of their bodies which must not be named.[3] (Kramer and Sprenger 226)

Keep promising her that a confession will save her soul and stave off torture (but still end in death). Bind her. After she has had time to think, apply the torture. The torturers must appear saddened by their grievous task. Tight bands about the head, limbs stretched from their sockets—these must be periodically interrupted with assurances that there will be relief if a confession is made. Promise her life in prison, rather than burning (note: it is not necessary to keep one's promises to a witch, the text states), if she names her confederates. If she does name people, she'll burn anyway. If she will not confess:

> while she is being questioned about each several point, let her be often and frequently exposed to torture, beginning with the more gentle of them, for the Judge should not be too hasty to proceed to the graver kind. And while this is being done, let the Notary write all down, how she is tortured and what questions are asked and how she answers. (Kramer and Sprenger 223)

After three days of torture, they are to take a break and set a date for the resumption of torture. The prisoner should always be guarded against suicide, for the Devil tempts them to it.

The Inquisitor will succeed: "there are so many means open to us which we may use either in their own proper form or in some equivalent form, so that the truth will be had from their own mouths and they can be consigned to the flames; or failing this, God will provide some other death for the witch" (Kramer and Sprenger 227). Just ask her if she is willing to undergo the trial by red hot iron rather than confess.

---

3. "Now in the parts of Germany such shaving, especially of the secret parts, is not generally considered delicate, and therefore we Inquisitors do not use it; but we cause the hair of their head to be cut off" (Kramer and Sprenger 227).

The Good Cop/Bad Cop strategy is suggested: i.e., getting a witch to talk with a trusted person while a hidden spy is listening. Should she confess *and repent,* she will be allowed to receive the sacrament and be prayed with before her execution.

III. The Hunters

Thus, Kramer and Sprenger, the men who wrote the book (literally) on witch-hunting, spawning a genre of popular literature. It seems that people have always needed their fix of sex and violence in their reading (look at ancient pictographs on cave walls), and when sensational literature served the needs of the church, the X-rated literature was officially sanctioned. Kramer is responsible for the text of *Malleus Maleficarum,* and he took his show on the road, applying the principles he espoused to wipe out the witches. Sprenger was later added as a co-author to lend a greater degree of credibility to the text. Between 1645 and 1645, Matthew Hopkins found his calling in cleansing his own neck of England, and witch-hunting made him wealthy. He traveled with his assistant, John Stearne, who identified 300 possible witches and was responsible for gathering evidence against them, and with his female prickers, to towns that would tax their citizens to pay for Hopkins's extermination services. Some towns refused him, however.

The afflicted girls of Salem were also witch-finders: acting as witch Geiger counters, they convulsed and screamed when touched or looked upon by a witch. Their show was taken on the road, too, to Andover and Ipswich and other towns, where they provided their services to other communities (Hill 93–94). Cotton Mather continued to write and preach the theory that validated the bloodbath of neighbor against neighbor in Salem, and which continued on until the wives of a minister and the governor were accused, at which time the proceedings ground to a halt. In 1706, Ann Putnam's confession was read to the Salem congregation by the minister, while she stood silently:

> I desire to be humbled before God for that sad and humbling
> providence that befell my father's family in the year about '92; that
> I, then being in my childhood, should, by such a providence of
> God, be made an instrument for the accusing of several persons of
> a grievous crime, whereby their lives were taken away from them,
> whom now I have just grounds and good reason to believe they
> were innocent persons; and that it was a great delusion of Satan
> that deceived me in that sad time, whereby I justly fear I have
> been instrumental, with others, though ignorantly and unwitting-
> ly, to bring upon myself and this land the guilt of innocent blood;
> though what was said or done by me against any person I can truly
> and uprightly say, before God and man, I did it not out of any an-
> ger, malice, or ill-will to any person, for I had no such thing
> against one of them; but what I did was ignorantly, being deluded
> by Satan. And particularly, as I was a chief instrument of accusing
> of Goodwife Nurse and her two sisters, I desire to lie in the dust,
> and to be humbled for it, in that I was a cause, with others, of so
> sad a calamity to them and their families; for which cause I desire
> to lie in the dust, and earnestly beg forgiveness of God, and from
> all those unto whom I have given just cause of sorrow and offence,
> whose relations were taken away or accused. (Hill 108)

She is so sorry, but she is not responsible for her actions, the Devil
made her do it—and God allowed it!

In the 1920s, Montague Summers was still concerned about
witches: "the same quintessence of sacrilege persisted throughout
the centuries, even as alas! In hidden corners and secret lairs of in-
famy skulks and lurks this very day" (146). Furthermore, "Satanists
yet celebrate the black mass in London, Brighton, Paris, Lyons,
Bruges, Berlin, Milan, and alas! in Rome, itself. Both South America and Canada are thus polluted" (151).

It is not the purpose of this study to moralize about the witch
hunts, because everyone knows that human beings have always
tended to persecute those whom they consider different or when
profitable. Our species still devours entertainments concocted of sex
and violence, especially the mingling thereof, in fantasy or in newspaper articles and true crime television—and we still thrill to witch-

hunting literature of old, whose themes culminate in the torture of (mostly) women and ends with their death, an early form of what today we call snuff literature. The witch-hunting manuals, however, did not come with "Do Not Attempt This at Home" labels affixed to their covers, but were sanctioned by church and state as a way to eliminate deviants and to strengthen central control through a system of horrible punishments and lurid rewards.

Works Cited

Baker, Emerson W. *A Storm of Witchcraft: The Salem Trials and the American Experience.* Oxford: Oxford University Press, 2015.

Boguet, Henri. *An Examen of Witches.* 1603. Tr. E. Allen Ashwin. Ed. Montague Summers. London: John Rodker, 1929.

Hale, John. *A Modest Enquiry into the Nature of Witchcraft.* 1697. Bedford, MA: Applewood Books, n.d.

Hill, Frances, ed. *The Salem Witch Trials Reader.* New York: Da Capo Press, 2000.

Hopkins, Matthew. *The Discovery of Witches.* 1642. Project Gutenberg. https://www.gutenberg.org/files/14015/14015-h/14015-h.htm

Kramer, Heinrich, and Jacobus Sprenger. *Malleus Maleficarum.* 1486. Tr. Montague Summers (1928). Paris: Adansonia Press, 2018.

Summers, Montague. *The History of Witchcraft and Demonology.* 1925. New York: Bristol Park Books, 2010.

Trask, Richard B. *"The Devil Hath Been Raised:" A Documentary History of the Salem Village Witchcraft Outbreak of March 1692.* Danvers, MA: Yeoman Press, 1997.

Tyson, Donald. *The Demonology of King James I: Includes the Original Text of Daemonologie and News from Scotland.* Woodbury, MN: Llewellyn, 2021.

The Keeper of the Lighthouse at Land's End

Kendall Evans

Sometimes he feels as if he's still a sailor
        navigating treacherous shores
Of some remote uncharted sea
    upon a starless, storm-cast night that lasts forever

His hands have grown all knobbed at joints and knuckles,
        stiff and arthritic
"It's only rheumatism," he mutters, as if the truth
        could thus be compromised
The lies he tells himself (the keeper tells himself)
    help him to survive out here
Alone, at land's end

Taking up his box of tools and lantern, the keeper of the lighthouse
        climbs around and 'round the ever-turning stairs
As he has climbed before, five thousand times and more
Until it's difficult to separate this present moment
        from so many memories
At fifth turn, mid-way up, he hesitates
    peering thru the recessed thickly-glassed embrasure
Where a close wing startles as it razor-cuts
    across his shrouded view
And the retreating shriek of the demented beast
    might be the sound of that serrate wing slicing air
Afterwards, mere emptiness; what roils there beyond the glass
        is like a mix of smoke and fog
Confusing place of changing shapes he cannot say with surety
    he's truly seen; vague shifting forms, ephemeral

*   *   *

"I am numb with the cold of chaos,"
                              he wrote in a letter to his sister, Isabelle,
"Yet doing well as be expected. Please do not bring
                              my niece to stay, as you suggested.
This is a hellish place to visit. I fear an uncle's love
                              might prove too brutish.

I am not myself. Forgive me.
Love,
Isaiah"

What are these fierce and monstrous hungers come to gnaw upon him?
                              the keeper wonders
As he spirals up the final turning of the tower's stairs
What heinous thoughts and energies that fill him
With the bile of heartfelt rage? And who but he, the keeper
                              keeps these forces dire at bay?

In the windowed chamber at the top of the stairs, he trims the wick
And lights the light, to the accompaniment of shrieking birds
Infrequently he sees their demon faces, framed by wings
        like pterodactyl wings, like elbowed arms bent wrong
Flesh fabric-taut upon a web of bones all spindle-thin
As they fly past the lighthouse tower, diving, looping, rising, turning
                              like outsized flies caracoling about a corpse

For this is the shore of Chaos, where vile birds
                              of discord and disorder congregate
And not some northern sea
This promontory the terminus of man's dominion, the light in the
        tower warns
Beacon at the gateway to a realm of lawlessness
                              principled by uncertainty

Beyond it only dervish skies, and struggling half-born forms

at war with what is real

Where true sky meets the chaos sea, all manner of tumult ensues
    Constant storms and hurricanes of unlike atmospheres op-
        posing
Sometimes the tides of chaos rise, and lap like waves all 'round the
    tower
                        and break upon the tower's outer walls

During the squalls he never acknowledges what knocks
                        to be let in, pounding,
Pounding again and again like some loose shutter
                    banging in the wind

Did he dream one recent night
        discordant birds all in a frenzy
Flying full-out at the lighthouse windows
            explosive crack and splintering of brittle panes
Berserk attack, birds dying on the spears and shards
            of broken glass, plummeting to rocks below
While others follow squirming thru the crook-toothed gaps
            of shattered glass and hollowed frames

Flames! Mouth-like beaks and talon-claws all biting,
                    gnawing, prying, clawing
At stacked but toppling, tumbling, rolling, tar-sealed barrels of lamp oil
The barrel staves prized open, broken
            oil flowing everywhere
Disordered senate of mad birds all soaked in it, wings coated
                    with flammable sheen of oily fuel
Clawed pinions blundering, blundering into the burning beacon light
The lighthouse tower become a flaming torch,
            a bright inferno in the darkness

And he himself there somewhere
                    in the fractured dream, the turmoil
Of beaks and talons, battling fiery man-sized birds that bite and scratch
Fighting to contain the hellish flames
All ending in illuminating scalded inhalation
of infernal sulfurous fumes . . .
"Only a dream," he mutters to himself
                    in hopes grim possibilities will not be realized

Plagued by rages, sweating fevered dreams and visions,
He is *not* himself, the keeper
His hair and beard have grown all wild, unkempt and colorless
As chaos frothing at the rocks below. His eyes are frayed
                              with lines of red,
The pupils slowly changed until their shape resembles
                    markings on a spider's underbelly

He fears it is not age that stoops him, but some bestial form
                    intruding, and his hands all knobbed and claw'd
—Might these painful, bone-hard nubs upon his forehead be
                    Azazel-like horns aborning?
What are these fears, these loathsome appetites
              that gnaw at him, and feed his rage?

Despite the sickness in him, he does his duty as he sees it
Climbs the stairs and trims the wick and lights the light
                              and oils the gears,
And lights the light and trims the wick, time after time,
                              night unto night

For it is nearly always night
              At land's end

Fierce-eyed, by lantern's light
              Isaiah climbs

Garden Statuary

John Shirley

A Friday afternoon in November.

"I've denuded the Victorian Lady for you," Garreth said, leading Bryan across the creaking wood floors of the kitchen, with its ceramic-coated cast-iron sink, its brass fixtures blue-green with age. "We've seen every room—and obviously this old house is going to be a bit of a squeeze. Only room left is damned small. Everything else is filled with dad's old junk, or just unlivable. Moldy. Rooms with broken windows repaired by cardboard. So unless you want to live in a root cellar . . ."

"Trying to persuade me not to move in, Garreth?" Bryan asked almost casually, following him onto the Harrow House's splintery back porch. The cousins were both in their early thirties, Bryan younger, but Garreth had a springiness to go with his long legs, the aggressiveness of his step, that Bryan envied. Bryan had steadily gained weight on his dull, dispiriting summer of tutoring.

"Just being real, Bryan. It's . . . impractical."

"Is it the girl? You need my room for the baby?"

Garreth seemed to freeze in place. "She died." He looked down at the floor. "The birthing went bad."

"Whoa! I'm sorry, man. I didn't see an announcement."

"We just didn't feel like announcing it. Just trying to put it behind us. Anyway, there's something you should see out back. Our latest backyard oddity."

Outside it was early November in New England but didn't feel like it. Half the leaves were fallen from the elms and sycamores, but the humid air was oppressively warm. The cloud cover was an opaque, featureless gray, as if horizon-to-horizon it was but one flat sheet of cloud, like a waterpot's lid seen from inside.

Sweat started out on Bryan's forehead, as he followed his cousin down the groaning back porch steps, and he regretted putting on the knit wool sweater. "The air out here," Bryan said, wiping his forehead, "feels like a damn sauna."

"Think of it as an Indian sweat lodge." Garreth winked. "You'll have visions!"

"I can do without visions."

"Hey, the weather'll change and maybe you'll wish for the sauna when the cold starts. If you're really taking this on, you've got to get some serious work done out here before it comes to freeze."

Bryan nodded resignedly. Uncle Clive had left the house to Garreth with the stipulation that Clive's nephew, Bryan, be allowed to live here free, as long as he worked in the garden at least an hour a day, five days a week. Bryan had paid his way through some of college as a gardener.

Garreth had not encouraged the move-in, but Bryan needed it. He was working as a substitute teacher while trying to sell his poetry and lyrics on the side. The substitute gig wasn't steady. The Harrow House offered free rent—with a little labor required. Living here he could save money for a modest place of his own.

But the back half-acre was a sad wreckage. From the top of the slight slope, the broad garden was beyond unkempt and cryptically humped with outcroppings. Following Garreth between the tangles of shrubs, Bryan found that what he'd taken for outcroppings were the crumbling, time-worn bases of marble and granite statues. On one pedestal he could see a pair of chipped carven marble feet along with the hem of a missing toga, and on another an effigy's granite boots. Other statues were fallen, broken apart, their faces pitted.

"The boxwood's gone wild," Bryan pointed out. "Some of it's got to be uprooted. You've got a big patch of Tree of Heaven there too. Crazy invasive stuff. And there's no order to the hydrangeas and the rose bushes."

"It used to be about the sculptures, mostly," Garreth said, looking pensively around.

"Why the ruins? Haven't seen it since I was twelve, but I remember a pretty fine display of philosophers and fairies . . ."

"The statues started to fall apart over a period of two months. We brought a specialist out, a geologist—he said the granite ones were corroding from some kind of acid coming off a fungus, and the marble ones must have been vandalized. It started after Elias Bierstone took on the gardening. Maybe it was the weird little herbs he grew here, in his personal plot, over against the fence. Mandrake for one." He pointed at the wrought-iron barrier, black where it wasn't rusted, decorated in iron ivy, topped with black spearheads. Beyond it was a rubbly field, and then a railroad track. "Elias could've brought some contamination in with his oddball herbs. Some fungus that damaged the statues."

"Never heard of a fungus that eats granite," Bryan murmured. "Nor this Elias either."

"Elias is . . . a pretty eccentric old geezer." Garreth ran the palm of his hand from his forehead to his chin—a tic of his, as if he were trying to erase a facial expression. "Dad hired him. Elias claims to be a bastard child of Aleister Crowley. For a while, out here, he dug and planted, put in a sort of design. But it went to hell fast. We had to fire him. I'm pretty sure he was doing heroin on the job. I found a syringe, for one thing. He'd just sit out here on the bench, slumped over and muttering to himself. Anyway, I think he's been mucking about in the yard again. Maybe at night when Mimi and I are asleep. Come and look."

He led the way through ivy-strangled statuary stumps to an open space in the middle. In the center of the garden stood a middling marble fountain, long dry, now choked with fallen leaves. The eroded figure of a lonely-looking dryadic nymph was frozen in mid-frolic over the bowl.

"Well *she's* intact, anyway," Bryan said, looking at the nymph. He reached out to the bowl of the fountain, to test its stability.

"Don't touch that!"

Bryan was surprised by the sudden sharpness of Garreth's warning. "Is it fragile?"

"It's . . . quite old. I don't want it to crumble like the others. It could fall over, too."

Bryan glanced at the base of the fountain—and noticed a semicircular mark of displacement on the soil. "Seems like it's been moved."

"Moved? Hasn't, no. That's not what I wanted to show you. It's—these sculptures." He stepped in front of the fountain and pointed toward the other edge of the clearing: two marble busts sitting near each other, not quite aligned. They weren't visibly mounted on anything. Their bases seemed hidden in ground moss, like old gravestones.

"Yeah, I noticed those. Busts, I guess. So at least you have some small statues, still intact."

"Not still intact. They weren't here. They just showed up."

"Showed up? This Elias brought them in?"

Garreth wiped a hand down his face. "I don't know."

"Maybe they were in the shed and he dragged them here."

The marble figures were clean, almost new, expertly formed images of a proud-looking bearded man and a handsome woman, both in Edwardian garb, about two yards apart, half turned as if looking at each other. The figures were a little more than two feet high from elbows to the top of the head. It took Bryan a long moment to recognize the faces. He'd seen them in antique sepia-toned photos. "That's Old Ethan, isn't it? And his wife?"

Garreth nodded. "Ethan Harrow and his wife Edwina. My great-grandparents. Your grand-uncle and aunt."

Bryan had used a search engine to get clearer on that part of his ancestry. *Ethan Marshall Harrow.* Patriarch of a New England family, heyday late nineteenth and early twentieth centuries. An investor in lumber and furs and railroads; some called him a "robber baron." Made a fortune. Put some of it into Nikola Tesla's research—and lost a bundle. Ethan was a eugenicist, like Tesla, and a Hoover booster. His wife Edwina, however, got caught up with the suffragettes. Got the vote and impudently insisted on using it. Ethan thereafter tried to keep Edwina locked in the house. She broke a window and ran away to a freethinker commune, never to be heard from again.

"And look at you now, Ethan," Bryan said, "reduced to a little stub of marble in the ground. You know what, Garreth? I haven't been here in twenty years but . . . I don't remember these statues."

"I told you—they're *new*. I found them last weekend when I came out to see what shape the garden was in."

Bryan snorted. "New! Been vaping something again, Garreth?"

"I'm serious. These just weren't here. Not on the property."

"Could've been brought in from a cemetery at some point. What's that?" He'd noticed two twisted pillars protruding from the ground, sickly pallid and hinting of human shapes, to the right and left of the bust-like statues of Garreth's ancestors. "Some kind of fungal growth?"

"Yeah. Look closely at those things."

They walked over to the white figure. Bryan caught its distinct mushroom odor, noticed a pittedness about it. It was about sixteen inches high and looked like a half-finished sculpture of a writhing infant clutching itself. Was that a face on top? Not really. But it implied one.

Garreth waved a hand vaguely at the shape. "Doesn't it look sort of like a person?"

"That's just pareidolia—like seeing a cloud that looks like a bird or a face."

"But fungus doesn't get so *big!*"

"Some fungi get big. Belts of honey mushrooms get so big they kill trees."

"If you say so. You sure you want to do the gardening here?"

"Was the garden tour supposed to discourage me? I need to save up money, Garreth. I can manage an hour or two of gardening a day. Maybe on a Sunday I'll put in a little extra time. In a week I can get the garden into some kind of shape."

Sunday morning, half past eleven. November.

A cooling mist fell as Bryan set to digging out another overly ambitious boxwood and the blackberries entwining it. He'd been working since eight-thirty, using the rusting tools in the leaning garden shed, working his way from the brambly outer edges toward the center. He was prying at boxwood roots with the rust-tinted shovel. He'd gotten up three of them—but now the roots refused him, the shovel blade's collar broke off from the handle's half-rotten wood. Shaking his head, Bryan tossed the handle aside. He'd have to bring some of his own tools out. "Vectors for tetanus," he muttered, kicking at the pitted shovel blade.

Stretching to get a crick out of his back, he decided to have another look at the garden. He picked up his clippers, strolled along the sparse paths, clipping back bramble vines, deadheading browned roses, till he came to the open space around the fountain.

He stared. The busts of Garreth's great-grandparents were no longer busts; they were complete statues from feet to heads.

They were taller than Bryan, life size—and new-looking, if a little stained by rain streaking through dirt in the lower parts, as if they'd worked their way up out of the soil. Old Ethan Harrow, wearing his Edwardian suit, his beard lifted, eyes squinting in anger at his wife, his right hand fisted. Edwina Harrow was in a long, flowing walking-dress, a parasol in one hand, held out like a sword between her and Ethan. She was frozen in the act of drawing back from him, her eyes meeting his with their own fierceness, her prim lips firmly set.

Byran's rationality huffily demanded he shrug off astonishment. Casting about, he remembered that Garreth had brought him to this spot to point out the upper parts of the statues, the "busts" that supposedly appeared overnight. Could Elias, an elderly pretender of magical workings, a faux groundskeeper, have suggested the hoax to

Garreth? *"You don't want him staying in the house? Scare him off!"* Was that it?

Yet the ground around the base of the statues looked undisturbed. Bryan knelt, felt about the moss and weeds encircling the sculptures. All seemed firmly rooted, long since grown thickly in place.

Bryan shook his head. Someone must have brought in mossy sod and worked it in to make it look as if these things had just popped up out of the soil.

Then he heard a soft moan and caught peripheral movements: a kind of writhing on the left and the right. He glanced left and saw that the twisted white pillar—the supposed fungus—was replaced by the bust of a man. It seemed to shrug a little, to turn its head slightly his way. Must be some illusion of the light.

It was Bryan's grandfather. Marcus Harrow. Son of Ethan Harrow.

Bryan stepped over and bent close. What had been fleshy white fungus before was now marble. Unmoving, silent—*stone.*

Straightening up, Bryan said, "No. Just—no."

He started along the thready path to the house.

Bryan found Garreth's wife drinking tea at the polished-oak kitchen table. Mimi was a bleached blond round-faced pop-eyed woman, heavy-set, about five years older than her husband. She wore a pink turtleneck sweater and puce leggings. Her large pale blue eyes tracked Bryan as he came in. "You wipe your feet on the mat?" she asked. "All that dirt and mud out there."

"Yes I did. Is Garreth around?"

"And wash your hands before you touch anything."

"I was wearing gloves. Garreth—is he around?"

"No. He's at Eye to Eye."

"I thought you guys went to that together."

She frowned and tapped her fingers on the table. The large pink diamond in her wedding ring flashed. He saw that the toenails on her stubby sandaled feet were painted pink too. She made him think of a Pepto-Bismol bottle. "Since there was that vandalism in the garden," she said at last, "we decided one of us always has to be here. He has to go: they made him a group leader last month." She glanced away, as if trying to hide the smirk of satisfaction on her thin, satiny lips. Mimi was glad to be spared attending Eye to Eye.

Bryan nodded. Garreth had talked him into going to Eye to Eye once. A kind of fusion of *est* and Scienetics, it had been co-created by Garreth's late father, Bryan's Uncle Clive. It was "confrontational therapy," leader and learner eye to eye for five-hour sessions—dragging out secrets, demanding a new state of "Individualist Realization." Bryan's dad had called it a "factory turning out glib manipulators." To get through Eye to Eye without melting down you became fiercely defensive—or you learned to tell lies with exquisite skill. And Garreth's day job was working in online marketing. Bryan had actually dealt with it another way: after an hour and a half of sitting almost noses-touching close to a man staring at him and demanding to know what he was afraid to talk about—ninety minutes of "How is it crippling you, Bryan! How can you grow without owning your trauma? Tell me!"—Bryan simply patted the man on the shoulder and left the building.

Now he asked, "Mimi, this vandalism, the old broken statues—*is* that what it was? Or some kind of set-up?"

She frowned. "Meaning what?"

"Have you been in the back garden lately?"

"*God,* no. I—nope. I never go there. Not since I first moved in, anyway."

"When you moved in, were there marble statues of great-granddad Ethan and his wife anywhere on the property? In a basement maybe?"

"I didn't see any. There was a statue of Julius Caesar, don't ask me why, and one of I think Nietzsche and some dancing fairy person. All busted up now."

"You haven't seen the *new* statues?" He watched her face closely now.

Her head ducked back, and she gave a little snort. "New ones? You mean like those gnome things at the Garden Store with the pointy hats and beards?" She seemed genuinely puzzled.

"This stuff is marble. Looks expensive. And it's of great-grandfather Harrow and his wife. The sculptures started out like busts and now they're full size."

"Bullshit!" she blurted, shaking her head.

Bryan shrugged. "You want to go see them?"

"I really don't." She sipped her tea, staring into space. "I just don't go out there. It's . . . gross. If there are new statues, then probably that Elias put them in."

"I thought you guys got rid of Elias."

"We did. But maybe he's back. Weird that Garreth didn't tell me."

"When does Garreth come home?"

"About nine-thirty tonight."

"I need to talk to him. Because someone's pranking me. Statues don't grow . . . in stature. Go and look! It has to be Garreth doing this. I don't know if he's trying to get me to leave so he can rent the room or sell the place or what. But something's going on."

"Um—Bryan? You're freaking me out. I'm not sure I want to be alone in the house with you."

"Come off it, you've known me for years."

"Known you? Barely."

He put his hands up between them. "Never mind. I'll be in my room. Tell Garreth I really have to talk to him. Seriously. Tonight." Bryan turned away—and then turned back to Mimi. "And I'm ordering some pizza. Don't let it 'freak you out' when the delivery guy comes to the door." He strode to the stairs, suddenly very tired. He was remembering the look on Marcus Harrow's smoothly carven marble face. Cold hostility.

* * *

Penumbra

Almost nine, and autumn gusts were rattling the window glass.

Bryan lay on his bed, fingers linked behind his head, studying the rococo pendant light hanging from the peeling yellow ceiling. Trying to drive the sculptured visage of grandfather Marcus from his mind.

But the face was insistent; it was bitterly resentful, its empty eyes somehow finding room for cold fury.

Bryan had been brought to meet Grandfather Marcus when he was four. The old man was a centenarian, and he claimed to be long-lived thanks to eating smoked oysters. Bryan had wandered about the kitchen as the adults talked, and found the oyster jars lined up above in the closet-like pantry. Row on ugly row of oysters, like big gray navels packed in brine, utterly enigmatic. Then Marcus stalked suddenly in the dusty little room, to loom scowling down at him, snapping, "What are you getting into, boy?"—and Bryan burst into tears. Marcus gave him a look of raw contempt.

It was Bryan's earliest memory, and the only one he had of Grandfather Marcus. But he knew the family stories. As a young man Marcus Clay Harrow had been a gambling addict and womanizer, squandering his modest inheritance. He married a dance-hall girl, and she helped him spend his money. Penury loomed, and he turned desperately to the most conservative Lutheran synod, becoming a rigid teetotaler and white-knuckled businessman, selling nine acres of family property and investing in oil. Marcus took a lucky oil strike as a sign. Over time he devolved into a wealthy miser, icily ruthless, sending thugs with lead pipes to crush labor strikes.

Marcus had two boys—abandoned by their mother when she ran away with the pastor's son. Bryan's father, Adrian, left home as soon as he could, becoming a community college English instructor. Bryan grew up in a household that was always one paycheck away from the street.

Clive Harrow, Garreth's father, remained in the decaying house. He worked for his dad but mutinied when it came to Lutheranism. He made a hobby of the occult. Bryan had learned not to talk social philosophy with his uncle. Clive was a eugenicist like great-grandfather Ethan.

Fueled by Adderall, Clive was prone to staying up for days at a time, obsessing about family history and Enochian graphs. But he had a softer side—an affinity for nineteenth-century Romantic poetry, especially Shelley and Swinburne, which he shared with Bryan.

He could hear Mimi climbing the stairs. Bryan remembered a social media announcement that a baby was expected, followed soon by another announcement about Uncle Clive's death. Mimi and Garreth moved into the old house, as per the will. Then, it seemed, she'd lost the baby. Bryan winced: he should have been kinder to her.

A sharp, impatient rapping came at the door. "Bryan?"

"Yes, Mimi." He answered the door. "I left some pizza for you on the table."

"Bryan—did you set up some lights in the garden? Around that fountain?"

"What? No!"

"*Someone* did." Mimi chewed her lower lip, and hugged herself. She seemed upset. "Well . . . maybe Elias came back. Put up some lights."

"Show me."

"I'm not going out there, but you can see through the window."

He followed her downstairs. They looked through the kitchen window.

A general glow, soft green and cold blue, was being emitted from globes of light around the fountain clearing. Moths fluttered around the lights.

"I am so totally *not* going out there," Mimi whispered.

"No chance this is not a goddamn prank," Bryan growled, balling his fists. "It's Garreth trying to drive me out of the house."

Her mouth dropped open and she turned away, shaking her head. "Freaking me out again, cuz. I am going to lock myself in the bathroom."

Bryan went to the coatroom, put on his jacket, and hurried out to the back porch. Cold night air stung his ears and nose. But when he descended the stairs, into the garden, he found the air was warm here. Uncomfortably close. He fumbled out his cell phone, his hands trembling.

He turned on the cell phone's flashlight to negotiate the path, but—"*Shit!*"—still got raked across a cheek by thorns on a bramble vine.

He made his way to the soft blue-green glow at the center of the garden and stopped by the fountain, looking at the light source.

It was the statues themselves. The glow was diffused, each statue illuminated in phosphorescent acid-green, surrounded by a faint methane-blue halo. Moths fluttered about the halos of blue light, but seemed unable to get closer.

Bryan looked around in confusion. The statues had multiplied. There were now four more statues. One was of the late Clive Harrow, Garreth's father. Across from him, in the circle forming from statues, was Tilda Harrow, who'd run off with one of Clive's occultist friends—who'd introduced her to opiates. The Harrow men had a history of alienating their wives, of somehow driving them away. She'd died of a fentanyl overdose in a homeless encampment.

Clive's statue, looking much like his grandfather Ethan, was staring across at the sculpture of Tilda—who had shoulders hunched, her eyes closed in sobbing.

The other new marble figures stood opposite the great-grandparents, almost completing a circle of statues. More distant ancestors, early nineteenth century. Bryan didn't immediately recognize them; the woman in a bonnet and a long dress with puffy short sleeves—the man, heavily bearded, wearing a three-corner hat. The woman looked sterner than the man, who was almost jolly, carved with a beer stein in his hand.

There were two more fungus-like stubs in the ground, like half-finished gravestone figures. They completed a circle of statuary around the fountain.

Marble couldn't glow, could it? Perhaps some synthetic resembling marble, infused with phosphors? But as he stepped closer to the phosphorescent statues of his grandparents, reached out to touch his grandmother's face, he saw the outer shape of the glow change; saw it react to his hand, rippling in subtle waves. That wasn't what phosphors did.

He raised his cell phone and took a photo, framing his grandmother's glowing, carven face. He checked the photo—just a blurry circle of sickly green and blue. The statue wasn't visible.

Bryan heard brisk footsteps behind him.

"This is *sick!*" Garreth snarled, striding up. He whirled to face Bryan. "You! This is you! You must've . . ." Then the absurdity of the accusation struck Garreth and his face went slack, his eyes widened.

And with that brief window into Garreth—his cousin's undeniable astonishment—Bryan realized that this was no prank. Garreth was as bewildered as he was. The statues were a real, organic outgrowth of the garden itself. But who was a gardener of statues?

"If it's not me and it's not you," Bryan said, looking around at the marble faces, "was it Elias—working at Uncle Clive's behest?"

"Behest?" Garreth said, staring at this father's marble face. "Who says behest anymore?"

"Are you, sir, making a mock of me?" Bryan asked. Then he put his hand to his own mouth and muttered, "What did I . . ."

Garreth gaped at him. "You didn't say that on purpose?"

"It just . . . came out that way."

"You're the very beast your great-grandfather was," Garreth said. And then clapped both hands over his own mouth. He spun around, looking at the statues. *"They're in my head!"*

"They are but things of marble," Bryan muttered. But he was looking at Great-Grandfather Ethan's face—hadn't it just changed its expression a little? The white-marble face looking right at him now, eyebrow arching.

There was something in that expression he'd seen in his Uncle

Clive, and in his grandfather's face too—even in his own father's face. But when his father, Adrian, had behaved that way he'd later come to apologize. The way of most Harrow men was a poised, almost passive insistence on domination; an emanation of entitlement to power. A willingness to manipulate to get it. To endlessly deny. He had certainly seen it in Garreth over the years. And perhaps—

But that thought came asunder at the sounds of groaning and sobbing moans, coming from behind. He and Garreth whirled to see two more statues rising up, completing the new fungal growths, pushing the ground aside as they widened and filled out. The upsurge of marble resembled fast-action footage of plants growing.

Another new statue shuddered into view and then froze into a marble sculpture of a man with long hair, thick beard, craggy face, and bushy eyebrows. He wore late seventeenth-century breeches and a long, heavy coat. In one hand was a flintlock pistol. Standing at his side, clearly a companion, was a Native woman with braided hair and wearing an Iroquois robe.

"So it's true," Garreth whispered. "Some Native blood. Dad tried to prove it wasn't true. His eugenics trip. They—"

A groan from behind—and they turned to see that the other statues were closer together now.

And closer to Bryan and Garreth.

Garreth took a step back. "Bryan, we need to get out of here."

"Oh, yeah," Bryan said, nodding vigorously. "Come on." He started to sidle past the statues of the settler and his Indian wife—and the man's statue *moved,* a quick gliding motion accompanied by a grating sound, the sculpture blocking Bryan from the path.

Startled, Bryan stumbled back and saw that the settler's marble gun-hand was now raised, flintlock pointed at him, his head tilted, one eye closed.

From the corner of his eye Bryan caught another white-marble motion. He turned to see Garreth trying to rush past the figure of his great-grandfather Ethan—the statue gliding to block the way. Garreth yelped in fear and fell back, landing on his rump. "Bryan—!"

The other statues were gliding closer—and the white-marble women were now pointing, with outstretched arms and stabbing fingers, all at once, at the base of the fountain.

"He insisted!" Garreth shouted, his voice taut with hysteria. "Dad insisted! He said he'd leave me with nothing if I didn't do it!"

Bryan offered a hand to help Garreth—but there was a flash of white stone and a painful thud and Bryan was struck down. He fell heavily on his left side. A woman's white-marble hand closed around his wrist, pulled him roughly to his feet; another stony hand pushed him from behind and he fell on his face, outside the closing circle of statues.

There was a scraping, a gliding.

Bryan got painfully up, turned to see the statues closing around Garreth; creaking, cracking a little as they piled on, wrapping their arms around him. Constricting as one. Great-Grandfather Ethan raised his head to show Bryan bared teeth and blank white eyes narrowed with warning.

The statues clenched together like the fingers of a cruel boy crushing a moth. Garreth screamed.

Blood spurted between marbled limbs and torsos. Another scream—from the window overlooking the garden. Bryan dimly heard Mimi shrieking, *"Garreth!"*

The garden seemed to spin, and then Bryan realized he was running for the house, gasping, his head seeming to ring metallically, like a stone struck by a chisel.

Inside, Bryan went to the fridge and walked past Mimi, who was hunched over, hands covering her eyes, her shoulders shaking.

He found the Stolichnaya vodka, poured himself a drink with shaking hands. He drank it down and poured one for her. "Here." He put a hand on her shoulder, led her to the kitchen table, and she sat down, taking the drink from his hand. She couldn't yet drink it because the almost silent weeping contorted her mouth so.

Bryan went to the window and saw that the green and blue glow

Penumbra

was now centered in one place, one ball of light—and it was diminishing. He watched it shrink down, swirling like water in a drain. Then it was lost behind a shield of hydrangeas. There was a faint aurora—and then it blinked out entirely.

Mimi drank her vodka off noisily and coughed. Then she asked, "Is he dead?"

"I'm not exactly . . ." With a sickening inner lurch Bryan realized he had to go back out there. "Is there a real flashlight around here?"

"Um—yeah. Under the sink."

He took the black Maglite flashlight to the back porch and switched it on. It felt reassuringly like a cop's flashlight in his hand. It was metal. If he swung it, could it crack marble? Probably not.

Shivering in a damp November gust, he descended the complaining stairs and followed the yellow-blue flashlight beam down the path, the overgrown shrubs lit from beneath, shadows impenetrable between stalks. He wended along the path and stopped, not quite inside the clearing, feeling an icy tingle on the back of his neck, and scoured about the old fountain with the flashlight beam.

The statues were gone. There was no sign of Garreth.

Bryan shook his head. It was all too much to take in. The light had gone out in the garden—the blue-green phosphorescence had vanished, the marble sculptures with it. Even Garreth's blood was gone—sunk eagerly down into the earth.

Yet the soil was thoroughly disturbed, muddy and black where Garreth had died, as if something had been dragged down and covered over.

Clearly, in his mind's eye, Bryan saw the statues of the women all pointing at the fountain. Was there a faint wisp of acid-green over the fountain? Perhaps.

Shivering, he went to get the rusty, broken-off shovel blade. He had to force himself to return to the fountain. He looked around—half expecting the statues to rise up again—and then turned doggedly to the fountain. It took considerable effort to push it over.

It fell with a cracking clunk onto the ground. He leaned the flashlight up on the base of a clipped shrub so it pointed at the ground, and he went to his knees, immediately digging where its base had stood. Six inches, eight inches, twenty inches down. Then an acrid smell wafted up, and thick red fluid welled around the shovel blade. He scraped more dirt away—and hesitated. He'd uncovered a layer of blood, two inches deep. Fairly fresh. Pulpy bits of something in it, along with shreds of cloth.

Garreth.

As a boy visiting the Gulf of Mexico he quit digging for clams in the beach when he came to a black layer of petroleum, from oil spills, spread uniformly about eight inches down.

The blood, too, had its own layer, spreading out in the garden, twenty inches down.

But he remembered the pointing fingers of white marble, and he resumed digging, feeling sweat going cold on his forehead, his fingers aching. Another two feet—a substantial hole. Blood seeping down into its deeps, puddling.

Then he uncovered a hand—a woman's hand, pale and elegant, palm downward. Made of white marble, the hand of a statue, its arm extended away into the dirt. Just beneath it was a thick cloth. A muddy pink blanket. He dug around the hand and the blanket—found the blanket was bundling something. He stared.

"Just get it done," he told himself, through grating teeth.

The hand was stretched over the muddy blanket as if trying to protect it. Garreth's blood encircled it.

Bryan tapped the hand, waited for it to react. The marble hand remained motionless.

I should get up, I should go back to the house. Call the police.

But he resumed scraping dirt away, exposing the bundle. It was just the right size.

He tugged the bundle out from under the marble hand, laid it on the ground outside the hole, and covered up the sculptured white fingers with bloody mud and then black mud and clay and dirt.

It took them two hours to decide what to do.

It was almost midnight. Bryan sat at the table across from Mimi, the vodka bottle and glasses between them.

"When I saw the women pointing at the ground," Mimi said hoarsely, as she poured another Stolichnaya, "I got this theory: that Clive couldn't live with what he made his son do. So he had to die. And then Garreth too."

Bryan glanced toward the wicker basket on the floor. They'd covered it in a checkered red and white table cloth. Under the cloth were the bones, and a little of the shriveled flesh and brittle hair of the baby that had been buried under the base of the fountain, wrapped in two baby blankets.

He looked back at Mimi. He didn't want to look at Delilah's remains again. "You're saying Clive was . . . paying penance?"

"After he had the stroke, he said they were there. Granddad and Great-Granddad and the others. Said they were watching as he died. He could barely talk, but he whispered it in my ear. I figured—you know. Guilt—delusion."

Do you want another drink?" she asked dully, pushing the bottle toward him. Her hair was mussed, her makeup streaking her face. "You look like you need one."

"Not yet." His voice didn't come out quite audibly, and he repeated what he'd said.

"Bryan, will the police arrest me?"

"The police . . . I don't know. Did you help Garreth do it?"

"No! He smothered her with a pillow. I tried to keep him away from her. But then he just did it when I wasn't in the room and I—" She let out a long shaky breath and brought a hand down on the table in a single hard slap. "But I didn't tell anybody!" She drank a little vodka and wiped her eyes. "So maybe that makes me—what do you call it? In complicity. And—I was sort of *relieved*, too. Delilah was always wheezing and squirming and crying, and the doctor said she had brain damage from that stupid Eye to Eye midwife, the woman used some kind of tongs on the baby's head and squeezed too hard. But Clive said it was because of 'bad blood, bad genes,' and she had to be culled, and he badgered Garreth into it. And I did nothing, just *nothing*. But I am *so scared* to be alone in a jail cell. I'll wake up and they'll be there, Bryan! White and hard and with nothing in them at all, nothing but *stone* . . ."

After putting the baby in the basket and washing his hands, he had called the police. Now he could hear their radios talking as they pulled up outside. If the police dug down and found the statues—let them figure it out. He would say Garreth had told him where to dig before running away.

"I really don't know what the police will do," he said, his voice a rasp. "But I won't be digging in your garden again. I'll take that drink now."

Brian Aldiss: "A Border-Jumping Effrontery"

John C. Tibbetts

> "This making and unmaking of ideas doth very properly denominate the mind active."
>
> —George Berkeley,
> *A Treatise concerning the Principles of Human Knowledge*

The bemused figure peering at us over the cover of his book, *Frankenstein Unbound,* is a man named Brian Aldiss. Both book and man are together bound by the proposition that to be "unbound" is to be extravagantly human. Attend to him in these pages, but be watchful of the wit, even wickedness, that is both confounding and all too familiar.

I first met Brian Aldiss in July 2004. The noted British writer, critic, anthologist, poet, painter, essayist, Fellow of the Royal Literary Society, and recipient of the Order of the British Empire had long held an esteemed position in the ranks of science fiction littérateurs.[1] He had come to the University of Kansas to be inducted into the Science Fiction Hall of Fame and to meet his friends and colleagues, Greg Bear, Gregory Benford, Harry Harrison, and James Gunn. In the midst of it all, he agreed to sit down with me and talk shop. My surprise at his generosity was only confirmed by the ensuing sequence of events and the correspondence that followed for several years thereafter.

Immediately upon sitting down for our conversation, he expressed dissatisfaction with the label that popularly is ascribed to his work, "science fiction." It is a term too often reduced to galactic empires, technologies run amok, planetary romances, bug-eyed aliens, and the like. "If you get that label put onto you," he declared, "it deters you from having your own voice. Which can destroy you. If you're going to be a writer, but you don't find your own voice, you're nothing. There was a time in the sixties, when science fiction was achieving a sort of 'New Wave.' People insisted I subscribe to that label. But no. I told Judy Merrill I wanted nothing to do with that.[2] I could easily have joined, and it might have gained me a lot of publicity for my career. But I'm a non-joiner."

If Aldiss is dissatisfied with the term, he is no less uncomfortable with the label "Gothic," popularly reduced to the trappings of haunted houses, family curses, implications of the supernatural, doppelgängers, rampant seducers, and fainting maidens. Rather, with the unrelenting zeal of an obsessive—a descriptive he happily admits—he pursues a synergy that he defines in the introduction to his book of essays, *The Detached Retina,* as "a literature dealing with mankind's attempts to come to terms with new powers and to over-

---

1. In the face of the many honors that have come his way, Aldiss has described himself in the mildest of terms, as "the adventurous small boy, the unhappy lad at school, the macho soldier in the war, the wage slave, the lover, the traveler, the timid scribbler, the family man, and now the most unlikely avatar of them all—the established writer" (*Detached Retina* 193).
2. Judith Merrill (1923–1997) was an influential SF writer, editor, and political activist.

come those aspects of nature reckoned to be impediments to progress" (3). Together, they offer new ways, as he explains, to discuss old topics, like "the sense of the alien," the "unease generated by religion and the failure of religion," our "ambiguous feelings concerning technology," and "the importance of gender roles." His own work, as we will see demonstrated in the three novels under consideration here, stands as a demonstration of that interplay.[3] "Both worlds have shaped him," declares critic John Clute, "and he has shaped in turn both worlds. . . . It has always been absolutely central to his art . . . His contents glow with the speculative dash, the border-jumping effrontery, the natural tale-teller's voice, that supercharge his work even now . . ." (258).

But we're getting ahead of ourselves. Aldiss has explored all this in great detail in his two seminal literary histories, *Billion Year Spree* (1973) and its follow-up thirteen years later, the Hugo-winning *Trillion Year Spree*. Hovering over those pages is the seminal figure of Mary Shelley, whom he pronounces "the mother figure of SF," and the novel she wrote at age eighteen, *Frankenstein*. "After I had written *Billion Year Spree* in 1973, I thought that of all the thousands of novels that I had covered, the one that continually engaged my interest was Mary Shelley's *Frankenstein; or, A Modern Prometheus* in

---

3. Apart from this discussion but related to his syntheses of Gothic and SF tropes are two important works. First, the Hugo-winning "The Saliva Tree" (1965) successfully crosses H. G. Wells's *War of the Worlds* and Lovecraft's "The Colour out of Space" in a tale of the catastrophic effects of a meteor crash in an English village. Wells appears as a character. Second, Aldiss's eight-page story "Super Toys Last All Summer Long," which played a part in the Kubrick-Spielberg Gothic fantasy, *A.I.* (2001), reimagines the classic Gothic trope of E. T. A. Hoffmann's many stories about automata. The character of David in Aldiss's original story is unaware that he is an android. "It comes as a shock to realize he is a machine," writes Aldiss in the foreword to the story. "He malfunctions. . . . Does he autodestruct? The audience should be subjected to a tense and alarming drama of claustrophobia, to be left with the final questions, 'Does it matter that David is a machine? Should it matter? And to what extent are we all machines?'" (*Supertoys* vii–ix).

1818. The movies have always played it for the horror element. I hoped in a way to 'redeem' the Book." (Tibbetts, *Gothic Imagination* 330).

Although *Frankenstein* derives from the standard Gothic tropes in works such as Horace Walpole's *The Castle of Otranto*, Matthew Gregory Lewis's *The Monk*, and Ann Radcliffe's *The Mysteries of Udolpho*, he insists it also brings these melodramatic trappings into a new consideration, with science replacing supernatural machinery. This controversial partnering of the two has by no means been universally accepted. Howls of protest have come from colleagues, such as his friend, James Gunn: "The experienced science fiction reader keeps wanting Victor Frankenstein to behave rationally . . . but he shrinks from his creation" (Gunn 47). Darko Suvin, former professor of English and Comparative Literature at McGill University, likewise protests "the irruption of an anticognitive world into the world of empirical cognition" and regards the impact of Gothic horror on science fiction as "pernicious" and a "parasitism" (quoted in Gunn 226). On the other hand, writers such as Greg Bear, renowned for his galaxy-hopping narratives, defends the proposition and pursues it in many of his own ghost stories: "Science is not usually thought to cross over into fantasy because it's constrained from it by cultural prejudices . . . What I want to do is use a scientific theory to give you experiences you've never had before, but in a familiar way, and what is that but the ghost story?" (Tibbetts 100).

Moreover, as we will see in our conversation that follows, he brackets *Frankenstein* with two late-century novels whose Gothic machinery is likewise undercut with science, Bram Stoker's *Dracula* (1897) and H. G. Wells's *The Island of Dr. Moreau* (1896). Although the former can be regarded as a supernatural "resurrection" story with Christian overtones, *Dracula* is only "metaphorically and euphemistically about vampirism." More to the point, "it is the great Victorian novel about venereal disease, for which vampirism stands in as Stoker's metaphor" (*Trillion* 144–46). Beneath its trappings of Faustian man, *Moreau* is really concerned with the confrontation of religious and evolutionary theory. The doctor stands in for God, whose church is the House of Pain, and whose flock are beasts subjected to surgical procedures that accelerate their evolution. Wells, writes Aldiss, "was one of the first writers to use evolutionary themes directly in his work, but he was here using them against the grain of his generation's perception of the meaning of evolution." Whereas evolution could be understood as that which had carried man to the top of the tree, *Moreau* demonstrated that evolution was as likely to work against mankind as for it. The revelation is that in the bestial are the potentials of the human and in the human lurk the traces of the bestial. "The beast in the human," concludes Aldiss, "the human in the beast—it's a powerful theme, and one which seems in Wells's case to owe as much to inner emotion as to evolutionary understanding" (*Detached Retina* 117–22).

Which brings us to the reimaginings of Shelley, Stoker, and Wells in the three books at hand, *Frankenstein Unbound*, *Dracula Unbound*, and *An Island Called Moreau*. There is a temptation—and I have been guilty of it—to call them a "Gothic Trilogy," but by now we know how problematic that label is. In their synergy of Gothic and SF tropes and subjects they are best defined as . . . *something else?* But what?

"The impulse behind my writing *Frankenstein Unbound* [1973] was, in a way, exegetical," he says. "I hoped to explain to people what the story was really about. Mary Shelley says she wants to deal with the 'secret fears of our nature.' I've always thought yes, that's one of the things that real science fiction does, is treat 'the secret fears of our nature.'"

Enter filmmaker producer Roger Corman.

"My Frankenstein book was picked up by Roger Corman. He was a very nice man. He came to my house with his producer, and they had dinner with me. At the end of the meal, I suggested that if he made *Frankenstein Unbound*, he would then have to film its sequel, *Dracula Unbound*. In a moment of foolish generosity, he said, 'You write it, I'll film it.' So I had to go ahead and write *Dracula*

Unbound [1991], a sort of continuation of the earlier book, in which I retained the character of 'Bodenland.' But in fact it was far too long and needed too many special effects. And so when I sent it to Roger, he didn't say anything. I never heard back from him. Later, I got him to be invited Guest of Honor at the Conference of the Fantastic. And he came along with his charming wife. I sidled up to him and said, 'What did you think of *Dracula Unbound?*' All he said, 'You know I can't film that, Brian, I'm just a cheapo outfit.' This from a guy whose autobiography was entitled, *How I Made a Hundred Films in Hollywood and Never Lost a Dime!* But he was a charming man."

From there it was only a step from Shelley and Bram Stoker to H. G. Wells.

"You would think with my writing *An Island Called Moreau* that I would be proceeding with some sort of plan to finish a trilogy started by the Frankenstein and Dracula projects [in Britain it was published under the title *Moreau's Other Island*]. No, there was no plan. There was too much time between the first two, and the third came even later. But certainly I saw that the things that had been done in Wells's original novel by vivisection could be done in a more sophisticated way by genetic mutation. Mind you, I got my one and only Nebula for a novella called *The Saliva Tree,* in which H. G. Wells was a real character. The central character is a farmer whose farm is being invaded by aliens. He's writing Wells about these terrible events."

The threat of some sort of global holocaust hovers over them all. In *Frankenstein Unbound* nuclear explosions in the stratosphere have brought about "timeslips" that threaten to tear apart the fabric of history, space, time, fiction, and reality. In *Dracula Unbound* vampires are stalking history and threatening the very survival of their prey, mankind. In *An Island Called Moreau* a global war is also threatening to annihilate mankind, unless Moreau/Mortimer Dart can create a race of mutants to repopulate the planet.

In each novel a protagonist encounters and intermingles with fictional characters and situations. The stories are "Gothic" not only in that they invoke three classic Gothic novels but the Faustian figures in them—Victor Frankenstein, Bram Stoker, and Dr. Moreau (Mortimer Dart)—who indulge in unholy experiments with artificial and/or inhuman creatures without soul or spirit. These transgressions against the natural order—a monster stitched out of cadavers and given life by electricity, an "undead" vampire who subsists only by preying on mankind, and beast-men who are neither man nor beast—threaten to procreate and replace man.

Thus, Aldiss's fictional Frankenstein creates a monster and a mate to populate the world with monsters. The real-life Stoker creates Dracula and his minions to "infect" the rest of humanity. The fictional Moreau/Mortimer Dart creates beast-men and a race of creatures, the SRSRs, intended to take over the planet.

Each of Aldiss's narrators, Joe Bodenland and Calvert Roberts, are themselves "creators" in the sense that they also meddle in things with disastrous consequences. They find themselves justifying their destruction of things in their efforts to improve the human condition. In *Frankenstein Unbound* Joe Bodenland is thrust into Switzerland in 1816, where he tries to subvert the consequences of Frankenstein's experiments by tracking him and his monsters down and destroying them. Has he become the unwitting artificer of their actions and their fate? In *Dracula Unbound* Joe invents a time-displacer that he thinks will allow mankind to dump toxic waste safely. But this device in turn triggers the invention of a "time train" that takes him back to the era of Bram Stoker and Dracula—only to find that it was this very time-travel device that was seized by vampires, permitting them to stalk their prey across the vast spectrum of history. He travels further back in time to a prehistoric age, where he destroys a gathering of the original vampires with a nuclear bomb. In *An Island Called Moreau* castaway Calvert Roberts finds himself on an island dominated by the scientist Mortimer Dart, only to realize that his own country has funded Dart's unholy experiments. He destroys Dart's compound. In each of these three stories, however, we wonder if the destruction wrought by Bodenland and Roberts is final and complete. There are hints in each case that it is not. In the last book, particularly, Dart escapes in a submarine, heading toward a future fraught with uncertainty about his beast-creatures.

And what about the authors of these stories, Mary Shelley, Bram Stoker, and H. G. Wells? What fates did they incur in their own creative energies?

And finally, what about Brian Aldiss? He, too, is a creator, presuming to tinker with all these literary and fictional worlds, blending them, confusing them. What consequences has he incurred? Has he, too, found himself the victim of—*what?*

Why should something dreadful come out of good intentions?

Let's take a closer look at Aldiss's Gothic Trilogy.

FRANKENSTEIN UNBOUND

Aldiss prefaces *Frankenstein Unbound* with lines from Lord Byron's *Manfred:* "Alas, lost mortal! . . . I tremble for thy sake . . ." And in proper epistolary fashion, letters and taped journal entries by Joe Bodenland and an assortment of newspaper reports and cablegrams propel the narrative. It is the year 2020, and the nuclear explosions in the stratosphere occasioned by global war have caused "time slips," or ruptures in space and time. The concept underlying the book is immediately announced:

> "We can no longer rely [announces a *New York Times* article] even on the sane sequence of temporal progression; tomorrow may prove to be last week, or the last century, of the Age of the Pharaohs. The Intellect has made our planet unsafe for intellect. We are suffering from the curse that was Baron Frankenstein's in Mary Shelley's novel: by seeking to control too much, we have lost control of ourselves." (9)

One moment your neighborhood is in 2020, the next, it's a decade in the past, or a century previous.

In several letters from Joe Bodenland to his wife, Minna, he urges her to return from New Houston. He describes "time slips" in the area that temporarily throw the region into an unknown space and time. We learn Joe is taking care of their grandchildren (the parents have died).

A telegram reveals that Joe has disappeared. When last seen, his farm had been plunged into a time slip, into a region resembling Switzerland.

The rest of the story is drawn from Joe's "Tape Journal." Joe goes exploring in his car and he finds out that he is stranded in 1816. He references H. G. Wells:

> "As far as I knew, I was the first man ever to be displaced in time, though no doubt the timeslips were now making a regular thing of it. I remembered reading the old nursery classic, Herbert Wells' *The Time Machine*, but Wells' time-traveler had gone ahead in time. How much nicer to go back. The past was safe!" (28)

At a tavern in the little town of Secheron, near Geneva, Joe is astonished that the person he meets is none other than Victor Frankenstein. No fictitious character he, this is a flesh-and-blood person. He is agonizing over the murder of his six-year old brother, whose alleged killer is Victor's nursemaid, Justine Moritz. Joe follows Victor into the forest, where he witnesses Frankenstein's meeting with the huge monster he has created. Meanwhile, Justine is convicted at the trial. But the real killer, Joe realizes, is this monstrous creature.

Immediately Joe feels shifts in his sense of identity, a feeling that will grow and grow, until, later, he begins to feel that his identity is dissolving. He says:

> "The time distortions might cause mental illusion in their own right. One of those illusions was my persistent sensation that my personality was dissolving. Every act I took which would have been impossible in my own age served to disperse the sheet anchors that held my personality." (108)

Moreover, for the first of several times he muses on the improbability of witnessing and interacting with fictional characters from Mary Shelley's 1818 novel, *Frankenstein*, and declares that he feels himself "in the presence of myth and, by association, *accepted myself as mythical!*" (34) Later he repeats:

> "I had accepted the equal reality of Mary Shelley and her creation, Victor Frankenstein, just as I had accepted the equal reality of Victor and his monster. In my position, there was no difficulty in so doing, for they accepted my reality, and I was a much a mythical creature in their world as they have been in mine." (89)

And Mary admits the same thing: "Enchanted indeed! You and I are under an enchantment, Joe. We do not exist in the same world! Both of us are spirit, though you kiss my flesh" (97).

Needing some money, Joe pawns his watch. And here is the first reference to another theme of the book, *time* . . .

> "Its undeviating accuracy in recording the passage of time to within a twenty-millionth of a second was a joke in a world that still went largely by the leisurely passage of the sun . . . That wretched obsession with time which was a hallmark of my own age had not yet set in; there were not even railway timetables to make people conform to the clock." (42)

Mary Shelley and Lord Byron enter the story. With them, Joe reflects further on the modern invention of time:

> "That straightness of time, that confining straightness, was one with the Western picture of setting the world to rights. Historically, it was easy to see how it had arisen. The introduction of bells into all the steeples of Christendom had been an early factor in regularizing the habits of the habit—their first lesson in working to the clock. Next would be the complex railway timetable which 'would reinforce the lesson of the factory siren: that to survive, all must be sacrificed to a formal pattern imposed impersonally on the individual.' That leads to the 'horrible clockwork universe of Laplace and his successors. That image of things would dominate men's notions of space and time for more than a century.' For po-

ets, however, time 'would always be a wayward thing, climbing over life like a variegated ivy over some old house.'" (75–76)

Joe confronts Victor and demands that he confess that the monster was the murderer of the child. Victor rejects this, voicing another theme of the book, the ambition to improve mankind through the intellect, through science: "'Truth was everything to me! I wanted to improve the world, to deliver into man's hands some of those powers which had hitherto been ascribed to a sniveling and fictitious God! I made my bed in charnels and on coffins, that a new Promethean fire might be lit!'" (54). Joe muses on the folly of this attitude, and he again references Mary Shelley's novel:

> "Whatever previous generations made of it, Mary Shelley's *Frankenstein* was regarded by the twenty-first century as the first novel of the Scientific Revolution and, incidentally, as the first novel of science fiction. Her novel had remained relevant over two centuries simply because Frankenstein was the archetype of the scientist whose research, pursued in the sacred name of increasing knowledge, takes on a life of its own and causes untold misery before being brought under control. How many ills of the modern world were not due precisely to Frankenstein's folly." (61)

And later he tells Mary that her book will be prophetic: "Man has power to invent, but not to control. In that respect, the tale of your modern Prometheus is prophetic" (102).

To his astonishment, Joe learns from a newspaper that three months had vanished in a twinkling, and he is now in Geneva in August, three months later than when he arrived (and after Mary's inspiration for the novel had arrived).

At the Villa Diodati Joe meets Shelley, Byron, and Mary Godwin. He argues with them about the consequences of technological experimentation. Shelley predicts the triumph of science in the service of mankind, declaring, "We are marching towards an age, a realm of science, in which goodness will not be trampled underfoot by despair! Everyone will be a force to be heard!" (81).

Joe has reservations, and hints—

"Culture will become enslaved by the machines. The second generation of machines will be much more complex than the first, for it will include machines capable of repairing and even reproducing the first generation! Not only will human goodness be unable to operate effectively in such a system: it will become increasingly irrelevant to it." (84)

Mary joins in, and she is sympathetic to Joe's views:

"Our generation must take on the task of thinking about the future, of assuming towards it the responsibility that we assume towards our children. There are changes in the world to which we must not be passive, or we shall be overwhelmed by them. . . . When knowledge becomes formulated into a science, then it does take on a life of its own, often alien to the human spirit that conceived it." (86)

Later, Joe and Mary fall in love and spend delicious hours of sexual ecstasy together. He tells her he has come from the future and that her book will become world-famous. She in turn tells him that she is toying with the idea of having Victor create a mate for the monster.

Believing that altering the course of events in Mary's novel and in Victor's experiments will change the technological nightmare of 2020, Joe determines to destroy Victor and the monster. But before he can encounter either, he goes through a nightmarish sequence of events in which he finds himself imprisoned in a Geneva jail on suspicion of murder. It is here that he writes a long letter to Mary, in which he admits that his condemnation of his own twenty-first century was too harsh, that there have actually been civil and social improvements:

"In the Western democracies, those masses have never again suffered the dire oppression that they suffered in England until almost the 1850s, when sometimes laboring men, particularly in country districts, might never have a fire in their hearths or taste meat all week, and faced death if they trapped a rabbit on the local lord-of-the-manor's land. People have been able to become softer since those ill times, thanks to the great abundance for which technology is directly responsible . . . Thanks to the work of your moral forces, powered by the social change which always and only comes from technological innovation, the future from which I come is not entirely uninhabitable. On the one hand, there is the sterility of machine culture and the terrible isolation often felt by people even in overcrowded cities; on the other hand, there is a taking for granted of many basic rights and freedoms which in your day have not even been thought of." (118–20)

Moreover, "It is your husband-to-be who declares (or will declare, and of course I may misquote) that poets are *mirrors of the tremendous shadows which futurity casts upon the present* and the unacknowledged legislators of the world. He is absolutely right, save in one particular: he should have specifically included novelists with poets'" (119).

He makes his escape when a winter blizzard suddenly hits the area, attended by a flood, another space-time collapse. Everything is strange. Lake Geneva has disappeared. The town has been half submerged in mud. Other cities in the world may have disappeared. It appears as if he now inhabits a polar region. He reflects upon these additional space-time slips:

> "I was eager to discover what dreadful catastrophe had overtaken this part of the world. I could only suppose that the collapse of space time in my own day was slowly spreading outwards from the source, like a bloodstain oozing across an old sheet, threatening many deep-seated continuities. The very idea raised an image of a gradual disruption of the whole fabric of history until, at some stage, the rupture would seriously interfere with the creative processes of Earth themselves." (133)

After surviving in the snows, he makes his way back to the town, where he confronts Victor and accuses him of tampering with natural laws and morality. They argue. Victor again justifies his work: "My responsibility must be to that truth, not to society, which is corrupt. Moral considerations are the responsibility of others to pontificate on; I am more concerned with the advancement of knowledge" (148). To which Joe replies: "It is useless for me to point out that scientific curiosity by itself is as irresponsible as the curiosity of a child. It amounts to meddling, no more. You have to accept responsibility for the fruits of your actions" (149).

Victor informs Joe that when his monster escaped, it acquired education and literacy, a dangerous thing, since "education should only be bestowed on the few" (150):

> "So it befell that he read Goethe's *The Sorrows of Young Werther* and discovered the nature of love. He read Plutarch's *Lives* and discovered the nature of human struggle. And, most unfortunately, he read Milton's great poem, *Paradise Lost,* from which he discovered religion. You can imagine how damaging such great books were, casting their spells on a completely untutored mind!" (150)

The two men go to Victor's tower laboratory, a veritable charnel house, where Joe is horrified to see that Victor is working on a female mate for the monster. At this point Victor's thoughts of benefiting mankind with his experiments are replaced by the fear that if he doesn't do this, the monster will destroy him. So he has set to work and create a female, but whose form and biology are altered to create a more purely procreative creature. There are six extra ribs, increasing the lung cage. Air can be breathed in through the nose and through apertures behind the ears. The vagina is designed purely for procreation (a vestigial penis serves to eliminate waste). There is a twin backbone and a fortified pelvis, allowing for greater leg musculature. And, most horrifying of all, it possesses the face of the dead Justine Moritz. Joe feels pity and dismay at this creature who possesses no spirit or soul (a prophecy of the controversy attended by today's cloning science), and it sparks in him a glimmer of religious sentiment:

> "Victor's plan for this creature's coming resurrection would be a blasphemy. What had been done, in this inspired cobbling together of corpses, was a blasphemy. And to say as much—to think as much—was to admit religion, to admit that life held more than the grave at the end of it, to admit that there was a spirit that

transcended the poor imperfect flesh. Flesh without spirit was obscene. Why else should the notion of Frankenstein's monster have affronted the imagination of generations, if it was not their intuition of God that was affronted?" (160).

The monster arrives, and Joe is astonished to gaze upon his machine-like beauty. He expected the erroneous description offered in Mary's novel; instead, he confronts something beautiful, but not human, a face like a "helmet":

> "The eyes were there, glaring down at me from behind defensive cheekbones, as if through the slits of a visor. The other features, the mouth, the ears, and especially the nose, had been blurred in some fashion by the surgeon's knife. The creature that now stared down at me looked like a machine, lathe-turned." (163)

The creature declares that his life is one of woe: "'I have no life while everyone's hand is turned against me. As I am without sanctuary, so I am without gratitude. My creator gave me life, and the profit of it is I know how to curse; he gave me feeling, and the profit of it is I know how to suffer! I am fallen! Without his love, his aid, I am fallen'" (165). He promises Victor that if he finishes the female creature, they will disappear north and never bother Victor again.

What follows is the most horrific scene in the book. Everything seems dislocated and out of joint. As two moons sail in the sky above, Joe watches as the monster and his bride dance around each other and then couple violently, brutally. Then the two monsters depart toward the frigid lands.

Narrowly escaping the monster's clutches, Joe flees the tower and finds his car outside. It is armed with gun mounts. He confronts Victor and brandishes a revolver at him. Victor pleads for understanding. He babbles that he might create a *third* monster, which will arouse jealousy in the first, and that the two will kill each other. Crazily, he shrieks out more words, again, a blend of self-justification and compelling logic:

"Did you ever think it might be life that was the pestilence, the accident of consciousness between the eternal chemistry working in the veins of earth and air? So you can't—you mustn't kill me, for a purpose must be found, invented if necessary, a human purpose, *human*, putting *us* in control, fighting the *itness* of the great wheeling world, Bodenland. We have to be above the old considerations, be ruthless, as ruthless as the natural processes governing us." (186)

Joe shoots Victor at point-blank range and sets fire to the tower and laboratory. He sets out in pursuit of the monster and his bride. He reflects on the paradoxes of events around him. Yes, he has killed Victor and therefore wrecked the *fatalism* of coming events. But, he reasons, Victor was not real to his world of the twenty-first century. Yet he had been real to the world of 1816 ("and there might be countless other 1816s of which I knew nothing"):

"Such thought opened dizzy vistas of complexity. Possibility and time levels seemed as fluid as the clouds which meet and merge eternally in northern skies, forever changing shape and attitude. . . . Somewhere there might be a 2020 in which I existed merely as a character in a novel about Frankenstein and Mary . . . There was no future, no past. Only the cloud-sky of infinite present states. Man was prevented from realizing this truth by the limitations of his consciousness. Consciousness had never evolved as an instrument designed to discover truth; it was a tool to hunt down a mate, the next meal." (190)

Joe continues his pursuit across a bleak and frigid landscape. There is a protracted dream sequence that is a brilliant Dali-esque exercise in its surreal blending of disparate elements and fugitive visions. Shelley and Mary appear, vanish, and reappear, fantastic events transpire in quick glimpses. The sequence is for me reminiscent of Ken Russell's freewheeling depiction of events at the Villa Diodati in the film *Gothic*. Examples of Joe's visions: "[Shelley] sat on a mossy stone and wept, refusing to be comforted. I offered him a bowl of something, but a raven ate it, whatever it was. He flew a kite and climbed swiftly up its string." And this: "[Shelley] picked Mary up and put her in his pocket." Moreover—"I found there were many infants in the great heap, all with wakeful eyes." And, finally, "I thought [Mina's] hair was on fire. A pig ran past, although we were in a crowded room. A man she knew was pulling a piano apart" (199–200).

Meanwhile, back at the narrative, Joe comes at last to what seems to be the end of the world, and there on the heights is what appears to be a gigantic walled city. From within comes ruddy glows of light and the sense of a celebration of some kind:

> My speculation was that this was the last refuge of humanity. The place was so remote that I could only believe the timeslips to have delivered me at a point many centuries—maybe many thousands or even millions of centuries—into futurity. So that I might be witnessing the last outpost of mankind after the sun had died, when the universe itself was far gone towards the equipoise of its death. (207)

Joe spots the monster and his bride about to enter the city. He picks up his rifle and targets them through the telescopic sight. He fires, killing the female. The male then lopes rapidly toward him. Joe fatally wounds him before being crushed before the onslaught. The dying creature mutters enigmatically:

> "This I will tell you, and through you, all men, if you are deemed fit to rejoin your kind: that my death will weigh more heavily upon you than my life. No fury I might possess could be a match for yours. Moreover, though you seek to bury me, yet will you continuously resurrect me! Once I am unbound, I am unbounded!" (211)

Joe fires again at the creature. He settles down to wait for whatever will happen next. He wonders if the inhabitants of the city will come for him. Their celebration seems to be dying down. "They would know where I was," he reflects, "and what I had done." Then come the final lines: "So I would wait here until someone or something came for me, biding my time in darkness and distance" (212).

In her commentary on the novel Wendy Bousfield notes, "Bodenland's references to myth suggest how historical and fictional
figures may coexist on the same plane. In Western consciousness,
Byron and Shelley exist as mythic figures, as Frankenstein's monster
does. There is a hint of the metafictional here. . . *Frankenstein Unbound* explicates Mary Shelley's novel as a work of prophecy, though
it at once invites and resists hard and fast conclusions about the
dangers of technological advancement" (359–61).

Note: *Frankenstein Unbound* was made into a 1990 movie
adapted and directed by Roger Corman, starring John Hurt as Joe
Buchanon, Raul Julia as Victor, Nick Brimble as the monster, Bridget Fonda as Mary Godwin, Jason Patric as Byron, and Michael
Hutchence as Shelley. It was Corman's first directorial effort in
twenty years. Music by Carl Davis. A quick synopsis reveals the
scope of the free adaptation:

In Los Angeles in 2031, scientist Joe Buchanan develops a
weapon that can destroy an object by molecularly imploding it. But
his experiments are causing strange pink clouds to appear in the sky,
causing objects to disappear. One of them swallows up Joe and his
car, and he finds himself back in 1816 in Switzerland. He meets
Victor Frankenstein in a tavern. He follows his carriage into the forest, where he first sees the Monster. Wandering into the town, he
learns about the trial of Justine Moritz for the murder of Victor's
younger brother. He tries to persuade Victor into saving Justine by
confessing to the identity of the Monster. Victor gives Joe a letter to
take to Elizabeth exonerating Justine. But the letter actually contains a warning to Elizabeth to leave town. Seeking more help, Joe
goes to the Villa Diodati, where he meets Byron, Shelley, and Mary
Godwin. He had assumed that Mary knew about the Monster, since
she had written *Frankenstein*. But Mary explains she has *not* written
such a book yet. She marvels at Joe's admission that he's from the
future. There's a romantic interlude.

Back in the town, Justine is hanged.

And the Monster slays Elizabeth, who is fleeing by carriage.

The Monster reappears, demanding a mate. Victor exhorts Joe to supply him with the necessary electricity to do the job. But Joe has other ideas, and while Victor sets about to create the mate (using Elizabeth's corpse) he sets the controls to his automobile to blast Victor's tower laboratory. So, just as the switches power the mate with electricity, the automobile's lasers implode the laboratory. Amidst the rubble, the Monster and his mate meet. But in an accident, Victor's pistol fires and kills the mate. The enraged Monster turns on Victor and kills him. He flees, Joe in pursuit.

Across the snowy mountain peaks Joe follows the monster. He comes across an underground laboratory, a kind of power plant. He also finds the Monster. Joe finds a way to level the underground lasers at the Monster, eventually frying him to a crisp. Joe emerges from the underground power plant and spies a strange city in the distance. He walks towards it with the Monster's last words echoing in his ears: "You can't kill me. I am *unbound*."

No, the story doesn't really flow. The last scenes with the Monster's mate, the destruction of the tower lab, the slaying of the mate and of Victor, and the final confrontation between the Monster and Joe in the futuristic underground power plant are ridiculous. Byron and Shelley are present only a few minutes. The affair with Mary is perfunctory and irrelevant. The paradoxes about time and her being made aware of her novel-to-be are contrived. There are a couple of feeble attempts at dream sequences, but they have nothing to do with Aldiss and anything else, for that matter. Above all, the dialogues between Joe and Victor about science and humanity, about the disasters of a materialistic, mechanistic spirit, are gone. Joe's own growing obsession with killing the Monster himself is never apparent. He just kills the creature, and that's it. We desperately need more of Joe's *narrative voice* to sift through the complexities and subtleties of the story.

Contemporary reviews of the film were generally dismissive and failed to acknowledge Brian Aldiss as the story source. Writing in the *New York Times,* Vincent Canby wrote, "It is the conceit of Mr.

Corman and his associates that when Mary Godwin was writing 'Frankenstein,' she wasn't writing fiction but only a thinly veiled account of a rather rude if well-to-do neighbor named Victor Frankenstein. More about the story you need not know. The movie, actually filmed in Italy around Bellagio and in Milan, looks fine, and the performers are mostly good. Bridget Fonda, ordinarily a charming actress, plays Mary as if she were Annette Funicello in an early-19th-century blond fright wig. Mr. Brimble's Monster looks the way Alexander Godunov might look after a failed face-lift. The special effects are nicely spaced out, and the laugh lines fairly funny."

DRACULA UNBOUND

Prologue: In the far future only a handful of human beings survive in a world that has been devastated by vampires, called "The Fleet Ones." The vampires are draining the sun of its energy in order to fuel a "time train," with which they can shuttle back and forth in time, foraging for victims and gathering armies for a final decimation of the earth. One of the surviving humans, a scientist named Alwyn, prepares to travel back into the past to warn mankind of the approaching evil. One of his intentions is to alert writer Bram Stoker about vampiric evil, so that his novel will alert the world to its dangers. The prologue ends with Alwyn soaring into the air on his mission.

The story proper begins with the discovery in 1999 in Utah of two coffins buried in a strata of land that dates back to Cretaceous period of prehistory. The coffins and the two corpses are marked with symbols and silver bullets identifying them not only as humanoids that lived at the time of the dinosaurs but as vampiric creatures. Could it be, the world wonders, that *Homo sapiens* are much older than their presumed two millions of years? The discovery is made by Bernard Clift, an archaeologist. His friend is Joe Bodenland. Joe has made a discovery of his own. His "inertia reversal" process is a kind of time machine that has been developed to dispose of toxic waste. This process halts time-decay, much as refrigeration delays bacterial action. Bodenland sees this as a way of disposing of nuclear waste, of isolating it and suspending it in time.

At the excavation site Joe and Bernard make yet a third discovery. The exhumation has somehow triggered a strange phenomenon: a "ghost train" is seen traversing the site at night. "And it was there in the darkness, like something boring in from outer space, a traveler, a voyager, an invader: full of speed and luminescence" (31). The two men, using Joe's "inertia reversal" machine, manage to board the train. And thus begins the major portion of the novel's narrative.

On the train the men are attacked by vampiric creatures. Bernard is killed. Joe survives and kills the engineer. Upon learning that the train had let off an agent in 1896, he backtracks the train to 1896, where (and when) Bram Stoker is working on his new novel, *Dracula*. He leaves the train, visits Stoker, and is taken into the household. Stoker is only mildly incredulous about his visitor from the future. Joe realizes that Stoker's nightly adventures with London prostitutes have left him with syphilis. Outside Stoker's mansion, meanwhile, another danger is gathering. Vampires, including Count Dracula himself, are in the area. A beautiful woman—or is "she" really a monstrous "he"?—tries to entice Joe to her "undead" embrace. Indeed, she bites his neck. But although he is weakened, he manages to turn a crucifix on her and destroy her.

Joe and Stoker determine to use the time train to destroy the vampires. First, they journey to the future, C.E. 2399, where only a remnant of mankind—survivors of a colossal collision with a meteor—living in what is called the "Silent Empire" of Tripoli, Libya, awaits certain extermination from the vampire hordes. The two men procure an "F-Bomb," a mighty explosive device, which they take with them back to prehistory. They also take with them two vampires that have been destroyed. They will bury the coffins there. (And, of course, those are the two coffins that we saw exhumed in 1999 at the story's beginning.) There they observe the proto-vampires, a race of pterodactyls whose bloodlust has transformed them into a semi-human state of immortality (a kind of immortal death, as it were) and who herd the dinosaurs as fodder for their thirst. Joe and Stoker want to detonate the bomb and destroy the vampires before they can continue their existence into future time. Interestingly, the vampires exist openly under the sun. It is only when the bomb goes off and the brilliantly destructive light and heat destroy them that an aversion to light is "inherited" by the survivors. That is why vampires have come to avoid the day and come alive only at night.

The bomb is detonated. The ensuing catastrophe precipitates the death of the Cretaceous period and the age of dinosaurs.

Joe and Stoker return to the present. Several time-travel paradoxes now come into play: 1) Joe's wife, Mina, who has been infected by a vampire, is brought "back to life" by traveling a few days back into the past in order to prevent the vampiric attack in the first place. 2) Joe realizes that his invention of the "inertial reversal" process was the very process by which the vampires had been able to develop the "time train." Joe is responsible, in effect, for the very means by which vampires had traversed time to wreak havoc across the ages. 3) Joe realizes he must destroy the time-travel device and the time train. He arranges to have the two trains meet each other, going and coming through time, so that they will collide and destroy each other.

Bram Stoker, meanwhile, is administered penicillin against his syphilis and taken back to 1896. He signs a copy of *Dracula* to Joe and dates it "1897." Hence the mystery of how a book could have been signed to a twentieth-century Joe Bodenland in the time of 1897.

Vampires here are construed as predatory machines, evolved from bloodthirsty pterodactyls, animals without the "neocortex" that allows humans to think and differentiate themselves from animals: "All those little plagues to human life were originally innocent suckers of fruit juice and plant juices. But the taste of blood proved addictive and they had become enslaved by parasitism" (103). They regard themselves as the true inhabitants of earth. Human beings are but a short-lived anomaly who came and will go in but a blink of time. In other words, they see humans as monstrous and themselves as the norm. By destroying mankind they restore the balance of nature. Dracula at one point ridicules Bodenland's petty humanity:

> "Your scientific view has blinkered you, Joe Bodenland. You should open your mind to a darkness wider than your petty light. This is a turning point in history, when the human race become mice again, not pretentious creatures who dream of visiting other planets . . . Man, you have a brain, yet you cannot feel with it how short life is, and how long death." (160–61)

Dracula also rejects Joe's assertion that he is "evil":

> "Your kind regards my kind as evil. I have been forced to observe your kind over the centuries, since you huddled in caves against the ice. Has ever a day gone by, or a night, in all those centuries, when you have not put someone to death? . . . a litany of murder in more various forms than we of the Un-Dead could ever command. Your sins are endless and committed willfully. What we do we cannot help." (166)

Yet, without intellect themselves, they are threatened by mankind. ("For all our strengths, we remain forever slaves to the human imagination," Dracula says [119].) Indeed, it was the coming of Jesus Christ and humanity's own self-awareness with the dawn of history that separated humans from the vampires and targeted them as the vampire's enemy:

> "An individual consciousness had been slow to dawn. Signs of dawn came in the sixth century B.C., with such great men as Confucius, the Buddha, and the classical Greek philosophers . . . After Moses, Christ embodied what was new and revolutionary— the value of the individual. The idea of individual salvation was consciousness-raising. It had changed the world, or most of it. It was an idea for which the time was ripe—hadn't other great religions sprung up in the same period? All with the same emphasis? Originally the Ur-vampires had preyed on creatures without individual consciousness. Such was their natural prey. The dangers

hugely increased when they found themselves attacking an unpredictable individual—and the Cross was the symbol of that very danger. The Cross embodied all they most dreaded." (125)

Thus, they fall back before the trappings of Christianity. Their infected blood is likened to the syphilis of the nineteenth century and the AIDs of today. Unable to have sex themselves, they "preyed on humankind by activating one of the strongest instincts below the neocortical level, the great archetype of sex" (102), and in their dark appeal to immortality through eternal death.

Stoker explains:

> "My Christian belief is that there are dark forces ranged against civilization. As the story of the past unfolds, we see there were millions of years when the Earth was—shall I say unpoliced? Anything could roam at large, the most monstrous things. It's only in these last two thousand years, since Jesus Christ, that mankind has been able to take over an active role, keeping the monsters at bay. . . . Only piety can confront them." (91–92)

Note: The "time train" is a wonderful conception. Dim and clouded and infested, it elongates and compresses as it accelerates and decelerates through time. It is invisible to the outside world, unless it slows its journey through time to let an agent off.

Aldiss maintains a wry, almost skeptical tone throughout the story. Bodenland and Stoker both believe and disbelieve in time travel and vampires and the events unfolding around them. He and Stoker trade quips at oddly inappropriate times. Aldiss himself is playing tag with the narrative, both exploiting vampire legend and satirizing it:

> Although [Bodenland] admired Stoker's courage, he still could not persuade himself to believe in vampires. His experience told him they existed, his intellect denied it. Of course, that paradox played to the advantage of vampires, if they existed. But they did exist—and somehow below the level of human intellect. (101–2)

Historical, "real" characters include Bram Stoker (he is called "the ginger man"), his wife Florence, and the actors Henry Irving and Ellen Terry (there is even a scene where Bodenland accompanies Irving to receive a knighthood from Queen Victoria). They interact with the fictional characters of Dracula, Renfield (who languishes in a lunatic asylum next to Stoker's house), and Van Helsing.

In his critique of the novel, Thomas Dubose observes that the novel "is a wry satire of the way in which industry and government appropriate and make use of the discoveries and inventions of men and women of science, work that others cannot accomplish on their own and cannot fully appreciate beyond their potential for exploitation. Perhaps the novel's greatest feat of imagination is the Fleet Ones themselves. In them, Aldiss has interwoven three subjects that have been dear to writers and readers of fantasy and science fiction for decades: dinosaurs, vampires, and time travel" (249–50).

AN ISLAND CALLED MOREAU

The year is 1996. The world is in the grip of a rapidly escalating global conflict. Aldiss's narrative strategy is straightforward and the timeline is chronological.

Calvert Roberts is an American under secretary of state whose space flight on the shuttle *Leda* ends in disaster as it crashes into the Pacific. After days of being stranded on his small raft, he sights an island. A blond man named Hans Maastricht pulls him aboard his boat and takes him to the island. A gigantic "M" marks the cliff face. After marveling at sights and sounds of beast-like creatures populating the island, whose human-like speech and manner identifies them as transitional states between animal and man, Calvert is taken to meet the Master of the island.

The first sight of the Master is a shock. He is a helmeted, robot-like humanoid. It turns out that inside the body armor he is a mutant, a genetically deformed man as a result of the thalidomide drug. His name is Mortimer Dart. Now obsessed with hate and vengeance for what has happened to him, he conducts drug experiments on the beast people that were left over from the island's former dominance under the legendary Dr. Moreau. Dart explains that H. G. Wells based Moreau on a real Edinburgh doctor named Angus McMoreau, notorious for his vivisection experiments. After disaster befell McMoreau, the island was left to the remnants of the beast people. Now, Dart continues the experiments for purposes that for the moment remain shrouded in mystery.

> "Wells may have been writing an allegory, but his island was firmly based on a real one—just like the island on which Defoe's Robinson Crusoe was shipwrecked was based on a real one. . . . The real Moreau . . . was a pupil of Thomas Huxley—Wells met him. His life is well documented. Wells did very little to camouflage the real situation, beyond some overdramatizing. In fact, McMoreau brought a lawsuit." (41)

After McMoreau's death, an assistant carried on his vivisection work. Later, offspring were born to the hybrid stock, Dart continues, but through genetic experiments not vivisection. Calvert speculates about Dart's motives:

> It was not hard to understand how an intelligent man afflicted by his disabilities might be obsessed with the function of those disabilities and their cause. I knew how erroneous was the popular view of scientists as being "detached," of science as being "pure"; scientists, like artists, were often obsessionals, and the most outstanding work came from obsessionals. Dart would have as strong a drive as any man to comprehend the mysteries of genetic structure and programming. (67)

Calvert insists, to no avail, that he be permitted to send a radio signal to the American government. Dart distrusts him and claps him into jail. Later, Calvert is released to explore the island further. He visits some sort of fortification and learns of the existence of another race of Seal People, who swim the waters just off the island.

Dart conducts convocations of the beast people in the manner of a church service, with this chant-like invocation:

> The Master's is the Head that Blames
> The Master's is the Voice that Names
> The Master's is the Hand that Maims
> The Master's is the Whip that Tames
> The Master's is the Wrath that Flames (100)

Things turn nasty when, during the Master's presiding over the burial of Maastricht (who has died in a tractor accident), the beast people begin to revolt. They are led by "Foxy," a precocious fox-like human (or human-like fox) who has stolen a carbine rifle and stirred up resistance. Dart flees, leaving Calvert to fend for himself. Calvert finds refuge among the Seal People, where he indulges in a four-day idyll of sexual ecstasy.

Back on the island, Calvert finds Dart's compound under siege. In the laboratories, he learns that Dart's final series of experiments involves the creation of a "subrace" of gnome-like creatures who are designed to prevail long after humankind is destroyed by the global holocaust.

> The creature confronting me was even more of an aberration of the human form than [the beast people]. It stood under one and a half meters high and was disproportionately thick of body. It had extremely short legs, so that the arms trailed almost to the ground. Its head was distorted into cephalic form., the skull tapering almost to a point at the rear. . . I was reminded of drawings of the faces of seven-month fetuses. (147)

They are called "SRSRs" (Standby Replacement Subrace). Dart explains:

> "They're what this island's all about. McMoreau's crude vivisection techniques were just an amateur beginning. After that came my early experiments in genetic surgery. . . . When total war wipes out humankind, A world of want is going to result—that's the cost of victory, and that's where it's at. The human race will be decimated, air and ground will be radioactive . . . But if we can breed up the SRSRs, they can take over the enormous tasks of reconstruction. . . . They will be less vulnerable to radiation than the

rest of us, will propagate faster, will consume less supplies because of their smaller bulk. They are, in fact, our survival kit into the future; they may even replace us." (153–54)

Calvert realizes these experiments must be stopped. But the American government intervenes. He is dismayed to learn that the government has been subsidizing and promoting Dart's island experiments all along. Indeed, as the compound goes up in flames, a submarine arrives and dispatches a contingent of men to rescue Dart and his assistants. But before Dart can board the ship, he is badly wounded by Foxy.

Calvert watches while the submarine and its occupants sail away. The compound burns to the ground. Only Calvert and a number of Seal People remain. As the book ends, he awaits an arriving helicopter to carry him back to civilization.

An Island Called Moreau is suffused with Aldiss's characteristic mordant view of life. Late in the story Calvert observes: "I agree that many aspects of human life have always been wretched. Sometimes it seems that the most promising advances of science merely leave us with more problems—just as lowering of the infant mortality rate landed us with world overpopulation" (111). Still later—

> This hasn't been the best-ever century for faith, and some would say hurrah for that. No, I believe in a sort of abstract God, remote and not particularly comforting, whose specialty is continuity rather than succor. The universe is his—I mean, it makes more sense to think of a consciousness behind creation that to imagine that it all grew in its complexity out of nothing, like a mushroom out of concrete. But now that the universe is a going concern, my God is aloof from it—maybe he is now powerless to interfere. You could say he was more of an Artist than an Administrator. (119)

And, as in *Dracula Unbound,* it turns out that the narrator was the agency of the events of the novel. Because of his arrival on the island, Calvert had unwittingly brought about Dart's downfall and the uprising of the beast people: "My arrival on the island had been the signal for a chain of death" (150). At the end of the book Calvert muses: "I recalled how the fable of H. G. Wells, when the beasts on his island had slowly degenerated from the human back to the animal, sounded a note of melancholy. These actual beasts were slowly advancing from the animal to the human; and I could not find it in my heart to think that less melancholy" (165).

"Books like this are all over the place, now," says Aldiss. "You find Jane Austen as a character in a series of detective novels. And there's *Wide Sargasso Sea,* by Jean Rhys, which is a 'prequel' to *Jane Eyre.* It speaks to something of the way in which the generic divisions have dissolved under the excitements and pressures of modern life. Having written my own autobiography, I realize that it's a part of my own mythology. It's changed me in a way, made me feel that I'm free now to do what I like, win or lose. I wonder if authors in the future will reference me as a character in their own fictions. What a terrible fate! There's a story by Max Beerbohm, 'Enoch Soames,' where the title character makes a pact with the devil to go into the future to see if he's referenced in the histories of literature. And he finds he's only a fictional character in a work by Max Beerbohm! Hilariously wonderful! The trouble is, critics take this sort of thing and call it 'postmodern' and serve it up with all kinds of academic phraseology and references to Derrida and all that. It's unreadable. What would George Orwell make of it?"

Epilogue

Consider Aldiss's trilogy as Frankensteinian creations in themselves, stitching together fact and fancy, giving new life to the authors and the characters in the novels, and setting them on the course of further adventures in time and space. Binding them together is a profound anti-establishment and anti-religious commentary placed into the mouths of the characters.

The great paradox that is Brian Aldiss indulges, on the one hand, in a deeply rooted pessimism about the human condition that surfaces in the three novels under discussion here. Consider this admission in his essay, "The Veiled World":

I'm for blasphemy. I am for doubt and disbelief and all those un-comfortable things. We'll need them if we are to get far into the future in any useful way . . . I'm also for the shedding of god and gods. We need to understand ourselves, to come to terms with our own mystery, not the assumed mystery of some assumed godhead. God was mankind's greatest imaginative invention. We've got to survive without him (198).

On the other hand, the Brian Aldiss I came to know that sunny day in July 2004 and in the years of our correspondence that followed—and which constantly surfaces in all his writings—was one of the kindest, most genial persons I've ever met, controversial at times but generally beloved by his colleagues.[4] At the time of our interview he was about to turn eighty and was living comfortably in Headington, "a comfortable part of Oxford," where he confessed the satisfaction of a life that "has rarely been better." He had just published *Affairs at Hampden Ferrers* ("An English Romance"). He continued a corre-spondence with me until his death in 2017. I had the honor to read and comment on the manuscript of one of his last novels, *Walcot* (2009). He called it his "Magnum Opus." But that's another story.

Works Cited

Aldiss, Brian. *Billion Year Spree.* New York: Doubleday, 1973.

———. *The Detached Retina.* Syracuse: Syracuse University Press, 1995. [Contents include "The Veiled World" and "Wells and the Leopard Lady."]

———. *Dracula Unbound.* New York: HarperCollins, 1991.

———. *Frankenstein Unbound.* New York: Random House, 1973.

———. *An Island Called Moreau.* New York: Simon & Schuster, 1981.

———. *Supertoys Last All Summer Long.* New York: St. Martin's Press, 2001.

———. *Trillion Year Spree.* New York: Atheneum, 1986.

---

4. See the obituary by Christopher Priest: www.theguardian.com/books/2017/aug/21/brian-aldiss-obituary

Bousfield, Wendy. *"Frankenstein Unbound."* In *Magill's Guide to Science Fiction and Fantasy Literature.* Englewood Cliffs, NJ: Salem Press, 1996. 2.359–61.

Canby, Vincent. "Corman's 'Frankenstein Unbound.'" *New York Times* (2 November 1990). (www.nytimes.com/1990/11/02/movies/review-film-corman-s-frankenstein-unbound.html)

Clute, John. *Look to the Evidence.* Seattle: Serconia Press, 1995.

Dubose, Thomas. *"Dracula Unbound."* In *Magill's Guide to Science Fiction and Fantasy Literature.* Englewood Cliffs, NJ: Salem Press, 1996. 1.249–50.

Gunn, James. *Alternate Worlds: The Illustrated History of Science Fiction.* Englewood Cliffs, NJ: Prentice-Hall, 1975.

Tibbetts, John C. *The Gothic Imagination: Conversations on Fantasy, Horror, and Science Fiction in the Media.* New York: Palgrave Macmillan, 2011.

———. "Music in the Blood: Greg Bear and the Gothic Imagination." *Penumbra* No. 2 (2021): 90–110.

When Dawn Came at Last to Vandajhar

Darrell Schweitzer

There are dangers in dreaming. I can tell you that much.

Take this, if you will, as a warning:

In dreams I have seen the fabulous city of Kladion, inhabited solely by golden metal birds that sing so piercingly, so alluringly, that the dreamer strives to linger and hear them forever; but always persistent winds carry me away, and, upon awakening, I have never been able to recall a single note or lyric of the songs of Kladion, just a painful emptiness from their memory. This is probably just as well. I am certain that the sirens who tormented Odysseus learned their art in Kladion.

And there is a city of black stone in the midst of a blood-red desert, where even the dreamer must tread in absolute silence, lest a single cough or scraping footstep awaken the winged vampires that hang sleeping in the city's towers and they burst forth in such numbers as to shut out the sky and devour the world. I have been there. So far, I have managed to escape each time.

Yes, I have seen . . . an endless sea haunted by diamond-studded leviathans . . . villages of ghouls on the far side of the moon . . . but most often I dreamt of holy Vandajhar, which lay beyond the Hills of Hesh, on the bank of the river Falnos.

Much has been written of this city in ancient and secret books, how it existed in a state of eternal darkness, beneath brilliant stars; yet was not haunted nor dead, but alive and filled with joy, which is only appropriate, since the very name of Vandajhar translates as "joy" (or perhaps "beauty") in a dozen languages long forgotten by mankind and a dozen more no human being has ever spoken. It is also known as the city that never sees the dawn, for such would be an absurdity, an impossibility; for its very perfection is in that changeless, starry night.

There in Vandajhar a King and Queen sat exquisitely on their thrones, flawless in their countenances and their robes and their crowns and in the splendor of their throne room. Such was the firm faith of the people of Vandajhar that these two would remain forever thus, with the serenity of their thoughts would infusing the realm, bringing changeless peace and contentment to all.

There could be no death in Vandajhar. Never did a soul need to shed its body in order to rise to Paradise. Never was anyone reincarnated. There was no need.

Yet the King and Queen were not totally timeless. It may be that they existed on a vastly different scale of time, so that for them centuries seemed like seconds, and a hundred years might pass before they could be seen to nod or turn their heads, and a thousand before they might speak.

Now, at the very moment of which I write, they felt a certain disquiet, some lessening or faltering in the perfection of their kingdom, like a tingling at the extremity of a limb.

Therefore they summoned before them the great Zathanos, the grand vizier, poet, sage, philosopher, author of many books of wisdom and interpreter of many more, magician, tamer of demons.

The King and Queen spoke within his mind, not with sound, but as though their speech had been implanted in his memory long ago and he only now recalled it.

There is that which was not before, said the King. *Go,* said the Queen, *to the great window, look out, and tell what you see.*

So Zathanos, who had knelt before them, rose. He was neither young nor old, but pale of face and iron-gray in his hair and beard. He strode with firm strides, his starry cloak trailing behind him. He stood before the great arched window opposite the throne, and he looked out over the darkened kingdom of Vandajhar. He saw the perfect stars. Sometimes he had contemplated them at length, to read secrets in their courses and turnings, but now he saw just the stars, as they had always been, gleaming, their reflections like rippling jewels above and in the river below. He saw the rooftops and battlements of the city. He saw a few drifting lights, where revelers made their way across a public square. He heard laughter and common songs from a tavern. He saw, far off among the hills, the Tower of Nightmare, where monsters were kept bound by the power of his own spells. A dragon slept there, wrapped around the tower like a thick growth of leaves, its scales gleaming in the starlight like brazen shields.

He returned to the throne sand said merely, "All is as it has always been."

But the King said, *There is change.*

Look again, said the Queen.

So he looked again and thought he saw, far beyond the hills, on the most distant horizon, a light that had not been there before, as if a star had fallen to earth, or perhaps common folk, rejoicing in the midst of some festival, had lighted a bonfire.

He described this to his Lord and Lady.

Even so, said they. *We feel an unease in our flesh. Go and put an end to it.*

Zathanos could only obey. He bowed three times in ritual fashion, then backed out of the royal chamber, not because it was disrespectful to turn one's back on the King and Queen but because no one, whether lord or wizard, servant or commoner, would ever want to gaze upon their rapturous perfection for a second less than was possible.

Yet he made his way down a winding stair, through a passage lined with stone creatures (that sometimes spoke to him but now were silent), until he came to his own chamber, which was both library and laboratory. With a snap of his fingers he summoned those bound spirits and tamed demons and golden automata which were his servants, and bade them prepare for a journey. While he was capable of enduring great hardship, of crossing the world alone and in disguise, he preferred to travel in a style befitting his rank. There would be a great pavilion set up wherever he chose to rest, and ghostly musicians to entertain him, with his magical books floating in the air, should he wish to consult them, while golden, mechanical warriors patrolled the periphery of his camp, with their flaming swords held before them against any dangers.

So Zathanos set out, in a carriage drawn by horses of living flame and driven by a coachman made of some gleaming, liquid metal; and behind him came his golden warriors with their swords, and his ghosts and tame demons to carry all that he might need or fancy. He encountered a mass of revelers in a public square. They parted before his caravan like the sea before a great ship, their lanterns bobbing and scattering the way tiny, luminous sea creatures do the ocean on a dark night, insignificant, sparkling, then gone.

He paused before the city gate and spoke to the captain of the guard. He ascended with the captain to a high battlement. His long staff clacked on every step as he went.

He pointed out the strange light on the horizon, which he had seen from the throne-room window. It looked a little brighter now, a little larger.

"What do you make of that?"

The captain was so abashed to be addressed by so great a one as the illustrious Zathanos that he stammered like a child.

"I . . . I . . . think it is the dawn."

Zathanos thumped his staff angrily. The captain barely got his foot out of the way.

"Ridiculous! How can there be a sunrise in Vandajhar? That implies *change*. Is not Vandajhar eternal and unchanging?"

So it was recorded from time immemorial, in languages known and unknown, spoken and forgotten, in numerous ancient books, many of which Zathanos had authored himself.

He didn't bother to explain further that the very notion of dawn was not even a legend, but merely a foolish thing spoken of to frighten children and idiots.

He left the captain without another word, descended the stairs, and commanded that the city gates be opened, so that he and his retainers might pass through. Meekly the captain complied, and when the last spirit or automaton or goblin was gone from his sight, the captain muttered softly to himself, "Nevertheless, I think it is the dawn," and he was much troubled that this might be so.

Zathanos, too, was troubled, as he traveled along the road, through villages and towns, where the people seemed to move furtively, and there was no rejoicing, no occasion for which the common folk might have lit a bonfire. From within the taverns came only flickering lights and no songs.

Having traveled for an interval, Zathanos called for a halt, and his pavilion went up, and he feasted, and his musicians played softly, and he consulted his books; and he confirmed what was written therein, that all the land of Vandajhar should never know a sunrise or the day, for the perfection of its beauty lay in the night, beneath the brilliant stars. It always was so and always would be. So it was written in the books, often in Zathanos's own hand.

Yet when he arose, it was from a restless sleep. He had dreamed of blinding light and fading stars, a condition he knew to be impossible, and all the more terrifying because it was impossible.

He took his breakfast. His pavilion was folded up, and while he was waiting for all to be set in order, he climbed a low hill nearby and looked to the east, where he saw that, indeed, the light upon the ground in the distance was brighter than before and more widespread. It was a low, steady glow, as if a fire had been set and was spreading below the edge of the darkened world and was just now beginning to creep over the rim.

"I defy anything that was not before," said Zathanos. "I will extinguish it."

Indeed, this was his oath. He had sworn as much before the King and Queen.

He journeyed for another interval of travel and sleep. Now he met people on the road, who parted to let him pass, but he saw that they were frightened and bore what belongings they could carry on their backs, and were fleeing in the direction opposite to that in which he came, westward, back toward the capital city of Vandajhar with its King and its Queen and its sacred perfection.

"I defy this," said Zathanos.

Once more a magical book hovered in the air before him like an enormous moth, and its pages turned themselves and he saw what was written there, that dawn should never come to Vandajhar. Perhaps it was a promise from the gods; perhaps it was merely the eternal nature of things. This was something he and other philosophers often puzzled over and debated. Was eternity not eternal? Could perfection be less than perfect?

He had no time for that now.

"I defy and deny," he said.

Yet when his pavilion was folded up, he saw that the whole eastern horizon was faintly alight, and overhead some of the stars had truly, if blasphemously, begun to fade.

The magical book fell to the ground like a dead thing.

Now Zathanos grew angry, and he proclaimed yet again that he would defy this new thing, and deny it, and destroy it.

So he summed his automata warriors with their flaming swords, and he marched at the head of them, his staff now swollen with potent magic. Overhead there was faint thunder, from the passing of thousands of night birds, which had abandoned their roosts in the forests and the cliffs of the Hills of Hesh and fled ever westward, into the fading darkness.

He marched, and did care to notice that many of his ghostly servants, when their eyes caught the first gleam of that strange and oncoming light, lost their enchantment and drifted away like smoke, abandoning his luggage. Some of the goblins he had bound broke free and scampered away into the underbrush like enormous rats.

He climbed the Hills of Hesh with his golden, clanking army. There was no time for leisurely meals in his pavilion or musicians or reading from levitating books. Now he would bear all hardships with strength and courage in the service of his Lord and Lady. He would play the hero.

He struggled onward, down the far side of the hills, across the barren lands, as all the while the sky grew brighter and the whole of the horizon before him was unquestionably aflame.

"No," he chanted to himself. "No, no, no, no. There cannot be that which was not before."

He knew that this would be the end of perfection and beauty, if he allowed it to be so.

"No," he said.

His automata soldiers began to fail. Steam hissed out of their joints. One by one they collapsed in useless heaps.

In the end it was only Zathanos himself who reached the world's edge, amid blazing light, and he stood defiant on the rim in his dark and starry cloak with his magic-swollen staff in hand.

But then he could only drop to his knees and let his staff slide from his fingers and tumble into the abyss.

He knew that perfection had ended, however much he might try to deny it.

Yet he was not without resources even then, and he reached up and seized by the legs the very last of the birds of night that fled westward from the terrible fire. Black it was, with enormous gleaming wings, now aflame at the tips and the tail, and shrieking with pain. But still it flew, and Zathanos clung to its legs and it bore him up, beneath the failing stars, over the Hills of Hesh where the shadows faded. He saw the villages and towns now empty. He saw his own Tower of Nightmares in ruin, split open like a ripening seedpod, but there was no sign that the horrors he had trapped therein had escaped to ravage the land. He did not think that the dragon set to guard the tower had gotten very far either. He saw a few of its scales scattered forlornly on the ground.

Then, by a transition he could not follow, Zathanos found himself once more in the throne room of the King and Queen of Vandajhar.

They were still magnificent in their glory, but even here the shadows were in full retreat. The great window blazed.

He brought out from within his cloak the last of his magical books. It fluttered weakly in the air like a dying bird.

"It is written here," he said, "the most terrible of all truths, simply this: that Vandajhar is and always has been a dream, an ideal toward which mankind has always aspired, an impossible phantom thing, a dream—and when the dreamer awakens, and Vandajhar shall be no more."

Now the King and Queen leaned forward on their thrones.

"I pray you forgive your servant, who has failed you," Zathanos went on, almost babbling. "I went to the edge. I beheld the dreamer. It is even possible that by looking on him I woke him up. No, I cannot believe that. Nevertheless, *he is awake*. What is written is written. I think it is in my own handwriting."

The King reached out and the book drifted into his hand. He looked at it and said, with an actual human voice, which Zathanos could hear, "But there is nothing written here."

And the book crumbled into ashes.

Still denying it could not be so, defying, denying, but powerless to destroy what he saw, Zathanos ran to the window and looked out. And he beheld the dreamer fully, as he had barely glimpsed him at the world's edge. Then the dreamer had been only stirring, and now he was fully awake, an ordinary man, who had dreamed such marvelous fancies as Vandajhar and its infinitely beautiful King and Queen, and the Tower of Nightmares with its bronze-scaled dragon, and the goblins in the underbrush, and the ghostly bearers abandoning the luggage, and all the rest. For just an instant the two of them, Zathanos and the dreamer, seemed to recognize each other.

Zathanos saw nothing more, ever.

And the King and Queen of Vandajhar rose from their thrones and likewise went to the window to look out. They at the last conducted themselves with indescribable grace and dignity.

Whatever they saw, whatever they understood, was only for an instant.

Then there was only blue sky.

*   *   *

And when I awoke I was lying in my own bed, gazing out the window at that blue sky. I had a fleeting feeling that someone was staring at me with amazement and alarm and despair.

But that quickly faded.

In the street below a car alarm went off.

I still manage to dream of such places on rare occasions, glimpsing even Kladion or the vampire city in the red desert; but never again have I beheld holy Vandajhar. I write down what I can remember. It seems unsatisfactory, like a shape seen in dissipating smoke.

And despite diligent researches I have been unable to find in any reference work, however esoteric, even a single reference to the city that had never known the sunrise.

August's Pumpkin

Scott J. Couturier

August's pumpkin, plumpen on greening vine!
Beneath sterling Sturgeon Moon you ripen,
Clammy with dew; Summer's too-dry design
Cannot stop your swell, seeds thriven within.

August's pumpkin, flushing with orange flame!
Bee's busy buzz accentuates your drowse,
Sun crowning you in aureate acclaim:
Faeries rouse by nightfall to swear you vows.

August's pumpkin, Autumn's emissary,
Augury of Winter's oncoming reign:
Almost you seduce lost souls to tarry,
Though as Jack's lantern you become their bane.

Ghost Park by Moonlight

Carl E. Reed

Wake up, Danny! Wake up!

Ten-year-old Danny Mitford moaned in his sleep and turned over to face the wall.

C'mon, Danny! Oliver tugged on his brother's pajama sleeve. *Wake up!*

"Don't want to," Danny mumbled, pulling a pillow over his head.

Sure you do! Get up! Let's go to the ghost park.

Danny moaned again.

Oliver removed the pillow from Danny's head and tossed it against the wall.

The moon's as bright as the sun! I don't know how you can sleep on a night like this! Honestly, I don't!

"Because I'm tired," Danny grumbled. "Aren't you tired?" He sat up in bed and rubbed his eyes. A rabid fan of all things that took place "a long time ago in a galaxy far, far away . . .," dark-eyed, somber-faced Danny wore short-sleeve pajamas whose chest top bore a silk-screened image of a Star Wars X-wing emerging from the fireball of an exploding TIE Fighter. "You should be."

But I'm not tired!

"No kidding."

There had been another single bed stacked above him not long ago, with a guardrail to keep Oliver from rolling off the top bunk onto the floor in his sleep.

I'm not tired at all!

"Keep your voice down or Mom and Dad will hear you." Danny's eyes blink-blinked in the penumbral darkness, focusing on his brother.

Oliver wore the striped collared shirt, elasticized waistband with drawstring shorts and high-top sneakers he'd been wearing when the car broadsided him. He was small and frail, even for an eight-year-old. His delicate-boned physiognomy, close-set, darting eyes, and nervous mannerisms had earned him the nickname "bird-brain" from his brother.

Oliver had been right behind Danny when he was killed. They were doing laps around the block on their BMX-style bikes that spectacular summer day in the city—73 degrees, light breeze blowing, not a cloud in the sky—shouting to each other and giggling as they raced along. They pumped the peddles of their bikes like madmen, rushing past scolding pedestrians and barking dogs lunging at the ends of leashes; feeling the rush of joy, freedom, and exhilaration only pre-pubescent boys freed from the imprisonment of adult-policed housing could feel. They were midway through lap five when Danny was hit.

Mother had repeatedly cautioned them: *Stop your bikes and check both directions before crossing the alley. Look for cars that might be turning into you, or barreling down the alley, to ensure that the coast is clear.*

And they *did* stop—the first dozen times they encountered the T-section alleyway exits opening onto Jefferson Street, Balmoral Avenue, and Selnick Boulevard. But what fun was that? Braking and losing all forward momentum and speed—coming to a complete halt—having to start up again from a wheel-wobbling standstill. Bogus, man! Total drag. Serious Bummersville.

So that thirteenth time (unlucky number indeed) they came to an alley, Danny raced right across, catching an onrushing dark blue mass in his peripheral vision even as a squeal of brakes pierced his ears and the acrid smell of burnt rubber fouled his nostrils. Danny glanced over his shoulder in time to catch the four-door sedan with the tan soft-top and thin white-wall tires slam into his brother with a shriek-crunch of buckling fender and hood. The impact catapulted Oliver into the air off his mangled cherry-red bike even as he hit his own brakes and skidded to a stop. The scream that reverberated in the air? His own.

That last freeze-frame image of his brother was burned into memory: Oliver suspended above a disintegrating bicycle—auburn hair hanging down obscuring his face—hands and arms thrust out, fingers clutching . . . for what? Handlebars? His brother? The safety and security of the world a second ago? Danny's shock froze time into a snapshot of horror.

For an instant. Then Oliver bounced off the hood of the hard-braking car, smashed into the spider-webbing windshield, and rolled off onto the pavement in a crumpled, limbs-akimbo heap. Dark-red arterial blood spread from beneath his corpse . . .

C'mon! urged Oliver. *Let's go to the ghost park!*

Danny jolted back to himself. His reverie had lasted but a second. Blood pounded in his temples and he found that he was breathing in rapid, shallow breaths. "I said keep your voice down!"

Why? asked Oliver. *You worried about Mom and Dad? They can't hear me.*

Danny had nothing to say to that. He had no idea why only he could see and hear Oliver's ghost—for that was what was surely standing before him now.

The ghost of Oliver. Oliver the ghost.

No matter how many times he recited some variation of this phrase to himself, the situation still struck him as unreal. His brother—no longer among the living—returning to visit. This peculiar state of affairs did not horrify so much as fill him with a terrible, desolating sadness.

This was the fourth time Oliver had called upon him since his burial a month ago. In truth, these early-A.M. visitations had become somewhat routine. The first time Oliver came to see him—the day after interment—Danny hid beneath the covers and moaned and shivered until his brother went away again. *Why, you would have thought* you *were the ghost!* Oliver rebuked him on his second visit a week later, the night they talked for an hour.

On the third visit (second week after interment) Danny and Oliver quietly played together till diffused light from the master bedroom down the hall warned of their parents' awakening. Oliver retreated to a corner of the room beside a dresser whose top was crowded with an alarm clock, Godzilla coin bank, 1/32nd–scale model of a World War II P-47 Thunderbolt fighter plane, and battered baseball glove. Danny scrambled back into bed, closed his eyes, and pulled the covers up to his chin. But his parents weren't fooled when they hove into view. The floor was littered with toy cars, trucks, and airplanes—toys that had been put away when he first climbed into bed.

"What's going on in here?" his father called out from the doorway. This was clearly a rhetorical question. "It's two in the morning, for god's sakes!"

Christopher Allen Mitford—a thin, chain-smoking man who'd only grown more emaciated and hive-ridden (face, neck, and arms) since Oliver's death—shuffled into the bedroom in threadbare slippers and loosely belted robe. His wife peeked out from behind him, similarly attired in robe and slippers, angling for a better view of the room in the soft gray light that filtered through the drawn curtains of the double-hung window.

The jig was up. Why not confess?

Danny sat up in bed and swung his feet to the floor.

"Don't get up," Christopher said, "unless"—relenting—"you want a drink of water or need to use the bathroom."

Danny considered. "No," he said. "I'm okay."

Gail Mitford stepped around her husband. A Rubenesque, once raucous-laughing, life-of-the-party type, she'd undergone a startling transformation since Oliver's death. Her eyes had sunk into dark hollows; deep grief lines wrinkled the skin around eyes, nose, and mouth. "Why were you out of bed this late at night, honey? Couldn't you sleep?"

Danny hesitated a second before answering. He glanced over at Oliver.

His brother held a finger to his lips, then faded into the wall.

"Son, your mother asked you a question."

Danny switched his gaze back to his father. Might as well just come out with it. Hadn't he resolved to tell the truth? "Ollie was here again," he said.

Gail gasped.

"I wasn't afraid, though!" he hastened to reassure his mother. "We played together, as quietly as we could."

"Danny . . ." Christopher breathed, looking stricken.

Shame flooded Danny as his face flushed. He knew—in a way he couldn't articulate or even fully comprehend—that he'd just said something unspeakable.

"'Again,'" Gail said. "You said 'again,' Danny! How many times . . ." She faltered.

"Three," Danny said. He winced at seeing his mother's distress. "Counting tonight, Ollie came here three different times."

Gail put a hand to her mouth.

"I'm sorry!" Danny blurted. "I should have sent him away, not played—"

"Hush, Danny." Christopher glanced at his wife, then advanced to the bunkbed. He dropped to his knees, gathered Danny in his arms. Hugged him fiercely.

Danny hugged him back.

Christopher stroked Danny's hair. "You know that can't be true, right, champ?" His voice broke. "That just can't be true—no matter how badly we all might wish Oliver alive again."

"Ollie isn't alive; he's a ghost," Danny corrected.

Christopher broke the extended clench, grasped his son by the shoulders, and gazed meaningfully into his eyes. "Now listen: we all miss him terribly—"

"Ollie was here," Danny averred.

"A dream," said Christopher. "You had a *dream*, Danny. Then your imagination took over and you got up, pretending—"

Danny shook his head in negation.

"It *had* to be a dream, honey. Can't you see that?" Gail's hands twisted together before her, waist-level. "There's no other explanation, there just isn't!"

Danny glanced again at the corner of the room where Oliver had faded into the wall.

No sign of his brother there.

Christopher and Gail tracked Danny's gaze to the corner of the room, studied the dresser and its environs.

"What?" asked Christopher. "You want that fighter plane?"

"Your baseball glove?" Gail hazarded, improbable as that seemed.

"No," said Danny. And sighed. "I guess he's gone now."

Christopher stood up, exchanged looks with Gail.

Danny lay back down. He tucked the sheets and cover up under his chin.

Christopher refocused his attention on his son. "No more playing with toys in the middle of the night—or rather, early morning," he commanded with a weak smile. "And no more bad dreams, okay?"

"It wasn't a bad dream," mumbled Danny. "Wasn't a dream at all."

"Danny . . ." began Gail, only to stop herself. Then, turning to her husband: "We need to take these bunkbeds apart. We should have done it before the funeral, right after . . ." She gestured helplessly. "But I just couldn't, Chris. I couldn't . . ."

"I know," said Christopher, not unkindly. "We'll talk about this in the morning, hmm?"

Gail nodded, not trusting herself to speak further.

Christopher laid a consoling hand on her shoulder.

They turned and drifted out of the room.

Danny waited till he heard the box springs under his parents' queen-size bed give out a mattress-dampened squeak from down the hall. Then he sat up in the lower bunk and directed his gaze to the corner of the room where Oliver had faded into the wall.

"Ollie?" he whispered.

No response.

"Oliver?" he whispered again, slightly louder this time.

No further sign—visual or aural—of his brother's presence.

The spectre. The spirit. The ghost.

Danny lay back down, turned on his side, and pulled his knees up to his chest.

Sleep was a long time coming. When it arrived, he spiraled down into a dreamless black void—limbs lead-weighted, mouth slightly agape—as if pole-axed. And whimpered.

Danny awoke groggy and out of sorts in the morning. He remembered his parents coming into the bedroom—their initial confusion and consternation at discovering the floor littered with toys—the ensuing discussion. Oliver coming to see him again; vanishing when mother and father entered the room.

Or . . . had it all been a dream, as his father suggested? Was he losing his mind? Seeing and hearing things that weren't there?

No, Oliver had called upon him; he was certain of it. As certain as he was that Oliver would call upon him again—soon.

Come on, Danny! Let's go to the ghost park!

Back to that again.

We can play there! Tag, hide-and-seek, statues. Other games!

Oliver stood beside his bed, earnestly entreating, on his fourth and final visit.

"Ghost park" was his brother's phrase for "cemetery." *The* ghost park (emphasis on that leading determiner) could only refer to East Lawn Cemetery—where Oliver was buried, a short five-mile drive away. His forearms and the back of his neck prickled with goose-flesh every time Oliver uttered those two words together.

"No," said Danny. "I'm not going with you to the gh-ghost park. Not now; not ever." Alarm and exasperation caused him to stutter. He was already sitting up in bed; now he swung his feet to the floor. "Never."

Why not?

"Because you're dead and I'm still living."

Oliver frowned. *That's not a nice thing to say. That's not a nice thing to say at all!*

"I know it isn't." Danny climbed out of bed as quietly as possible, taking care not to let the frame springs beneath the mattress squeak more than absolutely necessary. "But it's true. You're the one who's dead; not me."

Oliver gazed at him blankly. *Hey, I'm still your bird-brain baby brother though, right? We can pl—*

"You can't keep coming here like this. It isn't right. You're upsetting Mom and Dad."

Only because you keep telling them I come here! Oliver flung his arms wide, as if to embrace his brother, though it was a gesture of despair and confusion. *Where else am I supposed to go, Danny?*

Where else, indeed. God, he had no answer to that. Didn't even want to think about it.

"I'll tell you what," Danny said slowly, mulling it over. "We can hang out in the treehouse, like we did last summer. One last time, okay, Ollie? We'll stay there till dawn. Read comic books, and talk and stuff. How does that sound?"

Oliver put a hand to his chin, in imitation of their father pondering a momentous decision. Took his hand away. *Okay,* he said.

"Great!" Danny said with false enthusiasm. He strode to the double-hung window and pushed the curtains aside, raised the shade to let the light of a full moon brighten the room with silvery radiance.

See? I tole ya—bright as the sun!

"Sssh!" Danny cautioned. He wasn't sure if his parents could hear Oliver or not, but he wasn't taking any chances. He undid the window locks and slid the half-screen and bottom sash up as far as they would go, revealing a rectangular escape space roughly four feet across by three feet high—large enough to allow the egress of little boys intent on hijinks.

He and Oliver had gone out this second-floor window in just such a manner a couple of times last summer. They'd clambered down the extruded brick exterior to the ground-floor cement patio and crossed the yard to climb a rope ladder to the ramshackle tree-house built amongst the thick and gnarled limbs of the centuries-old oak beside the back fence. (Extruded brick walls were meant for climbing, they felt—else why build them, if not to challenge the agility and daring of adventurous squirrels, energetic monkeys, and daring little boys?) There they had stayed till dawn, just hanging out for the illicit thrill of it. Once—feeling especially adult and criminal with their taboo-breaking—they'd shared a cigar up in the tree-house, feeling just as mighty and fine and overall pleased with them-selves as any latter-day Tom Sawyer and Huckleberry Finn.

"You go first," Danny said. He stepped away from the window.

Sure, said Oliver with a shrug of his shoulders. And walked through the wall.

"Oh!" said Danny, thinking *duh!* to himself. What did he ex-pect? He kept forgetting Oliver was a ghost. He stepped back to the window and looked out.

Oliver waved to him from the patio below.

Danny waved back—then wriggled out the window.

The tricky point of a successful house escape came midway through the egress, when you had to reach for the gutter a couple of feet away to secure a handhold, simultaneously twisting your torso while pulling your legs through the open sash as your feet felt for purchase on the extruded bricks. Once you had oriented and bal-anced yourself properly it was then a simple matter to descend the wall to the ground.

Except this time it all went wrong. Danny moved too quickly, driven by equal parts impatience, excitement, and a stomach-clenching foreboding he didn't have long to contemplate. He reached for the gutter, pulled his legs through the window—and caught the tip of one toe against the sash as the gutter gave way. For a second Danny hung precariously upside down against the side of house, flailing arms scrabbling for purchase on the extruded bricks. Then his foot slipped off the sash and he dropped straight down to the cement patio thirty feet below with a startled cry.

"*Danny!* Oh my god! Don't move, honey!"

Danny looked up at his mother and father peering down at him through the open sash of the window: hunched-over figures outlined against the brighter light of the bedroom's two-bulb ceiling fixture, their faces pale and gaunt in the moonlight.

He felt warm. Incredibly sleepy. Something very bad had happened, that much was clear. He couldn't move, though he tried. And his skull felt . . . wrong. Broken. *Shifting* with every rasping breath. His face and pajama top were damp with blood. There was no pain.

His father's face disappeared from the window even as his mother screamed down again: *"Danny!"*

He tried to speak, but his tongue was a stone in his mouth.

Don't worry, he wanted to cry out. *I'm okay—really!*

But he couldn't.

His dulling eyes fixed on the stars. Strange, he'd never really noticed their magnificence before. Such beauty and mystery, spread across the sky. An entire universe up there . . . Had he been blind?

No, he'd been ten. Distracted. Busy. You know, with . . . stuff.

Well, he'd pay attention to the stars now. Yes sirree Bob! He'd make a point to glance up at those bright, twinkling lights every night he dashed in and out amongst the tombstones, giggling, with Ollie. Forever innocent. Gleeful. Ignorant of the horrors of the world. A rustle amidst the autumnal wind making whirlpools of brittle leaves, tiny twigs, stray trash. In the ghost park by moonlight.

Mirror Falls

Debra K. Every

The forest surrounding Mirror Falls was a little dark, a little scary, and a lot wonderful. Dierdre grew up taking long hikes to the top while her parents made up ghost stories along the way. But that was years ago. She had her own daughter now. Dierdre figured a day at Mirror Falls was just what Marie needed after the year they'd had.

There's nothing harder for a thirteen-year-old than getting uprooted in the middle of a school year. But after John's sentencing, getting uprooted was the least of it. Their neighbors had been heartless with their stares and whispers, particularly after Dierdre returned home from her month at St. Francis. Just because she'd needed a little help didn't mean she was cut from the same cloth as her husband. But the worst of it was poor Marie having to manage in foster care without her.

Once her daughter had been brought back home, Dierdre decided to pack up their belongings and move to Brockton ten miles from where she grew up. It would be their fresh start. She'd found an adorable little cape at the end of a quiet lane with not a neighbor in sight. With their unpacking now behind them, it was time for a bit of fun. It was time for Mirror Falls.

The tires crunched on the gravel parking lot as Dierdre coasted in. It was a little more overgrown than she remembered, but that was all right. There was still a trail map posted under its own tiny roof with pamphlets stuck in wooden holders along the side—not that Dierdre needed any of that. She could hike Mirror Falls in her sleep, even now, after all these years.

"You're going to love it, hon," she said. "When I was growing up, I'd pretend that Mirror Falls was an elegant lady with a new dress specially made for each season. At this time of year the water will have dwindled down to a trickle. I know that doesn't sound very exciting, but once we get onto the bridge you'll get a bird's-eye view of the creek bed. The rock formations from that height are really something special."

Marie turned to her mother with an indulgent look—as if Dierdre was the daughter and Marie the mother. Dierdre couldn't help but feel ashamed, but now that she was well and they were back together, things were sure to get better.

"It sounds like fun, Mom." Marie patted her mother's hand with a trace of sadness pulling at the corners of her mouth. "I love you," she said with a smile.

Dierdre felt her throat catch. "I love you, too."

Marie gathered her chestnut hair into a ponytail and got out of the car. Dierdre loved watching her daughter move—more colt than little girl. Her legs had become too long for her body, and her hips, while still slim, were just beginning to round out. But no matter how much she'd grown, she would always be Dierdre's Sweet Pea Marie.

She joined her daughter at the trail head and they set off. It was a glorious day, just cool enough for a hike and warm enough to have fun. Dierdre was struck by the symmetry of a mother sharing a memory with a daughter. She had waited patiently for Marie to be returned to her, all the while fantasizing about this very moment: hiking along a familiar trail with her daughter by her side.

"I used to think Mirror Falls was the most exciting place in the world," said Dierdre. "I'd run ahead of my parents on this very path with my mother yelling to come back and my father laughing at his feisty daughter."

"Hard to imagine you feisty," said Marie, suddenly serious.

Shouldn't have said that, thought Dierdre, with a grab at her stomach. Comparing her happy childhood to Marie's was thoughtless. Her daughter had borne the brunt of John's anger and darkness and recriminations no matter how hard Dierdre had tried to protect her.

Today would be the first step toward changing all that. And it would be good for Dierdre as well. No more pills. No more hospitals. No more endless conversations about what was and wasn't real.

They hiked for nearly a half hour, barely saying a word. Every once in a while Marie would pick up an interesting stone and tuck it into the pocket of her jeans, just like when she was four, with her porcelain face and easy smile. By the time she was six, Marie had amassed quite the collection. She kept her *jewels* in a treasure box hidden in the back of her closet next to an old tea party set and a pair of patent leather shoes. To see Marie picking up stones now gave Dierdre hope.

They eventually came to a fork. To the right was the public trail; to the left, a little-used path leading to a footbridge that spanned a deep ravine.

They turned left.

In another half hour they were staring down at an ancient creek bed some eighty feet below, with a footbridge thrown across the expanse. Along the bottom lay a cityscape of jagged rocks jutting out, here and there, with just enough water flowing through the crags to highlight the beautiful sculpture nature had created. It was just as Dierdre had remembered. This was going to be great.

"All right then, hon. Ready for that bridge?"

Marie looked at the footbridge draping across the ravine with its six-inch wooden slats two inches apart and its rope railings on either side. There was a quick twitch of worry between her eyebrows, but to Dierdre's delight Marie nodded and said, "If you think it's okay, sure."

It was as if Dierdre had been there only yesterday. The key was to keep her eyes forward—to put one foot in front of the other without looking down. She counted the planks laid out like a bolt of fabric ready for inspection. Thirty-two planks, just as she remembered.

Okay. Here we go.

First plank.

Looking good.

Next.

Couldn't be easier.

Eight planks now. Eight steps. But with each foot forward Dierdre felt a growing uncertainty. It surprised her. She never worried when she and her parents crossed the bridge. Her father would be in the lead, then Dierdre, then her mother. They laughed and joked with every step.

Not now. The bridge swayed with her slightest movement. Could there have been additional supports back then? Maybe. Come to think of it, Dierdre remembered a safety net stretched underneath.

She looked down. The netting hung in tatters, rotted away long ago.

"Are you sure about this?" called Marie.

No, thought Dierdre. *Not sure at all.*

And then, for a quick second, the annoying doctor from St. Francis was standing in front of her wearing that condescending look on his face. The one that said she'd gotten something confused; something wrong; something—

Forget about it. Dierdre couldn't let Marie know she'd made a mistake. They were now in it and it was up to Dierdre to get them out.

"Just keep your eyes focused ahead," she said, a little too cheerfully. "You're going to love when we get to the other side."

She snuck a peek at how high they were. The eighty-foot drop seemed bigger than she remembered, and the planks were in terrible shape. Every time she stepped down she could feel the wood give way.

"Are you all right back there?" she called to Marie.

"I guess."

Dierdre could hear how nervous her daughter was by the tremor in her voice. If she could turn them around and go back, she would, but going back would now take longer than going forward. And why the hell hadn't the park built proper railings? The damn rope rails swung every bit as much as the rest of the bridge.

Dierdre put her foot down on the eighteenth plank and heard a crack. She froze. The rocks below seemed to open wide, ready to swallow them whole. Her nervousness broke into panic. She brought the right and left ropes close to her body with so much force, the bridge started to swing. The more it swung the more frightened she became.

"Mom! You've got to hold still!"

"It's okay, sweetie," she called, with her voice high and tight. "Just stay calm."

She over-corrected one way and then the other. Dierdre felt Marie's hand on her shoulder and, as a reflex, shoved it away. Then the whole bridge tipped to one side.

Her feet slid toward the left, now nearly a foot lower than the right. She looked back to check on her daughter and—*oh, no!* Marie was grappling for the rope rail as she slid off the edge!

"Help!" she screamed.

But Dierdre would have to let go of the rope to help her.

No, she thought. *I can't.*

Marie's legs were now dangling helplessly off the bridge with her eyes wild and her mouth stretched into a scream.

"Mom, please! Pull me up!"

Dierdre shook her head awake. *What am I doing?* She reached with her right hand as her left held onto the rope. But her daughter was too far away. If Dierdre leaned any further, she'd fall off as well.

Dierdre lowered her arm, as if she had no choice in the matter, and then straightened up. Once her arm had taken its place by her side she leveled her eyes on her daughter and watched—just watched—as Sweet Pea Marie, her blessing, her pride, her light, hung helplessly in the air.

And then . . .

And then . . .

And then . . .

. . .

It was as if Dierdre had been there only yesterday . . . and it confused her. *Oh, yes,* she thought. *I'm on the bridge.* The key was to keep her eyes forward—to put one foot in front of the other without looking down. She counted the planks laid out like a bolt of fabric ready for inspection. Thirty-two planks, just as she remembered.

Okay. Here we go.

First plank.

Looking good.

Next.

Couldn't be easier.

And all the while, Marie hurled insults.

"Look at you," said Marie. "You're so scared I can see your stupid shoulders up around your ears."

"Don't talk to me that way. Let's try to have fun."

"Fun? What a joke. No way would we be doing this if Dad was around."

Dierdre had suffered her daughter's escalating rebukes for the past ten months. There was no getting around it. Marie had become a younger version of the frightening man she had married. John may have been charming when they first met, but after five years living within his orbit, she'd come to the disturbing realization that her husband was ill. It was the way he laughed at other people's pain, his lies, his exaggerations . . . and his frightening temper. It was that viciousness that had landed him in prison on a manslaughter charge.

"Jesus, Marie, he was convicted. What do you expect me to do?"

"How about making a lousy phone call or maybe even go for a visit? You were his wife, for Chrissake."

Dierdre tightened her grip around the rope rails. "We'll talk about this when we get off the bridge."

"Look at you," she laughed. "You're scared shitless."

"Marie, please."

Her daughter grabbed hold of Dierdre's shoulder, brought her lips to her mother's ear, and whispered, "I hate you." Then, against all reason, she pushed Dierdre toward the left edge.

"Stop!" said Dierdre, as the bridge swayed. She turned to look at Marie and, when she did, let out a gasp.

Her daughter's face was different—dark and sunken. Her eyes were shadowed by her furrowed brow, and the edges of her mouth were twisted into a sadistic smile. Dierdre tried to shake the image from her head. This isn't real.

That's right, Dierdre. It isn't real. It isn't-t-t-t-t. Isn't—

But that didn't stop Marie from grabbing Dierdre by the hair and jamming her knee into the small of her back.

"What are doing?" cried Dierdre. "Let me go!"

The bridge swung wildly as she kept a grip on the rope, trying desperately to hold on.

"Marie, please. I'm going to fall."

"And what a terrible accident that will be, Mother dear. I'll just cry and cry."

Dierdre sunk to her knees with the rope held in her fists. Marie scrambled on top, trying to pry Dierdre's fingers open, all while the bridge tipped to one side. Marie managed to release her mother's right hand and was now working on the left. Dierdre clamped her free hand onto the front of Marie's neck and squeezed.

"Let go!" rasped Marie.

Dierdre marshaled her strength and, without hardly thinking, pushed her daughter with so much force that Marie skidded away, grabbing hold of the handrail as she did. But she couldn't hold on. She couldn't hold on.

As Marie fell, her face flickered in and out, first angry, then featureless—as if every bump and crevice had been wiped smooth—back and forth, getting faster and faster, stopped only by the impact of her body echoing up from the creek bed, hitting Dierdre in the face with a cruel slap.

It was as if Dierdre had been there only yesterday . . . and it confused her. For a frightening moment she thought Marie was—

But no. Marie is right behind me. The key was to keep her eyes forward—to put one foot in front of the other without looking down. She counted the planks laid out like a bolt of fabric ready for inspection. Thirty-two planks, just as she remembered.

Okay. Here we go.

First plank.

Looking good.

Next.

Couldn't be easier.

"Gee, Mom, maybe we shouldn't do this."

"It's okay, honey. We'll take it slow."

But with each step Dierdre was regretting it. The whole point of walking across the bridge was to help Marie with her confidence. She'd thought that with John locked away, Marie would regain some of her old self, but the abuse her father had laid on the thirteen-year-old wasn't going away. She had become as timid as a four-year-old child and every bit as dependent, looking to Dierdre for help with the smallest of things. Even so, walking across a footbridge eighty feet above a ravine was turning out to be a stupid idea.

"Look, sweetheart, we're halfway across. You're doing great."

Dierdre hoped her voice sounded steady but she sure as hell didn't feel that way. The planks were in terrible shape. Every time she stepped down she could feel the wood give way. She kept her eyes focused front. The rope rails felt rough and prickly in her fists.

Twelve planks.

Sixteen.

Halfway there.

A thick forest waited for them on the other side, with a path leading back down the mountain. There was a collection of hidden shapes deep within its shadows—hard to tell what they were. But Dierdre's imagination was playing tricks on her. (*This isn't real . . . isn't real.*) The trees seemed to part, revealing a tableau in diffused light flickering like an old-time movie. It was a mirror image of the very bridge they were standing on. In the reflection Marie was behind her, wearing a grim expression as she struggled to keep her balance.

But the mirror showed something more. Hovering over Marie was a shadowy figure, growing taller, its face twisted into an expression of . . . hard to tell. Wait. Hunger. Yes, hunger—as it stared down at her daughter. The sky in the reflected image darkened, growing ominous.

Dierdre turned her head to check on Marie. There *was* someone behind her. Someone or some*thing*. It wore a robe of moss and twigs. Its face was collapsed in on itself; eyes empty, hair long and caked with mud, mouth open wide revealing a large tongue and rotted teeth.

She had to get Marie away from it.

"Honey, I need you to keep your eyes on my face."

"What? Why? What's the matter?"

"Just keep looking at my face, and as you do, walk past me so you're in front."

"I can't do that," said Marie with a whimper.

"Yes, you can."

"Why? Is something wrong?"

The dark figure grew taller.

"Just do as I say and everything will be fine."

Marie nodded and grabbed her mother's outstretched hand. But when she stepped onto the plank next to Dierdre's foot there was a loud crack. The plank broke in two, leaving Marie's and Dierdre's legs dangling in the air.

She grabbed Marie's arm. "I've got you, baby." But her daughter was shaking so hard, Dierdre was having a hard time keeping hold. "We'll pull our legs out together," she said. "Ready?"

Dierdre did her best to keep her face calm, but in her peripheral vision she could see the rocks below change shape and size until they stood upright like a field of jagged spears, growing taller, coming closer. She had to reach the other side before the spears got to the bridge. They couldn't go back the way they came. That *thing* was blocking their way.

With a great deal of struggling and even more coaxing, she

managed to get Marie back onto the bridge. Marie was now first, Dierdre second, and the dark figure last, breathing with a kind of gurgle, smelling of old leaves and moldering earth. Dierdre tightened her grip on the rope rails, praying the planks would hold. She could feel the creature's body pressed against her back. She could smell its fetid breath as it leaned its cold cheek into the crook of her neck. Its two arms, as white as death, reached out on either side of her, trapping Dierdre in a horrible embrace.

The creature combed its bony fingers through her hair and brought its mouth close to her ear. "Not you," it whispered. Then it flipped up and over both Dierdre and Marie until it stood directly in front of her daughter.

Marie let out a scream. It wrapped its arms around her and squeezed as she struggled to get away—her face buried in its chest, her arms pinned to her sides. With a giant leap it dove off the bridge, taking Marie with it. But they didn't fall. They hung in the air, two halves of a whole, suspended in time. Then with a quiet pop, time caught up with them and they fell down, down until the creature faded away, leaving Marie alone in a freefall to the bottom.

Dierdre watched helplessly as her daughter's terrified face grew smaller and her arms and legs stretched out wide like a child making snow angels on a quiet winter's day.

It was as if Dierdre had been there only yesterday. *Marie?* The key was to keep her eyes forward—to put one foot in front of the other . . .

It was as if Dierdre had been . . .

It was . . .

Echoes of the Self: Fitz-James O'Brien's Literary "Other" as Ontological Inquiry

John P. Irish

> "May the reader never be haunted by Shadows!"
> —Fitz-James O'Brien, "The Man without a Shadow: A New Version"

Speculative fiction writers frequently employ the concept of "the other" in diverse and intriguing ways. While much literary analysis has focused on categorizing these different types,[1] a more compelling question arises: why do writers incorporate "the other" into their narratives? This inquiry transcends mere identification, aiming to uncover the underlying messages or philosophical insights that the introduction of "the other" seeks to explore within a story. Fitz-James O'Brien (1826/8–1862), a notable figure in speculative fiction, utilized "the other" not merely as a narrative device but as a tool to delve into profound questions of identity and ontology. This essay will not catalogue the types of "others" in O'Brien's work; instead, it will explore how he used them to examine and articulate deeper ontological questions and themes of being.

Long before Sigmund Freud, C. G. Jung, and Otto Rank delved into the psychology of "the other" and the mental bifurcation of the human psyche, O'Brien was already exploring this concept through his fiction, poetry, and essays.[2] Although his reflections lacked the

---

1. For a strong overview of this scholarship, the reader is directed to the important essay by Tony Fonseca, "The Doppelganger."
2. I acknowledge the complex nuances of classifying literary elements, yet for the scope of this essay I treat concepts such as the other, the double, and the doppelgänger as interconnected and interchangeable. As highlighted in the opening paragraph, the central exploration of this essay is not merely to categorize these elements, but to delve into how O'Brien employs the concept of the other to engage with autobiographical and

support of psychological data or experimentation, O'Brien's assumptions about the composition of the human psyche were remarkably prescient, emerging well before Freud, Jung, and Rank began publishing their groundbreaking theories.

In February 1853, shortly after arriving in America following a brief stay in London, O'Brien wrote a compelling essay on the philosophical concept of "the other" (or alter ego) and its potential relation to human nature. Titled "The Two Skulls," the essay delves into philosophical notions of doubling and how perception influences both the perceiver and the perceived. In it, O'Brien presents initial insights into "the other," which he later employed in his fiction.

First, he explores the idea that physical closeness enhances clarity. This proximity, however, also magnifies imperfections and uncovers shortcomings, offering multiple perspectives of the observed subject. O'Brien observes, "we never see a great man who did not disappoint. . . who did not lose something of his magnitude by near approach" (*The Best of O'Brien* 21).[3] Perspective adds to or detracts from identity. Second, he contends that we often impose our values on others, attributing qualities they may not possess and exaggerating their virtues. This leads to disillusionment when genuine flaws emerge: humanity is "disappointed if they find him manifesting any of the ordinary every-day traits of humanity" (21). This implies an imposition upon the world around us, where our understanding influences our perception of others. Third, he discusses significant distinctions between external and internal traits, noting fundamental "differences in the external position of men . . . [compared to] their intrinsic qualities" (21). Inherently, there are multiple "others" with-

philosophical questions. This approach allows us to probe more deeply into O'Brien's thematic intentions, exploring how these manifestations of the other contribute to discussions on identity, existence, and the human condition within his speculative fiction.

3. This collection contains a sampling of O'Brien's best fiction, poetry, and essays. I have edited a one-volume edition of O'Brien's best speculative fiction for Hippocampus Press, *The Lost Room and Other Speculative Fiction* (forthcoming in 2025).

in each of us. Fourth, he highlights individuals' extreme positions, including ethical behaviors, and points out the hypocrisy often seen in religious figures who preach one set of values while acting contrary to them. Finally, O'Brien touches on the compartmentalization of human existence. Individuals present varied facets of themselves to different audiences and the external world. Here he introduces the concept of the shadow, where these multiple selves can become external entities that still influence the individual: "It became a thing outside himself, but it pushed him along" (23).

In O'Brien's work, "the other" serves as a vehicle for probing various philosophical questions: epistemological, metaphysical, ethical, phenomenological, and ontological. However, for the purposes of this essay we will specifically examine how O'Brien employs the literary "other" as a means to explore autobiographical questions of identity through the lens of ontology—the philosophical study of the nature of being and existence. Several self-referential questions emerge from his fiction: Who am I? What defines my identity? Am I a being subject to change? Does free will truly exist? What happens to me when I undergo change? How do I ascertain my own identity?

O'Brien categorizes the narratives in his fiction into two distinct realms, focusing on the concept of "the other": the external "other" and the internal "other." The external or physical "other" is a metaphysically real entity with a physical presence. The internal "other" manifests itself within the mind's consciousness, not real in a metaphysical sense but still very real within the protagonist's mind, influencing the physical world and its inhabitants. The distinction between these two can blur or remain distinctly clear within his works. The physical "other," which can be either malevolent or benevolent, often serves as a catalyst, prompting the protagonist to question something fundamental or to initiate significant change. The internal "other," emerging as a projection of the inner self, frequently allows for the expression of suppressed desires—desires that social norms might otherwise inhibit or reflect actual behavior. Additionally, this internal aspect can provide a means of escape for protagonists from overwhelming emotions or situations they find themselves incapable of confronting directly.

This paper will explore six of O'Brien's stories featuring main characters who grapple with "the other." Half of these stories address "the other" as an internal manifestation, while the other half present "the other" as a physical presence. All incorporate autobiographical elements, utilizing various literary techniques to delve into self-referential ontology. In one story O'Brien employs a method that would become a hallmark of his writing: the dream sequence, where a character encounters his future self in a dream. Another story uses the traditional motif of the shadow to explore identity. We will also examine a pair of stories (a diptych) that highlight contrasting images and messages about "the other" and ethical action. Additionally, we will analyze one of his best speculative short stories, where "the other" is employed with the most sophisticated use in the whole of O'Brien's fiction—the uncanny and "the other" collide in a powerful example of loss on multiple levels. Finally, we will look at a relatively unknown story where O'Brien narrates the tale of a child with an unnatural affection for the dead. These stories not only explore deep philosophical questions about identity but also reveal important autobiographical elements about O'Brien himself.

In 1852, O'Brien's inaugural year in America, he wrote a series of stories centered on the theme of "the other," displaying a distinctiveness within the literary exploration of "otherness." In August, within the pages of the *American Whig Review*,[4] O'Brien published a noteworthy tale titled "The Old Boy."[5] The narrative revolves around the

---

4. This publication served as the primary vehicle for O'Brien's early works in America. Over the first few years he gradually transitioned to other venues for his writing. Unfortunately, much of what O'Brien published in America was done anonymously, making it challenging to establish a definitive canon of his work. The *American Whig Review* was a significant source of his early publications and featured some of his best initial efforts.
5. This story was not identified by Francis Wolle as part of the O'Brien canon; however, Wayne R. Kime did identify this as an O'Brien story. I

protagonist, Lionel Darkman, whose surname subtly hints at a shadowy presence. Echoing a passage from his essay "The Two Skulls," O'Brien begins the story with a profound declaration: "Every man is a double. He is what he knows himself to be, and what others think of him. The two men—the outward and the visible, and the inward and invisible man—are often very different sorts of people" (149).

Darkman, a teenager at a boys' boarding school, awakens from an extraordinarily long sleep—a motif O'Brien often uses to explore liminal spaces within his fiction.[6] The dream that grips Darkman is vividly detailed, presenting a future in which he becomes a celebrated novelist, resonating deeply with his existing passion for literature. This scenario aligns with Clifford Hallam's exploration of Freud's concept of the uncanny, where familiar experiences become unfamiliar and unsettling, akin to the phenomenon of déjà vu (14–15). The dream's vividness and the subsequent disorientation Darkman feels upon waking echo this uncanny sensation. Additionally, Paul Coates's analysis connects the appearance of the double in literary iconography with the Romantic belief in the mutability of character, suggesting that one can look into the future and see oneself (2). Darkman's vision of his future self as a renowned author reflects this Romantic notion, blurring the lines between his current identity and his potential future, thus deepening the story's exploration of the self and "the other." Darkman envisions himself as "a great and distinguished man, accustomed to receive the consideration due to my position" (149). The dream, extremely vivid, leaves Darkman wondering about its nature. Was his dream a premonition of his future, suggesting supernatural foresight? Could it represent a form of time travel, where Darkman lives out his future only to be returned to his

agree with his assessment, based on the fact that the topic and wording were almost identical to his essay "The Two Skulls."

6. Here O'Brien plays with Washington Irving's story of "Rip Van Winkle." While Rip falls asleep and wakes up in the future, Darkman falls asleep and dreams about the future but returns to the waking world with foreknowledge of what is to come.

present upon waking? Alternatively, might the dream signify an out-of-body experience, providing him a glimpse into what could be? Or perhaps, the dream is merely a vivid fabrication of his subconscious?

Upon realizing what has happened, Darkman finds himself trapped in the body of a teenager, yet possessing the mind and years of experience of a man. Those around him will not accept his dream; they laugh at him and mock him, forcing him to navigate a hostile environment intent on making him conform and act like a teenager. Aware of his predicament, Darkman escapes the confines of the boarding school and attempts to live out his life as presented in his dream. Despite his mature mind, his physical presence remains that of a young boy, and no one takes him seriously. Consequently, Darkman creates a *nom de plume,* an alter ego—"the other" within "the other"—adding intriguing multi-layers of reality within the story. He invents a fictitious persona, Percy Egremont, and acts as the literary agent for this mysterious writer. The first publication is a huge success, and through his alter ego Darkman achieves literary success, fame, and fortune.

This dream of Darkman reflects interesting autobiographical elements from O'Brien's own life and underscores the profound influence of literature on him. Growing up in affluence in southwestern Ireland, O'Brien had ample access to great literary works, particularly drawing inspiration from the poetry of the Romantics. In his dream, spanning a decade, Darkman envisions himself a great writer, embodying the aspirations and inner life of his creator. The autobiographical elements in O'Brien's story are pronounced. He knew from an early age that he aspired to be a writer, having achieved publications in a major periodical, the *Nation,* during his teenage years.[7] His first publications were poetry, focusing mostly on political and economic themes, demonstrating a keen sense of cultural and political awareness. O'Brien's lifelong interest in themes of justice is evident throughout his work. However, the story also reflects

---

7. Wolle 1–29. This is the only full-length biography of O'Brien to date and, as such, is the main source of O'Brien scholarship.

struggle, as Darkman faces physical limitations due to his youth and a societal reluctance to take him seriously because of his age, mirroring obstacles O'Brien himself encountered.

Darkman's creation of a fictitious persona, Percy Egremont, to get published further mirrors O'Brien's own experiences. Notably, O'Brien initially concealed his identity under the pseudonym Heremon[8] or simply used his initials FJOB in his early publications.[9] This tactic speaks to the broader theme of identity and recognition that permeates his work. Additionally, O'Brien's publishing career was marked by consistent struggles. His personality often led him to abandon projects midway, leaving others to complete them, before he would move on to new endeavors brimming with potential. This pattern of behavior reflects not only the challenges he faced in his career but also adds depth to his exploration of identity and personal evolution in his fiction.

The story of Darkman intricately weaves ethical and existential questions into its narrative, particularly concerning the nature of reality and free will. First, if Darkman's dream truly is a premonition, it raises the troubling suggestion that his future is predetermined, thus casting doubt on the reality of free will. This scenario proposes

---

8. According to medieval Irish legends and historical traditions, Heremon was one of the chieftains who took part in the Milesian invasion of Ireland, which conquered the island from the Tuatha Dé Danann, and one of the first Milesian High Kings.

9. The poem, "Oh! Give a Desert Life to Me," which promoted leaving Ireland because of the current political troubles and difficulties caused by the English, was commented on by the editor of the periodical, Charles Gavan Duffy, a man dedicated to the cause of Irish patriotism: "This might be called 'The Coward's Resource' . . . we recommend our friend not to come again when the work is over. He will get a cold welcome from the men he left to bear the heat of the harvest." This is the first known published work by O'Brien. The name was printed without the hyphen, as "Fitzjames O'Brien." The second poem published by O'Brien in the *Nation* was signed with the initials "T.J.O'B.," no doubt a misprint by the editors of the periodical. Further publications were either anonymous or published with the name "Heremon."

that the experience of free will might be an illusion—a phenomenological falsehood—that prompts deeper metaphysical inquiries about
whether our experiences accurately reflect the true nature of the
world. Second, Darkman's vision of the future introduces a classic
existential dilemma regarding the concepts of essence and existence.
If his future is indeed fixed, the question arises: does he possess the
capability to alter this predetermined path? This consideration
touches on existential angst—knowing one's possible future and
questioning the role of free will that can either paralyze or motivate
an individual. For Darkman, this knowledge could be a profound
burden, potentially shaping how he perceives and interacts with the
world. Is his life devoid of authentic choice and control? And if so,
does this realization help him by relieving the pressure of decision-
making, or does it harm him by stripping away his sense of agency
and purpose?

The story also explores the complicated notion of identity. The
internal and external struggle between the boy and the man is intri-
cate, posing the question: what makes us who we are? As O'Brien
questioned in his essay "The Two Skulls," is it the outer teenager or
the inner adult man that defines a person? Can both identities coexist within the same individual? Darkman's memories are real and integral to his identity, yet the outside world refuses to acknowledge
them, seeing only the teenage body. For those around him, this external perception becomes the sole source of his identity and ontological reality. However, for Darkman it is the internal reality that
determines his being and identity. These conflicting perceptions of
identity—the external world's refusal to accept his internal experiences and his own conviction of their reality—create an unresolved
tension. Despite this, the story concludes with Darkman achieving
the success he envisioned in his dream, suggesting that internal
identity and personal truth can ultimately shape one's destiny, even
if they are not recognized by the outside world. This resolution
highlights the theme that true identity is defined internally, irrespective of external perceptions.

Through these themes O'Brien not only explores the complex interplay between predestination and free will but also challenges the reader to contemplate the implications of a life where future events are already scripted, questioning the very essence of human existence and autonomy. In this story, "the other" serves as a foil to explore critical concepts of identity while also revealing significant autobiographical elements from O'Brien's own life.

In 1852, O'Brien's exploration of otherness produced a lighter, more humorous narrative compared to "The Old Boy." Published in the *Lantern,* the story titled "The Man without a Shadow: A New Version" serves as a playful parody of Edgar Allan Poe's 1835 tale "Shadow: A Parable." O'Brien's narrative humorously subverts the traditional notion of a shadow by introducing an unusual and troublesome shadow that becomes an unwelcome companion to the protagonist, persisting in both daylight and moonlight. As O'Brien describes it, "It is not my natural shadow I speak of; but an unnatural, an impertinent Shadow, which of late attached itself to my person, and could not be shaken off whether in the glare of sunshine or the pale moonlight" (91). This deviation from the norm invites readers into a playful examination of identity and presence, challenging conventional perceptions of the self and its darker counterparts. Through this imaginative reinterpretation O'Brien engages with but expands upon Poe's thematic legacy, infusing it with his distinctive literary style and philosophical inquiry.[10]

The whimsical elements of "The Man without a Shadow" also humorously reflect O'Brien's own life and habits. The story's shadow not only follows the protagonist to dinner, engaging in human-like activities, but also incurs double charges at the restaurant and borrows items—behavior that comically mirrors O'Brien's reputed tendencies. In a particularly amusing scenario, the shadow acts as a separate entity, borrowing one of the protagonist's shirts and a five-

10. This is a uniquely O'Brien style of writing and the reason why he can be considered an important bridge between the romantics of the early 19th century and the realist of the late 19th century.

dollar bill, only to disappear afterward. This playful depiction aligns closely with anecdotes from O'Brien's life, as related by his first biographer Francis Wolle, suggesting that the shadow acts as an alter ego. Known for his financial escapades, O'Brien's arrival in America is marked by his renting a room at New York's finest hotel and then evading the bill (Wolle 30). Moreover, he once borrowed money from a friend under the pretense of settling debts but instead used it to host a lavish party, notably excluding the lender. Wolle notes: "O'Brien during the rest of his life was always living beyond his means; indeed, he became a typical example of the impecunious Irishman, and when he did receive money for his writings was much more likely to spend it in giving extravagant dinners for his friends than to use it in payment of his debts" (31).

O'Brien's fiction not only serves as a canvas for the exploration of metaphysical and existential themes but also provides a deeply autobiographical glimpse into his own life and struggles. Through characters like Darkman and personas such as Percy Egremont, O'Brien artfully mirrors his personal journey in the literary world—his early ambitions, the societal challenges he faced as a young writer, and the identity obfuscations necessary for his initial literary engagements. The use of literary devices such as dreams and shadows further enriches his narrative approach, allowing O'Brien to weave complex questions of identity and existence into the fabric of his stories. These elements not only enhance the literary depth of his works but also offer a poignant reflection on the personal trials and tribulations he endured throughout his career. Thus, O'Brien's stories are not merely tales of fiction; they are narratives steeped in the realities of their creator's life, presenting a compelling fusion of art and autobiography.

The year 1855 was pivotal in O'Brien's exploration of "the other," marked by the publication of two significant stories, "The Bohemian" and "The Pot of Tulips." These narratives extend his early literary experiments, blending autobiographical elements with profound inquiries into identity and ontological questions. Both stories, while thematically aligned, offer a nuanced contrast in terms of character development and the moral implications of their actions, reflecting O'Brien's personal preoccupation with the pursuit of wealth. These stories not only showcase his skill in crafting engaging tales but also his ability to embed deeper philosophical questions within his works. By juxtaposing these narratives, we can better analyze how his personal ambitions and existential reflections manifest in his characters. Each narrative explores different facets of ambition and consequence, mirroring O'Brien's own life struggles and his continuous quest for financial and literary success. This comparison enriches the reader's understanding of O'Brien's work, highlighting his complex approach to themes of wealth, identity, and morality in a Victorian context.

"The Bohemian," published in the July 1855 issue of *Harper's New Monthly Magazine,* marks an important milestone in O'Brien's literary career, three years after his arrival in America. By this time, O'Brien was well on his way to establishing a formidable literary reputation, in part due to his strong professional relationship with Harper's—a publication that regularly featured his work, along with its sister publication, *Harper's Weekly*. Set against the backdrop of Pfaff's Beer Hall in New York City, "The Bohemian" is a tribute to the American Bohemian movement, of which O'Brien was a significant part.[11] This vibrant and influential community, akin to its European counterparts, was a hub for some of the most avant-garde writers and artists of the era (see Parry). Notably, Walt Whitman, another prominent figure of this group, was a frequent visitor to Pfaff's, further highlighting the pub's central role in the cultural and social interactions of these American Bohemians. O'Brien's connection to this community is evident in his writings, which often reflect the ideals and the aesthetic of the Bohemian movement. Through "The Bohemian," O'Brien not only pays homage to this influential circle but also integrates his experiences and observations into the

---

11. See John P. Irish, "'Of Nobler Song Than Mine.'" Part of this dissertation was published as "Fitz-James O'Brien Hands In His Chips."

narrative. This story, therefore, serves as both a piece of literary work and a cultural artifact, encapsulating the essence of an era defined by its radical and revolutionary ideas in art and society.

In "The Bohemian," O'Brien weaves a captivating tale around Henry Cranstoun, a young lawyer; his fiancée, Annie Dean, who is clairvoyant; and Philip Brann, a self-styled Bohemian with a penchant for the mystical arts. Brann, who prides himself on his ability to mesmerize people and read minds, approaches Cranstoun with a proposition. He introduces himself as someone who aspires to amass wealth with minimal effort—a lifestyle he believes Cranstoun also desires. Initially skeptical, Cranstoun's doubts are dispelled when Brann demonstrates his powers by mesmerizing him. Convinced of Brann's abilities, Cranstoun becomes curious about how Brann might assist him. Seizing the opportunity, Brann suggests that Cranstoun's fiancée, Dean, possesses untapped magical powers that, with the right guidance, could lead them to hidden treasures. Brann proposes to meet Dean to unlock her potential by reading her mind, which he claims can access information about these hidden riches, promising immense wealth for all involved.

The story takes a tragic turn when the mesmerism experiment, despite its initial success in uncovering a hidden treasure, results in dire consequences. Cranstoun and Brann extract the location of a vast treasure from Dean's clairvoyant abilities, leading them to wealth beyond their imaginations. The thrill of their success, however, is short-lived. Contrary to Brann's assurances, the process of mesmerism severely impacts Dean's health. Brann had promised that while the procedure might cause temporary illness, Dean would recover swiftly. Unfortunately, the reality proves devastatingly different. Within a day of the procedure, Dean falls gravely ill and succumbs to the effects, dying unexpectedly. This outcome leaves Cranstoun in a profound state of shock and remorse upon his return. "Below stairs, in the valise, lay the treasure I had gained. Here, in her grave-clothes, lay the treasure I had lost!" (242). While he now possesses immense wealth, the cost of this fortune is the life of his fiancée—an irreversible and tragic price. This twist in the narrative underscores the ethical dilemmas and unforeseen repercussions of tampering with supernatural forces, highlighting the profound moral of the story: that the pursuit of wealth, especially through unconventional and risky means, can lead to unforeseeable and often catastrophic consequences.

In "The Bohemian," O'Brien cleverly employs the concept of "the other" as a philosophical and ethical juxtaposition through its characters. Philip Brann and Henry Cranstoun, as doubles, reflect each other's desires and ambitions, prioritizing personal gain and wealth above all else. This shared attribute is epitomized in their willingness to exploit Dean's supernatural abilities, despite the risks involved. Dean, as Cranstoun's fiancée and another double, embodies a starkly different set of values. She represents selflessness, loyalty, and the willingness to sacrifice for those she loves. Her tragic fate highlights the moral cost of Cranstoun's and Brann's actions, serving as a stark contrast to their selfish motivations. Dean's character underscores the ethical implications of using others merely as means to an end, a theme that resonates deeply in the story's tragic conclusion. Through these characters O'Brien explores deep ethical questions about the nature of desire, the morality of ambition, and the consequences of using people as tools for personal advancement. The juxtaposition of Brann's and Cranstoun's selfishness against Dean's altruism provides a rich tapestry for examining the conflict between personal desires and moral responsibility. This interplay not only drives the narrative but also invites readers to reflect on the cost of unchecked ambition and the value of human relationships.

This narrative also serves as a poignant autobiographical reflection on O'Brien's involvement in the Bohemian movement. Known for his relentless pursuit of the next big score, O'Brien's personal desires for wealth and prosperity were evident from his youth. Upon receiving a large inheritance as a young adult, he promptly moved to London, where he squandered his entire fortune within two years. His expenditures on books, food, clothes, theatre attendance, and travel highlight his indulgent lifestyle. Consequently, O'Brien was compelled to turn to writing as a means to sustain his lavish habits. While writing allowed O'Brien to engage in intellectual pursuits, it also served more pragmatic purposes for him: it was a way to maintain a life of luxury. In this regard, "The Bohemian" can be seen as embedding autobiographical elements within his fiction, mirroring his own life's pattern of seeking pleasure and financial gain, even at significant personal cost. This story not only delves into themes of ambition and the supernatural but also reflects the Bohemian ethos of defying conventional societal norms and seeking life's pleasures without succumbing to the drudgery of traditional labor. Through the character of Philip Brann, O'Brien explores the allure and the moral ambiguities of such a bohemian lifestyle, posing questions about the ethical implications of using supernatural powers for personal gain.

Published in the November 1855 issue of *Harper's New Monthly Magazine*, "The Pot of Tulips" stands in stark contrast to "The Bohemian," yet it similarly explores speculative themes. Unlike most of O'Brien's work, which often veers toward the weird and philosophical, this narrative is a traditional ghost story, offering a different perspective on the theme of "the other."

The story follows two friends, Harry Escott, the narrator, and Jasper Joye, who purchase a historically significant house that once belonged to old man Van Koeren of New York, a house admired by Escott since his youth. The house carries a storied past, having once hosted George Washington. However, its more recent history is marred by the dark legacy of Mr. Van Koeren, known for his abusive treatment of his wife, Marie, and his distrust toward their son, Alain, who he suspected was not his own. This suspicion fueled further abuse toward Marie, who eventually passed away. Mr. Van Koeren then largely abandoned Alain, who spiraled into a life of depravity and eventually fathered a child, Alice Van Koeren. Tragically, both Mr. Van Koeren and Alain died simultaneously, leaving Alice with minimal inheritance and a cloud of mystery surrounding the family's fortune.

This backdrop sets the stage for a haunting exploration of the sins of the past and their repercussions on the present, as the protagonists navigate their new home's eerie atmosphere and unravel its grim history. The ghostly elements of the narrative serve as manifestations of unresolved historical traumas, making "The Pot of Tulips" a poignant commentary on legacy, memory, and the lasting impact of familial strife. Through this tale O'Brien not only contributes to the genre of ghost stories but also embeds deeper reflections on the nature of inheritance, both material and emotional, and the shadows that past misdeeds cast on subsequent generations.

Escott reveals that his fiancée is none other than Alice Van Koeren; it was this circumstance that motivated his purchase of the ancestral home. However, lacking sufficient funds to marry Alice, Escott continually seeks ways to increase his wealth while remaining loyal to her. The two main characters are puzzled about what might have happened to the old man's wealth. One night, both men retire to their respective parts of the house for bed, and Escott experiences a strange and otherworldly encounter with a ghost—the ghost of Mr. Van Koeren. The ghost, unable to speak, is holding a pot of tulips. Tulips, emblematic of the old man's Dutch heritage, were abundant throughout the house and garden. Before a second encounter, Escott convinces Joye to join him in the bedroom, where both men see the ghost again, but this time accompanied by another spectral figure—it is Marie, Mr. Van Koeren's wife. The old man, still holding the pot of tulips, gestures insistently toward it. Recalling a similar pot on the mantelpiece in the waiting room, the two rush there and realize that the old man was signaling them to turn the pot. When they do, a side panel opens, revealing documents that provide information about the old man's hidden wealth.

Both stories, "The Bohemian" and "The Pot of Tulips," explore themes of wealth and desire, yet they diverge significantly in their portrayals of intentions and outcomes. In "The Bohemian," Cranstoun is depicted as someone willing to endanger his family and sacrifice his fiancée's well-being to amass wealth, reflecting a reckless and selfish pursuit of financial gain. His use of supernatural means to achieve this end ultimately results in tragedy and loss, illustrating the perilous consequences of prioritizing wealth over human relationships. Contrastingly, in "The Pot of Tulips," Escott demonstrates a commitment to his fiancée Alice, showing his loyalty by purchasing a home that connects her to her ancestral roots. His intentions are rooted in care and preservation of family heritage, rather than sheer greed. While supernatural elements also play a crucial role in uncovering hidden wealth in this story, the outcome is vastly different. Escott's actions are rewarded not only with material wealth but also with the preservation of personal relationships, highlighting a more balanced and ethical approach to the pursuit of fortune. Thus, while both characters employ otherworldly means to acquire wealth, the stories underscore contrasting moral lessons about the impact of one's intentions and actions in the pursuit of riches. "The Bohemian" serves as a cautionary tale about the dangers of greed and self-interest, whereas "The Pot of Tulips" offers a more uplifting narrative about the rewards of loyalty and the preservation of personal integrity.

Both stories incorporate autobiographical reflections on O'Brien's early life experiences, particularly highlighting the impact of wealth and family dynamics. O'Brien's father passed away when he was a teenager, after which his mother remarried and moved the family from County Cork to County Limerick in southern Ireland. The psychological effects of these significant changes in his formative years, though not explicitly documented, probably had a profound impact on him. The introduction of a new paternal figure and the relocation could have been sources of emotional and psychological upheaval for the young O'Brien.

Wealth plays a central role in both "The Bohemian" and "The Pot of Tulips," reflecting O'Brien's own upbringing in affluent settings. This background would have instilled in him an appreciation for the comforts and cultural enrichment that wealth can provide, such as access to literature, poetry, music, and quality clothing—

luxuries to which he grew accustomed in his youth (Wolle 31–33). These stories suggest that for O'Brien, wealth was not just a means of attaining material comfort but also a crucial element for a stable, secure, and fulfilling life. His narratives often explore how wealth can act as a stabilizing force, offering safety and enabling access to higher cultural and intellectual pursuits, while also acknowledging the potential moral and ethical dilemmas it can provoke. Through his fiction, O'Brien seems to wrestle with the dual nature of wealth, recognizing both its empowering qualities and its capacity to inspire greed and corruption. But access to wealth comes with great difficulty, especially for a young man relying solely upon his artistic talents. As Wolle notes: "The numerous stories which he tells of a young man in debt, humorous and withal a bit pathetic, almost invariably show their hero—the author under various disguises—as vexed and troubled by tailors' bills . . . reduced sometimes to poverty-stricken makeshifts to hide or disguise the meagerness of his wardrobe" (31). O'Brien was perpetually living well beyond his means. The conflict between the young O'Brien and the older O'Brien echoes themes found in "The Old Boy," where the young and old serve as mirror reflections of desires versus the realities of the situation.

The characters of Cranstoun and Escott in "The Bohemian" and "The Pot of Tulips" serve as autobiographical doubles that reflect the significance of the literary "other" in his fiction. These characters not only mirror aspects of O'Brien's personal experiences and his contemplations on wealth, but also engage with the philosophical and ethical dimensions of their desires through their interactions with other characters in the stories.

In "The Bohemian," "the other," represented by Philip Brann, acts as a malevolent force that taps into the darker aspects of human nature. Brann's influence leads Cranstoun to act on his baser instincts, prioritizing the accumulation of wealth over moral considerations and the well-being of his fiancée. This portrayal of "the other" as a corrupting influence reflects a critical view of unchecked ambition and the moral degradation it can cause. Conversely, in "The Pot of Tulips," "the other" is embodied by Mr. Van Koeren, who, despite his past as an abusive and destructive figure, ultimately seeks redemption. His posthumous appearance as a ghost who guides Escott and Joye to the hidden treasure represents his desire to atone for his past misdeeds. This act of revealing the treasure to his granddaughter and her fiancé can be seen as a final, redemptive gesture to ensure their future prosperity and happiness.

Andrew Webber argues that "the other" as double, or doppelgänger, represents "a figure of visual compulsion" (3), highlighting a power play between the ego and alter ego. Dimitris Vardoulakis expands on this by asserting that the double is a distinct being, perceptible by the senses and existing independently of the original. O'Brien's stories, "The Bohemian" and "The Pot of Tulips," anticipate these theories by exploring the complex interplay between self and "other." In "The Bohemian," Philip Brann acts as a doppelgänger to Henry Cranstoun, embodying the moral conflict driven by the allure of wealth and power. This relationship exemplifies Webber's idea of visual compulsion and Vardoulakis's notion of the double as an independent entity. Similarly, in "The Pot of Tulips," the ghost of Mr. Van Koeren serves as a spectral double, guiding Escott to hidden treasure and challenging his sense of identity. Through these narratives, O'Brien delves into the ethical and existential implications of encountering one's double, reflecting his engagement with philosophical questions of identity, morality, and the human condition.

Through these stories O'Brien uses the concept of "the other" not just as a narrative device but as a means to explore deeper questions about human nature, ethics, and the consequences of our choices. The "others" in these tales serve as foils that prompt the main characters to evaluate their priorities and the lengths they are willing to go to achieve their goals. Thus, the accumulation of wealth, while a central theme, is intricately tied to broader questions of moral integrity and redemption, highlighting the complex interplay between personal desire and ethical responsibility in O'Brien's work.

This lack of personal stability, driven by desires for wealth and affluence, led O'Brien to live in a constant state of flux and insecurity. This insecurity is directly related to the ontological concept of identity, particularly the identity derived from place and home. O'Brien's personal experiences of displacement and the impermanence of residence in New York profoundly influenced his exploration of "the other" in his speculative fiction. In his standout story, "The Lost Room," O'Brien delves into this theme from a unique angle, shifting focus from a human or ghostly other to a more abstract yet equally poignant other—the idea of home itself.

"The Lost Room," published in *Harper's New Monthly Magazine* in September 1858, is an exceptional piece in O'Brien's body of work.[12] It follows his notable success with "The Diamond Lens" earlier that year and precedes other famous tales such as "What Was it? A Mystery" and "The Wondersmith" in 1859.[13] This story exemplifies O'Brien's evolved storytelling prowess, particularly highlighting his improved ability to craft compelling endings—a significant leap from his earlier efforts. In "The Lost Room," O'Brien deftly

---

12. For similarities to this story, see H. P. Lovecraft's "The Music of Erich Zann" (published in 1922). I believe that Lovecraft was influenced by O'Brien in the construction of his story. Lovecraft was familiar with and admired O'Brien's work as evidence in his observation on the writer: "O'Brien's early death undoubtedly deprived us of some masterful tales of strangeness and terror" (65).

13. "The Diamond Lens" and "The Wondersmith" are two of the three stories upon which O'Brien's reputation as a writer of speculative fiction rests today. Alongside "What Was It? A Mystery," these three works are solid pieces that deserve a larger audience. "What Was It?" was one of the first stories to explore the concept of invisibility. "The Wondersmith" was among the earliest tales to delve into the concept of robots, featuring wooden carved puppets imbued with evil spirits. I have explored O'Brien's reliance on Mary Shelley and her classic *Frankenstein*, particularly in his two stories "The Diamond Lens" and "The Wondersmith": see "Stories of Genius and Madness."

employs the themes of the uncanny and "the other," integrating them seamlessly into the fabric of the narrative. The "other" is intriguingly represented through various figures and symbolically through the apartment itself, which becomes a character in its own right. This integration enhances the eerie and unsettling atmosphere of the tale, drawing readers deeper into its mysterious world. This story not only reflects O'Brien's mastery in handling suspense and the supernatural but also marks a high point in his creative output, demonstrating his ability to engage readers with a well-executed conclusion.

"The Lost Room" opens with an unnamed narrator who, troubled by insomnia, begins to survey his surroundings in meticulous detail. This introduction serves multiple purposes in the narrative. By describing items that also appeared in O'Brien's personal life, the story blurs the lines between fiction and reality, enhancing the autobiographical undertones. Additionally, the narrator shares an anecdote about a great-grandfather who was knighted by the English queen—a detail that, while seemingly extraneous, subtly prepares the reader for a shift in the story's setting. This shift is crucial as it not only alters the physical space but also deepens the thematic exploration of the story.

This background sets a foundation for understanding the story's deeper layers, particularly its exploration of identity and ontology. As the story unfolds, these elements of autobiography are not just narrative embellishments but are integral to the overarching theme: O'Brien's use of "the other" to probe questions of self and existence. The detailed setting and personal history imbue the narrative with a sense of authenticity and introspection, reflecting O'Brien's ongoing engagement with themes of personal and existential significance. Through this approach, he skillfully intertwines the external environment of the apartment and the internal world of the narrator, creating a rich tapestry that challenges the boundaries between the self and "the other."

Unable to sleep, the unnamed narrator decides to take a journey outside into the garden of the apartment complex, hoping the night air will clear his mind and help him relax. However, this turns to fear when the narrator encounters his first "other" within the story narrative. Because the night is so dark, it is impossible for the narrator to get a clear glimpse of the unwanted guest. When the guest asks for a light, the brief burst of illumination reveals "the other" as a ghastly figure with a ghoul-like visage. The guest warns the narrator about the inhabitants of the apartment building, claiming they are ghouls intent on devouring him: body and soul. Refusing to believe this fantastical story, the narrator bids goodnight to the guest and re-enters the apartment building. Here is where the story really begins to take a dark turn.

This dramatic sequence in "The Lost Room" deepens the story's exploration of the uncanny and the supernatural. The narrator's nocturnal encounter in the garden significantly shifts the narrative tone, introducing a palpable sense of dread and suspense. The mysterious figure, resembling a ghoul and warning of other ghouls residing in the apartment, serves as a chilling herald of the transformations that follow.

Upon returning to his apartment, the narrator experiences a profound disorientation from an overwhelming burst of light—a motif that captures the essence of the uncanny in Gothic literature. The once-familiar and comforting space is altered in ways that are both surreal and disquieting. This transformation of common objects into unfamiliar versions of themselves—the piano into an organ, a painted tree into a real one seen through what was once a wall—effectively destabilizes the narrator's sense of reality. This metamorphosis of the apartment challenges the boundaries between the known and the unknown, heightening the tension and mystery of the narrative.

Moreover, the sudden presence of six strangers eating strange foods at his table where his books once rested amplifies this sense of intrusion and displacement. This scene not only intensifies the eerie atmosphere but also embodies the theme of "the other" infiltrating the personal and private spaces of the protagonist. These "others," possibly the ghouls referenced by the mysterious figure, represent external manifestations of inner fears and anxieties, blurring the lines between external threats and internal psychological turmoil. They, like the unwanted guest in the garden, also represent a physical threat to the narrator.

This turning point in "The Lost Room" further intensifies the narrative's surreal and unsettling qualities. The confrontation between the protagonist and the strangers encapsulates the theme of reality versus perception, challenging the protagonist's—and the reader's—understanding of what is true. The strangers' insistence that the apartment belongs to them shakes the protagonist's conviction, introducing a layer of doubt and questioning the reliability of his own senses. The decision to resolve the dispute through a game of chance symbolizes the arbitrary nature of truth in this transformed reality. The protagonist's loss in the game and subsequent expulsion from the apartment is a poignant moment, highlighting his helplessness and the loss of control over his surroundings. As the door shuts behind him, sealing off what he believed to be his own space, the fleeting glimpse of the apartment reverting to its original state before transforming into a mere wall is a powerful visual metaphor for impermanence and loss.

This final transformation, where the door is replaced by a wall, leaving the protagonist isolated from a place he once considered his sanctuary, encapsulates the existential dread and the theme of alienation central to the story. It confronts the protagonist—and the reader—with the unsettling possibility that our grasp on reality is not only fragile but can be irrevocably lost, echoing broader existential concerns about belonging, identity, and the elusive nature of truth. O'Brien's philosophical skepticism reaches its high point in this story, where the narrator has no reason to trust anyone or anything. His senses provide contradictory information, leading to an existential paradox about reality.[14]

---

14. O'Brien's best story exploring this philosophical skepticism is "What Was It? A Mystery." In this story, the narrator's senses provide contradic-

"The Lost Room" not only explores the theme of "the other" through its characters but also significantly through the apartment itself, which initially provides the protagonist with identity and comfort. This sense of security is dramatically upended when he returns from the garden to find the apartment transformed into an alien and hostile environment. The once comforting space now opposes him, filled with strangers who challenge his ownership and sense of belonging. This unsettling transformation causes the protagonist to deeply question his identity and his very existence. The apartment, a key element of his personal and ontological foundation, becomes "the other" that disorients and alienates, turning what was once a sanctuary into a source of profound existential crisis.

Like the other stories explored in this essay, "The Lost Room" also reflects autobiographical elements from O'Brien's own life. His consistent financial instability and the resultant lack of a permanent home are mirrored in the protagonist's loss of his apartment, which symbolizes a deeper loss of identity and security. As Jessica Amanda Salmonson has noted:

> [The] story could be interpreted as a fable about Fitz's own lost room when, in poverty, he was forced to give up his board and move in on friends ... Autobiographical references riddle Fitz's stories. The objects lovingly described in the opening third of this tale almost certainly belonged to him. The living situation—two rooms rented in a large mansion—were typical of his own generally impoverished circumstances. The discussion of Sir Florence O'Driscoll is taken directly from Fitz's family tree on the maternal side. (O'Brien, *Wondersmith* 255)

This theme extends beyond the personal to encompass O'Brien's broader sense of dislocation from his homeland of Ireland, intensifying the narrative's exploration of loss.[15] The apartment, as "the oth-

---

tory information about the reality of the world, forcing the protagonist to grapple with unexplained epistemological and metaphysical paradoxes.

15. There is some debate among O'Brien scholars about the extent to which he felt the loss of his native land of Ireland. I believe there was pro-

er" in this story, represents not just a physical space but a profound sense of being uprooted, illustrating how integral a stable home is to one's sense of self and belonging. Through this narrative O'Brien articulates a dual loss—both personal and cultural—that deeply affects his characters' identities and life experiences.

In "The Lost Room," O'Brien probes what happens to one's sense of self when this anchoring presence is disrupted or absent. The story articulates a deep-seated anxiety about the loss of a stable home and, by extension, the erosion of the sense of self and continuity. This reflects O'Brien's own struggles with finding a permanent residence and his feelings of being unmoored from a stable, consistent home environment. This theme resonates on a broader scale, touching on the universal fear of losing one's place in the world and the existential dread that can accompany such loss. O'Brien's choice to personify the apartment complex as "the other" encapsulates the profound impact that our living spaces have on our psychological and emotional well-being.[16] "The Lost Room" thus serves as a poignant reflection on identity, belonging, and the deeply human need for a stable place to call home. In "The Lost Room," the apartment complex becomes a metaphor for the instability and transience of home. For many, home is not merely a physical space but a pivotal component of identity; it anchors individuals in a familiar context, enriches their life with memories, and fosters a sense of belonging and continuity. Home forms a core part of one's ontological foundation, influencing how one perceives oneself and interacts with the world.

---

found loss, despite the fact that being Irish in 19th-century New York could be a liability. He found it necessary to include Irish themes and topics in much of his writing throughout his American publications.

16. Similarly, Blake Crouch's *Dark Matter* (2016) echoes O'Brien's themes of alienation and the dislocation of home as they relate to personal identity. In the novel, the main character, Jason Dessen, experiences similar displacement and alienation when he is thrust into an alternate reality. When he returns to his apartment, it is uncannily similar yet different. I have not ruled out the possibility that O'Brien, in this story "The Lost Room," has crafted an early tale of interdimensional travel.

The final story explored in this essay also uses "the other" as a way of examining the loss of home and the deep yearning humans have for a stable place of security and identity. O'Brien experienced physical and mental displacement throughout his life. As a young man, his world was thrown into turmoil by the early death of his father, which uprooted him from his home. The transformative experience of receiving his inheritance, moving to London, and quickly spending it forced him to find other sources of revenue. O'Brien turned to what he knew: writing, which became a source of both intellectual growth and physical security, providing him with the means for survival and a material standard to which he was accustomed. Additionally, O'Brien's sudden and abrupt move from London to America also leads to displacement of home. Only living there for just over two years, O'Brien's leave this time was triggered by rumors that his involvement with a married woman, whose husband, a British officer in the army, was on his way back home to London to settle the score. O'Brien felt it might be a good time to continue his journey, and he finally immigrated and landed in America in 1852.

Youth plays an important role in many of his stories, and "The Child That Loved a Grave" stands out as one of his most profound meditations on the ontological nature of loss and identity. Written shortly before O'Brien's death in 1862 and published in the April 1861 issue of *Harper's New Monthly Magazine*, "The Child That Loved a Grave" is a poignant exploration of loneliness and isolation through the lens of "the other." Unlike many of O'Brien's stories that incorporate elements of the supernatural, this tale employs a physical yet unconventional "other"—the grave and the corpse of a young child. The narrative centers on an abused child who, devoid of companionship and affection, finds a somber comfort in the secluded environment of a long-forgotten churchyard. The child forms an unlikely attachment to a grave, specifically to the remains of another unnamed child buried there. This attachment symbolizes not only a connection with someone who the protagonist imagines might have shared a similar fate but also serves as a stark representation of the protagonist's profound loneliness and yearning for friendship.

The story's setting in the neglected graveyard further amplifies the themes of neglect and abandonment, both physically by society and emotionally by the child's surroundings. The child in the grave, as "the other" in this story, is not just a physical presence but a poignant symbol of the child's emotional state—forgotten, overlooked, and yet a sanctuary where the child finds a silent companion. O'Brien's use of the grave as "the other" challenges conventional narrative elements by personifying a place of death as a source of comfort and connection, reflecting the depths of the child's solitude and despair. "The Child That Loved a Grave" stands out in O'Brien's oeuvre as a deeply melancholic and powerful narrative that delves into the impact of neglect and the unconventional ways in which the human spirit seeks connection and solace, making it a subtle yet significant exploration of the themes of loneliness and the human condition.

The child visits the grave daily, refusing to spend time with living people and seeking solace and comfort away from his abusive parents. When other children try to include him in games, he refuses to participate, choosing instead to stay with his companion, the grave. One day a group of men intrudes upon the graveyard, searching for the grave of the unnamed child. Frightened by their presence, the protagonist hides behind a tree. Realizing that the men are digging up the grave, the child reveals himself and begs them to leave it alone. The men, unyielding, explain that the grave contains a child who was well endowed with means and that his family now wants him moved to the family graveyard. Once they are finished and the grave is empty, the child, weeping at the loss of his friend, returns home. "When he went to his little bed he called his father and told him he was going to die, and asked him to have him buried in the little grave that had a gray headstone with a sun rising out of the sea carved upon it. The father laughed and told him to go to sleep; but when morning came the child was dead" (684).

This story is imbued with "the other" from several different perspectives. The two unnamed children have a symbiotic relationship, with the protagonist viewing his companion as essential to his existence. Once that connection is removed, life becomes untenable for him. This extension of the self beyond the physical individual to another being is a powerful image and a profound statement on relationships. It suggests that without something or someone to give us life, only death will follow. This concept strikes at the heart of identity and being.

"The Child That Loved a Grave" resonates with autobiographical undertones reflecting O'Brien's own life experiences, particularly his detachment from close familial and social ties. When he departed Ireland in 1849, it marked a permanent separation from his homeland and his family, a separation that, despite his never returning, continued to permeate his literary work through persistent Irish themes and nostalgic references to his childhood. This separation and the consequent emotional detachment are poignantly mirrored in the story through the motif of the grave. The grave symbolizes not only a physical but an emotional distance, representing O'Brien's complex relationship with his past and his homeland. Just as the child in the story finds solace in the silent companionship of a grave, O'Brien's writings suggest a yearning for connection with his Irish roots, albeit from afar. The grave thus becomes a powerful metaphor for O'Brien's longing for Ireland and the impossibility of his return—whether due to personal choices, his pursuit of a literary career abroad, or financial constraints. The story encapsulates themes of isolation and the melancholy of exile, reflecting O'Brien's own life as a diasporic figure who, while physically distant from his origins, continually sought to reconcile his present with the memories of his past. This narrative layer adds depth to O'Brien's exploration of "the other" as a theme, highlighting the personal and existential dimensions of separation and belonging.

"The Child That Loved a Grave" also eerily parallels O'Brien's own life and death, resonating with the gloom and philosophical contemplations that marked his later years, similar to those experienced by his literary predecessor, Edgar Allan Poe. O'Brien's struggle with depression and his preoccupation with death deeply influenced his writing, imbuing it with a haunting introspection about mortality and the human condition. This thematic focus is vividly reflected in the somber tale of the child's connection to a grave, which becomes a symbol of the protagonist's isolation and melancholic longing. O'Brien's reported conversations at Pfaff's Beer Hall, where he expressed a weariness with life and a desire to uncover the meaning of existence, highlight the depth of his existential ruminations, which often permeated his literary work (Wolle 220). Such reflections underscore the profound sense of inevitability and resignation that O'Brien felt towards life and death, themes that are central to the story (and most of his publishing output).

Theories abound about why O'Brien enlisted in the American Civil War. I have argued elsewhere that his decision was influenced by an existential sense of duty, stemming from the rebuke he received for his first published poem, in which he suggested that men should leave Ireland due to the troubles caused by the English. This critique, particularly from Charles Gavan Duffy, left a lasting impression on O'Brien. As an adult, he felt he could finally address these issues. His maturity, mental growth, and patriotic feelings for his adopted homeland compelled him to join the war (see Irish, "Fitz-James O'Brien Hands In His Chips").

Furthermore, the narrative of loss and identity in "The Child That Loved a Grave" gains additional significance from the fact that O'Brien's own gravestone has been erased and, in a sense, lost over time. This loss symbolizes a further erasure of his physical identity, mirroring the story's themes of forgotten existence and the ephemeral nature of life. Thus, the tale not only explores the loneliness and existential dread experienced by its young protagonist but also serves as a poignant metaphor for O'Brien's own fears and the eventual obscurity that enveloped his final memory. Through this story O'Brien confronts the somber realities of death and identity, crafting a narrative that reflects his personal struggles and philosophical inquiries into the meaning of life and the inevitability of death.

The final chapter of O'Brien's life and the subsequent handling of his burial site reflect a poignant commentary on the remembrance and legacy of literary figures. Lieutenant O'Brien's death in April 1862, following injuries sustained at one of the early battles of the American Civil War, marked the end of a vibrant but turbulent life. Initially placed in the receiving vault at Greenwood Cemetery, his body was later moved to a grave near the southwest corner of the graveyard on 27 November 1874. The original marble headstone was inscribed with a tribute to his genius and character, acknowledging both his imperfections and his admirable qualities.

However, the transformation of his grave marker over time, as noted by his biographer Francis Wolle in 1944, highlights a broader narrative about the fading memory of historical figures. Wolle discovered that the original eloquent epitaph had been replaced by a simpler stone bearing only O'Brien's name (251). This change might reflect the erosion of his literary reputation or perhaps budgetary or familial decisions regarding the upkeep of his grave. Regardless, this evolution from a detailed epitaph to a mere name underscores the transient nature of memory and recognition, mirroring the themes of identity and obscurity prevalent in O'Brien's own writings. The simplicity of the new gravestone could be seen as a stark reminder of the inevitable decline in the public memory of even the most colorful and influential figures. This real-life detail of O'Brien's forgotten grave adds a layer of historical authenticity and melancholy to the contemplative and often somber tones found in his literary work, further enriching the interpretation of his stories and their reflections on life, death, and legacy.

In an essay published in the *New York Times,* titled "The Way to Get Buried" (19 March 1853), O'Brien reflected on the nature of death and, interestingly, on the nature of burial. In the article he contemplates the meaning of life and the nature of death, as well as how humans commemorate this significant event. The piece commences with a profound question: "The question arises some time or other in the mind of every man as to the best means of disposing of that corporeal skin which falls like a cerement when the chrysalis bursts and the Psyche soars into the sunshine of the eternal." Continuing with contemplations on the essence of burial, the historical importance of burial rites, and the practical obstacles associated with the disposal of deceased individuals, O'Brien reflects on his visit to Greenwood Cemetery, his ultimate resting place, and discovers a place that aligns perfectly with his view of death:

> Here, I thought, it would perhaps be pleasant to rest; at the foot of one of those large trees with plenty of moss on the grave, and no tombstone to call a blush upon my mouldering cheeks by challenging the world's esteem for virtues that I never possessed. Here where the distant sea gleams through the branches . . . of that endless ocean on which all sail—here, where the robin sings in Summer sweet carols for the dead—here, where there is no brick and mortar splendor to attract the vulgar crowd.

Perhaps the change in the gravestone was the result of a visitation by the ghost of O'Brien, ensuring compliance with his wishes in this article. The glowing epitaph changed to just his name, simple and plain. A man who wished to be forgotten?—not likely. O'Brien planned an edition of his collected writings, but unfortunately this never came to fruition. O'Brien yearned for the spotlight and desired fame for his literary accomplishments. The autobiographical elements in his stories, along with his poetry and essays, depict a figure mired in existential crisis and bewilderment about his own literary reputation.

The concept of "the other" in O'Brien's fiction serves multiple functions. This paper has explored just a fraction of his works that rely on this concept. The questions raised by these literary techniques serve several purposes. Throughout his fiction O'Brien was deeply influenced by and interested in philosophical questions. "The other" gave him the opportunity to explore profound metaphysical, epistemological, ethical, phenomenological, and ontological questions of existence and essence. What does it mean to be human? O'Brien's fiction also serves as ontological self-referential reflections on identity. Whether intentional or not, his fiction incorporates elements of his own history. Subtle manifestations of his personal experiences work their way into his stories, exploring themes of what it means to be an author and the relationship between the author and their work.

Writing long before the psychological theories of "the other" were developed by leading psychologists, O'Brien, in his typical fashion, anticipates modern ideas of the human psyche. Though his literary reputation rests upon a handful of speculative fiction, his literary and philosophical depth is only now being recognized as cutting-edge and at the forefront of contemporary ideas and thought. He serves as a literary bridge between the Romantics and the Realists. Through his exploration of "the other," we see his profound philosophical insight into the human psyche and his deep understanding of what it means to be human. "The other" in O'Brien's work serves as both a philosophical journey and an autobiographical exploration of human existence.

Works Cited

Anderson, Douglas A. "Questioning Attributions of Stories Supposedly by Fitz-James O'Brien." *Green Book* No. 23 (2024): 22–32.

Bleiler, Richard. "Fitz-James O'Brien (1828–1862)." *Green Book* No. 18 (2021): 37–51.

Clareson, Thomas D. "Fitz-James O'Brien." In E. F. Bleiler, ed. *Supernatural Fiction Writers.* New York: Charles Scribner's Sons, 1985. 717–22.

Coates, Paul. *The Double and the Other.* New York: St. Martin's Press, 1988.

Corstorphine, Kevin. "Fitz-James O'Brien: The Seen and the Unseen." *Green Book* No. 5 (2015): 5–25.

Fennell, Jack. "Mad Science and the Empire: Fitz-James O'Brien and Robert Cromie." In *Irish Science Fiction.* Liverpool: Liverpool University Press, 2014. 32–61.

Fonseca, Tony. "The Doppelganger." In S. T. Joshi, ed. *Icons of Horror and the Supernatural.* Westport, CT: Greenwood Press, 2007. 1.187–213.

Hallam, Clifford. "The Double as Incomplete Self." In Eugene J. Crook, ed. *Fearful Symmetry: Doubles and Doubling in Literature and Film.* Tallahassee: Florida State University Press, 1981. 1–31.

Irish, John P. "Fitz-James O'Brien Hands In His Chips: His New York Writings on Slavery and the Civil War." *New York History* 103 (Summer 2022): 104–22.

———. "'Of Nobler Song Than Mine': Social Justice in the Life, Times, and Writings of Fitz-James O'Brien." Ph.D. thesis: Southern Methodist University, 2019. scholar.smu.edu/simmons_gls_etds/3

———. "Stories of Genius and Madness: Fitz-James O'Brien's Laboratories of the Mind." *Green Book* No. 23 (2024): 33–44.

Joshi, S. T. *Unutterable Horror: A History of Supernatural Fiction.* 2012. New York: Hippocampus Press, 2014. 2 vols.

Lovecraft, H. P. *The Annotated Supernatural Horror in Literature.* Ed. S. T. Joshi. 2nd ed. New York: Hippocampus Press, 2012.

Moskowitz, Sam. "The Fabulous Fantasist—Fitz-James O'Brien." In *Explorers of the Infinite: Shapers of Science Fiction.* New York: World, 1963. 62–72.

O'Brien, Fitz-James. *Behind the Curtain: Selected Fiction of Fitz-James O'Brien, 1853–1860.* Ed. Wayne R. Kime. Newark: University of Delaware Press, 2011.

———. *The Best of Fitz-James O'Brien.* Ed. John P. Irish. Bridgeport, TX: A Bit O'Irish Press, 2018.

———. "The Bohemian." *Harper's New Monthly Magazine* 11 (July 1855): 233–42.

———. "The Child That Loved a Grave." *Harper's New Monthly Magazine* 22 (April 1861): 682–84.

———. "The Lost Room." *Harper's New Monthly Magazine* 17 (September 1858): 494–500.

————. *The Lost Room and Other Speculative Fiction*. Ed. John P. Irish. New York: Hippocampus Press, 2025 (forthcoming).

————. "The Man without a Shadow: A New Version." *Lantern* (4 September 1852): 91.

————. "The Old Boy." *American Whig Review* 16 (August 1852): 149–54.

————. *Poetry and Music*. Ed. John P. Irish. Bridgeport, TX: A Bit O'Irish Press, 2018.

————. "The Pot of Tulips." *Harper's New Monthly Magazine* 11 (November 1855): 807–14.

————. *Thirteen Stories by Fitz-James O'Brien: The Realm of the Mind*. Ed. Wayne R. Kime. Newark: University of Delaware Press, 2012.

————. "The Way to Get Buried." *New York Times* (19 March 1853): 2.

————. *The Wondersmith and Others*. Ed. Jessica Amanda Salmonson. Ashcroft, BC: Ash-Tree Press, 2008.

Orford, Pete. "Unfamiliar in their Mouths: The Possible Contributions of Fitz-James O'Brien to Household Words." In Hazel Mackenzie and Ben Winyard, ed. *Charles Dickens and the Mid-Victorian Press, 1850–1870*. Buckingham: University of Buckingham Press, 2013.

Parry, Albert. *Garrets and Pretenders: Bohemian Life in America from Poe to Kerouac*. 1933/1960. Mineola, NY: Dover, 2012.

Vardoulakis, Dimitris. "The Critique of Loneliness." *Angelaki* 9 (August 2004): 81–101.

Webber, Andrew. *The Doppelgänger: Double Visions in German Literature*. Oxford: Clarendon Press, 1996.

Wolle, Francis. *Fitz-James O'Brien: A Literary Bohemian of the Eighteen-Fifties*. Boulder: University of Colorado Studies, 1944.

The Man Who Keeps Halloween

John C. Tibbetts

No one knew anything about The Man Who Keeps Halloween, where he came from, and where he went afterward. His trim little cottage tucked away at the end of Larkspur Lane had seemed to appear overnight, although some of the elders had a dim memory of a similar dwelling many years ago. The overhanging trees gently caressed the gabled roof, and a liberal supply of leaves and pumpkins neatly decorated the lawn. His name, Josiah Frietchie, seemed, well, familiar, but no one knew just why. Certainly there was nothing memorable about him, unless it was a pipe that seemed perpetually alight, and unless it were the peculiar hat that perched perilously in a rakish tilt on his head. Even in the high wind that came that night, that hat remained stubbornly in place. Otherwise, his trim little beard and sparkling blue eyes bespoke humor and kindness.

The children who came trick-or-treating that Halloween night were understandably nervous. He was a stranger, after all, even if he seemed entirely familiar with the town. But the quaint little "Welcome" sign on the lawn was reassuring. And certainly the man who greeted them at the door with a gentle smile put them instantly at their ease. Would they like a spot of hot mulled cider beside the crisping fireplace to ward off the chill?

In the snug parlor he looked around the circle of plastic ghoul and ghost costumes with a mild reproof. Things were different in the Halloweens of the past, he remarked, his pipe smoke spiraling lazily toward the ceiling. "I keep Halloween in my own way," he continued, passing around a tray of dark chocolates. "We used to sew our costumes from old clothes passed down the generations— not like the dimestore costumes you're wearing," he added. He chuckled, pointing his pipe stem toward a little witch girl in the corner. He stood up and proudly gestured toward an enormous pumpkin on the mantle. "And here's a *real* pumpkin, not like those silly plastic jack-o'-lanterns you're carrying." At that moment the candle flame inside flickered and flared up briefly. The orange light poured through the eyes, nose, and yawning mouth, throwing his crooked shadow against the wall.

The children stirred then, a trifle uneasy, but relaxed when another round of cider appeared. He picked up a little flute from the table next to him and blew a silly little tune. The children giggled, and one of the boys turned a few steps there in the firelight. No one offered to leave. Soon it was time for ghost stories. He invited them to tell a few, and he smiled tolerantly at their foolish whimsies. "Now," he said at length, "I have a ghost just for you."

The evening lengthened, the shadows deepened, and the starlight grew cold. A few notes from a flute were heard, whispering down the wind.

In the days that followed, anxious parents grew distraught at the disappearance of their children. Visits to the house found only a deserted ruin. The police were puzzled. Several of the moms and dads grew ill and went mad.

Meanwhile, The Man Who Keeps Halloween puffs away at his pipe. He settles back in his little hut in a faraway forest. He pulls from his cloak a small vial containing a rich, orange-colored fluid. With a smile, he uncorks it. Placing it near his ear, he chuckles at the tiny, plaintive cries the emanate from it. Behind him the pumpkin winks. On the whole, he muses with a sigh, this Halloween had been barely satisfactory. Not like in the old days. They knew how to do Halloween then.

He places the vial on a little shelf where he keeps his other Halloweens.

"Better luck next year," he smiles.

Notes on Contributors

Jason V Brock is a writer, editor, filmmaker, composer, scholar, and artist. His fiction and nonfiction works have appeared in many venues; his books include *Disorders of Magnitud*e (about horror and science fiction in culture), numerous anthologies, and two fiction collections. He has been nominated twice for the Bram Stoker Award, and his documentary about *Forrest J Ackerman, The Acker-Monster Chronicles!*, won the Rondo Hatton Classic Horror Award for Best Documentary in 2014.

Frank Coffman is a retired professor of English, Creative Writing, and Journalism. He has published four major collections of speculative poetry—*The Coven's Hornbook & Other Poems, Black Flames & Gleaming Shadows, Eclipse of the Moon,* and *What the Night Brings.* His formal verse and short fiction spanning the popular genres has appeared in many magazines, journals, and anthologies. His collection of occult detective stories, *Three Against the Dark,* was published in 2022.

Scott J. Couturier is a Rhysling Award–nominated poet and prose writer of the weird, liminal, and darkly fantastic. His work has appeared in numerous venues, including *The Audient Void, Spectral Realms, Tales from the Magician's Skull, Space and Time, Cosmic Horror Monthly,* and *Weirdbook.* Currently he works as a copy and content editor for Mission Point Press, living an obscure reverie in the wilds of northern Michigan with his partner/live-in editor and two cats.

Kendall Evans's stories and poems have appeared in nearly all the major science fiction and fantasy magazines, including *Asimov's, Analog, Weird Tales, Strange Horizons, Weirdbook, Mythic Delirium, Dreams & Nightmares, Space & Time, Nebula Award Showcase* (2012), *The Magazine of Speculative Poetry, Amazing Stories, Fantas-*

tic Stories, and many others. He is the author of the novels *The Rings of Ganymede* and *The Adventures of Ching Shih, Pirate Princess.*

Debra K. Every is an author of horror, thrillers, and stories that make the heart beat fast. Her debut novel, *Deena Undone,* was a double winner in the 2024 IAA competition: Best Debut Novel and Best Horror Novel. It also won gold in the 2023 Pitch Week XXIX competition and was shortlisted for a 2024 Hawthorne prize. Debra lives in upstate New York, where she endlessly strives to write one perfectly balanced sentence.

Wade German's most recent full-length poetry collection is *Psalms and Sorceries* (Hippocampus Press, 2022). His first collection, *Dreams from a Black Nebula,* is available from the same publisher. Other titles include four slim volumes of his selected poems with Portuguese translation: *Incantations, Apparitions, Phantasmagorias,* and *Chapel of Celluloid* (Raphus Press).

James Goho is a researcher and writer with many publications on dark fiction. In 2014, Rowman & Littlefield published his *Journeys into Darkness: Critical Essays on Gothic Horror.* McFarland published his *Caitlín R. Kiernan: A Critical Study of Her Dark Fiction* in 2020. His higher education research is found in academic journals, and his infrequent short stories appear in literary magazines. He lives in Winnipeg, Canada.

Maxwell I. Gold is a Jewish-American cosmic horror poet and editor, with an extensive body of work comprising more than 300 poems since 2017. His writings have earned a place alongside many literary luminaries in the speculative fiction genre. His work has appeared in numerous literary journals, magazines, and anthologies. Maxwell's work has been recognized with multiple nominations including the Eric Hoffer Award, Pushcart Prize, and Bram Stoker Award.

Joshua Green is an author of weird fiction, fantasy, and science fiction. His work has appeared or is forthcoming in *British Fantasy Society: Horizons, Strange Aeon, Spectral Realms,* and elsewhere. Currently he is working on the narrative-driven expansion for the critically acclaimed board game *Beast.*

John P. Irish is an independent researcher specializing in nineteenth-century American literature. His dissertation explored the philosophical ideas of Fitz-James O'Brien—the "Irish Poe." He is also interested in the intersection of pop culture and philosophy. He has contributed articles to *Philosophy Now* and chapters in the book series on "Philosophy and Pop Culture." He lives in Texas with his wife and three pets: Teddy, Lucy, and Holly.

Katherine Kerestman is a debased, quasi-pagan thing, and the author of *Lethal* (PsychoToxin Press, 2023), *Creepy Cat's Macabre Travels: Prowling around Haunted Towers, Crumbling Castles, and Ghoulish Graveyards* (WordCrafts Press, 2020), and *Haunted House and Other Strange Tales* (Hippocampus Press, 2024), as well as the coeditor (with S. T. Joshi) of *The Weird Cat* (WordCrafts Press, 2023) and *Shunned Houses: An Anthology of Weird Stories, Unspeakable Poems, and Impious Essays* (WordCrafts Press, 2024).

Marcos Legaria is a scholar of H. P. Lovecraft, R. H. Barlow, Clark Ashton Smith, and related writers. He is a member of the Esoteric Order of Dagon and a contributor to *William Hope Hodgson: Voices from the Borderland,* the first full-length study devoted to the life and work of Hodgson. His articles have appeared in the *Crypt of Cthulhu, Lovecraft Annual,* and *Spectral Realms.* He is the author of *L'Affaire Barlow: H. P. Lovecraft and the Battle for His Literary Legacy* (Bold Venture Press).

Ngo Binh Anh Khoa is a teacher of English in Ho Chi Minh City, Vietnam. In his free time, he enjoys daydreaming, reading, and occasionally writing poetry for personal entertainment. His speculative poems have appeared in NewMyths.com, *Heroic Fantasy Quarterly*, *The Audient Void*, and other venues.

Manuel Pérez-Campos of Bayamón, Puerto Rico, is a longtime poet in the tradition of the weird, with work published in several venues.

Carl E. Reed is currently employed as a call center agent at a retail fixtures company just outside Chicago. Former jobs include U.S.M.C. photographer, long-haul trucker, stage actor, cab driver, construction worker, and door-to-door encyclopedia salesman. His poetry has been published in *The Iconoclast, Spectral Realms, Black Petals,* and *Deathlehem: Holiday Horrors;* short stories in *Black Gate, newWitch, Sci-Fi Lampoon, Penumbra, Eldritch Tales,* and elsewhere. He is a member of Frank Coffman's Weird Poets Society. *Dark Matter: Weird Stories and Poetry* was published by Hippocampus Press in 2024.

Geoffrey Reiter is Associate Professor and Coordinator of Literature at Lancaster Bible College. He is also an Associate Editor at the website *Christ and Pop Culture,* where he frequently writes about weird horror and dark fantasy. As a scholar of weird fiction, Reiter has published academic articles on such authors as Arthur Machen, Bram Stoker, Clark Ashton Smith, and William Peter Blatty. His poetry has previously appeared in *Spectral Realms* and *Star*Line,* and his fiction has appeared in *Penumbra* and *The Mythic Circle.*

Ann K. Schwader lives and writes in Colorado. Her collection, *Unquiet Stars,* is now out from Weird House Press. Two of her earlier collections, *Wild Hunt of the Stars* (Sam's Dot, 2010) and *Dark Energies* (P'rea Press, 2015), were Bram Stoker Award Finalists. In 2018, she received the Science Fiction and Fantasy Poetry Association's Grand Master award. She is also a two-time Rhysling Award winner.

Darrell Schweitzer is a former editor of *Weird Tales* and the author of four fantasy novels and about 350 stories. His most recent collection is *The Children of Chorazin and Other Strange Denizens* (Hippocampus

Press, 2023). PS Publishing issued a two-volume retrospective of his work, *The Mysteries of the Faceless King* and *The Last Heretic*, in 2020. He has published books about H. P. Lovecraft and Lord Dunsany.

John Shirley is the winner of the Bram Stoker Award for his story collection *Black Butterflies: A Flock on the Dark Side*. He has been guest of honor at the World Horror Convention and a special guest at H. P. Lovecraft Film Festival. His novels include *Demons*, *Cellars*, *Wetbones*, and *Stormland*. His most recent story collection is *The Feverish Stars*. His first collection of weird poetry, *The Voice of the Burning House*, was nominated for an Elgin Award.

Oliver Smith is an artist and writer from Cheltenham, Gloucestershire, UK. His poetry has appeared in *Dreams & Nightmares*, *Eye to the Telescope*, *Illumen*, *Mirror Dance*, *Rivet*, *Spectral Realms*, *Star*Line*, and *Weirdbook*. His collection of stories, *Stars Beneath the Ships*, was published by Ex Occidente Press in 2017, and many of his previously anthologized stories and poems are collected in *Basilisk Soup and Other Fantasies*. Smith is studying for a Ph.D. in Creative Writing.

John C. Tibbetts is Professor Emeritus at the University of Kansas in Film and Media Studies. His books include *The Furies of Marjorie Bowen* (McFarland, 2019), *The Gothic Worlds of Peter Straub* (McFarland, 2016), *Those Who Made It: Conversations with the Legends of Hollywood* (Palgrave Macmillan, 2015), *Peter Weir: Interviews* (University of Mississippi Press, 2014), and *The Gothic Imagination* (Palgrave Macmillan, 2012). In 2008 Governor Kathleen Sebelius presented him the Kansas Governor's Arts in Education Award.

Short story author and occasional poet **Carla Ward** is a Pushcart Prize nominee. Her work has appeared in over a dozen publications, including the *Saturday Evening Post*, *Dark Horses Magazine*, *Modern Magic Anthology*, and *Night Picnic Journal*. She was a semifinalist in

ScreenCraft's 2024 Cinematic Short Story Competition and is currently ranked in the top 10% of The Red List.

Lee Weinstein is a retired Philadelphia librarian with a lifelong interest in science fiction, fantasy, and horror. He has edited a collection of Edward Lucas White's horror stories, and his essays have appeared in *Studies in Weird Fiction, Supernatural Fiction Writers*, the *New York Review of Science Fiction*, and elsewhere. He was a contributor *to Horror Fiction through History* and is an ongoing contributor to the online third edition of the *Encyclopedia of Science Fiction*.